FLASH POINT

LANCE CORPORAL MATT CROUCHER grew up in the Midlands and joined the Royal Marines aged sixteen, passing through the legendary thirty-week training pro-gramme and into 40 Commando despite a series of injuries. He served two tours with the Marines in Iraq, was awarded the George Cross for gallantry in the face of the enemy for putting himself between a Taliban booby-trapped grenade and three of his fellow marines in Afghanistan in February 2008, before transferring into the Royal Marines Reserves and returning to Iraq as a private security contractor with the United Nations. He re-joined 40 Commando for the ultimate challenge of a tour of duty in war-torn Afghanistan in September 2007.

Also available by Matt Croucher

Bullet Proof

MATT CROUCHER GC
FLASH POINT

arrow books

Published in the United Kingdom by Arrow Books in 2010

3 5 7 9 10 8 6 4 2

Copyright © Matt Croucher 2010

Matt Croucher has asserted his right under the Copyright, Designs and Patents Act,
1988 to be identified as the author of this work.

First published in the United Kingdom in 2010 by Arrow

Arrow Books
The Random House Group Limited
20 Vauxhall Bridge Road, London, SW1V 2SA

Addresses for companies within The Random House Group Limited can be found at:
www.randomhouse.co.uk/offices.htm

The Random House Group Limited Reg. No. 954009

www.rbooks.co.uk

A CIP catalogue record for this book
is available from the British Library

ISBN 9780099543138

The Random House Group Limited supports The Forest Stewardship
Council (FSC), the leading international forest certification organisation.
All our titles that are printed on Greenpeace approved FSC certified paper
carry the FSC logo. Our paper procurement policy can be found at
www.rbooks.co.uk/environment

Mixed Sources
Product group from well-managed
forests and other controlled sources
www.fsc.org Cert no. TT-COC-2139
© 1996 Forest Stewardship Council

Typeset in Palatino by Palimpsest Book Production Limited,
Falkirk, Stirlingshire

Printed and bound in Great Britain by CPI Bookmarque Ltd, Croydon CR0 4TD

PROLOGUE

'**G**O! GO! GO!' Coldrain shouted.

There were three two-main lock points on the door. Two were at waist height, the other higher up, which Coldrain figured was a sliding-lock mechanism. Kymor Haydarov, the stripey in charge of Uzbekistan's elite counterterrorists, took the top lock first because it was always quicker to raise a weapon from a lowered stance than an elevated one. With the bitch aimed at the top right corner Haydarov depressed the trigger. There was a short, sharp flash accompanied by a thunderous bang as the Hatton round's metal powder and wax combo tore into the lock structure and the whole frame of the door shuddered. In one smooth move the stripey pointed the gun down at the main locks and fired a second breaching round. The locks were blown clean off, and the force of the round saw the door swing open back into the hallway.

As soon as the door was free of its hinges, Coldrain pulled the pin from the flashbang and tossed it into the hallway. Two seconds later the grenade detonated, creating a deafening sound like a clap of thunder striking on top of them. Their ears were cushioned by the walls. Whoever was inside wouldn't be so lucky.

Taking advantage of the small window of diversion afforded by the flashbang, Coldrain was first in, MP5 raised at shoulder level, eyes darting from left to right as he scanned for targets, quickly shadowed by Haydarov at his five o'clock.

The hallway was narrow and sparsely decorated with hardwood flooring, glossed and covered in burgundy and gold stencil patterns. To the immediate left was a room with a white door frame. At the opposite end of the hallway from Coldrain and Haydarov were doors to the left, centre and right, all closed. On their left, past the white door, was a narrow staircase leading upstairs to a landing that was out of his line of vision. There was nobody in sight.

Coldrain surged forward and shouted, 'Clear left!' as he turned towards the white door. He gave it a kick and it flew open. Haydarov tossed another flashbang into the room. This time the bang was louder. Coldrain's ears were ringing, but he shook his head as he entered the room and swiftly hooked his MP5 from left to right, ready to slot any lethal threat.

The room was empty. No problem, guys.

He shouted, 'Room clear' and ducked back out to the hallway just in time to see Steve Waterford and the rest of Bravo team storm past and head directly for the staircase. Coldrain wasn't a hundred per cent sure, but he could swear that Waterford had been sporting a wide, manic grin as he bounded towards the carpeted steps.

Alpha still had three more rooms to clear on the ground floor. Coldrain directed Haydarov to the room at the rear centre of the hallway, a pair of frosted glass doors flanked by tacky panelling in the same style. Haydarov didn't mess about; he swung the bitch down against the handle and followed through with a solid kick. They were out of BFGs so Coldrain rushed straight in and found himself in a dimly lit dining room, an imposing, long dinner table in the middle, stretching back to the rear.

Coldrain saw movement. One, no two shapes at the far end of the room coming towards him. He brought his Heckler & Koch MP5K (PDW-type variant) to bear and locked onto his first target.

He was poised to let rip when he heard a voice scream, 'Orange! *Orange!*'

Coldrain understood the term instantly because he'd taught it himself. It was the warning to make clear they were friendly forces. NATO strapped orange panels onto their vehicles to alert trigger-happy F-16 pilots to the presence of friendlies. It didn't stop blue-on-blue incidents but right now it worked just fine.

He eased his finger off the trigger and watched as the two shapes came forward into the fluorescent light that seeped into the dining room from the hallway, and finally identified the men as Temur Denisov and Ahmed Soliev. There were glass shards around their feet and resting on their shoulders like sharp, glistening chunks of ice. Behind them he saw a hollow sliding door, the glass punched wide open into a man-sized oval hole.

'All clear,' Soliev said.

Coldrain frowned. This didn't make any sense. Where the hell was everyone? According to Waterford's mark-one eyeball there should be six X-rays inside the house – the two guests, Uzbekistan's most notorious drug barons, codenamed Vegas and Rio, their drivers, and the two men waiting to greet them in the safe house. And all of a sudden the ground floor was empty. No more than three seconds had elapsed between Haydarov breaching the door and Coldrain making his entry. They would have to be quicker than Usain Bolt to all flee upstairs in that short space of time. Suddenly he felt nauseous. He had a bad feeling about the whole set-up.

His sense of unease just kept growing. Coldrain knew even as they went through the motions of clearing the rooms to the left and the right that no one was lying in wait inside them. Just an empty living room with a plasma TV hanging from the west wall, well-worn armchairs and the thick stench of Arab cigarettes in the air, and to the right a kitchen caked in dust.

He wondered what Bravo team had discovered upstairs. No gunshots so far. He found Soliev at the foot of the staircase.

'Anything?'

'Nothing.'

Coldrain turned to Haydarov.

'I'm going up. Secure the perimeter.'

Coldrain started to climb the stairs. He could see a door to the left at the top of the staircase, and from the boot mark embedded into its centre he knew that the room had already been cleared. He also saw that the landing panned off to the right, leading in the opposite direction and parallel to the stairs. Coldrain could hear multiple voices. One sounded like it belonged to Waterford, aspiring alcoholic, working-class Clapton operator and former Cherry Berry in 2 Para. Waterford didn't trust the Uzbeks an inch.

He was screaming at something. It sounded like he was swearing. There were other voices too, hectic, rushed, foreign. The other guys in Bravo, he guessed. *Or the targets.* The shouting became more frantic as he neared the top of the stairs. Someone screamed at the top of their voice, a high-pitched yell.

Then he heard two sharp gunshots.

Crack, crack.

Coldrain was almost at the landing. His MP5 swung by his right side. It was a knock-off Pakistani model, not the trusty original, which didn't fill him with confidence in the sub-machine gun. The mags were also chad, held together by black maskers tape to stop them from splitting open and the rounds falling out.

The view across towards the far end was blocked by the ornamental black railings that tapered off above the stairs and ran parallel to the landing.

Just three more steps to go.

He kept his head turned to the right.

As the landing came into view, clear of the railing, he stopped dead in his tracks.

A pair of boots were lying on the floor.

Bates Defenders.

Attached to a body smeared in blood across a khaki shirt and jeans.

Coldrain leapt the final step and charged down the landing, shouting, 'Man down! *Man fucking down!*'

He reached the body in three sprinting strides. He knew it was Waterford, even before he had a confirmed visual on the face. The big man was lying face down and the pool of blood covered the whole area beneath his torso and legs. Blood trails were splashed down the beige wall. Coldrain saw two exit wounds. One was on the left side of his neck; the second at the rear of his right tricep. They were the size and shape of walnuts, the skin torn back exposing a deep tunnel of shredded membrane, burst blood vessels and distressed muscle tissue.

Coldrain felt around Waterford's neck and legs. Nothing. Then he ran his hands up and down the obliques, and his fingers hit a sticky, thick substance, like mercury-red glue. Coldrain saw the entry wounds. They had penetrated to the right of Waterford's abdomen, their course deflected as they smashed into bone and vital organs, and finally tore out of his body. He must have been shot from the side, with two well-aimed rounds. That was the only way to inflict a chest wound when someone was packing a ballistics vest.

Whoever shot him knew he was tooled up with body armour.

It was obvious the guy was wasted. Coldrain could hear further shouts and shots. Rising to his feet, his bloodied hand firm on the MP5 trigger, he moved down the landing. There was a white door at the far end, ten metres away. The voices were muffled, coming from behind the door. Bravo and the targets must be in there, Coldrain thought. He kept his MP5 trained on the door as he closed in. He was six metres away now. The shouts grew louder, interrupted by the crack of rounds being put down, a three-shot burst then a two-shot and a single crack. Some serious shit was going down in there. Behind him he heard footsteps bounding up the stairs. One of the Uzbek lads trying to get in on the action. Coldrain cursed them for disobeying orders. He'd told them to secure the perimeter.

He turned around to face the stairs.

And felt something hot brush against his back.

The next thing he knew he was being banged out against the rear wall, his face smashed into the plaster. He felt a couple of teeth loosen with the impact. There was no sound for a moment, and then the silence was replaced by a roaring, violent wind that sucked the air out of his lungs. He felt his stomach compress, as though a pair of giant hands were squeezing his sides. The world turned pitch black. He could feel ash in his mouth. He tried to breathe through his nostrils but it felt like he was snorting lava.

Coldrain was laid out on the floor, facing the stairs. His vision was blurred. He blinked and rubbed his eyes and things became a little clearer. He looked at his hands. They were pockmarked with cuts, bits of glass and wood and metal. Tiny shards of shrapnel lined both of his legs, leaving small dark red patches along his combats. He could taste blood in his mouth. His left shoulder stung badly.

The next thing he knew Haydarov was kneeling down next to him. Coldrain couldn't move. Everything ached and throbbed with pain. His muscles shook from the vibrations caused by the explosion. Haydarov grabbed Coldrain's head and looked into his eyes. Coldrain coughed violently and spat blood onto the floor. He was in a bad state, and the Uzbeks were only packing limited trauma. They would have to rush him to a hospital, and fast.

Then he blinked again and focused on Haydarov's face.

He was smiling.

Haydarov released Coldrain's head and his skull hit the ground with a thud. He could barely believe what was happening. At the end of the landing he saw Bravo team stroll coolly out of the room.

They escorted Rio and Vegas out of the room. The smug bastards beamed triumphantly and were followed by their drivers and the two hosts. They stepped carefully around Waterford's bloody corpse, now slumped against the western wall, opposite the railings. His neck had been lacerated in the blast, and blood oozed out of his perforated throat and gushed down his body armour.

Coldrain doubled over, clutching his guts and coughing up more blood. Breathing was a tremendous effort. He recalled training courses in the Alps, deep-cave explorations, finding small pockets of air to survive on; holding his breath underwater for minutes at a time. This was harder. He hurt all over.

Haydarov stood over Coldrain's struggling, prostrate figure, lit a Lucky Strike and took a swig from a hip flask.

'It's funny, I was just thinking, you know, the grenade should have killed you. If this had been any other day I would say you were a very lucky man. But today, as it happens, you are not so lucky.'

Coldrain wiped his mouth. His lips were dry, his throat so scorched he couldn't speak.

'If you weren't about to die, you would ask me what happened. What can I say? This is nothing personal, just business. We all have money to make. These people,' he continued, referring to Rio and Vegas, 'pay more than those bureaucratic pieces of shit in government. That's all.'

The pain in Coldrain's shoulder returned with a vengeance, a sharp electric shock that ran across his back and neck. He arched his head to the left to get a better look at it, and his eyes widened when he saw a large, triangular-shaped piece of shrapnel buried deep in his shoulder blade. The tip was still pretty wide at the entry point, almost two inches. Coldrain started to panic. He could visualise the shrapnel tip, glistening hard and sharp, pressing against his lungs like a knife point resting on a balloon. He was seriously fucked.

Denisov came back upstairs clutching a gasoline can. He started tossing the liquid over the landing, making sure Waterford's body was dripping from head to toe. He let the gasoline trickle onto the floorboards and trailed it back down the stairs. The kid was whistling all the way.

'No hard feelings,' Haydarov said.

Then he stepped back, heading down the stairs.

With a casual flick of his fingers, Haydarov tossed the tab high into the air. It fell onto the floor slap bang next to Waterford and ignited the petrol. The fire quickly swallowed up Waterford's corpse and spread across the landing. Flames licked the walls and doors. The heat singed Coldrain's eyebrows and scalded his arms and face.

He watched Haydarov's lanky frame disappear. Saw the flames crawl closer towards him. The same words rattled around his numbed skull.

No hard feelings.

It's nothing personal.

Only business.

PART ONE

ONE

Three Months Later

It was gone 3 p.m. when Coldrain rolled up at the red-brick semi-detached at the end of a quiet residential road in Colchester. It was grey and cloudy, as though the sky was covered in dirty blankets. He eased his lime-green Kawasaki Ninja ZX-7RR into the narrow driveway and slipped it into first gear, kept his balance dead on straight so he wasn't leaning and employed his rear brake. Placing his left foot down on the ground as he hit the clutch, in one smooth move he jumped off and kicked up the foot stand, leaning the bike onto it. The Ninja was awesome and well worth the cash he'd laid down on it, although he'd just had to shell out for a shit-ton of repairs after a recent collision. He'd been cruising it at ninety on a dual carriageway when a BMW M3 had pulled out in front of him without looking. Not for the first time in his life, or in the last six months, Coldrain was lucky not to be browners. The motorist claimed Smidsy after the crash – 'Sorry mate I didn't see you'.

The only thing that distinguished this house from any other on the drive was the number on the letterbox. That, and the dark memories lurking inside. Coldrain stepped up to the porch and rang the doorbell. Through the patterned glass he saw a gloomy figure slowly shuffle forwards and waited a seeming eternity while the multiple locks were undone. Finally the door creaked open.

'Hey, John,' he said in his best cheery voice. The girls in Hooters sounded less fake.

'You're back.'

The old man looked like crap. The beer gut was so prominent he looked as though he'd shoved a pillow down his shirt. His face was pale and waxy. Clutching his can of lager he looked like he truly couldn't give a toss about anything. His breath reeked of cheap booze.

The old man didn't invite him in but he stepped inside anyway. The house was a mess. Days' old post lay scattered across the doormat and reception. The carpet was covered in crumbs and dark stains. A stale, milky smell lingered in the air.

Coldrain walked through into the living room. There were two tattered beige leather sofas that were older than him, the material worn down to the nub. They faced a TV that was permanently switched on, tuned in to Sky News. A faux Victorian mantelpiece was lined with cards. They all looked basically the same. Pictures of flowers, blue skies and clouds with shafts of light, with messages in tacky fonts like 'May Memories Comfort You', 'In Sympathy' and 'He Will Be Remembered'.

Pam was slumped on the sofa closest to the TV, her dim eyes fixated on the screen while she chained a twenty pack of Bensons. The sombre news report was about some kid from the Sappers who'd been zapped in Helmand.

Roadside bomb, the weapon of choice for today's courageous martyr.

Coldrain took up a seat next to her on the sofa.

'He was nineteen,' she said in her raspy voice, eyes dead centre on the TV set and yet somehow gazing beyond it, into a well of misery. Her eyes feasted on the depressing images. The parade photograph of the dead kid. Coldrain was inured to most death and barely batted an eyelid at the stabbings and shootings that were a regular feature of the news. But another dead soldier in the Afghan always unnerved him, belt tightening across his chest, his arms and legs shaking, as if he was standing at the epicentre of an earthquake.

Another dead soldier, another reminder of Jamie.

'It's so sad,' she said, finally ungluing her eyes from the box. And something about the pity in her voice made Coldrain angry. Her sentimental tone drew anger from him like a needle drawing blood.

'It's been a while now,' he said. 'We've got to move on. I'm still here, I'm part of the family.'

'Yes,' her head angling back at the TV. 'We have you.' But her eyes told the full story. An adopted son isn't the same. Since he was eight years old, Coldrain had lived with John and Pam Reese after his dad had walked out on them and his mum committed suicide, but they had never made him feel like a true part of the family. He kept his surname and grew up as a kid on the outside looking in. It wasn't for lack of trying, he figured. They treated him and Jamie equally, spent the same on them at Christmas and birthdays, and made all the right noises about loving them equally. Good intentions, however, were no match for biological reality. Jamie was their son, and they loved him the most. And he'd been snatched from them in the cruellest way.

'Our Jamie was the same age as this lad,' she gulped. 'You know, when it happened.'

Coldrain gritted his teeth. He felt less like a son and more like an unwelcome guest. Not their fault, he told himself. That was beside the point. A part of him dared to wonder, *If John and Pam had the choice of which son to lose, their adopted one or their real one, who would they have picked?*

He already knew the answer.

It was this, or the fact that Jamie looked like another kid who was browners, or another corps-pissed sprog fresh out of CTC, Commando Training Centre. Like the woman was actively seeking out signs. And she was so caught up in this crap now, he didn't even recognise her any more. Before the incident she'd been happy and outgoing. Always had a smile on her face. But now, this. Coldrain realised that coming here was depressing the hell out of him. All it did was open up a can of worms that he'd spent the past three years trying to keep closed with a combination of freelance work, booze and uber-cool bikes. He couldn't take much more of this.

'Where are you going?' Pam asked as he stood up. It was the first time she'd looked at him since he'd arrived.

'To Jamie's room,' he replied.

It had once been as much his room as Jamie's. As kids they spent every minute playing football, chasing each other round building sites and having a laugh. At weekends, when Jamie's parents were out, they would find an 18-rated horror or action movie and watch it in their room with the lights turned off. They were best mates as well as adopted brothers, had been since the day they were lumped together in primary school. Since Jamie's death, however, the room had been turned into a sort of shrine. Frozen in time, untouched since the moment Jamie had shipped out to the Afghan. Stacks of books on the Marines and a DVD of *Black Hawk Down* were still lying on the bottom bunk. It was all just as Jamie had left it, except that the desk where the Xbox used to sit had been cleared to make way for a display of photographs and cards. His pass-out snap was prominent among them.

He found himself staring at the other item that had been changed in the room. The Union Jack, neatly folded into a square, upon which lay the Dog and Basket, or to those on Civvy Street, the Lion and Crown, badge of the Royal Marine Commandos. Kind of ironic that Jamie's insignia was so perfectly preserved, Coldrain mused, seeing as he'd trashed his own in disgust shortly after things went pear-shaped.

Memories came flooding back. Bad memories. The type you'd sink a quart of Johnnie Walker straight to get rid of. Images that had been seared into his consciousness, no matter how hard he tried to forget.

He needed a drink. The old man was a beer drinker, but Coldrain had the thirst for something a bit stronger than that. He sodded out of Jamie's room and went back downstairs to the kitchen. He opened the cupboard above the untidy bench and, behind the vinegars and other condiments, located the bottle of Nelson's Blood he was looking for. He tore the cap off the rum and took a long neaters swig. It warmed him up and made him shiver at the same time. Then he opened the back door and stepped into the garden, overrun with weeds and grass longer than Terry Waite's beard. Once upon a time the old man had taken great pride in his vegetable plots and fruit trees and gnomes, but now it was merely a testament to long-term neglect.

He took another gulp of the rum.

Three years, but sometimes it felt longer than that, and sometimes it felt more like three days. At least he didn't immerse himself in misery and self-loathing like Jamie's parents, but he'd be lying if he said it wasn't at the back of his mind most, if not all, of the time. After all, when you stripped away the pain, it was Coldrain who'd seen Jamie die. He'd been there.

TWO

They had been based at Forward Operating Base Sangin, in Helmand Province, along with the rest of Charlie Company, 40 Commando. Dispatched there on a wave of gung-ho euphoria in September 2007, the lads had become embittered by the tedium and slow nature of life in-country. Life in those first few months had settled into a depressing monotony of mortar attacks and skirmishes with the Taliban in the few kilometres surrounding the base. The weather was icers and protection from the freezing cold nights was non-existent. Despite the hardships of life in Afghanistan, the lads were well looked after. They had cooked meals, centrally sourced, and access to clean water and showers. For some of the other boys in Afghanistan it was not so cosy, and Coldrain was thankful for these small luxuries. Still, having a hot shower and some decent scran didn't make the time pass any quicker.

Jamie was still uber-corps-pissed when they rolled into Sangin. Just nine months after pass-out, he'd been a stand-out candidate over the course of the selection process at the Commando Training Centre. On the legendary commando tests, Jamie had completed the nine-mile speed march down Heartbreak Lane with a fractured metatarsal, the sort of nails performance that put English footballers to shame.

That was Jamie all over. He wasn't the most stacked Marine, but he had the biggest heart. He was always looking out for his oppos and doing his best to maintain morale with a good joke about the Sweaty Socks or which Wrens the lads fancied the most. On nights out on the piss he'd defend any Royal if a fight broke out. He was an all-round good guy, smarter than the rest, and Coldrain was proud as punch the day Jamie was sworn in as a proper Bootneck.

'Morning, Royal,' Coldrain said, gently kicking Jamie. 'Fancy some scran?'

'Yeah, mate.'

'Then get it yourself.'

'Bastard.'

'I aim to please.'

Jamie rubbed his eyes.

'Let me guess what's on the menu for today,' he said. 'It's either a sixteen-hour patrol with about five seconds of zeds, followed by an all-night barrage of mortar fire from those Taliban wankers. Or it's another day of sitting on our arses doing fuck all except taking the piss out of the Cloggies and Poles and choosing from either *Hamburger Hill* or *Saving Private Ryan*. Again.'

'Welcome to the world of war, lad.'

'I wouldn't mind if it wasn't so bloody cold.'

'Got sore toes again, have we?'

'I'd be a lot less cold if I had a nice warm wet inside me.'

'Put the kettle on then, young 'un.'

'*Bastard*'.

As the winter thawed, word got back to the media in Britain that the Taliban were proving hard to break down. They were using words like 'resurgence' and 'Vietnam' to describe the current state of affairs. Predictably the ruperts all of a sudden passed down the message that forces at FOB Sangin should take the fight to the enemy. They forgot that was what the lads had been doing from the moment they arrived. Still, anything for a decent photo-op and a good piece on the evening news.

Operation Solvent would see 40 Commando, alongside US Marines, breaking the Taliban stranglehold on Kandahar, which was at that time tighter than a Randy Couture headlock. The objective was to launch an assault on the village of Ghorak in Kandahar Province, located in the south-eastern corner of Afghanistan. The Taliban were using Ghorak as a weapons cache for launching attacks deeper into Helmand Province. Lads from Charlie Company would carry out the raid. If they were lucky they would find a stash of weapons and High Explosives that would put a severe dent in any attempts to cause mayhem.

Kandahar was the poster child for the giant clusterfuck that Afghanistan had become in the years following the 2001 invasion. On the one hand it was a province of breathtaking beauty. Coldrain wasn't the type of guy who wrote poetry and admired the sunset, but even he was stunned by the natural landscape. Pomegranate trees blossomed in between the purple rock faces and along the verdant green basin of the Arghandab Valley, the horizon dominated by the valley mountains, above an ultramarine dome. The air carried a scent of tangerine and at night you could see the most incredible star constellations. Unlike London, where light pollution made even the moon all but invisible, here the Milky Way cast shadows on the ground. The air was so pure that sound would carry for miles, but the darkness was absolute; you couldn't see your oppo, even though he was right next to you.

Way back in the day, before the Soviets rocked up, Kandahar had been the breadbasket of Afghanistan. The Russian invasion, civil war and drought had changed all that and the place was now a thin collection of settlements that tried to get by on their wheat crops and fruit orchards, a little water and the occasional internecine conflict, when they weren't busy trying to plant IEDs and sniper pongoes on patrol. The atmosphere was one of pure fear. The locals were terrified of the Taliban and lived in a state of constant anxiety about reprisals if they were disovered to be co-operating with the coalition forces. About the only thing different from Iraq was that the Afghan National Army and Afghan National Police could be trusted, which represented a step up from the insurgent-infested Iraqi security forces. The ANA and ANP were peopled with good blokes and willing soldiers, fighting to give their country some kind of a future and not drag it back into the dark ages, where the Taliban wanted it to be.

Everything that could have turned shitty in Kandahar had. The beauty hid a nightmarish reality that was playing itself out in front of Coldrain's eyes.

'We're rolling out at 0200 hours,' Sergeant Charlie Wheater, the resident off, said, addressing the lads. 'Moving nice and early, so we minimise the chances of the Taliban assaulting us along the way. For the next eight hours we will move slowly but surely forward, checking for tampering and being especially vigilant against IED attacks. At 1000 hours we will group up at the forming-up point, on this rocky rise to the north-west of Ghorak. The FUP codename is Stamford Bridge. Once there, we will prepare for our assault.'

'Finally,' Jamie said. 'A bit of action.'

'Just watch your back,' Coldrain replied. 'No funny business out there.'

'I'll be fine. Still, can't wait to get stuck in. A chance to take the fight to the enemy for a change, awesome.'

'Charlie Company will split into two teams,' Wheater continued. '5 Troop will enter and storm the village from the west, carrying out house-to-house searches before any locals sympathetic to the enemy have the chance to hide the arms stash.'

'Or before the dickers themselves pepper-pot out of the village and up into the mountains,' Jamie cracked.

'I heard that, Marine Reese. Quieten it down back there or I shall set Dan on you. Now, the second team, 6 Troop, will make an eastern approach, securing the perimeter while Team Alpha clears the buildings, looking out for possible Taliban scouts or snipers and making sure none of the villagers get any dumb ideas.'

'Anyone tries any shit with me, they're browners.'

'Any questions? Apart from who gets to slap Private Coldrain first?'

The boys laughed and displaced, but beneath the jokes everyone was deadly serious. This was it. They wanted in. Back home the press and general public had the barmy notion that soldiers didn't like fighting in wars. Bullshit. Coldrain, Jamie, the rest of the Royals, they were desperate to get some. A war without fighting wasn't really a war.

The equipment they had for the operation was top-of-the range stuff. A troop of Viking all-terrain vehicles (ATVs) fully equipped with .50 cal Browning heavy machine guns and capable of operating in environments from below minus forty degrees to almost fifty-degree heat and came fitted with hard-core bolt-on armour plating to protect it against anti-personnel mines. It was part of a Troop, and each ATV would transport eight Marines to the RV point. If all went to plan, the lads would seize the cache, gather the village elders around a table and give them a good bollocking, and the dickers would be down on guns, ammo and explosives. Result.

Ghorak was a small village even by the threadbare standards of war-torn Afghanistan. Population 122, it was essentially a loose arrangement of mudbrick houses built from water, mud, sand and clay and mixed with rice husks, and connected via a series of plain low arcs and narrow paths strewn with rocks, straw and the occasional rotting dog corpse. Everything was sandy brown, even down to the weather-beaten wooden doors on each house and the flat roofs covered in layers of branches and woven mats. The only object breaking up the monotony was a large bank of poppies growing to the north of the village with their distinctive pink buds turning rose red atop long green stalks. Branches hung overhead, and loose rags dangling limply from these makeshift clothes lines.

Ghorak was considered hot. Recent int suggested that Taliban forces had been seen in the area and to emphasise the level of threat Charlie Company was also packing some heavy firepower backup in the shape of grenade machine guns mounted on the Vikings. And just in case the shit was well and truly flung against the fan, they would also be able to call in an airstrike courtesy of an AH-64 Apache attack helicopter kitted out with AGM-114 Hellfire anti-tank missiles, 70mm Hydra rockets and a

30mm M230 chaingun to teach the Taliban a lesson or two. If they did have to call in a strike, filling in the insurgents was going to cost a couple of million quid in munitions. Taliban dickers, it seemed, were worth more than gold. Coldrain was of the opinion they were worth considerably less.

Charlie Company moved on from the FUP at 1305 hours and made their approach to the village, Coldrain riding in the Viking.

'Bloody hell, I thought Bootle was crap, but this place takes the fucking piss.'

The voice belonged to Andy Tyrell, a sprog with the thickest Scouse accent he'd ever heard. He was driving the Viking, which was always the sprog's job. A more experienced Royal, Denison, was on top cover.

'First tour for you, Royal?' Coldrain shouted up above the engine roar.

'First and last, mate. After I'm done, there won't be any Taliban left for you to fight.'

'Sure, mate. I suppose we should just pack you off to Waziristan with a pistol and wait for the good news to come through about Bin Laden's death.'

'Where's Waziristan?'

'Forget it. How are your teeth?'

'What the fuck. Everyone's asking me that. Have I got some shit on them or something?'

'Nah, you're just paranoid, mate.'

It was Tyrell's first tour with Charlie but the new Bootneck had taken like a duck to water. Tyrell could be a bit hotheaded and was always the victim of C Company pranks. The previous week a few of the other Bootnecks had taken Tyrell's toothbrush and given it to one of the dogs on camp trained to look for explosives. They planned to email Tyrell the camera snap the next morning – after he'd given his teeth a good clean with a dog-licked brush. He wasn't a happy mucker. But for all that he was a good Bootneck in the making.

The Viking came to a halt at the edge of the village and Coldrain debussed along with the rest of 5 Troop. Denison stayed on the .50 cal ready to unleash some serious fire-power. He shouted something to Tyrell once the last man was unloaded and the Viking roared into life and started to flank around the village. Coldrain led the way into Ghorak.

Ghorak was laid out exactly as Coldrain remembered it. Shaped like a quadrangle, the western edge of the village presented a wide courtyard the size of half a football pitch with a clump of naked trees in the middle of it and a few hedges and thin strips of grass. To the left and right of the courtyard was a waist-high wall and behind that ran a strip of small single-room buildings. At the far end the yard opened up into a wide, bumpy dirt track that passed for a street and was lined with ancient-looking mudbrick buildings. An Afghan Main Street. There was rubbish all over the place, and ditches ran parallel to the dirt track, carrying raw sewage directly out of the homes. The street ran for two hundred metres and terminated at the foot-steps of a mosque. Low walls straddled around the edge of the houses on the northern and southern fringes of Ghorak, insulating the village from the outside world. The one new addition to the location was a series of three piles of rock and mud to the left of the courtyard. They looked like oversized rabbit mounds. A pencil-thin tree was planted atop each one with scraps of brightly coloured rags tethered to them, red, yellow, blue, white. Coldrain knew instantly that they were burial plots. The coloured bits of cloth were martyrs' flags. That meant they had probably been killed in a recent airstrike. Like the crucifix planted in the middle of FOB Sangin, it was a stark reminder of the human cost of war.

The villagers stood by silently as 5 Troop flooded through the courtyard. That was the first sign to Coldrain that something wasn't quite right. Usually when they rolled into an area the locals came right up. It was either to greet them or to complain. Maybe someone had warned them in advance of the mop-up job. Or perhaps they'd experienced this so many times it was just as much a part of their daily routine as forced marriage and beheadings.

They split into eight-man teams, equal to a single section, and went from compound to compound. Building clearances were stressful and every Bootneck needed to have his wits about him. Coldrain was looking out for his muckers as much as his bacon.

'Let's fucking do it.'

'Stay calm, Belham.'

Adam Belham was a Lympstone lad born up the road from the CTC. He and Coldrain set to the right and approached the first housing unit. Each house was surrounded by an outer perimeter wall. They had to be careful as a Taliban could be lurking just inside the walled area, waiting to ambush them.

'On my count,' Coldrain said.

'Ready.'

'Three . . . two . . . one . . . go!'

Coldrain booted the brightly coloured wooden door in, his foot crashing into it so hard it collapsed in on itself. Inside he found a typical Afghan dwelling: silk rug on the floor, narrow shelves lined with copies of the Qur'an, old posters of Muslim clerics and Hollywood movies tacked onto the walls side by side and a stove in one corner bearing five or six large metal bowls. Something was cooking; the scent reminded him of the awful chickpea stews the locals served up during the hearts-and-minds gatherings. They offered the Royals a taste whenever the village elders fancied a chat, but the lads always refused. Quite rightly, they didn't trust anything that didn't come from a ration pack or Marine camp. The last thing a Bootneck needed in Afghanistan was a bad case of the shits.

The home was empty. Not much sunlight got into these places and Coldrain had to squint to readjust his eyes to the filmy darkness, but it seemed to him that whoever had been in here had upped sticks just a few minutes prior.

'Clear!'

'All clear!'

'Move, move!'

They came to the next home.

And crashed the door in.

Inside there was a group of four young girls sitting around a half-finished rug which they were weaving. They were wearing the salwar kameez dress of loose pyjamas and a long tunic with a chador blouse wrapped around their faces. The girls looked startled and stopped their craft-work. Coldrain felt sorry for them. They were no older than thirteen or fourteen. Soon these poor young women would have to deck themselves up in the full-length burqa, or the black letterbox treatment as some of the lads termed it. All they had to look forward to was a future husband who could rape them whenever they wanted, and slap them about if they resisted. It was a hard-knock life and although Coldrain didn't give a toss about the locals as long as his muckers were all safe and sound, the sight of

28

subdued Afghan women always left him with a strong sense of injustice.

The room was boiling hot. Coldrain gave a cursory look round but there was nothing to see here.

It was the same for the other homes in Ghorak. Team Alpha turned them over, but there was no sign of a cache anywhere. The locals just stood back and watched. Out of the corner of his eye, Coldrain spied a group of young men lurking in the shadows of the compound. They were wearing the black turbans that marked them out as Talibs.

'What do you reckon their game is, mate?' Belham asked Coldrain as they passed by a group of bearded old men.

'No idea. But I don't like it one bit.'

It took an hour for 5 Troop to complete the village search. The temperature was forty in the shade. If there had been any. As it was they were redders and they were hanging out of their arses with all the kit they were having to patrol round in. Body armour, knee pads, elbow pads plus the SA-80s they were packing and their back-up Browning Hi-Power pistols, the lot. Coldrain carried his spare ammo, 66mm LAW, trauma kit, 51mm mortar rounds, PMG link and spare rations. It was a shit-ton of gear to carry around in such unrelenting heat. He took a stop and necked some water from his camelback. He squeezed the droplets into his mouth. They were warm.

And where the fuck was the cache? D Company were damned if they were going to sod off out of Ghorak empty-handed. The wary looks they were getting from the locals told Coldrain they were definitely hiding something. He just couldn't figure out what it was.

Coldrain saw Jamie and another Royal, a stick-thin Bristol lad called Phil Hardman, standing in the courtyard.

'Perimeter's clear,' Jamie said. 'No sign of dickers.'

'Yeah, and not a gun in sight here either.'

Jamie looked up at the sun and squinted. He hadn't even broken out in a sweat.

'It doesn't look good,' he replied.

They'd covered every inch of every building. That meant the weapons cache had either been moved uber-quick, or that the int guys hadn't done their job properly. Neither was very likely.

Coldrain was bang out of ideas.

'You heard of any air strikes here lately?' Jamie piped up.

'Round these parts? Not a word. Why?'

'You see any buildings damaged?'

Coldrain looked around him.

'Me neither.'

Jamie nodded towards the graves.

'Look at the soil.'

The mounds of earth were coffee-coloured and distinctly drabber than the surrounding sandy terrain. That meant the soil was freshly dug up. Given how blazing hot it was Coldrain guessed the mounds were no older than two days. And there had definitely been no activity around Ghorak in that time frame.

Jamie was grinning.

'Got to be it,' he said, already on the net calling for the explosives detection dog. Coldrain thinking, *Always wanted to be the man of action*. He had an optimism and go-get-'em attitude that bordered on naiveté. As if he was trying to prove something to his best mate and adopted brother.

Coldrain cast another skeg around the area. In the distance, four hundred metres beyond Ghorak, he spotted

30

two blokes on motorbikes at the top of a hill overlooking the village. The men were shadowed behind the sun, and they were too far away to tell if they were armed or not, whether they had bad intentions, or good. Coldrain kept an eye on them for a moment longer, let them know he was aware of them and that he wouldn't take any crap.

A couple of the village elders had been standing a few metres away watching this shit unfold. Their faces had more creases than a newbie in a game of poker, and they were each wearing the trademark beige pakul so beloved of the old Mujahideen.

The two village elders turned jittery. They started shouting and gesticulating, first to each other, and then to Coldrain and the rest of the Charlie oppos. Soon others joined in the commotion. Jamie was thirty metres from the graves. Coldrain started to get anxious. Belham had walked over to the two elders and was shouting at them to shut the fuck up.

The other guys in 5 Troop had now gathered in the courtyard. They, too, sensed that they were in the rattle. Without prompting they formed a thin semi-circular cordon in front of the crowd, putting eight metres between themselves and the Afghans. Above the wall that ran around the yard Coldrain could see Denison's head bobbing along on the .50 cal on top of the Viking. Coldrain shouted to Belham.

'Keep these people back. I don't want this getting out of control.'

Belham nodded.

'Where's that fucking translator? Tell these people to lift up their clothes and prove they're not suicide bombers.'

The explosives detection dog and its handler arrived at the courtyard. The lads stayed well clear. Chances were high that the cache was booby-trapped with an IED to ward off coalition soldiers prodding at the mounds. But the Royals were one step ahead of the Taliban dickers. No Bootneck in his right mind would go anywhere near the cache until it had been cleared of explosives.

Coldrain found the situation distressing, but he had very good reason to suspect that the weapons cache was buried in the graves. He'd never been so certain of anything in his life. There was no other logical explanation on the location of the stash. The absence of a crater in the ground merely confirmed his thoughts. Just because there might be a weapons cache in the village didn't mean the locals were on the side of the Taliban. In fact, the opposite was true. A lot of Afghans couldn't wait for the Taliban to be booted out of their region. But as soon as their patrols left town, the locals were defenceless. That was when the Taliban made their move, threatening violence on anyone who dared talk to the Coalition, or refused to let the Taliban use their home to store munitions.

Jamie was now ten metres from the burial site. The thin trees cast a sliver of a shadow over him. Bright cloths flapped in the mild breeze. Belham returned with the translator, some Pashtun kid from the ANP who looked like he was ready to piss himself. His voice was shaking as he spoke. The kid could barely make himself audible above the hysterical crowd.

Coldrain and the 5 Troops lads pointed their guns at the crowd to get them to simmer down. They quietened. Funny the power an SA-80 had over people. A few retreated into their homes. Others stood around but stayed quiet, scratching their elbows and muttering under their breath.

Coldrain thought about all the taxpayers safely tucked away in their semi-detacheds back home. He hoped they were enjoying Ant and Dec and tucking into a nice plate of fish and chips.

He glanced over his shoulder at Jamie. He was patrolling around the edge of a nearby compound. Checking out possible threats and managing the locals.

The next few seconds had become a blur in Coldrain's mind and it was difficult to separate them out. He could remember the dog handler confirming that there was a device around the weapons cache. Meaning they would need to Op Barma the site to clear the IED. Op Barma drills were painstakingly difficult and the guys in the team were among the bravest Coldrain had ever met. He was going to wish the Barma lads luck. But he never managed to finish the sentence. Midway through he felt a sudden belch of hot air behind him, and a fraction of a second later came the deafening sound of the explosion. The ground around Coldrain shook. Rocks and fist-sized clumps of dirt were blown past him like projectiles fired into the crowd.

Spinning around Coldrain dropped his rifle and was rushing towards the explosion. His heart sank when he saw where the smoke was coming from. The compound Jamie had been adjacent to was obscured behind an expanding mushroom of debris and smoke billowed into the sky, blocking out the sunlight. It was oozing violently like a blackened thermal spring from the exact spot he had seen Jamie a moment earlier. He couldn't see him anywhere. As if he'd spontaneously combusted.

Coldrain got to within fifteen metres of the compound before Belham grabbed a hold of him.

'Oh no you don't, mate,' Belham said. 'Stay the fuck away!'

He struggled against his oppo's bear hug but deep down he knew his mucker was right. The Taliban used primary and secondary IED these days and there was a decent chance that Coldrain could get himself zapped as well if he ventured any closer to the explosion. Two birds, one stone.

As he was wrestled to the ground by Belham, he thought about the promise he'd made to Pam to bring Jamie back home alive. He had let her down.

'Man down! Man down!' he heard Belham scream into his radio. 'Need immediate medevac, T1 casualty.' A T1 was the most critical type of casualty and indicated that the victim had an hour before he was browners. But every lad there knew the call was made out of protocol rather than hope. Jamie was zapped. Coldrain had seen explosions on patrols along the roads of Kandahar and Helmand and he knew the extent of the kill zone on such incendiary devices. There would be nothing left of his best mate.

Coldrain found himself looking back to the hill spot, where the two figures had been watching. He glimpsed their retreat, the two shadows sinking behind the other side of the hill, as the motorbikes sped off into the distance. Most people's lives gradually get shittier over a prolonged period of time. Coldrain was able to pinpoint the exact moment when his life turned gash.

The effects of the rum began to wear off. Coldrain suddenly didn't feel like drinking any more. He screwed the top back on the bottle and dumped it back in the kitchen cupboard. Headed for the front door.

'Off already?' the old man asked.

Coldrain shrugged.

'Jamie's anniversary next week,' Pam said.

Other families, regular folk, had anniversaries for

marriages or engagements or the birth of a kid. John and Pam Reese had one for the day their son was incinerated by an IED hidden in a weapons cache thousands of miles from home, in the middle of a shit-hole wadi in some godforsaken corner of Afghanistan.

Coldrain said nothing, slammed the door behind him and hit the road.

THREE

Smiling was not something that came naturally to the Sandman. Nor was it a requirement for the industry he operated in. Paranoia, yes. Mistrust, certainly. But a good sense of humour, no. He found the smile awkward to maintain. His facial muscles ached, a relic of the shrapnel fragments buried deep inside them, the shards of hot metal that had perforated his cheek flesh as bombs rained from the sky and slammed into his village. That had been a very long time ago, but the scars still felt fresh. Smiling was a reminder of the terror that had been inflicted all those years previous. It was for this reason he chose not to smile, even when social situations required it. But today, at lunch, he was prepared to accept the pain and smile. Principally because the man opposite him was asking for help, and that in itself was quite improbable and not a little amusing.

He sipped his latte and listened to the sweaty man opposite talk. He was not asking for the Sandman's assistance. No, this was a man who was begging. The Sandman had seen plenty of those in his time, and the man before him, in his crumpled suit and crinkled shirt, was displaying all the hallmarks of a classic beggar. Pleading eyes that flicked from left to right, hands clamped together on the table to hide their sweaty palms, all accompanied by a general nervousness and agitation. Combined, these signals communicated the man's deep anxiety, betrayed his desperation to the Sandman. Brown, for that was his name, was a man in a dire position.

Brown. The Sandman wasn't even sure if that was his opposite number's real name. Somehow he doubted it. He couldn't have looked less like a shadowy government player. No cigarette hanging from his lip, no black suit, no trilby hat. Just a podgy middle-aged man with a badly disguised bald patch and jowly cheeks. Anyone else would have taken one look at Brown and arrived at the perfectly understandable conclusion that he was a used-car dealer. Then again, one lesson the Sandman had learned over many years in the game was that drawing unwanted attention to oneself was not the mark of a good operator. He lived in the world of the grey men, people who had perfected the art of not standing out. James Bond's fantasy approach was best left to Hollywood. And the fact that Brown was so inconspicuous allowed the Sandman to construe that his credentials were genuine, even if his name were not.

Brown was a fixer for the British government. The title was unofficial and so was the job, organising third parties to do the bidding of Whitehall when the assignment was too dirty for Downing Street's fingerprints to be found on the murder weapon. The Geneva Convention, the Human Rights Act and an increasingly emboldened twenty-four-hour media circus had reduced the government's room for manoeuvre on such issues. Certainly when it came to the torturing of suspects, or the elimination of key terror targets in Afghanistan or neighbouring Pakistan, Brown was the man who would find someone to do the work. All for a good price, of course.

The Sandman was a contractor on the circuit, but he had never been offered work by Brown before. That was because the government tended to work with one or two very loyal contractors, the kind who had long-standing relationships with Whitehall and could be trusted in the event that things turned ugly. Combined with the fact that Brown's employers tended to pay less than the Americans and private organisations such as oil firms meant that, although the two men had worked for many years in the same arena, they had never once shaken hands on a deal. Instead they had circulated each other, like wary neighbours.

'I'm sorry, Brown,' the Sandman said. 'But I can't help you.'

'But – you agreed to meet. Surely you're interested in our proposition?'

'Nigeria,' the Sandman replied firmly.

'I beg your pardon.'

'Nigeria is a bad country. A dangerous place for a white security adviser, but I'm sure even you realise that. Ever been there?'

'No.'

'Then you are lucky. Now, my biggest problem is that my boys know how bad it is over there. A civilised man such as yourself couldn't even begin to imagine the squalor and violence that infests every inch of that continent, like a terminal cancer spreading across a weak body. So when I am offered business in Africa, I am faced with a dilemma. Which of my boys will accept the work? It's hard enough as it is to get good men.'

Brown lowered his gaze.

'In Nigeria last month I dispatched a four-man team to Port Harcourt to provide protection to three executives from a well-known oil company. Tell me, Brown, are you familiar with the NDV?'

'Not really.'

'As I thought. As with most British you pretend to know everything about the rest of the world, but in reality your knowledge is as thin as your hair. The NDV is the Niger Delta Vigilante. They are an armed militia group whose only interest is in causing as much havoc to the oil infrastructure as humanly possible. Three days ago the NDV launched wave after wave of attacks on the city. Your "employers" wouldn't know about this, of course, having withdrawn all but the most basic support services from Nigeria over the past several months.

'The NDV raided the city police stations first. They knew that by overrunning the rudimentary police they would be free to cause chaos throughout the rest of the city. My boys were based in a hotel near the city centre when the attacks happened. They didn't have time to react. The reports I have indicate that they tried to fashion an escape from the hotel by shooting their way out of the fire escape, but they were apprehended by the NDV and taken away. The oil company people were executed on the spot.

'Unfortunately for my boys their fate was not so pleasant. For the crime of killing NDV soldiers, they were subjected to horrific torture at the hands of their captors.

'A witness described the executions on the phone to me personally. The first man was skinned alive, salted and then burnt as the others were forced to watch.

'The second operator was tied upside down to a thick tree branch, ropes bound around his ankles. He was left like this for an hour, until most of his blood had gone to his head. Then two NDV soldiers took a long saw and hacked him in half, sawing down from his groin into his stomach cavity. Because most of his blood was lower down, the man did not die until they had reached his lungs.

'The third man had his ears and nose hacked off with a machete. The severed features were wrapped inside a cloth which was then stuffed into his mouth. The man's mouth was sewn shut, and the NDV soldiers took it in turns to punch him in the stomach and shoot him in his legs and arms. Eventually he choked on his own blood and vomit.

'The last suffered the worst. He was taken over to a spot next to a truck used by the NDV to transport soldiers. His captors pinned him to the ground and four other men then lifted the truck off the ground. They slowly dropped one of the front wheels on top of the man's head. His jaw was crushed under the tremendous pressure, but worse was to follow. One by one the men climbed onto the truck, jumping up and down, increasing the pressure on the man's skull. Soon his eyeballs were bulging from their sockets and burst open.

'Finally, with more men climbing onto the truck, the pressure became too much. His brain oozed out of his ears.

'That is how my men died.'

Brown's mouth was agape. He looked like he was going to vomit.

'I don't understand—'

'Mr Brown, if that is your name, at some point today I have to call the wives of these men and explain what happened. Then I need to find a new team to send over there. This is a priority for me, if I am to continue doing

40

business with my clients there. My point being,' he added with a final flourish, 'I do not have the patience or the inclination to be patronised by your so-called government.'

A band of sweat had formed across Brown's forehead.

'I'm not being—'

'This is about the diplomat, it is not?'

'I'm sorry?' Brown flustered, stuttering badly.

'Don't play games with me. Christian Watts. The one killed in the bomb blast in Kabul a month ago.'

'Something like that.'

'It is either everything, or it is nothing. Which is it?'

'Yes, all right,' Brown acknowledged grudgingly. 'Watts is involved.'

'So you lose a civil servant. Now your men can perhaps empathise with the plight of the soldiers they send into battle. A little death can do wonders for a man's perspective, I have discovered.' He sighed. Leant back in his chair and twiddled his thumbs. 'And let me guess. Now your people wish for revenge.'

'An eye for an eye, isn't that what they say?'

'*An eye for an eye only ends up making the whole world blind.*'

'Mahatma Gandhi.'

'If you're familiar with the line, then you should take his advice. Leave vengeance to the soldiers. In your world, you lose someone like Watts, you wring your hands in that finest English tradition, and then you find some clone from Oxford or Cambridge to replace him. It is not so difficult.'

Brown shook his head. 'Please. Hear me out.'

The Sandman remained passive, folded his arms. Brown went on anyway.

'The point is, my various bosses want action and, yes,

it's true, they want blood. But that's the way it is. They won't take no for an answer. On the ground things don't look good. We've gone past the three hundred milestone for total losses incurred. We're getting a lot of flak over this, but equally we have been told, many times, by the generals that there is no quick fix. Sure, we can burn a few poppy fields, blow up some abandoned Taliban safe house or send another hundred troops, but the media see through those little tricks now. We can't pull a victory out of the hat on this one.'

'When even the newspapers see through your lies, the game is surely up.'

'But we can do something about the Watts case.'

'With your government's incompetence, I would not be so sure.'

'We can,' Brown insisted. 'We have a lead.'

Brown reached into the inside pocket of his cheap suit and pulled out a photograph. He laid it on the table, picture side down, and slid it across to the Sandman.

The photograph was six by four inches, green and black and grainy. The Sandman could tell it had been taken with a long-distance camera of the type used in covert observation ops, and consequently there wasn't much to look at. The photographer had captured the face and little else. There was a second head half hidden behind the central figure. The faint outline of mountains glowed in the distance and in the foreground there was a fire. Through the night-vision lens it resembled a burning orb.

The face had been snapped in front profile, looking up at something. He had a thin, wave-like moustache and what appeared to be a scar or dent on the left side of his forehead. The Sandman found himself drawn to the eyes. They were rugby ball-shaped and stood out because he had no eyebrows, just a slightly paler outline traced above.

'This man is big news, trust me.'

'For you, maybe. To me, this is just a face.'

He tossed the photograph back at Brown. Motioned to the Polish waitress to bring the bill.

'We're willing to quadruple the number I mentioned on the phone.'

The Sandman did a double take. Four times what was already an inflated figure, at least in government terms, what with all the fear about where taxpayers' money was being spent, and contracting third parties to do the dirty work being very low down the list of PR-friendly investments. *Four times.*

The waitress hovered by the table, card machine ready. When she stubbornly refused to move, the Sandman shot her a stone-cold stare that sent her scampering.

'His name is Dogan,' Brown said. 'Ali Dogan.'

'I am afraid that name does not ring a bell.'

'To anyone on the outside, it wouldn't. But trust me, this guy has been trailed for many months. He's been on the radar of MI6 for a while, which is how we know that Dogan is behind the Kabul bombing, as well as several others. The Tikrit explosion six months ago? Dogan. The Italian Embassy attack in Pakistan? That man Dogan again. He's no ordinary bomber. He's not interested in taking out civilians. Only those in power.'

'Some might argue he's doing everyone a favour.'

'I'm serious. Dogan's attacks are carried out with precision, planning and inside knowledge. His bombs are very advanced, and he has a small team working with him, funded partly by his association with the PKK, the Kurdish separatist group—'

43

'Based in the south-eastern tip of the country. Yes, I know they are. The PKK are heavily involved with the heroin trade, importing it from Afghanistan, up through Lice in Turkey and then smuggled north into Central Europe. Tell me something new.'

'Dogan is a man with means, and the ability to carry out devastating attacks on the political infrastructure. Already now we have other senior diplomats and foreign office postings worried about their safety.'

'He sounds like a very painful thorn in your side.'

'That he is. But our current difficulty is that resources are stretched to breaking point. If it was up to me, I'd have some of the lads from the SRR on the case as we speak. But they're working overtime on cases closer to home. MI5 likewise. And anyway, even if we did have the manpower, there's the whole question of ethics on this. We're preaching multilateralism and greater harmony between nations. If we were seen engaging in a stealth raid, in Turkey, a NATO country of all places, there would be hell to pay. You can imagine the sort of crisis that would ensue.'

'Only too well.'

'Intelligence has him down to complete a drug transaction in three days' time. It's a simple snatch and grab.'

For the first time in their entire conversation, Brown firmly held the Sandman's gaze.

'We need your help to apprehend Dogan.'

'Apprehend?'

'Take him down. Neutralise. Whatever you people call it these days.'

'Killing, mostly.'

Brown nodded awkwardly. 'So. Will you do it?'

'Four times?'

'You have my word.'

'Well then,' the Sandman said, gesturing for the waitress to come over again, this time beating over like a terrified rabbit, the Sandman paying in cash, with a generous forty-pound tip for her troubles. 'It is time we set about removing this particular thorn.'

FOUR

Coldrain sat in the reception, leafing through a copy of *Legal Business*. He'd toyed with the idea of going into the law profession when he was at school, enjoyed the sociology and history classes more than maths and the sciences. But reading an article on some obscure point of legislation, he was glad he'd never followed that career path. Coldrain had a good few brain cells on him and scored six A stars at GCSE. He had nothing on the legal babble on the page in front of him, though.

The reception looked like something out of a seventies sci-fi movie. White walls adorned with frames of Japanese characters, a high ceiling that echoed every set of clipped footsteps and a glass-walled front that gazed down onto Tavistock Square. A bank of pretty twenty-something receptionists were dressed in identikit black two-pieces and talking sternly into their headsets. Above the reception there was a large black-stencilled 'M' and 'T', the initials of the law firm. The place reeked of corporate bullshit.

And Coldrain stank of booze. He was beginning to regret the ten jars of Stella he'd shared the previous night with Victor, an old South African mate and a former Royal. Could still taste the kebab in his mouth, like he'd been sucking on an armpit.

'Miss Fisher will see you now,' one of the receptionists squawked.

He was signed in, a process that involved more paperwork and signatures than a move order for a Brigade deployment to Afghanistan, and leapt up the stairs two at a time to the fifth floor. He found Melanie's desk at the end of a long hallway. Melanie was sitting behind her computer, tapping away busily on her keyboard.

In the old days she smiled when she saw him. Now she had a look of concern on her face, and sadness too. The smile came later, and it was definitely forced.

'I thought I told you not to bother me at work,' she said.

'Just thought I'd swing by and say hello.'

'I would guess that depends who's doing the swinging.'

Melanie was the definition of 'petite', five foot three, although she looked taller. He guessed that was down to her well-proportioned frame. She had smooth, slim legs, a flat tummy, bazooka-sized warlocks and an arse that made grown men want to punch walls. She was wearing a white blouse and grey mid-length skirt.

She worked as a secretary at the corporate tax firm Mitchell Tasker, at the very bottom rung of a ladder she hoped to make her way up over the next few years. Coldrain respected her resilience and determination. He'd survived nightmarish firefights in the Afghan, but always suspected he wouldn't last five minutes if he worked in a corporate environment. Office politics wasn't his forte.

Every surface was clean and sterile. The lawyers were all immaculately dressed in Armani suits and obviously hit the tanning salon every other day in between grazing on tuna Niçoise salads. Coldrain was dressed in tattered pumps, torn jeans and a baggy Brown Job green t-shirt. He had a solid four days' of growth and maybe twenty quid in his back pocket.

Melanie didn't have an office. She had a pod, which was a fancy way of stating that she worked in a cramped two-by-four-metre area surrounded by Post-it notes, in-trays and Very Important Memos. He crouched low as he pulled up beside her, pecking her on the cheek.

'I'm busy,' she said.

'Wondered if you fancied grabbing some lunch?'

Melanie pointed to a pre-packed prawn sandwich sitting on her desk next to a low-fat bio yoghurt and a bottle of sparkling water named after some unpronounce-able Taff valley. It bested the bag-rat packed lunches he used to get in the Marines, which consisted of a squashed Cornish pasty, a packet of crisps loaded with enough sea dust to give you sodium poisoning and a can of foul-tasting, lime-coloured soda.

'How about we could go eat in the park?'

'Maybe after you tell me where you've been the last two weeks.'

He shifted uncomfortably. The walls of Melanie's pod were four feet high and Coldrain imagined the curious gazes of her co-workers, leaning in to catch whispers of their conversation.

'Sorry,' he offered.

'I tried calling, I texted, I left messages, I . . .' Melanie cut herself short, placing a hand to her chest and releasing a sigh as light as a zephyr. The office hummed with the noise of business: the faint rush of the air-con, the whirring of computer fans and the tip-tap of fingers on keyboards.

'Sorry,' he said again, but he offered nothing more. He had been off the grid, pissing his life up the wall. But he couldn't really tell her that.

'You can't just say sorry and hope it'll be better.'

He nibbled her left ear. Her feet slanted forward, toes pressed against the bland carpet. Her breathing became erratic, unsteady.

'I can do more than say sorry,' he said.

She flinched her head away from his, angled her body towards him, and gave him an arched eyebrow that reminded him of a schoolteacher frowning at an errant pupil. 'And *that's* not a universal fix either,' she said, barest hint of a smile at the corner of her lips. 'No matter how much you like to pretend otherwise.'

'That wasn't what you said last time.'

Her phone bleeped. 'Shit,' she said, distracted.

'Leave it. Come and have lunch.'

'I've really got to take this.'

'Dinner, then.'

'Maybe,' turning back to an array of papers scattershot over her desk. 'Let me see how I get on.'

They'd known each other for years, going back to secondary school. Some girls Coldrain knew had aged a lot in ten years. Not Mel. She was, if anything, getting more stunning with every passing year.

Back when he'd been a Royal, hunting down Taliban in Afghanistan and before that fighting the insurgency in Iraq, Melanie had been the only person who had kept in touch with Coldrain. Every month, just like clockwork, she sent him a letter. The letters themselves were nothing special, just a bit of goss and local news, but the fact there was someone back home who cared about him kept Coldrain going during the darkest periods. That was how they first got together. War had set him up with this bird. Maybe war was taking him away from her, too.

She was class and moneyed and read the *Guardian* and worried about climate change. He was broke and sometimes checked out the pools tips in the *Sun* and didn't even recycle. They'd somehow overcome their differences to become an item. And a good one, too. Coldrain had his fair share of disastrous hook-ups in the past and when things were good between Melanie and himself, they were really, really good. He hoped she wasn't slipping away from him.

'I guess you'll be off again soon?'

'Don't think so. I'm done with the circuit. Back for good,' he winked. 'More time for us.'

She shook her head.

'That's a lie. I'm training to be a lawyer, Dan. If you're going to fib, I suggest you take acting lessons.'

'You gonna bill me for that advice?'

'Take a long walk off a short cliff,' she said, winking back. 'And, anyway, how are you going to earn money in the future?'

'I've got loads of options. Bouncer. Male model. Professional midget tosser.'

'Goodness,' she said. 'Think of all the Stella that'll buy.'

One of the benefits of working the circuit was the low personal spend while on duty. He'd returned with a pretty decent stash in his bank account, but the money had not lasted as long as he'd expected. A lot of his old mates wanted to go out on the piss and hear his war stories. Or, to be precise, the comic-book version, the one that had all the nasty stuff edited out. He'd bought the bike and a few other things, and suddenly his paper was looking worryingly thin.

Reluctant to go back on the circuit, Coldrain had become a rubber dagger and joined the Royal Marines reserves, which paid him a big pile of fuck-all. Shifts operating the doors at a nightclub were worth a few shekels, which is how he met his flatmate Ricky, and they ended up sharing digs in the gash end of Willesden Junction with some jumped-up Irish woman for a landlady. If he was honest with himself, Coldrain was coasting at the moment, doing his best to keep his shit together and getting sandy bottoms on the sauce every other night of the week.

It was time for a reboot.

The phone insisted on Melanie's attention with a second ring.

'I really have to get on.'

'How about dinner?'

Melanie sighed. 'There's an absolute ton of work for me to get through, Dan.'

'I'll take that as a yes.'

'You're an arsehole.'

'I aim to please. I'll see you later,' Coldrain said, standing up to leave.

'You know what your problem is?'

'People tell me it's lactose intolerance.'

'You hate yourself so much it's impossible for anyone else to love you.'

Fuck me, Coldrain thought. *Spend half your bloody life hanging out with other Royals and talking about war, pornography and beer in that order, and then the minute you chat to a bird she figures you out like a beginner's Sudoku puzzle.*

FIVE

Coldrain chewed on his food and thoughts simultaneously as he rested on the bench in the small scrub of land that passed for a park in central London.

The sun was beaming and Coram Fields was filling up with posh mums and their screaming ankle biters. They looked like they were from a different world. He sometimes wondered how they would react if they knew what he'd done for his country. What he'd fought for, and what he'd lost. In the end, that was why he'd decided to go outside and jack in the Royals. He'd learned the hard way that the average person on Civvy Street didn't know about the reality of war, and didn't give much of a fuck either. They got spoon-fed some fantasy story in the press where words like heroism were bandied about by people who thought bravery was going out in Brixton on a Friday night.

A few others lay on the ground, lazy and still, letting the sun work their bodies.

He thought back to Jamie. Christ, the hour he didn't think of him had yet to be invented. Because Jamie was more than a mate. He was a brother.

An image seared itself into Coldrain's vision, like a rod of heated metal branding his skull. That fateful day at school. The bus ride home, arsenic clouds suffocating the sky. He went home on time that day, his mum having shouted at him the day before when he stayed out late with his friends, getting up to no good on a building site.

That day, he wished he'd never come home at all.

'Mum,' he shouted as he entered and saw no one in the living room and kitchen. 'Mum, where are you?'

His vision fast-forwarded to his new family, Jamie and his parents, the ones who'd rescued him and adopted him when none of his blood relatives wanted anything to do with the boy from that 'cursed family'. He never felt especially close to Pam and John; an eight-year-old boy is too far down the line to supplant his blood ties. But Jamie became a brother and made life bearable at first, in those difficult months.

The throbbing pain in his head had returned with interest since he walked out of the law firm. Probably all the organic air they had in that joint.

He swallowed warm mouthfuls of a rubbery hot dog and thought about how he'd make things up at dinner. It would have to be somewhere fairly cheap, as he was on a tight budget. He'd find somewhere decent. As a Bootneck on a salary of £17,000 a year he'd mastered the art of finding inexpensive but fancy-looking restaurants. The key, he'd learned, was to go some place where the food was good but they had a bottle of piss water. It was the wine selection that tended to bump up the bill. Stick to the red piss and he'd have some pocket shrapnel left over at the end of the night.

Coldrain finished off his munch and headed towards the exit. Someone was standing next to the gate. It took Coldrain a few seconds to recognise the figure, and then he froze. Anger washed over him like a seizure. The past was crashing back into the present.

SIX

'I should tear your fucking head off,' Coldrain seethed.

'Let's take a walk, Daniel,' the Sandman said icily. That accent was unmistakable, but impossible to place. No one knew where the Sandman came from. When Coldrain had worked for his company, Regulatory Services Ltd, the guys in the unit had a pool going. Fifty quid got you in, first person to guess the Sandman's nationality won the pot. He'd put his money down on Serbian. Others had staked cash on German, Russian, Argentinian and even Malaysian. No one ever claimed the pot.

'You know you shouldn't take all this so personally, Daniel. Tashkent was merely business.'

'Eat a dick.'

Coldrain began to walk away. Suddenly the Sandman reached out and gripped Coldrain's left wrist. Coldrain probably had more muscle in his little toe than the Sandman had in his entire wiry frame, but the old bastard had a fierce hold. He tried to shake himself free, but it was like his hand was clamped in a vice. Briefly, the thought crossed his mind of lamping the Sandman right on the kisser, but knowing the Sandman he probably had a whole platoon of crazed ex-Spetsnaz lurking behind the bushes.

'Walk if you know what's good for you,' the Sandman said in a severe voice.

'Staying as far away from you as possible would be a good fucking place to start.'

The Sandman was lean to the point of looking emaciated. His cheeks were pockmarked and his small, grey eyes had bags underneath so deep black you would mistake them for bruises. The whole package made him look creepier than a delegate a Tory party conference in election season. He was decked out in a posh-looking black Saxxon wool two-piece, white two-fold cotton herringbone shirt and blue sleek silk cravat.

'Nice threads, mate,' Coldrain said. 'Pay for them with the Tashkent job, did you?'

'I am very sorry I could not help on that situation. But the truth is, I did not even know you were alive.'

'Bollocks.'

Coldrain had had enough game-playing for one day.

'Just get this over with and tell me what the bloody hell you want. I got more important shit to being doing with my day.'

'I have a job for you.'

Rage flushed over Coldrain so quickly he nearly exploded. It took all his self-control to stop him from pounding the Sandman to shit. He fists were clenched so tight his nails were digging into the skin of his palms.

'You expect *me* to work for *you*? After you shafted me with those bent coppers in the Uzbek?'

'As I said, I'm very sorry about that.'

'Yeah, well, write a fucking letter and put it in the post. Waterford died. He might have been a twat but he still had a wife and kids. He said them guys were corrupt. You should have known. The whole thing was a cock-up waiting to happen.'

The Sandman sighed.

'You didn't even compensate the family. Me and a few of the other lads had a whip-round, couple of grand for her to pay the bills and that. But you're a rich mother-fucker, and yet you never gave Waterford's missus a penny.'

'If I looked out for the relatives of every employee killed in the field, I would have nothing left. I run a corporate enterprise, Daniel. Not some fucking social welfare group.'

'Yeah, I know. Remorse ain't exactly one of your strong suits.'

'Look, I am prepared to admit that what happened back there was, shall we say, a terrible accident. I would be lying if I said it did not make me sad. But you must understand, Daniel, it was not a mistake.'

Coldrain took a deep breath. He was incandescent with rage. Fuming, he stepped closer to the Sandman. They were eyeball to eyeball. The Sandman held his gaze.

'You mean to say you knew they were on the take?'

'I would not care to phrase it so carelessly. We, that is myself and the Uzbek authorities, were aware of a certain level of corruption within the paramilitary forces. It was, I have to say, the main aim of the mission. The Uzbeks were very keen on locking up corrupt police officers. Media-wise there was a lot of benefit attached.'

Coldrain felt his head spinning. He had never liked working for the Sandman. Too secretive, too elusive and too many people whispering in his ear that you should never trust him. Not for a minute. But now he felt a rising hate towards the Sandman. He wanted to get out of here and clear his head. He wanted a drink.

'You make me sick.'

'So you're not interested in making money?'

'I'm doing just fine.'

'That's not what the word on the street says.'

Coldrain looked away. 'You should take street talk with a pinch of salt. Just because I'm not bathing in Cristal at the Hilton, don't mean I'm skint.'

The Sandman ignored Coldrain. He pulled a packet of Russian cigs from his pocket.

'The mission is a simple snatch and grab. You and a partner. The other is American, ex-Delta. You'll like him. The fee is a million each, after expenses, on the condition that everything is under the radar.'

'Pounds or dollars?'

'Sterling, of course,' the Sandman said, eyes glinting.

A million shekels, he thought. That's way beyond the standard bill for this type of mission. Usually when someone was paying a whack over the going rate, there was a catch somewhere down the line just waiting to snap you on the arse. No doubt with the Sandman involved, there was some small print. But the pound signs kept doing little dances in front of his eyes. He pictured buying a Gucci pad in the Algarve, right next to one of those fuck-off golf courses that Premier League footballers played on during their hols. He had an image of him and Melanie strolling by the beach, sipping on a pair of ice-cold bevvies as the waves lapped against their feet. He pictured a better life.

Coldrain shook his head. He wanted to tell the Sandman to go screw himself. But instead he found himself asking for more int.

'Who's the target?'

The Sandman took a long drag on his cancer stick.

'He goes by the name of Dogan. He's a veteran on the global terrorist circuit. The people who want me to find him are desperate to get their hands on him. But they are also not the usual employers. These people are very important figures. Because of the urgency and because of the clients, I said I'd get my finest men on the case.'

'That's very flattering, but I don't work for you any more.'

The Sandman chuckled. 'You'd be surprised how many times I've heard that. You'd be even more surprised how many times those people have been wrong.'

Coldrain took a deep breath. A million. Christ. That was a hell of a lot of ducats, though working for the Sandman again would be like dry-humping the Devil. This guy had stabbed him in the back once already. He couldn't trust him not to do it again.

'I'm not interested,' he said flatly.

He turned to leave.

'If you change your mind, you know where to find me,' the Sandman called after him.

'Fat chance of that, mate,' Coldrain blasted back.

Deep inside, he knew that he didn't have much of a choice. It was only a matter of time when it came to the Sandman. He tried to clear his mind but last night's drink and this morning's hangover were draped over his brain like a hot flannel, clogging his thought processes. His phone cawed, awakening him from his fug. A text. Melanie. 'Sorry cant do tonite working late. Tomoz is bad but how about end of the wk xx.'

He went to text her back but discarded his message

halfway through. Much as Coldrain wanted to patch things up with Melanie, he couldn't concentrate. The Sandman consumed his thoughts.

Coldrain had a feeling they'd be seeing each other again before long.

SEVEN

The pub was a filthy den tucked away in the chad end of Walthamstow, sandwiched between a Kosher shop and a jerk chicken hut and overshadowed by a council block famous because the police usually gave it a wide berth after one of their own got the knife there a few years back.

When he was a kid, Coldrain's old man used to take him up to Walthamstow dogs on a Saturday. Coldrain would bring the pocket money he'd saved that month, usually amounting to around ten shekels, and have a couple of flutters. When the occasional dog came in a winner, he felt like he'd won the lottery. Now the track had closed down and in recent years the clientele had shifted once the gangs had taken up shop. Round this way, every pub was bent, all the money invested was from people on the make. It was the kind of joint where a bloke could smoke a cigarette inside and no one would ever come up to him and ask him to put it out. And if they did, they could probably expect him to comply and stub it out in their eye.

It was the kind of place that Coldrain knew someone like Dagenham Mick could be found.

If you wanted to find him.

Dagenham Mick was five-ten and looked like watered-down crap. He was skinny, pale and chewed frantically on gum. He only seemed to have the one piece, because every so often he would spit the gum into his hand, play with it like putty, stick it to the table to fester for a few minutes before popping it back into his mouth.

He was dressed in a whitish vest, over which he wore a purple pimping jacket. He was sporting four gold necklaces, two medallions and a gold ring on each finger. Underneath the rings were elaborate tattoos that covered every inch of his hands. Dagenham Mick had been a bare-knuckle fighter in his day, back when he was a traveller. Legend had it he'd killed a guy with one punch to the face. Stone cold. Now he was one of the biggest drug wholesalers in north London.

And he was also, according to Victor the South African, the source of some quick and easy cash.

'Name's Coldrain. Victor's friend. I heard you have work going.'

Dagenham Mick shoved a hand down his pants and scratched his balls. A towering hulk of a guy that Coldrain assumed was Mick's muscle brought over a beer to Mick.

'Drink?' he asked.

It was eleven thirty in the morning.

'I'm good.'

Dagenham Mick gulped down half his pint.

'Let me guess. Another ex-Marine looking for a quick buck?'

'Hole in one.'

'Well, I can't complain,' he said, digging into the back pocket of his green Adidas sweat pants. 'I mean, I thought these guys were tough,' he continued, nodding at the Incredible Hulk. 'But you boys? Jesus! Hard as nails.'

Dagenham Mick produced a wad of fifties from his pocket.

'This is four hundred quid. Yours nice and easy, son.'

'What do you need done?'

'Go over to Tower Hamlets. Find a guy named Darius He's a, uh, retail agent over that way and he owes me big time. I'm talking to the tune of twenty grand. I would like,' he said, finishing his pint with a belch, 'to get my money. Yesterday, like.'

'How am I going to find this guy? I'm a soldier, not bloody Morse.'

'Derrick here knows the address. He'll come with,' Dagenham Mick said, nodding to the hulking figure. Coldrain took one look at the guy called Derrick and knew he was on roids. He must have weighed north of twenty stone. Derrick had pecs that suggested he could bench-press a tank, with legs the size of tree trunks. He was big and wide and probably as dumb as a lump of day-old dog turd.

'What if your man hasn't got the money?'

'Then he needs to be taught a lesson.'

Coldrain nodded. He knew the kind of lesson Dagenham Mick was talking about, and it didn't involve blackboards or textbooks.

'Got a thing?'

'You what?'

'A gun, my man.'

Coldrain shook his head.

'I'll get one sorted.'

'No thanks, mate,' Coldrain replied. 'I'm good to go as I am.'

Dagenham Mick shrugged, like he didn't care one way or the other.

'You got wheels?'

'No.'

'Then take this,' Dagenham Mick said, chucking a set of Merc keys at Coldrain.

'Let's do this then,' Coldrain said, turning to Derrick.

'And, uh, Coldrain?'

'Yeah.'

'Make it slow.'

EIGHT

They pulled up outside a miserable grey estate that seemed to stretch for miles into the distance. Building after ramshackle building. Corrugated iron bars over the windows, cheap clothes draped on wire washing lines, mutt dogs chewing on old toys and a bum with a beer can pissing against a tree.

Someone, many years ago, had decided to call this place Summer Park and put a big bright sign welcoming people to it. Now the sign was tattered and covered in graffiti, like the butt of some bad joke. Coldrain was suddenly reminded of how Greenland got its name: some badass nutjob called Eric the Red was expelled from Iceland and sailed north until he reached dry land. Realising the place he'd pitched up was a barren hellhole, he decided that if people thought it was 'Green' he could trick them into thinking it was a great place to settle. Summer Park was no different. Pleasant name, shit place to live.

'Want to hear a joke?' Coldrain said.

Derrick said nothing. Maybe the big lunk had not yet evolved to speech.

'Priest checks into a hotel. He tells the receptionist, "I hope the porn on my TV is disabled."'

They got out of the car.

'Receptionist says back, "No sir, it's just ordinary porn. You sick bastard."'

Derrick didn't laugh.

He circled around to the trunk and popped the lock. A bulky grey blanket presented. Casting a suspicious eye left and right, Derrick peeled back the blanket, revealing a Browning 9mm pistol, a Benelli M2 tactical shotgun and two flashbangs. Shoving the Browning into the front of his trousers and the flashbangs into his pocket, Derrick inserted six fat slugs into the Benelli, Coldrain thinking, guy's got more firepower than the bloody Taliban.

Derrick finished arming himself. Coldrain remote-locked the Merc.

They walked across the estate, past the park with the shattered glass around the swings and the needles lying in the sandpit, and entered Sandwell House.

Back in Iraq, doing house-to-house had been a logistical nightmare. You went into the first house on the street in full-on mode, shotgun primed, and then you had a dozen grandmas, wives and children running about screaming at their tops of their voices. Shit was kicking off in a million directions at once, and even the best soldier needed eyes in the back of his head to stay alive. But at least the threat was clear. Here, you could get shanked by a nine-year-old kid.

Sandwell House was just like a dozen other estates. Thick front door with bars across the small window pane and graffiti scrawled on both sides. Flickering lights, the scent of freshly sprayed urine, weird stains on the linoleum stairwell and the faint sound of reality TV shows ticking behind bolted doors. If you brought your dog to this place for the holidays, you'd cancel your tickets.

'So you used to be a soldier?' Derrick asked. It spoke.

'Marine,' Coldrain answered. 'Delta Company, 40 Commando.'

'I always thought about joining up.'

'Never too late, mate,' Coldrain said.

Derrick gripped the jet-black Benelli by the pistol-grip stock, swinging it like a baseball bat.

'Ever use one of these bitches?' Derrick asked, lighting a cigarette.

'In Iraq,' Coldrain replied.

'To kill bad guys?'

'To blow open doors to kill bad guys.'

They reached Flat 9 and banged loudly on the door. Once, twice, three times.

'Open up, fuck face,' Derrick shouted.

Darius, aka Fuck Face, didn't answer.

The door was metal and scrawled with all but illegible graffiti. He could make out one word, CRYZTZ, in neon-pink lettering. There was a small spyhole at eyelevel. Coldrain watched Derrick press his eye up against the spyhole. This guy gets dumber by the second, he thought. He couldn't even be a Royal dishwasher.

'Open up,' Derrick boomed, eye glued to the spyhole. He tapped the base of the Benelli against the door frame.

Suddenly the spyhole exploded, torn out of its socket with a deafening boom and the force of the blast thrust the glass and surrounding wood splinters into Derrick's right eye. The big guy was thrown back and collapsed onto the floor. The whole stairwell shook like the early tremors of an earthquake. Recalling his Bootneck medic course, Coldrain scrambled over to Derrick's prone body and investigated the wound.

The whole area around Derrick's right eye was burnt

black. His eye was a mess. Like someone had cracked an egg yolk. Blown out of its socket, the eyeball was hanging out over his cheek, the retinal veins and arteries exposed too. The whole upper right side of his skull had been shaved off, leaving a crater of singed brain matter. He was browners.

Collecting the Browning, flashbangs and Benelli from Derrick, Coldrain turned back to scope the door. The area around the spyhole had been blown away, leaving a hole the size of an orange. Easily big enough for a gunman to shoot through at Coldrain. He withdrew to safe cover to the right of the door.

'Stay away, man! I'm warning you, I got six more bullets left and they all got your name on!'

Coldrain could see his options were limited. His only method of entry would be using the Benelli to blow the door open. Coldrain had another idea.

'Okay, mate, let's play it your way,' he shouted into the door. 'I'm backing off, all right?'

There was silence.

'Just don't shoot, okay?' Coldrain continued. As he spoke he adopted a crouch position, eased his fingers over the Benelli stock and pulled it towards him.

Still no response from Darius. Coldrain guessed he was surprised at his white-flag offer and was mulling over what to do. Often, in environments where people only understood violence, peace was something they had a hard time wrapping their brains around. It confused and unsettled them. Coldrain had seen that first hand in Iraq in the days after the fall of Saddam, when ordinary Iraqis misinterpreted democracy and freedom as an excuse to loot the National Museum of priceless artefacts and settle old scores.

Finally, Darius mumbled, 'Okay, man. Truce.'

He heard footsteps.

In one smooth motion Coldrain rolled his fingers around the Benelli trigger and moved a step to the right until he was directly beneath the exposed hole in the door. His balance firm and his feet planted firmly on the ground, Coldrain raised the Benelli up until it was pointing through the hole. He knew that he had only a split second to crack off the shot. Gripping the door frame with his left hand to counter the kickback the Benelli would give, Coldrain depressed the trigger. Even though he had big, strong wrists, he felt the shotgun buckle as the three-inch 12-gauge Magnum round was discharged. Coldrain dropped the Benelli and used the momentary surprise he had created to kick in the door. He busted it open in two fierce kicks with his Tims.

Coldrain had already brought the Browning to bear, ready to slot Darius if he tried to put him down. He quickly scanned the corridor from left to right. There was no sign of anyone. He guessed the guy had fled into another room.

The corridor was narrow. A strip of filthy lino floor was lined with sports bags filled with stuff that Coldrain guessed was pure, uncut horse. He'd never even dreamt of touching the stuff and adhered to the line that only losers took drugs, but Coldrain had known a couple of kids from secondary school who had started using marijuana and then turned to harder stuff in their late teens. It was a slippery slope and one of them was dead and the other in a mental home, doped up to her eyeballs on methadone and HIV positive from an infected needle, so Coldrain knew only too well the human damage that drugs did. This Darius guy had ruined countless lives and he was going to get what was coming to him. Coldrain was doing this for the cash, but if he was totally honest with himself, he was also getting a kick from dealing with class A scum like this guy.

Looking up, Coldrain spotted the damage rendered by the shotgun round. Just as he suspected, the kickback had proved too strong and had resulted in the round firing too high. It had torn a giant crater in the ceiling, revealing a network of wooden beams. Insulation material was falling from the hole, like dirty grey snow. He'd missed the target by a mile, but at least the distraction had allowed him to enter and get a bearing on his surroundings.

Coldrain identified three rooms feeding off the corridor. There were two doors to the right, at distances of five and ten metres respectively, and a single door on the left, also at ten metres. He moved forward. As Coldrain held the gun level, a knotted tension thrashed about deep inside his shoulder blade, a colony of ants burrowing into his lats. A random, tremoring pain that struck when he least expected it.

Finger on the trigger.

There were neat, isolated spots of blood dotted along the floor.

Coldrain entered the first room on the right. He found himself in the living room.

It was a stinking mess. Glasses and plates and empty pizza boxes everywhere, a scratched wooden coffee table covered in extra long green Rizla papers and rolling baccy and a giant plasma TV planted in one corner amidst some dead plants. He knocked over soggy Pot Noodles.

'You lied, man!' he heard a voice call from one of the other rooms.

Coldrain said nothing. Let the other guy keep talking. He shifted his stance and returned to the corridor.

'I'll drop you like a fucking bad habit, if you don't piss off right now!'

He checked the second room on the right. It opened onto a filthy kitchen, crawling with cockroaches and ants, dead mice on the floor, brown water in the sink. The walls were painted a fetid yellow.

Two rooms down. That meant Darius was hiding behind the closed door of the room on the right.

Coldrain eased towards the door and stood to the left of it. He stayed uber-quiet, breathing softly through his mouth and blinking sweat out of his eyes. His ears were pricked and close to the walls, listening for any sign of movement that could help him mark out the target's position in relation to the room.

Coldrain's heart skipped a beat. Then he heard a dull scraping sound. Like Darius was struggling to unlatch something. The smack dealer was trying to engineer an emergency exit through the windows. But they were on the fourth floor. He'd have to be incredibly brave, or unbelievably stupid, to jump out of the window from that kind of height.

Coldrain tossed the flashbang into the room. Closed his eyes and counted to three. The stun grenade cracked off, a flash of light Coldrain couldn't see but knew the effects of all too well. The light would disorientate the target for approximately five seconds, the loud bang upsetting the fluid in the ear. Five seconds to make his mark.

He burst into the room, bending his knees and keeping his posture low to make himself a smaller target. The bedroom was dark, putrid. Chaotic. He scanned the area quickly. There was an unmade mattress lying on the floor, covered in dirty clothes and cash

Adjacent to the mattress was a tall, old-fashioned sash

window, the white-painted muntin bars scabbed brown with rust and mould. In front of it Coldrain clocked the figure of Darius, struggling to slide the stiff panels open. One of his hands was in rag order, covered in splinters, frag blowback. Darius was short and squat and dressed in low-hanging black jeans and a grey hoodie with a giant gold 'G' emblazoned on the rear. In his right hand he held a Smith & Wesson 9mm semi-automatic.

Darius had been trying to jack the window, but the flashbang had unsettled him. He squinted, face locked in a grimace as he struggled to come to his senses. Two seconds since the flashbang had detonated. He started to turn.

'Drop it, mate,' Coldrain yelled and amid the echo of noise from the flashbang, it sounded like he was shouting underwater. Darius didn't seem to hear. He continued to spin around.

Coldrain didn't panic. He switched to left-hand only shooting, grasped the Browning as tightly as possible, thumb straightened, hand fully wrapped around the grip, eliminating any weak spots and building a stable fire position to increase his first-shot, first-hit probability. It was awkward holding the Browning left-handed, like kicking a football with his left foot. He felt off balance, and hoped that his aim would be true enough to compensate.

In quick succession Coldrain pumped two rounds into Darius's right leg. The first 9x19mm Parabellum round entered the target's left leg, creating a large crimson patch on his upper thigh. The second round struck lower, smashing into his tibia, exposing his patella. He saw shattered shinbone, covered in bloody muscle and tissue pulp.

The dealer was successfully incapacitated. He yelped in agony, dropped the Smith & Wesson and collapsed to the floor, his hands clenching his fucked-up leg. Tears welled in his eyes.

'Don't worry,' Coldrain said, picking up the spent shells from the floor. 'You'll live.'

'My legs, man! I can't walk!'

'Give it a few months you'll be up and about again.'

He looked down at the dealer. Up close the wounds were testament to a job well done. There was a bunch of muscle, bone, gristle and blood smeared up and down the dealer's jeans.

'You gonna kill me?' the dealer asked, breathing erratically.

Coldrain said nothing. He looked around at the dealer's shite surroundings. This was a gopping set-up if ever there was one. He guessed gangsters didn't really embrace the concept of personal hygiene. Then he looked back at the hole in the wall, where the bullet had whizzed over his head. He could even see the flattened round pressed into the hole. Coldrain thought, a little lower on his aim and that could have been my brains.

Even though a part of him was pleased to have taken down the dealer, a voice inside Coldrain's head questioned whether this was what he really wanted to do. Going around, settling someone else's beefs with drug dealers for petty cash. This wasn't right. It wasn't even okay.

He missed the buzz and the incredible adrenalin rush of the Royals, of fighting in the Corps, of being part of something special. The closest he'd come to recreating that feeling had been on the circuit, and that was gone now too.

'You gonna kill me?' the dealer repeated.

When he was first in Iraq with 40 Commando he'd bumped into a Yank in the 26th Expeditionary Unit, US

Marine Corps. The guy had told him the phrase 'ex-Marine' was taboo in Yankee Land, because once a Marine, always a Marine.

'There's no exit strategy to being a jarhead,' the guy had said.

Finally, Coldrain could relate to that.

He left the dealer lying on the floor. Stepped over Derrick's corpse. Called an ambulance on the way out and reported a shooting on the estate. They'd find the kid soon enough, and he'd be patched up in hospital with nowhere to go and plenty of time to think about the direction his life had taken. Coldrain had already thought about his, and as he fired up the Merc and drove out of the estate, he knew exactly what he was going to do.

NINE

He was playing with the other boys down by the beach when he saw it.

A long grey ship the size of many houses with guns on either side. The sun was behind it. The ship looked big and scary and he found himself looking back at the rusted wreckage that Abdi and Abshir were playing hide-and- seek in, the one the elders said was a boat that came from Russia and brought trouble with it. He thought to himself that they looked almost the same, like a brother and sister. But one had been rusting on the beach for as long as he had been alive, and was a good toy, with plenty of nooks and crannies to hide in. And the other was floating on the sea.

Ahmed whistled to the others. They too had seen the ship.

Ships meant bad news to Ahmed and the others. He had heard the stories. All the boys knew them off by heart. How the oil companies would use their coast to dump toxic waste, turning the blue Indian Ocean sickly green. The anger that the locals felt at being the world's dumping ground, while the great and the good leaders, powerful men able to destroy nations at the click of their fingers, looked the other way. How the brave men of their country took it upon themselves to punish these ships and kill their crewmen. It did not matter that the rest of the world dressed them up as thieves or pirates. To the people who knew them, they were heroes. Protecting their seas and taking what they felt the world owed them. Every boy wanted to be a pirate. Every boy wanted to be like Omar.

They all ran up the beach. Left their *xalwo* and *qumbe* and *lows* sweets and the camera they had stolen from the white woman who came to do a story on their lives, and left with nothing but empty threats.

They ran not because they were scared, but because they were in a rush to tell Omar about the boat. It was well known among the children that if you saw a boat and told Omar, he would reward you with a few shoots of *khat*, or even a little mobile phone called a Nokia.

For more than a mile they raced, up and inland, until they finally came across the big green tent guarded by two militiamen. Ahmed arrived first, his long legs carrying him quicker than the other boys. Breathlessly, he explained to the guards he had some news for Omar. One of the men checked him for guns, then waved him through. As he entered the tent, Ahmed stuck his tongue out at Abdi and Abshir and blew them both a raspberry. They shouted at him as he disappeared within Omar's tent.

There were several more militiamen within, and a strong smell of cardamom and cloves greeted Ahmed. Three of the men were standing guard while Omar sat on his chair, eating a chunk of *sabaayad*, using the bread as a scoop to collect some of the *maraq* cherry tomato stew and goat meat gathered on the side of his plate. Omar, as the leader, was granted this special luxury of meat for lunch. The others would make do with plain old *soor* cornmeal, mixed with a little *maraq* in the middle. If they were lucky.

He told Omar what he had seen, and Omar listened quietly, picking away at his food. Ahmed trembled as he spoke. Was Omar disappointed in him? He said nothing, and his face was hidden behind a pair of sunglasses, head wrapped in a bright red turban, and it was impossible for Ahmed to understand whether Omar was displeased. He suspected he was, and started to ever so slightly back away from the militia leader.

Suddenly Omar chucked his plate onto the floor, rose to his feet and grabbed the AK-47 propped against the side of his chair. Ahmed began to shake. His lips wobbled. He didn't want to die. He tried very hard not to cry, not to show Omar he was weak, because that was not the Somali way.

'When did you see this?' Omar asked.

'Only a few minutes ago,' Ahmed whispered.

He reached into his pocket for something. A gun, Ahmed worried. He closed his eyes and waited to die.

Except that he did not, and when he opened them again Omar was holding the gun out to Ahmed, offering him the pistol grip. He held it. It felt powerful in his hands, dark and light and lethal. He settled on tucking the weapon into the front of his jeans, like he had seen the older boys in the militia forces do. Omar smiled approvingly.

'If my best young lookout is to work, then he must have himself a gun,' he said through his wide grin. He patted Ahmed on his head, and the boy was beaming with pride. He had done a good job, Omar himself said he was the best. He looked on wide-eyed as the other militiamen took up their weapons. 'Tell the others to find us by the Old Port by the Abdul Aziz mosque,' Omar was saying to one of the men. 'Round up as many fishermen as you can. We will need GPS too. If we are lucky, we can get this done before *cambuulo*.'

The men exited the tent, one by one, cheering and whooping and spitting *khat* phlegm out from the sides of their mouths. Ahmed followed excitedly in their wake.

PART TWO

PART TWO

TEN

The wine was posh and the food was the kind of fancy nosh that celebs dished up on TV specials. The grub, the cutlery, the fucking contorted chairs. Yeah, this place was for the minted brigade all right, a Mecca for pretentious bullshit, but the real source of Coldrain's discomfort was the bloke sitting opposite him.

The Sandman was known for his love of food. A plate of Confit Loch Duart salmon sat in front of him at the table, elaborately decorated with foie gras, creamed leeks and soufflé potato. Occasionally the Sandman would slowly bring his napkin to his lips and delicately dab the white material across his mouth and take a gentle sip of chilled Grüner Veltliner white wine.

Coldrain had gone for the steak because it was pretty much the only thing in English on the menu. The waiter had turned his nose up when he asked if he could have chips with it, and screwed his face into an even tighter ball when Coldrain requested a cold lager to wash everything down. Part of him longed for the scran at bases. Beans, pies, mash and chips with Chinese wedding cake, aka rice pudding, for dessert. Better yet, a classic Bootneck banjo. Fried eggs in the perfect sarnie bap. That was tops.

They ate in silence, the Sandman nibbling at the fancy salmon and Coldrain attacking his steak with his yaffling irons. Nothing was said until dessert, which was some kind of brandy served with a tiny glass of sickly sweet wine and whose sole effect was to make Coldrain pine for a slab of Vienetta. Coldrain watched the Sandman finish his afters, wipe his lips once more, and then remove a small photograph from his jacket breast pocket. He paused a beat as the waiter took away their plates and placed the picture between them in the middle of the table. Coldrain found himself staring at an Arab man.

'His name is Dogan.'

'Al-Qaeda?'

'Not quite.'

Coldrain listened to the background int on Dogan, half-heartedly at first, but his interest grew as the guy's biography unfolded.

'He started out from humble beginnings,' the Sandman began. He sounded grand, like he was giving a lecture at some knob-jockey Oxford college. 'And over time, Alisan Dogan, known to his friends as Ali, has gone on to become a serious player on the terrorist scene. Uniquely among the key figures in the current insurgency in Afghanistan, Pakistan and the isolated pockets of resistance in Iraq, Dogan is not originally from the Middle East. In fact, our man comes from a Kurdish background. Word has it that Dogan grew up in Diyarbakir in the south-eastern corner of Turkey, the disputed area that the people living there called Kurdistan.'

'I thought northern Iraq was Kurd country?'

'It is, sort of. But the Kurdish diaspora is spread over a much wider geographical area than the northern side of Iraq. For the past forty years or so, the Kurds have been locked in battle with the Turkish military through their armed wing, the PKK. And that, Daniel, is where Dogan first cut his terrorist teeth.

'Born in 1950, by his early twenties Dogan had become one of the PKK's youngest and most enthusiastic soldiers, culminating in an episode when he burst into a local branch of the Turkish military and proceeded to open fire on soldiers getting their hair cut in the on-base barbers. Thirteen were killed, Dogan escaped, became a wanted man and a Kurdish *cause célèbre*.'

'So he's a freedom fighter, rather than a terrorist?'

'Two sides of the same coin, Daniel. In this case, however, it appears that Dogan's motivation was not, primarily, a free Kurdish state. By the early 1990s, Dogan was attempting to distance himself from the PKK. We think this was partly motivated by events in the Middle East. The Gulf War and so on.'

'Dogan became an al-Qaeda fan?'

'Not quite. Something a little more superficial. The evidence suggests that Dogan simply looked at the lack of international publicity around his own terrorist spectaculars and decided the only way to get widespread media attention was to target white Westerners. Americans and British. At that point, Dogan began seeking out honorary affiliation with a variety of extremist groups in the Middle East. He fought alongside the Syrian martyr brigades in Lebanon and took part in an ambush on Israelis working undercover with their border police, the Magav, assassinating three agents as they attempted to snatch a high-ranking Gaza official.

'Throughout the 1990s and into 2000, Dogan became a terrorist nomad. He emerged briefly in India, helping to launch attacks with radical Muslim separatist groups against Christian communities based in the south of the country, before heading up to Pakistan, where he made contact with local Taliban chiefs. There, he seemed to take on a new focus and murderous zeal. His activities became solely concentrated on assassinating important Western figures. Civilian casualties were of no interest to Dogan any more. Again, this is perhaps due to the fact that diplomatic hits garnered him more attention at a time when the slaughter of civilians was becoming a little too populist and clichéd for our man's liking. Each of the attacks he had perpetrated over the past four years was focused on a particular individual of importance. Collateral damage was acceptable, but it was not the main aim.

'In 2002, US envoy James T. Petersen arrived in South Korea to discuss policy towards its northern cousin. As he stepped into the chauffeur-driven limo, a bomb went off, killing Petersen and the driver, and wounding several more.

'Two years later, three members of the Coalition Provisional Authority in Iraq, aspiring young Republican staffers who had volunteered for the job, were cornered in a road block, a single bullet put through the back of each of their heads.

'The year 2006 was Dogan's busiest. A total of five attacks across the year, ranging from a daring hit-and-run in traffic in downtown Khartoum on a British diplomat sent for round-table talks over Darfur, through to an explosive device planted in the phone in the hotel room of America's overseas liaison to Israel. As he picked up the receiver in the hotel in Paris, the bomb detonated, taking his head clean off.'

'Bet that took him off the White House's Christmas card list.'

'Quite. Which brings me to Kabul, his latest attack. Are you familiar with the name Christian Watts?'

'The diplomat and former ambassador to the UN.'

The Sandman's eyebrows arched up a couple of miles. 'You've done your homework, Dan.'

'Politics isn't my cup of tea,' Coldrain said. 'He's the one who cheated on his missus with a bloke from his gym, right?'

'Moral muck aside, Watts was a senior diplomat with the brief of slashing Afghanistan's woeful recent record on poppy production. Dogan's attack was quite ingenious, by all accounts. The explosion was mixed into a cigar, the diplomat's favourite brand. When he lit up, in the hotel lounge, he was incinerated instantly.'

'Dangers of smoking.'

'And the realities of modern warfare. The Kabul attack displayed all the hallmarks of a Dogan operation. Precise knowledge of the target, such as whereabouts and habits, even down to their favoured cigar brand, an experimental explosive device, and a target who was high-ranking enough to send shivers down spines across Whitehall.'

'Let me get this straight. Some Kurdish terrorist is giving Foreign Office boys the jitters and they want him taken down.'

'That's part of it. But there's something else you should know,' the Sandman said.

Coldrain thought he saw the Sandman twitch.

'The information I have says that Dogan was working in Afghanistan some time ago, running a series of experimental bomb sites. He chose Afghanistan because the large proliferation of native IED attacks would mean he could carry out his, shall we say, tests without fear of being exposed. Any time his experiments worked, they would be blamed on local Taliban.'

Coldrain felt a sickness coming on.

'In particular, he set a trap that killed a young British serviceman. In a place called Ghorak.'

He saw what was coming next, even before the Sandman opened his mouth.

'Jamie Reese.'

Coldrain felt sick. He couldn't breathe. His palms became sweaty. Suddenly he was light-headed. It was like he'd just necked a whole bottle of JD straight. He closed his eyes, and when he opened them again he found his hands clamped tight around the dessert knife and pointing it directly at the Sandman's neck. The knife tip was pressing hard against his larynx. Coldrain was so angry he felt like he could easily plunge the end into the Sandman's throat. He remembered wishing that he had the steak knife to hand instead.

Then a voice inside told him to let go. Coldrain released his fingers and downed the knife.

Some of the other diners had turned round and watched in horror. *Yeah, well, fuck them. Something to talk about over a glass of sherry later on.* The waiter hovered close by. He looked pissed that it had all kicked off between Coldrain and the Sandman, but he was too scared to do anything about it. Coldrain didn't blame him. Coldrain himself was fourteen and a half stone of stacked muscle with wrists as thick as bricks. Put it this way: he was the kind of guy who always found it easy to reach the bar in busy night-clubs.

'Talk about my mate again, ever, you cunt, and I swear to God I'll kill you,' he said in a whisper.

But the Sandman was playing it cool. He even smiled. Bastard.

'Point that thing at me again and you won't get the chance,' he hissed.

ELEVEN

Coldrain nodded at the waiter to fetch him another beer. Trying to absorb the int was making him threaders and he took a long chug from the pint when it arrived. Didn't make him feel better. Coldrain imagined he was trapped at the bottom of a dark hole he couldn't crawl out of. All he could think was, if Dogan was behind Jamie's death, then there was only one thing to do. After thirty seconds of silence, he finally spoke.

'So this twat was responsible for the trap in Ghorak?'

'He was running tests, as they say. That bomb was one of them.'

Coldrain took another long swig of his beer. Thinking, *Those two men on motorbikes on the hill. The shadows. Watching the carnage unfold with intent. That was Dogan.*

For three years he'd punished himself for Jamie's death. He'd convinced himself that he had been the one who made Jamie become a Royal. He was responsible for his mucker being in Afghanistan that fateful day. *It should have been me.* Deep down he knew that such sentiments weren't true, that Jamie had been his own man and would have become a Bootneck one day sooner or later, with or without Coldrain's amateur PR guff, but it didn't stop those dark thoughts from plaguing him daily.

Dogan was his chance to exact his pound of flesh.

He tuned back into the Sandman's waffle.

'Normally this type of operation would be left to Special Forces. But the SAS, SBS and Delta are stretched to breaking point. Interpol have done their bit, but they're essentially a Brussels outfit and their reach doesn't extend beyond the cosy streets of Paris and Berlin. It's up to governments to get their hands dirty, and of course they'll pass the dirt onto us.'

Coldrain mulled over the Sandman's words. The story held together. Made sense. He still kept in touch with a couple of Royals who were now in the SBS and they were massively overworked. A lot of their activities were focused on the border regions of North and South Waziristan between the Afghan and Pakistan, since the Taliban leadership had basically upped sticks from the 'Stan and retreated after getting their arses handed to them on a plate. But fighting in Waziristan was a political hot potato and got the Pakistanis in a hissy fit, so the governments had to do it on the sly with Special Forces raids on strictly deniable ops. A lot of ground to cover for a very small fighting force. People imagined the Blades and the Sneaky Beakys to be massive regiments, but in truth there were only a couple of hundred SAS and SBS guys. If they were preoccupied with the task of hunting down Taliban leaders, it left the government no option but to farm dirty work like this out.

'Where is he?' Coldrain asked.

'I'm told that he relies on funding for his terrorist operations by working the drug trafficking network between Afghanistan and Turkey, in alliance with the PKK. It is, however, a very difficult network to infiltrate, because the Kurds trust only blood relatives and are hostile to outsiders. Rather like the Italian mafia.'

'No one on the inside then.'

'Afraid not. But my contacts have managed to bribe some good information out of the local police force, who are thankfully equally as corrupt. The Americans have reason to believe that he is currently in Van, in the south of the country, where it is understood Dogan is helping to organise a drug deal. There appears to be a pattern developing. He carries out an operation, then needs to replenish his cash. And he does that through taking a commission for drug trafficking.'

Coldrain eyeballed the picture. This Dogan prick was mean, busting the same look Coldrain had clocked on the streets of Basra, where the Ba'ath party had been determined to hang onto power, at least until the Challenger 2s with their L30A1 main armaments rolled into town. Not even nutcase Iraqi dictators were going to argue with a gun constructed from electro-slag remelting steel that unleashed 120mm HE rounds of death.

But in the days that followed Coldrain observed first-hand how the mood in Basra started to shift. The men, women and children who had greeted the Royals rolling into the city with warm smiles now shot them angry mob stares. The city had no electricity and no running water. The putrid smell of excrement hung in the air and permeated every building. Clung to his rig. With no aircon, families resorted to sleeping on the roofs of their bombed-out homes to escape the baking midnight heat. Coldrain had never experienced such sweltering temperatures. It was uber-redders, especially with all the body armour on, and during the day he'd shed his body weight in sweat. After a night's fitful sleep his pit would be drenched.

Almost overnight the population turned hostile. Dealing with trouble had meant dangerous patrols around the bad neighbourhoods of the city. The insurgency was gaining traction. Unruly gangs started to throw rocks at the convoys. After a few weeks the rocks turned into RPGs (rocket-propelled grenades). Coldrain encountered several of them when running ops on the ground. Many of the guys he didn't give two fucks about. They were ridiculous twunts, fired their AK-47s from their hips in the classic action-movie stance and predictably missed their targets by a country mile. But Coldrain remembered specifically a local Sunni leader who was unusually calm and pleasant. His manner unsettled Coldrain. The guy wasn't frothing at the mouth like the rest of them. He was cold and calculated, and he spoke surprisingly good English, in a posh, clipped home counties accent. The man told Coldrain he had even studied in Britain, as a dentist.

Coldrain recalled asking the man for his name. He wrote it down on a slip of paper and tucked it away in his pocket. Months later, he learned that the man was a British Iraqi called Amir Saeed Ishaq. He was responsible for a string of beheadings in Iraq over the next several months as videos of the executions flooded the web. Coldrain had seen one: some Korean guy pissing his pants and crying for mercy before his masked captor swung an old knife in the air and jabbed the tip of the blade into the Korean's back, making him raise his head. Then Ishaq brought the knife down against his nape, hacking back and forth, back and forth. Blood gushed out of the punctured neck. And Ishaq stood there, arms folded, proud of his handiwork. Like he'd slain a goat.

And now Coldrain found himself looking at a picture of someone with the same possessed stare. There was no fear, only an electric hatred burning in Dogan's eyes.

'When's the schedule?'

'Dogan must be in our custody in two days' time,' the Sandman said.

'That's impossible. Not enough time to prepare. No-where near enough time to sort out an assault.'

'It's non-negotiable.'

Coldrain checked his watch. 'Then you'll have to find some other mug. It's not for me.'

The Sandman leant in and Coldrain got a front-row seat to his blotchy, creased, old face. 'Look, I didn't come to you because I like you, Daniel.'

'Surprise, surprise.'

'But I do admire you. When it comes to snatching bad people, you happen to be one of the best. Sure, I have ex-MI5 and KGB spies who would peel their eyelids off for this assignment. But they're not field men. They like numbers and patterns and stats. You, on the other hand, you tend to excel at violence. Brute force. Think of it as your forte. I need someone who can stand the heat of battle. And think of the reward.'

Coldrain asked, 'You mentioned some Yank.'

'Yes. You will have company. An operation as high value as this, I can't trust to one man. Here,' the Sandman continued, removing an envelope from his breast pocket as he laid out his black American Express card for the bill. The card said it all. A gold AmEx would get you a business-class seat on Virgin Atlantic. Black would buy you a personal jet and a Thai masseuse.

Coldrain picked up the envelope and had a peek at the contents. Inside was a Turkish Airlines ticket to Ferit

Melen Airport in Van, east Turkey, with a stopover in Istanbul, a thick wad of bills in local currency, and a passport with his picture but with the name given as 'Stephen Jones'.

'Van is where the deal will go down. It's the heroin transit capital of the country. Everything has to pass through there before heading north to Serbia, where it is then transported into Western Europe. Your partner is already in situ and will fill you in on the details. Your flight leaves at eight o'clock sharp tomorrow morning, from Heathrow. Head across to the second airport on the other side of town for your connecting flight. From there, you'll head to east Turkey, PKK country. Your new friend will be waiting there for you. Questions?'

Coldrain gave it the Air Force shrug. Money, bad guy, snatch and grab. Pay day. What else was there to know?

If he had been sitting on the fence a few minutes ago, thinking about the million shekels had helped nudge him over. With that kind of dosh he could splash out on a brand spanking new MV Augusta F4 750 SPR complete with signature silver star rims. He'd treat his old folks to a round-the-world cruise, cheer them up a bit. And take Melanie on holiday somewhere nice. Canary Islands, maybe.

Then he thought about Jamie. Nah, he told himself, even if this gig was *pro bono* it would still be worth it. He thought back to the day Jamie stood up to Dean Skinner, the school bully. How he'd been unafraid, even though he gave up five inches and a couple of stone to Skinner and dished out a proper beating, the other schoolkids cheering on as Skinner's friends dragged him away, blood streaming from his nose. Jamie's clenched fists, blood on his white shirt, triumphant.

Bottom line, Coldrain was now doing this job purely for his mate.

TWELVE

Ferit Melen Airport had seen better days, Coldrain thought as he debussed from a mostly empty Airbus A319 and felt the stale, sagging heat smother him like a shroud. Above the drone of the engine, he clocked two runways and a series of low glass and concrete buildings. A security guard directed him along the tarmac to a rusted door. After a baggy-eyed official took a cursory glance at his visa, he was waved through into a terminal so small he'd need to step outside just to change his mind. He looked around for his new best mate and found himself staring at a familiar face next to the convenience store.

'Well, well,' Coldrain said, extending his hand for a man-shake. 'Small world, or what?'

'Not fucking small enough, you ask me.'

'Rod Outlaw. Long time no see, mate.'

'Not fucking long enough neither.'

Outlaw was African American, wiry and six foot two but if you asked him he'd swear blind he stood an inch taller. Former Delta Force, Outlaw was decked out in beige cargo slacks and a white t-shirt underneath a black down gilet, a pair of wraparound Oakleys surgically attached to his face. Short cornrow cut on top and pair of Converse

Chuck Taylor All Star Outsider boots down bottom. He was standing in front of a Coke machine, deciding whether to go Diet or Zero.

It had been two years since Coldrain had saved his life.

Madagascar. So hot the country blazed over as crimson as the red laterite soil, as though the island was caked in Mars dust. Coldrain and Outlaw were posted to defend a newly developed nickel mine in the Fianarantsoa region. The mine ought to have been good news, but in the capital, Antananarivo, soldiers were busy slaughtering members of the public protesting the ruling regime, the European Union had refused to acknowledge the Malagasy government and tensions were rising. It was the kind of set-up that would give a young BBC reporter a hard-on and some good footage for the news, but for Coldrain, Outlaw and the shit-scared mine foreman, there was a lot more at stake. The protests had spilled into the countryside, and to the new symbols of government prosperity and greed: the heavy oilfield at Tsimiroro and the coal development at Sakoa.

And the nickel mine they were based at. Coldrain and Outlaw versus more than forty guys baying for their blood. Outlaw had put down twenty of the fuckers while he manned the pod-mounted 'Ma Deuce' Browning .50 cal at the mouth of the gem mine, positioned on a slope fifty metres down from Coldrain's own position.

As he cut down the advancing militia, Outlaw had suffered a stoppage. He had been laying down more than fifty rounds in a single burst, causing the barrel to overheat. And five militiamen were bearing down on his position. They couldn't aim for shit but a lucky round from their AK-47 scratched his neck and left Outlaw in the rattle.

Showing disregard for his own safety, Coldrain abandoned his position and moved down the muddy slope under heavy enemy fire, using his Colt Commando to provide rapid covering fire. Then he checked the .50 cal. He had to be careful to avoid a cook-off, a situation whereby the chambered round was ignited by the heat of the barrel, causing the cartridge to explode. He waited a couple of seconds then pulled the bolt to the rear, checking for the ejection opening and the feed tray, released the action, relaid the Browning on the targets and depressed the bolt-latch release and locked it off, forcing the bolt to go forward upon pulling the trigger. The weapon sprang into life and the militiamen were ultimately repelled.

Coldrain had saved Outlaw's bacon that day. At nightfall, with the battle over and the gem mine secure, they had a laugh about it over a bottle of Glenlivet at a bar on Independence Avenue in Antananarivo. The bodies had been cleared from the streets, leaving faint blood washes on the walls and concrete, and spent jackets in the gutters. They drank and tried to make fun of the situation, but both men knew how close they had come to being zapped.

That was the last time Coldrain had seen Outlaw. Until today.

'Shit, I'm just playing with you. Good to see you, Danny boy. It's been too long.'

Outlaw tapped the Coke button again. The machine didn't deliver. He slammed his fist down on the tab, then tried the coin slot. The drinks machine was being tighter than a Sweaty Sock at Crimbo, keeping his drink and holding back his shrapnel too.

'So you're my new bezzy oppo, then,' throwing an arm around Outlaw's shoulder. 'How's the circuit been?'

'Same old shit. Journalists who think they're bulletproof. Operators who reckon they're Steven Seagal. Bad guys who reckon they got a hope in hell.'

'Hoofing.'

'Well, whatever the fuck that means. But, truthfully, it's been a little quiet lately.'

'Not much work going around?'

'The opposite. More work for fewer people. As for the Sandman, he's a shaver.'

'A what?'

'You know, shave a little of this shit off, shave some of that. Put some bullshit armour on the old BMW rather than upgrade to a new vehicle. Make it company policy that you pay for your own guns and ammo.'

'Christ. Add all that stuff up and you're in fucking trouble.'

'That's what I told the man. On email. Several times.'

He watched Outlaw give the drinks machine a kick. The machine shuddered. There was a slow rumble, and the glass bottle finally came tumbling out. Outlaw tore off the cap with his teeth and gulped some down. He pulled a face and spat the liquid out into a nearby bin, the bottle hot on its tail.

'Shit's fucking warm,' he gobbed. 'Come on chief, let's roll.'

He was glad that Outlaw was on-board for the op, and not just because they had a bit of previous and had built up a sharp, tight bond in those terrible minutes in the nickel mine in Madagascar. The Sandman, like a lot of PMCs, sought to cut costs by hiring advisers from non-elite back-grounds. On a four-man mission it wasn't uncommon to find himself with chefs and drivers and police officers. They were good men, and great at their jobs, but they weren't trained for operating in hostile environments, or standard tactics, techniques and procedures (TTPs). He had met one guy in Iraq who had been a bouncer at a club a matter of weeks beforehand.

'Check out the rims.'

'Very nice,' Coldrain nodding his approval.

Outlaw's motor was a light-brown Toyota Hilux, double-cab model. The 4x4 monster was legendary among PMCs for its reliability in the hostile terrains of Afghanistan. The Hilux was awesome at off-road driving and as it was a four-door vehicle it could carry more bodies, with ample space at the back for weapons. Even the Taliban used the Hilux as their makeshift WMIKs. The Hilux's biggest selling point, though, was its sheer indestructible nature. Coldrain had heard of instances where these bad boys had RPGs detonate right next to them and they'd still be working. Once a building even erupted right next to a Hilux and collapsed on top of it. After the rubble had been cleared, the Hilux worked smoothly, as if nothing had ever happened.

Outlaw lit a blunt and they drove from the airport towards the central districts.

'Admiring the view?' he asked.

'Yeah,' Coldrain said. 'I mean, there's got to be, what, six or seven shades of brown.'

Outlaw popped a laugh that reminded Coldrain of cracking open a can of beer. 'I call it Afghan-Lite,' he said, 'because it looks like the 'Stan minus the minefields.'

To the west were the striking deep blue soda and alkaline waters of Lake Van, its surface as still as a crust of ice. Across to the east a jagged row of monotone-grey mountains lingered on the horizon. And in the north stood Mount Ararat, hovering at 17,000 feet above sea level, its glacier-capped tip looking down ominously from above.

Squat orange and brown-coloured apartment blocks over-shadowed gloomy roads populated by old diesel motors chugging along and coughing out big plumes of tar-grey smoke.

They banged a couple of rights and found themselves on a bumpy, potholed single-lane heading south. Framed in the distance stood a massive stone fortification cut into a rocky hillside and surrounded by olive trees and scrubland.

They drove for several more minutes, crossing through a busy bus terminal that seemed to be where all the action was happening in town. Large coaches with names like Ulusoy and Yelgin steamed out of the station crammed with passengers, heading to far-off destinations like Antalya, Izmir and Ankara. People couldn't wait to get out of Van, it seemed. Bus drivers sat in plastic chairs on the tarmac in the middle of the hub, sipping copper-coloured tea with one hand and eating lemon-drizzled kebabs with the other. A Turkish flag flapped in the wind on a pole next to the station.

'Now, be warned. The hotel ain't exactly the Hilton,' Outlaw warned.

He wasn't wrong. The place looked like a festering sore. Three whitewashed buildings lined a rough, rubbish-strewn street. They all had blue tiled roofs. The bumpy main road had turned into a prehistoric dirt track.

'I've slept in some pretty rough places, mate.'

'Shit, even a jarhead would think twice about sleeping here.' He leant in to Coldrain, his eyes wide and round as golf balls. 'The roaches here got *wings*, brother.'

Outlaw parked the Hilux and they debussed. Coldrain heard chanting: a man performing the Adhan, the Islamic call to prayer, a familiar sound from his days in Iraq. His melancholic voice waffled away in the background, echoing off the city walls.

The hotel was beyond basic and Coldrain suspected the local prisons had more extensive facilities. A guy named Fatih was the manager, a man who had evidently never heard of the miracle of ear and nose trimmers. He had the staple thick black mo' compulsory for every bloke in Van and his shirt was one giant sweat patch. Coldrain signed in a tattered old logbook under the Stephen Jones moniker issued on his fake passport, and then followed Outlaw up an old wooden staircase.

There were four floors to the hotel. Outlaw had demanded rooms on the top floor.

'Better to be all the way up,' Outlaw quipped. 'Gives us some extra warning time in case anyone decides to pay us a friendly visit in the middle of the night. Plus, we're like practically the only guests.'

'Van's not the hot destination for the year then?'

'You kidding? It's on the top of the list of places *not* to go visit.'

'Won't we look a bit suspicious to the manager?'

'Yeah, maybe. In the alternate world where I didn't grease his palm with five hundred lira.'

'Good job, mate.'

'Always one step ahead, Danny boy. Let me show you to your room. And before you ask, there's no cable TV. No internet either.'

The grot resembled a scene from Alcatraz. There was a bed in one corner with a lumpy mattress and stained white sheets, no pillow. A knackered wooden desk was positioned to the right of a window. Coldrain tried the window lock. It was fixed fast. To his eternal disappointment, no towel or dark chocolate had been left on the pillow, no bottle of champers sitting in an ice bucket, compliments of the house. He checked the back of the door to see if they had left him an Egyptian cotton dressing gown with his initials etched into it. No dice there either.

'I'll be downstairs,' Outlaw said. 'Sort your shit out and meet me in five. I'll give you the heads-up.'

'Done deal, mate.'

He unpacked his gym bag. He hadn't brought much, just an extra t-shirt, some underwear, toothbrush, electric razor and a pair of NorthWest Territory waterproof hiking boots in case they needed to go off-terrain. There was also a state-of-the-art GPS navigator that the Sandman had given him, comprised of a thin strip of transparent, flexible and waterproof backplane that had an electronic e-ink display. The GPS functionality was touch-screen and allowed him to map out his position anywhere across the globe. In an instant he could switch to a variety of contoured and annotated maps and the navigator also included an emergency transmitter in case he became compromised and a Search and Rescue team needed to identify his position for an immediate evacuation. The wafer-thin nature of the backplane meant that it could, theoretically, be surgically inserted into the palm of his hand for added concealment, but Coldrain didn't feel like transforming himself into the Terminator just yet.

He'd also brought a rudimentary first-aid kit, Maglite torch and some trusty black maskers tape. No Bootneck worth his salt ever travelled without a roll of the stuff. It could fix pretty much anything, except maybe peace in the Middle East.

Then Coldrain remembered the other item he'd brought along for the trip. He dug something out of his jacket pocket and examined it. It was a BlackBerry Storm, one of the touch-screen jobs, specially issued to him by the Sandman. The phone had been modified so that the providers couldn't triangulate the signal and get a fix on his position. Well, no one except the Sandman and his employers, Coldrain would have bet his mortgage on that. If he had one.

He rolled the ball onto the Contacts icon. There were only three numbers in the folder. One read 'Home' and was to be called only once the target, Dogan, had been apprehended. That would put in motion a series of events that would give them a secure RV in order to complete the target handover, and, ultimately, a million big ones being shelled out to Coldrain and Outlaw.

The second contact was 'Upgrade' although this wasn't a number that would give him extra free weekend minutes. Texting a cash amount to this number would result in the required funds being deposited in a designated bank account, to which only Coldrain had access, as the team leader. The account was strictly only for mission expenses, such as weapons procurement and surveillance equipment. Bribes, too. Anything to get the job done.

The third contact, 'Taxi', was only to be used in extreme circumstances, when the team or the mission became compromised. If Coldrain dialled that number on his BlackBerry, a signal would be sent to a certain computer and alert the necessary people. The activation of the signal would alert the Sandman, who would automatically assume that the team had gone into Escape and Evasion mode, or, worse, been captured, and immediately shut the whole operation down. At that point, whatever shit Coldrain and Outlaw were in, they were on their own. Coldrain sorely hoped there wouldn't come a time when he'd need to call that number.

THIRTEEN

He did not think it was an unreasonable request.

Sir Hendry Thomas, senior envoy to the Iraqi government, and former UK ambassador to Libya, was fed up with the new emergency rules those bastard mandarins down at the Foreign Office had enforced upon him like an unwieldy and downright insulting straitjacket. No unauthorised trips outside the hotel. No use of public transport, no alcohol to be consumed, and absolutely under no circumstances any travel across the city without his security team seeking prior approval direct from Whitehall. They may as well have taken away his right to read *The Economist* as well.

He had been stuck in his hotel room at the Delphi hotel for more than three days straight, waiting for this blasted meeting. Twice he had been set to go and talk to al-Rakiri, and twice the meeting had been postponed because of 'security concerns', thus condemning him to a full seventy-two-hour stretch in a room that had a lumpy bed, poor lighting and only three TV channels, a choice between the liberal agenda luvvies on BBC News, CNN or the Al Sumaria station, which was wholly in Arabic and therefore utterly pointless. He had scrolled through his BlackBerry a thousand times and was tired of sitting around twiddling his thumbs.

Just wait till I get back to London, he thought. *I'll give that bastard Hanson what for, sending me on this wretched assignment. He'll get into the Cabinet over my dead body after this.* And as for al-Rakiri, insulting him like this, well, there would be hell to pay there as well.

But, right now, Thomas was locked in an argument with his security team. He wanted to go for a stroll outside, unaccompanied. They would not permit it.

Of course, he didn't really want to stretch his legs.

What Thomas really wanted was a boy.

'Just for half an hour, that's all I'm asking for.'

'I'm sorry, sir,' the chap in charge of the group of four thugs notionally defined as his security detail replied. He was startlingly muscle bound, well built, tanned and the right side of thirty, looked rather striking in the black suit, and, in a different environment, Thomas would have been keen to try his luck. But right now he was livid, and he did not shy away from showing it. After all, what was the bloody point of these foreign excursions if not to provide him with a bit of light relief and indulge in the odd fantasy?

'What's your name, please?'

'I've told you already, sir. Andy Rawbone.'

'Rawbone. Andy. Listen to me. If you do not let me outside for a brief wander, I shall make it my priority to have you demoted as soon as I return home. You will be sent on the most miserable postings imaginable, for as long as I shall deem fit. Am I making myself perfectly clear?'

'You can do what you like, but my orders are clear,' Rawbone replied with a straight face. If he was upset with Thomas for launching threats against him, he wasn't showing it. Or perhaps the chap had simply realised, from talking to the others, that there was very little Thomas could really do to make his life abominable. The MoD were notoriously inflexible when it came to accommodating the various demands and wishes of the other branches of the Civil Service. If they said something, he was hardly in a position to tell them to bloody well stick it, especially since these days ministers were in the habit of using the terrorism cachet to frighten the public into backing them. Now the MoD regularly beat their backs with the same rod, restricting their freedom and acting as the fun police on overseas assignments.

'I won't tell you what I think of your orders.'

'It doesn't matter to me either way you like 'em or not. I follow 'em, that's all there is to it.'

And with that, Rawbone, Andy, slammed the door shut, locked it from the outside, and left Thomas to sit on the side of the bed and ruminate.

Thomas waited several minutes, until he was confident the detail had trudged off to their own rooms, or the gym or their Nazi magazines, or whatever those beasts did with their spare time. Satisfied the coast was clear, he reached over for the telephone and dialled downstairs. Tariq answered first time. His feet were tapping away incessantly. Yes, all right, he was out on a bit of a limb here, but hadn't Tariq said just to ask him if he needed anything? Absolutely anything at all? Well, his definition of anything was about to be put to the test.

Two minutes of idle chit-chat about the weather and the on-off nature of the air-con and the hopes among the locals for a democratic future, utter nonsense the lot of it, and then he smoothly got down to business and explained what he was looking for. A boy, not too small, old enough to pass off as a waiter bringing up some food, but as young as possible. He added that he was willing to pay, then worried that he sounded a touch crass. All the while Tariq listened patiently, said nothing, and then at the end of Thomas's little spiel, he said to leave it with him and he would sort it all out. No problem.

His heart lifted. He was excited and thanked Tariq, four times when once or twice was really quite sufficient, and hung up.

The two hours took an eternity to pass. He whittled away the time by playing the games on his BlackBerry and fiddling with a presentation he was due to make at Yale the following month on how to effectively coordinate and manage relations in a shifting global environment. He checked his emails. Nothing in his work account, but in his personal file there was another message from the journalist. She was proposing to meet next Tuesday. She wanted to find out more, she said. She had not revealed anything else on the email, and that was good. Without even consulting his diary or his secretary, tucked up away safely back in Westminster, he emailed back to say that was fine, and he would see her then.

Finally there was a knock at the door. He leapt off the bed, adjusted his thinning brown hair in the mirror and then stepped to the door.

'Who is it?' he asked tentatively.

'Room service you ordered.'

The voice sounded young, innocent and when he opened the door he was not disappointed. The boy was no older than fifteen, perhaps even fourteen, but he had the build of a man. Tariq had done well. He told himself to give Tariq an extra large tip when he left this hellish place for securing him such a fine young specimen. He ushered the boy in and was surprised to see him undress without even prompting. Off came the tattered coat and the t-shirt.

And then suddenly Thomas was not smiling any more.

The boy had something strapped around his waist.

Thomas had never seen a bomb before, but the thing around the boy looked suspiciously like one. He looked to the door, as if to see Rawbone come charging through at any moment and rescue him. But the door did not swing open. Rawbone was not coming.

'No, no, no,' he begged the boy. 'Please don't!'

But the look in his eyes. It said something.

It told him he was too late.

FOURTEEN

Coldrain found Outlaw kicking back with a blunt and a soda at a table in the so-called hotel bar. It was a dimly lit room with four sets of tables and chairs. A woman with a face so creased it needed steam-ironing came over to deliver them some food. Lunch was sheeps' brains served with a leaf salad, kofte kebabs soaked in beds of rice and bread, and rolled vine leaves with an olive oil dip.

Coldrain attacked the sheeps' brains first. They were surprisingly light, and melted in his mouth like a lemon sorbet. Outlaw, fast food junkie, didn't touch a morsel, contenting himself with a bottle of cool mineral water.

He was pleasantly enjoying his sheep's brain feast when he spotted her in the corner.

The bad lighting had smudged the outline of her figure with the shadows, and only the backlight on her snazzy laptop provided any kind of illumination on her face. But that was enough to pique Coldrain's curiosity. She had wavy black hair that reached down to her shoulders, a button nose, eyes the colour of a moonlit lake and elegant, cherry-red lips that promised a smile without giving anything away. Take away the laptop and replace her tight jeans, green top and the shawl decorating the back of her head with a cocktail dress, and she could have passed for turn-of-the-century Russian nobility. But with the other clobber he figured her as some kind of journalist.

'I thought you said we were the only guests staying here.'

'No, I said we were *practically* the only guests.'

'Same thing. Practically.'

'All right. Cards on the table,' Outlaw said, taking a few dollar bills out of his wallet. 'Buck gets ten says I go over there and come back with a phone number.'

'Come off it, mate,' Coldrain joked. 'She's not the type.'

'*Every* girl is the type. You just got to know which buttons to press.'

Coldrain jerked his shoulders and tore off a chunk of bread, dunking the soft white dough into the olive oil. Outlaw waltzed over and touched the girl on her shoulder. Said something to her.

The old lady brought over his coffee. It was served in an espresso cup with decorations and shit down the sides. Coldrain took a swig and puked a little in his mouth. This was thick, bitter sludge. Like drinking mud. He laid the cup down again and swigged some of Outlaw's water to get the taste out of his mouth.

When he'd finished nearly gagging, he clocked Outlaw beating a hasty retreat to the table. Guy looked wounded.

'Your one-liner didn't work its usual magic then, mate?'

'Go stick it, Dan.'

'I thought you said every girl was your type?'

Outlaw grimaced, like he was trying to swallow glass. 'If you're so smug, why don't you go try your own luck?'

'No thanks. That ain't my style.'

Outlaw was about to protest when the girl saved him

the effort, slid casually out of her chair and paraded over to their table. Held out her hand to Coldrain, who stood up and accepted it. The girl was taller than he thought, five eight. Late twenties. She was proper blanking Outlaw.

'Anika Ischenko,' she said firmly, holding eye contact with Coldrain. He thought he saw a glimmer of something there, but it disappeared as quick as he had seen it. They shook hands for a second longer, before she asked, irritated, 'Are you going to tell me your name, or be as rude as your friend here?'

'Dan Coldrain,' he replied. 'Nice to meet you.' And then, 'Russian?'

'German, actually. But Ukrainian by birth.'

'And what brings you to Van?'

'I was about to ask you the same question. You are two serious-looking men, in east Turkey, and I am guessing you are not tourists here to see the ancient ruins.'

'You still didn't answer my question.'

'No, I didn't.'

'Not here to look at old rocks either?'

She shook her head, frowned, and Coldrain felt a little stupid. 'Not if old rocks aren't in the headlines.' Ischenko handed him a business card. A. N. ISCHENKO, it said. And below, JOURNALIST AND BROADCASTER. There was a fancy logo in the bottom right corner that Coldrain transcribed as DFB Channel 9. TV news.

'Reporter, huh.'

'Broadcaster and journalist,' she insisted. 'I'm actually researching material for a report.'

'What's the "N" stand for?'

'That's a secret.'

'Fair enough, we all have them. What kind of report are you working on?'

'Did you see the riots and murders in Berlin last month?'

Coldrain blinked. He rarely paid much attention to European news lately. His business was security and defence, and the countries he boned up on were the ones on the fringes, the countries ruled by despots or descending into anarchy, where the next generation of militants and terrorists fomented their hatred. The goings-on in Germany and Holland troubled him less.

'Well, if you had bothered to crawl out from your cave for a few minutes, you would have seen that there were five stabbings across the city, and this led to a full-scale riot, buildings destroyed, cars burnt, businesses ransacked. It was really tragic.'

Scratching his jaw, 'What's that got to do with Van?'

'Heroin,' she said.

Coldrain did a double take. He exchanged a look with Outlaw, who had emerged from his sulk, his eyes bright with interest.

'No shit,' he said.

She took a step back, eyed them suspiciously.

'Wait a minute. Are you police?'

'No, love. Do we look like police?'

'I guess not.'

'We're doing some research for an institute about the local drug trade.'

'What about, exactly?' Her eyes narrowed and she rested a dainty hand on her chin. Coldrain found himself looking, subconsciously, for a wedding band. His better nature made him quickly look away, remembering Melanie and the scent of jasmine in her hair, the way she held onto his upper bicep when they went out, as if Coldrain were her bodyguard.

'Just general research stuff,' he said, eyes taped to the floor.

'Right.'

The smile and warmth had receded from her face. He wasn't surprised. The few journalists Coldrain had ever met all tended to be paranoid, secretive and highly un-cooperative. They assumed everyone in the world was out to steal their story or stop them from running it. At this particular moment, Anika Ischenko was wondering which of the two categories he and Outlaw fell into.

But, unable to resist prying, she asked, 'Have you had much luck with your interviews so far?'

'Actually we just sort of got here,' Outlaw replied.

'Well, I hope you do better with the locals than I've managed so far,' biting her bottom lip with her top teeth and shaking her head. 'Kurdish men aren't exactly famous for their appreciation of strong, independent women asking them questions.'

'Like that, is it?'

Dismissing his concern – hers – with a wave of her hand, 'I'll get some quotes eventually.'

'Tell you what,' Coldrain said, tipping the cup of coffee-mud upside down onto the saucer. 'How about you come for a wander around town with us.'

Her eyes narrowed. 'Are you sure?'

Outlaw frowned, signposting the same question.

'Sure, why not? Maybe with the two of us around, some of those blokes will spark up a bit. They ought to; these people talk for a bloody living.'

She nodded and rubbed her chin. Stared out of the window. Coldrain followed her eyes. There wasn't exactly much to look at. A dirty wall, a pile of rotten wood, a three-legged dog licking at a puddle of something steaming and brown.

'Okay,' Ischenko finally said. 'It's a deal.'

'Great,' Outlaw added, about as enthusiastic as a cat at an arse-licking contest.

'So where do we start?'

'The streets,' he said. 'Let's go.'

'Now?'

'It's past afternoon prayer so should be quite busy.'

Coldrain wasn't one for cameras and pictures, but he wished he could have taken a snap of Outlaw's defeated mug. As for Coldrain, he was just saving up jokes for later, when he could rip the monumental shit out of Outlaw and his so-called player credentials.

A skeg around the streets with Ischenko would also give them the perfect cover to check out the scene of the raid and map out a plan in the small window of time they had available. A mission this complex, if the Special Forces guys were working it, would take months of preparation. Coldrain and Outlaw had less than forty-eight hours. It wouldn't hurt to let Ischenko tag along. Besides, as well as the journalist being hotter than Kim Kardashian in a swimwear catalogue, Coldrain needed a real cup of coffee, not some sour Arabic muck. Maybe he'd stumble upon a Starbucks.

FIFTEEN

Coldrain and Outlaw stood out like a couple of one-legged men at an arse-kicking competition. Only Ischenko, with the shawl wrapped tight around her head, made any attempt at going native, but with her luminous skin, striking eyes and perfect body, she blended in even less well among the locals than the two stacked operators by her side.

Locating the city centre was easy, mainly because there were only about four streets in Van selling shit. Capitalism was still in its infancy in east Turkey. Coldrain even spotted a bloke with a donkey and a cart during the ride north, reminding him of the old rag-and-bone man who used to call round his parents' way, back when he was a toddler.

While Ischenko was off talking to the locals, Coldrain and Outlaw sat on a couple of plastic chairs outside a café. Outlaw was caning back his fourth Coke of the day.

'Tell me something. Why'd you stay on the circuit?'

Outlaw frowned.

'You ever hear the one about the new Unit recruit?'

Coldrian shook his head.

'It goes a little something like this. There's three guys up for selection. They've done the training, passed the background checks, all they gotta do is pass this one last test. The examiner, now he takes the first guy to a large metal door. Hands him a Glock. Says to the guy, "Inside that room, you'll find a man tied to a chair. Kill the motherfucker." Now, the first guy looks back at the examiner and he's like, "You want me to go in there and shoot an innocent, unarmed man? No fucking way." Examiner says, "Fine, you're out."

'Second guy is taken to the door and is told the same routine. This guy goes into the room with the gun, but he comes out again a few moments later. He's crying like some broke-ass son of a bitch. "I can't go through with it," the guy says. Again, the examiner tells him he's failed the test and won't make the Unit.

'Okay, so the third guy steps up to the plate. He's given the same gun, same instructions. This guy doesn't blink. Straight up opens the door, steps into the room, boom. Shots fired. Followed by a bunch of screaming and banging. Couple of minutes later, the guy steps out of the door and hands the Glock back to the examiner. He's like soaked through with sweat. "This gun was loaded with blanks," he tells the examiner. "I had to untie the fucking bitch and beat the shit out of him with the chair."'

Coldrain was waiting for a punchline that never came.

'What's the moral of the story, mate?'

'There isn't one,' Outlaw cracked, punching Coldrain on the shoulder. 'I just wanted to remind you how bad we Delta boys were compared to you pussies in the Marines.'

'Did anyone ever tell you that you're an egotistical maniac?'

'Constantly.'

They wormed their way north, passing a street populated by angry looking Turks smoking fags and ranting about this, that or the other. There were no brand-name shops in Van, just a rabble of markets and battered shop fronts. Every third store was a mobile phone outlet or patisserie. Billboards overhead promoted local bistros and an upmarket new housing complex called Seven Hills. Lean, fox-tailed white cats roamed the streets. Coldrain noticed that they had odd eyes. Green on the left, brown on the right.

He located Ischenko and walked with her. A bony man was soon pacing alongside them. He looked about ninety. Raggedy clothes hung loosely on his skeletal frame. A traditional white pusi scarf embroidered with black Arabic writing was wrapped around his pinhead. The guy had maybe two good teeth, both of them rustier than a Ford Cortina in an Essex driveway. He shouted at them in broken English, offering phone cards, watches, mobile phones, SIM cards, cigarettes, batteries and a whole range of other junk. He was a one-man Nisa.

'I love you,' the Turk told Ischenko. She froze in horror.

Coldrain watched the old bloke repeat the phrase, Ischenko watching him warily, arms crossed. When he had enough fun, he ushered Ischenko to one side and Coldrain lifted a few lira from his pocket and stuffed the notes in the old man's hand. In return, Coldrain was given a symbolic gift. An international phone card that had a picture of a smiling girl on the front. She was ecstatic, apparently, that calls to Iraq were just five Turkish cents a minute, and Mr Phone Card was grinning at Coldrain like they were bestest best mates.

'How old you?' Mr Phone Card asked.

'Thirty.'

'Me too, boss.'

Bloody hell, Coldrain thought. Clearly the male beauty

companies should really get their act together. The Turkish market for anti-ageing gunk must be huge.

'What was that all about?' Ischenko asked.

'Little bit of baksheesh. Common as chips round these parts. Unless you pay up, they'll pester you all day.'

They walked on, working their way through the crowds. More people were selling crap. In the space of about thirty metres, Coldrain was offered a dozen different types of shisha pipes, from the smaller clay models with ten-inch long pipes right up to elaborate four-hose hookahs with green glass bases and ornamental bodies. If Coldrain had been a decade younger, he probably would've been interested in picking one up, but his smoking days and sly indulgence in the odd joint of wacky baccy were well behind him.

'It doesn't seem like a drug capital,' Ischenko said.

'Why do you say that?'

'I don't see any drugs.'

'You won't. Not around these parts.'

Ischenko pursed her lips, as if she was chewing broken glass.

'These people aren't users,' Coldrain explained. Across the street, two chubby men broke out into a heated argument. 'They couldn't afford to go on the gear all day, even if they wanted to. They're traffickers, shipping the stuff on to your people in Germany, who can afford to get high, and pocketing the proceeds.'

'So these people aren't drug addicts?'

'To them, doing the junk would be like sticking your hand into the sweets you're going to sell and eating a few on the side. You're losing profit, pure and simple. The action round here is deep underground, but it goes on all right.'

'But how can you be so sure?'

'Just look around you.'

He gestured to the guys at various sidewalks. There were local Turkish soldiers mincing about all over the place, dressed in their distinctive brown khakis, beige shirts and olive-green berets. They had holstered Browning 9mms in case any shit kicked off. In Coldrain's experience, overt military or police presences did fuck-all good in trouble spots. They merely sent the enemy underground and made it harder to smoke them out.

'Gendarmerie,' Outlaw explained. 'Here especially on account of the drugs issue.'

'That's a lot of soldiers.'

'Yeah, but you pay them enough cash and they look the other way. Just like our mate with the phone cards back there.'

'No wits, no crime,' Outlaw mused.

'Very true.'

Whilst Ischenko conducted her interviews, Outlaw and Coldrain made their way along the haggard streets, looking out for the ambush road as subtly as possible. They already stood out enough; the last thing they wanted to do was walk round with a really obvious map and point shit out in full view of the locals.

Coldrain had visited Istanbul once before and been intrigued by the fragrant, hectic metropolis, a true clash of cultures, with mega nightclubs and financial districts competing for a slice of the skyline with tall minarets, European and Asian styles blurred right down the middle. But if Istanbul was an intoxicating mix, Van had lifted its cultural heritage straight from the Middle East that Coldrain knew so well. Its elegance, devoutness, and its flaws.

A lot of the men looked the same. Grey or black flannel suit, white shirt, crocodile shoes coming apart at the seams. They all had identikit black hair, sideburn, 'tache. Even their faces were similar, with dark, sad eyes, bushy eyebrows and long noses. The only difference was that the older men wore dark flat caps that wouldn't look out of place in a Burnley factory whereas the younger guys went top-down. He saw few women on the streets, which didn't really surprise him. They were probably at home, performing their customary duties of washing, cooking and getting the shit slapped out of them for having an independent thought.

They hit the end of the market street with no luck. Outlaw took a side route and Coldrain backed up, trawling in the opposite direction until he came upon Ischenko. A hundred metres into their return trip, Mr Phone Card started pestering him again. It was like the guy had an endless supply of shit to sell.

'You buy Nokia!' he said. There were those teeth again, jutting out like a couple of soldiers on stag.

'No thanks, mate.'

'You buy DVD!'

'Not for me.'

'I have group! Anal! Gangbang!'

'This guy,' Coldrain talking out of the side of his mouth at Ischenko. They moved on.

'So I'm wondering,' Ischenko said as she reached for her bag and removed a packet of Marlboro Red cigarettes, lighting one. Coldrain caught the smell as it mingled with the baked air, bitter and sharp and choking.

'Me too,' Coldrain said. 'Back there in the hotel. Why'd you come up to us?'

She took a long drag on her cigarette. 'I told you. Two

Western males in a hotel in Van, having a furtive conversation? I'm a journalist. I get paid to be inquisitive.'

'But you knew all along we'd agree to escort you around town.'

Her silence gave the game away.

'Two free bodyguards,' Coldrain said. 'You played us well. We fell hook, line and sinker.'

'It's a dangerous thing to do, to trust a beautiful woman.'

'It's a dangerous thing to trust people, full stop.'

Ischenko stamped her cigarette out on the street. A dozen pairs of eyes gave her and Coldrain screw-faces, putting Coldrain on his guard. Ischenko was brazen, wilfully ignoring their evil eyes. Or maybe she just didn't see them; it was hard to tell how much was an act with her, and how much was genuine.

'You wondered something about me?' Coldrain asked.

Ischenko stopped at a bustling intersection where a large fruit and veg stall was erected. She cast a cynical eye upon ripe peppers, vibrant lettuce bundles and plump tomatoes. 'I find you interesting. That's part of the reason I came over too, you know. Your friend is a little, how do you say, aggressive? But you, I can see there is something different about you. Your eyes have seen much.'

'I don't think I follow.'

Smelling a bunch of parsley at the stall, Ischenko said, 'If you were the same as your friend, I'd say you were soldiers, no doubt. With him, it's obvious. But you make me question that.' She stood up and looked into Coldrain's eyes. 'I don't know who you are, or what you're doing.'

'Makes two of us,' Coldrain replied.

Ischenko got into conversation with the middle-aged woman behind the fruit and veg stall and Coldrain left them to it. He hooked up the street, banged a right and found Outlaw. Establishing their bearings, they beat a path down several winding roads and alleys until they came upon the street they were looking for, Selçuklu Boulevard.

The cobblestone street didn't end, it just kind of stopped and gave up, as though it couldn't be arsed any more. A hundred metres up and they had hit the jackpot. It was a street tapering off to the right, a dirt track really, and lined with tattered coffee shops that all kind of looked the same. Opposite the street, sandwiched between an internet café and some kind of hairdressers, was a rubble-strewn, hollowed-out, three-storey building.

'You see what I see?'

'Perfect firing point,' Outlaw said, nodding.

'If you can, have a closer look.'

'And where are you going?'

'Just for a bit of a wander, mate.'

Coldrain went for a skeg down the dirt track. It was a street with no name and no defining markers, until he walked directly past the target location. The Kevleri Kafe was a dive. Whoever owned this joint didn't make their money serving mud and baklava all day long. The name of the café was painted onto a wooden signboard above fog-like windows.

Outside the front door stood three men. A squat bloke with a unibrow and a nose the size of Brazil was berating two taller, younger men. One had a shock of silver hair and a goatee shaped like a heart, wearing a grey linen jacket. The other was younger, fatter, darker skinned to the point where he looked Indian. He wore a black tee that had printed on the front 'I ♥ NEW YORK'. Except the '♥' was replaced with the cut-out of a plane crashing into the 'N'. Coldrain figured that kind of design was a popular one on the black market. His shoulder brushed against New York as he walked on by.

'Fucking watch it, man,' the guy scowled, flashing his best angry face.

Coldrain said nothing, moved on, did a right at the end of the street and worked his way back up to Selçuklu Boulevard. There he found Ischenko. She was flipping through her notebook and looking well happy with her work.

'Get some good stuff?'

'A couple of locals gave me some reaction. That's all the material I need.'

'It's probably all you'll ever get out here, too. All the locals are tied up in the trade.'

'Everyone?'

'Look at the businesses around here. There aren't this many coffee shops in New York. And there must be more hairdressers than clients. All they're good for is laundering money. The locals get their fingers dirty with the trafficking and then they invest in a few businesses. They don't do much except make the paper trail hard to follow.'

'What about the police? Don't they care?'

'Deep State,' Coldrain said.

'Say what?'

'In Turkey, the Deep State is a collection of interests that exist within the government framework, but stay in the shadows.' Coldrain squinted at the sun. The heat was stifling, unrelenting. Claustrophobic. His forehead seeped sweat and his lungs burnt with the dry, heavy air. 'A sort of state within a state. As long as the Deep State feels drug trafficking is in Turkey's best interests, the police are kosher. And anyway, systematically monitoring the flow of money coming into the local economy, establishing which bits come from where, all that is far too much like hard work.'

'It sounds like the perfect place to do business if you are a drug lord.'

'You've pretty much hit the nail on the head.'

SIXTEEN

No answer.

Coldrain pressed Call for a sixth time and heard a series of clicks and screeches before his call was connected. The BlackBerry spat out the old, familiar ring. Five, six, seven ... then voicemail. He left a third message for Melanie and frowned at the screen when he hit End.

'Woman troubles?' Outlaw asked.

'Are there any other kind?' dismissing his concerns with a wave and a trite comment, and examining an AK-47 lying on the mattress. One of several pieces of kit Outlaw had retrieved, like an old man bringing down the presents on Christmas Day.

'Where'd you get this little lot, mate?'

'Couple of guys I hooked up with.'

There was more to it than that but long experience had taught Coldrain that sometimes it was better not to ask.

'There's enough clobber here for World Wars Three, Four and Five combined.'

'And then some.'

But no matter how Gucci the guns, neither Coldrain nor Outlaw would be fooled as to the use of the weapons. One of the best things about being a soldier was that bottom line, winning a fight came down to skill and cunning and preparation. The reality was that whoever they were coming up against tonight would be equally well equipped. If not better. They would have to go through the plan again and again, sort out every last detail, if they were going to get this one right.

Fail to plan, plan to fail, as the old Bootneck motto went.

Coldrain examined the Kalashnikov. One of two AK rifles that Outlaw had procured, both models looked in decent nick.

'The AK-47. Weapon of choice for bandits, insurgents, pirates and revolutionaries around the world. Boy, do I love this motherfucker almost as much as my late mom.'

'And popular for good reason too, mate. We used to practise with these out in Iraq. I reckon it's one of the most reliable toys in the business. You can freeze, burn or bury an AK and it would still work just fine.'

'That's why I chose them. The guy I bought them off, I didn't exactly have a lot of time to check that they had been properly cleaned and calibrated. Figured keep it low-risk and stick with the Old Reliable.'

'Good thinking.'

'That, and the guy was doing a two-for-one on Russian firearms.'

The downside to the weapon, Coldrain reflected, was the legendary inaccuracy of the AK-47. It was something he'd appreciated when Iraqi insurgents who fancied themselves as the next Daniel Craig fired off a few pray-and-spray rounds in his direction in Basra. Not so good when he was the one pulling the trigger.

He checked the rifle. There were a lot of cheap imitation models on the market, from Bulgaria and the like, and Coldrain wanted to make sure he was getting the authentic

IHZ Russian version. Using chad replicas would be like buying your Calvin Klein jeans from Romford market. They'd fall apart in five minutes.

Coldrain examined the other weapons. He wasn't disappointed. There was a gun he recognised as the AK-9 compact assault rifle. Coldrain had been introduced to this beauty by Russians on the circuit. The AK-9 was popular with the recon troops and specialist crime agencies in Eastern Europe, where a portable but deadly firearm was in big demand. At just over 700mm in length, with a side-folding polymer stock taking it down to less than 400mm, the AK-9 was as portable as a fucking GameBoy.

'Hands off,' Outlaw said. 'That's my baby.'

'I'm not fussed, mate. If you want to go around carrying a water pistol, that's up to you.'

He picked up a shotgun that he didn't recognise. It looked like an overgrown AK coated in cool black paint. It even had a scope rail fitted down the left-hand side to accommodate almost any regular AK optics.

'Now this is the Saiga. It's a 12-gauge, gas-operated combat weapon.'

'Russian?'

'Naturally, my man. The Saiga can do some serious damage. You don't want to find yourself on the wrong end of one of these bad boys. But check the sighting mechanism first. I want to show you something.'

Coldrain peered down the sights. The mechanism was high and the old practice of aiming off-centre and down from the target no longer applied.

'Not too precise, then?'

'The Saiga is about as accurate as a coin toss. But precision isn't something you need to worry about when the weapon is blowing open a hole the size of Africa in some poor bastard's gut. Note the Trionic stock attached to the end of it, along with the rubberised grip. This transforms the baby into a decent rifle with a lethal range of up to three hundred metres.'

Coldrain saw that the stock was foldable, so the weapon could quickly transition into a house clearance firearm.

'Not bad,' he said.

'Oh, it's all bad all right,' Outlaw said. 'It's so bad it's *sick*.'

Two Sig Sauer P229 pistols rounded off the gear. Sigs were famous for their resilience; an operator would be mad to go into a hostile situation without a reliable secondary weapon and the P229, the latest model, more than lived up to its predecessors. The Sig was as reliable as a weapon got. Any primary firearm could easily suffer a stoppage, and if you had just burst into a house full of X-rays and your tool jammed, there was no time to mince about trying to unfuck the gun. The operator needed to reach straight for his holster and switch to the secondary. In Coldrain's opinion there was no better backup pistol than a Sig. Comfortable to grip, as expected from a German-manufactured gun, it could also hit the head of a pin at ranges up to a hundred metres.

'I take it you're happy,' Outlaw said. The smug bastard.

'It's a hoofing haul you've got here, mate.'

'That's what I told the guy I got them from. Only I didn't use no stupid Marines' language.'

'Are they dirty?'

Outlaw screwed up his face, like someone had grabbed him by the bollocks. 'What do you take me for, D? Every-thing's clean as a whistle.'

Using clean firearms was essential. Dirty guns referred to ones that had been employed by previous users, so the chances were the police would have a bullet jacket on file somewhere that could be matched to the weapon. Clean weapons were brand new, fresh off the production line, and therefore a lot better for stealth hits where disguise and the ability to exfiltrate quickly were key factors.

'Tell me something,' Coldrain said, admiring the Sig, 'how did you get this job?'

'Like you give a shit.'

'Not really, but entertain me.'

'Last month I got the call, asked if I was interested in doing some gig down in DR Congo. I says fuck yeah. The company tells me, fly to South Africa and wait for instructions. So I do, and I have to pay for my own flight too. I get there, right, and they're supposed to have put a down payment in my account and given me details about a local arms dealer, too. Some Boer asswipe. Any sign of the paper or the guy? Not a chance. Three weeks wasted, fucking about in a country that looks like a pint of Guinness, white on top, and a whole lot of black beneath. But you know, work has been drying up ever since those assholes in Congress cut the budget in Iraq. So then I tell the company I quit. Next thing you know, the Sandman himself is on the line saying he's got a new operation and do I want in, and guess what I say?'

'Yes?'

'Fuck yeah.'

'So the Sandman personally contacted you?'

'Yeah, like that's the way he usually do business, right? It ain't like he sends out Christmas cards to his people. You know how he do. Guy doesn't like to get his hands dirty. A whole year I try calling him and he fobs me off on some bitch in the front office, Jane, or Janice, or whatever the fuck. And then out of the blue, this bony motherfucker starts acting like we're bestest best buddies. Make of that what you will.'

There was a knock at the door. Outlaw jumped and Coldrain reached for one of the Sigs.

'Who is it?'

'It's me,' a soft voice carried from the other side, 'I've just brought a little present along.'

Outlaw nodded to Coldrain and he opened the door a couple of inches. Kept his right boot the other side of the door, so she could not fully open it, force her way inside and discover the secret weapons cache bang in the middle of a near-empty Turkish hotel. That would blow a Saiga-sized hole through their bullshit university researchers story.

'It's late,' he said.

'I know, but I wanted to thank you both for earlier. I got some very good material, and it was all thanks to you.'

'Rubbish. You were the one who went and talked to people and made sense of their waffle. We just sort of hung around.'

'Can I maybe come in?'

'Bit busy at the moment.'

'I bought something to drink,' she added, revealing a bottle of Cockspur Fine Rum, the finest Nelson's Blood from Barbados. It was a high-quality brew that was one of Coldrain's favourite drinks, and Coldrain was impressed with Ischenko. Any woman who knew her rum, he thought, had his instant respect. He left the door ajar, and glanced back at Outlaw.

'You go,' he said. 'I'll take care of this.'

Meaning, give the guns a wipe down and a disassembly to inspect each moving part.

Meaning, he'd given up the ghost on Ischenko already.

Coldrain didn't care. When it came to birds, he was a go hard or go home type of guy.

'It's a bit cramped in here,' Coldrain making excuses so Ischenko wouldn't clock the armoury not ten metres from her position at the door.

'Well, how about my room?' she suggested.

SEVENTEEN

He took another swig of the Dark and Dirty, pusser's rum and Coke, and listened to Ischenko spin him the gen dit about her background. Coldrain had resigned himself to a tale of middle-class boredom and shitloads of cash splashed on her education, but the truth was different. In fact, she was, in some ways, similar to Coldrain.

'My father used to be a fighter pilot in the Soviet air force,' she said. 'After the collapse of the USSR, he retrained himself to learn to fly commercial aircraft. That meant we had to move to Oxford when I was five years old.'

Coldrain thinking, *that explains the weird accent.*

'But my family was not a happy one. My father was an alcoholic. On my eighth birthday I watched him kill himself. I can remember it clearly, even to this day, standing in the kitchen as he slit his throat with a bread knife. I called the ambulance and tried to save him, but it was too late. Afterwards my mother suffered a nervous breakdown. It was after the fourth or fifth suicide attempt, I think, I can't really recall, but then I was sent to Germany to live with my grandparents in Leipzig in East Germany. It's funny, everyone said socialism was dead, but for most of East Germany life was still very hard. My grandparents said there was no work, and all the money in Germany was in the West. For ourselves, we never had a car or even a television set. Lots of my friends had Western brand names like Barbie and Cindy, because that's how their parents rebelled during the regime. Can you imagine?'

Ischenko's luck soon changed. Her grades at school were exceptionally high. She worked her way through the education system and majored in International Relations at the Sorbonne, with the hope of getting a job at the UN, and spent two fruitless years working for a couple of charity organisations, which she hated.

'It's a dirty game, behind closed doors,' she said. 'Too much fighting over who gets the media coverage, who runs which part of the operation, and of course everyone wants to have the glamour jobs, handing out the food and giving medical supplies to refugees. It's incredibly cynical.'

So Ischenko used her initiative and set up a blog exposing some of the hypocrisy of the charity and aid circuit. There was a lot of bullshit, and, to be fair, Ischenko had taken a major risk, career-wise, by writing so candidly about an industry that was to all intents and purposes a closed shop to the outside world. Predictably, the charities concerned had promised sweeping changes on the back of the publicity the blog created. Even more predictably, Ischenko lost her job. But just as she was reaching a loose end, salvation came in the form of bloated Russian media tycoon Alexei Kornstov, who had just completed the acquisition of one of Germany's biggest media networks, Channel 9. He needed a fresh team of hungry, feisty field reporters for his round-the-clock news station, and young, ambitious and stunning Ischenko fitted the bill exactly. One signed contract and eighteen months later, however, the dream job had turned sour.

Marginalised by the other, male, anchors at Channel 9, Ischenko was given the assignments at the bottom of the pile. Like going to the eastern side of Turkey to find out more about the heroin trade.

'I mean, who really gives a shit where the heroin comes from?' she said. Her words were slurred at the edges. She'd obviously been tucking into the Cockspur before she came round to invite Coldrain for a taste.

'People are only really interested about the effect it has on their own community. I'll come back here in one month with a camera crew and a list of people to interview, and get three hours of great material, but the truth is, no matter how much good film I get here, my piece will only get the fifth or sixth slot on the main news programmes. If it even runs at all. Lately, they mostly delete the films and say they are saving them for later. Of *course* they are.'

She was lying on her bed, leaning against the wall, rolling a joint. Clinging to her youth.

'So what about you?' Damn, Coldrain told himself. Ischenko was a presser. She had more gumption than a Fleet Street dirt-chaser, and the more she talked, the deeper his admiration for her. 'You say you're here for the heroin trail too, but it doesn't take Sherlock Holmes to see that you don't look much like grad school researchers.'

She gave it the eyebrows.

'Even *I* can see that much.'

'We're sort of independent,' Coldrain replied, looking out of the window at the dark street below. Street lights appeared to be something of a rarity in Van, and that was a good thing, because reduced visibility would mean a low profile for himself and Outlaw the following night. Thinking, *an operator never switches off. Even when talking to a nine-out-of-ten bird.*

She sighed. 'Anyone would think that you were, I don't know . . . soldiers.'

Coldrain froze.

'I didn't say anything about us being soldiers. We're researchers.'

He heard a clink as Ischenko put her glass down, and the mattress gave out a squeak as she sat forward on the bed, cross-legged. Coldrain firmly directed his gaze through the smeared glass. Melanie invaded his thoughts. He was angry. With himself, for even entertaining Ischenko while Melanie was a part of his life. Angry, too, with Ischenko for being so bloody attractive. She seemed to have an electricity and energy about her that Melanie lacked. When they talked, the tips of his fingers crackled with electricity, and ants crawled over his chest.

Squash it, he thought. Melanie was there for you when you needed her the most, when you returned from the Afghan a human wreck, fatigued and crippled by a tour of violence and boredom, bloodshed and dust. She supported you better than any decompression course.

His mind played tricks. Another voice, unfamiliar to him, berated his loyalty. *You and Melanie don't have that special something no more. It withered and died on the vine a long time ago, pal. She dodged your dinner date. And why didn't she answer the phone today?*

'What about your background? You had a bad childhood?'

Coldrain arrowed his head to the right, looking at Ischenko through his periphery vision. She was twirling her hair with her index finger.

'It's very obvious,' she explained. 'Our parents do a lot of damage to us, you know.'

'Spare me the pop psychology, love,' Coldrain replied.

'I think we're old enough to take responsibility for our own actions.'

'But you had a bad one.'

He looked back at the street. So quiet outside.

'Dad walked out on my mum when I was eight and she was six months pregnant. Couldn't cope with the baby and me, I guess, because she drowned my little brother and hanged herself. I found them when I came home from school.'

Coldrain didn't need to look at Ischenko's face to see her reaction. Everyone responded the same. Open mouth, pitying eyes, struggling for words. Even two decades on, he recalled the odd smell in the house as he unlocked the front door and dumped his bag in the hallway. The sound of a tap drip-dripping, and an Arctic silence in the house. No TV on, no radio tuned in to Capital FM. No shouting or laughing.

And he climbed those stairs with a sinking feeling in his belly, as if his guts had turned to lead. Glimpsed something in his mum's bedroom, a ghost seemingly suspended over the double bed, the one she'd increasingly kept to in recent days, barely able to drag herself out of bed from one day to another. An eight-year-old boy sees a mysterious object in his house, he thinks, *Ghost. A monster or a bogeymen.* Not, *My mum's body hanging from the ceiling fixture, the life strangled out of her* ...

He sipped his rum, but there were too many voices inside for the liquor to make them go away.

'Look, Anika, I—'

Five delicate fingers rested on his right shoulder. He could feel them through the thin material of his shirt; they seemed to transmit a pulse of heat below the skin and into his shoulder blades. Coldrain let them rest there for a

135

minute, this channel of warmth between finger and bone flowing like a fast current and making him giddy.

'So much tension,' Ischenko said, her tone light and distant, but somehow caring. 'Your muscles are one giant knot.'

He said nothing. She began massaging his shoulders and half of him protested and kept rigid, the rest conceded, allowing her to unwind the stacks of stress and trauma that had implanted themselves in his flesh. With every rub he felt weaker and stronger. Ischenko had a way with her hands, as if she could push down all the way to his soul. He closed his eyes and saw Melanie's face. Opened them again. His skin was hard and rubbery from years of training and rugged existence.

'Come on, you can tell me,' Ischenko cooed. 'It's not going in a report or anything. You're soldiers, right?'

'Freelance,' Coldrain conceded.

'Like there's some big difference there? You both kill people.'

'You know being nosy isn't always a good thing.'

'Sure. But some habits you can't change. So what's your story?'

'Now that I can't discuss.'

She unbuttoned his shirt and peeled it off. He let her do it, without turning away from the window. Fought with all of his energy not to respond to Ischenko's advances. But he was powerless. She traced a finger over his shoulder blade and his chest seemed to explode with tension.

'That's a nasty scar. What happened?'

'Had an itch that wouldn't go away.'

'Very funny. If you don't want to talk about it, just say so.'

'Fine. I don't want to talk about it.'

She kissed the scar, legacy of the wounds he sustained in Tashkent. He felt nothing, because the tissue around the wound was numb, the nerve endings fried to shit.

'Tell me about why you're here instead. Is it because of drugs too? Something to do with the trade?'

It felt, suspiciously, to Coldrain as though Ischenko was sniffing out a story.

'It's nothing to do with anything.'

'That's a very specific answer. Is it terrorists?'

'No,' he replied, his tone hardening. He wasn't the type of guy to cheat on his girlfriend. Even if things weren't great, the memories of their honeymoon period, those first few months of being in each other's arms, formed a mental barrier. Every time his body cried out to be with Ischenko, he remembered the walks along the Thames, the weekends away in cottages in Bristol and Devon. He wasn't about to piss on those memories. Not now.

She was in close, examining every line of his face. 'I don't believe you.'

'Didn't say you had to. Just gave you an answer.'

'You gave me a lie. I'm very good at recognising bull-shit, as well as creating it.'

'I can't really talk about it,' Coldrain said.

He hastily threw his shirt on. Necked the rest of the rum, felt it instantly blaze up in his belly, and headed for the door.

A hand rested on his as he turned the knob. Coldrain felt her breath on his neck, a hot, intimate breeze that made his hairs tingle. Her lips were so close they were almost touching his skin. She was breathing fast, running her other hand along his shoulder, down his biceps and then smoothly along his back. She found the shrapnel point, ran her hand over it again, and then a third time, feeling the rough edges of the scar beneath the thin fabric of his polo tshirt.

'You could stay awhile,' she teased.

'I could.' And he wanted to. But he also wanted not to.

'We could talk some more. Among other things.'

'We could do.'

Her nose brushed against the back of his ear. Coldrain badly wanted to turn around and make out with her.

Melanie slipped from his thoughts, but her image was quickly replaced by Jamie. Dead Jamie, six-feet-under Jamie. And the mission.

'Maybe some other time,' he said as flatly as he could. 'I've got to take care of some stuff first.'

In a second, the hand was withdrawn, the warm breath gone sour and cold on his neck, and from a distance he heard her sink some neaters rum. 'Fine,' she said, suddenly brisk, snapping, her voice like wintry water splashed over his face. 'I'll see you around.'

And with that, he left.

Bollocks, he thought as he walked down the corridor, a severe case of blue balls brewing in his pants. *I'm never going to live this down with Outlaw.*

EIGHTEEN

The carnage on his TV left him cold.

Burning cars, men carrying the bloodied corpses of their wives and daughters through the streets. The wounded staring in a daze at the blazing fires and acrid smoke. Dismembered hands and feet set in a little pile on a street corner. He had seen it all before, and much worse, and he was inured against the horror-show reels the news teams enthusiastically poured over across the world.

He killed the sound, didn't want to listen to some wretched mothers wailing over sons who might or might not have died in the blast. The total death toll was either four or seven, according to different sources, and the reporters were displaying their customary journalistic zeal by 'revealing' that the target had most likely been the senior diplomat, Sir Thomas. A brief, gushing obituary on Thomas trailed at the ticker tape along the bottom of the screen, summarising his humanitarian achievements. He felt no sorrow for the man. He, like anyone in the game, knew the rumours about the extended trips to Thailand and Vietnam, the stories of children, sometimes five or six a night. In the old days, in the Sandman's motherland, the state church would cut off the hands of homosexuals and publicly hang paedophiles, punishments that he personally felt were appropriate for each crime. Of course, it paid to keep such thoughts to himself. Many in power had such tendencies. One of them being the man on the other end of the line. Not that he would ever admit to it, he thought to himself.

'We have to put an end to this now.'

'My men are on the case.'

'At this very minute?'

'As we speak.'

'Good. You know how important it is he is stopped. If word were to get out—'

'It won't,' the Sandman snapped. 'I'll make sure of it.'

NINETEEN

Coldrain was dying for some zeds, but he'd have to wait a while longer before he could hop into the bed for a spot of horizontal time acceleration. He sank some more green gunk in a can and shook his head. Come on, man, focus. The green shit was Turkey's answer to Red Bull. It had some semi-famous soccer player's face down the side of the can sporting a big fucking grin. No doubt laughing at the shekels he was raking in by sponsoring imitation energy drinks that turned your liver to mush.

'Run through it one last time. So we're sure,' Outlaw said.

'We keep it simple. The deal is going down tomorrow at midnight. Dogan is due to park his shit up outside the Kevleri Kafe at exactly zero hundred hours. Then he waits. Someone from the Kafe will come outside and Dogan then delivers the product inside to the owners in a set of suit-cases.'

'Do we know who he's working for?'

'Not sure,' Coldrain said, wearing a trench line into the floor. 'But the smuggling route has to go through the Balkans, just like every other kilo of heroin in the world. Have to imagine there's a connection between the Kurds and the Serbs, Russians or whoever. That's not our concern, though. Taking down Dogan is.'

'You'll be in the Toyota a couple of roads away. Meanwhile, I'll be stationed in the abandoned building opposite, eyes on the café. I will be in position from 2200 hours. That should give me plenty of time to note the protection and muscle at the location.'

Coldrain nodded. Splitting up their two-man team wasn't ideal, but in a situation with multiple bad guys and potential fire positions, they needed to disperse their own firepower as widely as possible. With Outlaw covering the café from a raised position across the street, Coldrain would be able to launch his own attack, confident in his bezzy oppo's ability to keep the enemy pinned down.

'Now we only have the smallest fucking window of opportunity for the snatch. It's got to be one hundred per cent shock and awe. Because no way on this green earth are we getting into some kind of OK Corral shit with a bunch of local drug lords. Christ, with the kind of manpower and money they bring to the table, only a crazy man would think they had anything less than the newest guns on tap.'

'Agreed, mate,' Coldrain staring out of the window, checking the roads for activity.

'So here's how it goes down. The moment our man Dogan exits from the vehicle, I start putting down some medium-range fire with the AK-9. Suppressive shit mainly, just to keep that bitch pinned down. At the same time, you pull the Toyota around, debus and apprehend the target, making sure to loose off a few warning rounds at the café. Then you focus on getting the fuck out of there before all hell kicks off. Simple.'

'It's a good plan. Daring, but not too complicated.'

'Yeah, but not a hell of a lot else going for it either.'

'Fuck it, mate. We've not the time to cook up something else. It's this or nothing.'

Yeah, but since when did doing nothing carry a real risk of being killed?

'Tell me something,' Outlaw said as he double-checked the Saiga shotgun. 'This Dogan bitch. I mean, respect to the guy for trying something a little different and targeting politicians, even though it's taking him on a one-way road to being a seriously dead motherfucker. But that kind of planning and execution, what's his beef?'

'Could be he doesn't have one, mate.'

'Like he's sort of in this for the fun.'

'Maybe, just because he can. Because killing people is always attractive to terrorists, whoever the target is and whatever the net result. Bottom line, mate, they just don't give a shit, as long they tear everything down. You know that as well anyone. We've both been there, mate. In the trenches.'

'That's a reasonable answer,' Outlaw said. He sat on the side of the bed and loaded cartridges into the Saiga mag. 'Let me phrase it another way then. What's *your* beef?'

Coldrain frowned, took a swig of green juice and checked the Sig. 'No idea what you're talking about.'

Outlaw slipped the last cartridge into the box mag.

'Come on, my friend,' he said. 'Everyone knows you were out of the game for good. The circuit ain't all that big. People talk. Word was, Dan Coldrain was finished. I mean, not to say I believe any of that shit, but a lot of the stuff they were saying, it sounded straight up like you were fucked up, feeling sorry for yourself and shit.'

'I was a little bored,' Coldrain conceded. He propped

143

his arse on the edge of the bed, looking at the assembly of firearms and equipment arranged on the floor.

'And I heard you liked a taste, too.'

Coldrain chose not to answer. He was uncomfortable telling Outlaw about Jamie, and how Dogan had been behind the attack. Part of him worried that his bezzy oppo would think he was acting on impulse. Emotion. The universal law among soldiers was never to act on a rush of blood to the head, because emotional responses to a situation had a knack of fatally compromising a mission. The thing was, deep down Coldrain was feeling lucid and sharp.

He remembered one epic night on the piss with Jamie, when a pair of Cherry Berrys from 2 Para challenged them to a drinking competition, not realising that, as well as being a top soldier, Jamie had an iron chest. When the two bottles of chilli vodka behind the bar were finished, the Cherry Berrys spewing on the floor, Jamie calmly stood up and shook their hands. Afterwards, even Coldrain had been stunned by his mucker's drinking feat.

'I didn't really cop all that voddie,' Jamie told Coldrain, grinning. 'Bribed the barmaid to pour me shots of water.'

But he was happy enough to let his legendary drinking marathon do the rounds of the barracks.

'If you've got your doubts,' Coldrain said slowly, 'you're free to walk out, and nobody says nothing.'

'I'm just fucking with you. Of course I'm down.'

'Good. Because we're in this together, mate, and I want you to know, I've got your back.'

'Likewise.' He was beaming. 'Seriously, you thought your crackerass was gonna have this gig all to yourself? She-eeeet.'

The P229 variant was fairly new and introduced to

replace the old P228 model worshipped by Marines and any police force worth a damn. The main difference with the new model was that it could hold a more powerful series of rounds than the standard 9x19mm Parabellum. The new Sig took .357 SIG and .40 Smith & Wesson rounds too. Named in honour of the .357 Magnum, the .357 SIG was essentially a .40 cal round necked down to a 9mm in order to be compatible with an automatic handgun. As it was a bottlenecked round, it wasn't as exposed at the tip as a lot of other revolver ammo, a smart design feature which meant the .357 would penetrate more deeply through light armour.

Coldrain slid back the milled steel firing mechanism to make sure the round was chambered. He saw the .357 SIG glinting like a filthy gold nugget. The increased velocity created by the .357 SIG round meant that the P229 was built with milled steel, which was necessary to help the sliding mechanism retract once the spring had recoiled. It looked a lot more hard core than the old stamped steel, alloy-frame crud the P226 was made with.

Outlaw chewed on an unlit blunt. He was packing his Bergen. It was a mountain-hiking model, not splashed in the usual digi-cam, and would draw less suspicion when he was moving about town. Coldrain had boned up on the old mountain ruins – they were a big tourist draw, being the only thing in a five-hundred-mile radius that wasn't a shit-stinking shack. If anyone was curious at Outlaw mincing about they would just assume he was some rich Yank tourist returning from checking out the citadel.

Into the Bergen went his Maglite torch, a compass, the folded-up AK-9, the Saiga plus a Surefire Saiga Tri Rail Forearm, a Picatinny rail that smoothly slid onto the barrel of the Saiga and allowed rail attachments to be added onto the shotgun. Outlaw had plumped for a black M50-D2L extendable bipod rail with a barrel mount to improve weapon stability across medium ranges, and a Kalinka optics mount to improve Outlaw's lock on the target. There was also some stuff they had picked up from a petrol station on the way back, bottled water, lots of, and some crisps and nutty. Junk food was loaded with sugar, so it was guaranteed to keep an operator alert. A waterproof smock and a fart sack to keep him warm in the OP were stuffed on top, in case a gendarme stopped him to search through his stuff.

He would leave two hours ahead of Coldrain and move in on foot to the empty building. That would ensure he was safely concealed in position way before any of the dealers carried out their own recce. If they were even that careful. And it would also enable him to closely observe the area, take note of potential obstacles or security threats via a very high-frequency (VHF) pair of two-way walkie-talkies Outlaw had also managed to scab.

Coldrain just prayed that the plan would work.

TWENTY

She blanked him in the hallway. Coldrain passed her on the way up, Ischenko heading for the stairs, notebook in hand. Ischenko, Coldrain realised, had her own defence mechanisms and the lukewarm response to her advances overruled any sympathy she might have for him. Their eyes shifted at the same time, focused on opposite points of the wall, and, when he was past, Coldrain resisted the urge to look over his shoulder. Did I make a mistake back there? he asked himself. Melanie hadn't responded to a second round of calls. In the end, Coldrain sent her a one-line text. *You're clinging to the past,* the unfamiliar voice said, rearing its head. *Move on. For both your sakes.*

No, Coldrain thought. No distractions. The plan has to absolutely be the only thing occupying your mind. He ran over the plan in his head, recalling the words of his first stripey, Colour Sergeant Jimmy Fleck, a mean Jock, teak-tough and seemingly able to subsist on about twenty minutes of sleep a night. And he drummed several important lessons into Coldrain. One of which was, *Don't think about how the plan can go right. Imagine the ways it can go wrong.*

That way, there are no ugly surprises.

He had a shower but decided against shaving, as a bit of gruff seemed to be all the rage in Kurdish male society. Then he spent half an hour figuring out how to use the toilet, which was nothing more than a tiled-up shit-pit. Relieved, he spent fifteen minutes doing shoulder exercises to warm the muscle groups up, when Coldrain heard a knock at the door. He towelled himself down and immediately tucked the Sig Sauer down the back of his combats, the grip cold against his wet back. He opened up to find Ischenko standing a couple of steps back from the door, almost as if she didn't want to be there.

'Have you seen the news?' she asked.

Coldrain gestured to the room. Not a TV in sight.

'Of course,' she said. 'Come with me.'

They walked back down to her room in a frosty, uneasy silence that pricked Coldrain's skin like a hundred needle points. She plonked her fancy laptop, a sleek white thing thinner than a credit card, on the side of the bed and pressed play on a news clip. Coldrain watched the grainy footage of downtown Baghdad, the sound of a bomb going off, the camera swinging up wildly to locate the source of the explosion, a hotel room five or six floors up, smoke gushing out of the windows, and then the usual sounds of Iraq, sirens and screams. It was the kind of event that would make headlines if it happened in London or New York, but in Baghdad, this was pretty much par for the course.

'Just another bomb,' Coldrain said, folding his arms in front of the laptop. Ischenko hadn't removed her eyes from the screen once. It was as if the earlier intimacy between them had occurred in some weird alternate reality.

'Keep watching.'

The report was brief and the standard journalistic

mishmash of bare minimum facts and maximum hysteria. Cutting past the bullshit, Coldrain could see this attack bore all the hallmarks of the Kabul assassination. Specific information on a senior diplomat's movements. Someone on the terrorists' side had to know that Thomas was a kiddie fiddler, in order for them to carry out the attack. As per usual, the report lazily ascribed the attack to local insurgents, without bothering to stop and ask themselves why the killers didn't just do the old-fashioned trick of ramming a truck into a crowded marketplace, if widescale destruction was their ultimate aim.

The news item ended.

'That's what you wanted to show me?'

'I've been thinking. What if this terrorist attack wasn't isolated? What if it was part of something bigger?'

'No idea. You probably know more about it than me.'

She paused the clip, closed the lid on her laptop and leaned in to him. The look in her eyes surprised Coldrain. It was inquisitive, searching, emotionally blank, almost as though last night had never happened.

'It's not just the story. You and your friend. The one who likes to check out my ass. You're both up to something here.'

'I don't get paid to ask questions or look good in front of a camera,' Coldrain said, raising his hands. 'I'm paid to do a job, and that's all I know. This other stuff, bombs in Baghdad and whatever? That ain't me. But you might want to check it out for yourself. You're the journo.'

She smiled.

'That's a good line. Very diplomatic.'

'I'm just selling it to you straight. If you're looking for the inside scoop, you won't find it here.'

'Bullshit. You know something. Something that links

these bombs with the drug trade. And I've seen the guns in your friend's room.'

'I'm just doing a job,' Coldrain said blandly.

He stood up.

'Wait. If there's something you want to tell me,' she was saying, a hand touching his elbow, a cheap shot, 'please, get in touch.' She slid another one of her business cards into his hand. He looked at it as he walked out of the door. From an offer of casual sex to formal card-swapping, all in less than twenty-four hours. Even for Coldrain, that had to be some kind of record.

TWENTY-ONE

Coldrain eased the Hilux down Selçuklu Boulevard. It was a muggy night, and the streets were empty. There were no bars or pubs round Van; everything just shut down in the evening. The only businesses open were the transsexual prostitutes stalking the back streets.

Game time.

He took a brief skeg at the hollowed-out building Outlaw was cased up in. He felt safer knowing that Outlaw was up there, scanning the area with his AK-9 locked and loaded and ready to rumble. Safer, but not by much.

There were very few street lights in Van. Selçuklu Boulevard was coated in a grainy film of darkness. Outlaw would have to cope with significantly reduced visibility, and without any night-vision gear to make his life easier. The dirt road straddling the Kevleri Kafe was blacked out, but closer to the Hilux was an electrical goods store throbbing with neon lights and flashing TV and computer monitors. Coldrain parked up the Toyota next to the shop.

He checked his Breitling. It was bang on midnight. Coldrain rubbed his eyes. He hadn't slept in twenty-four hours but he was getting a second wind now. Adrenalin pumping, he was buzzing and ready for action. Or maybe that was the after-effects of the third paint can of energy piss he'd chugged back at the hotel.

Coldrain kept the engine running. If he needed to make a hasty getaway, the last thing he wanted was to waste valuable seconds revving up the motor.

Outlaw was safely in position twenty metres to his left. The ex-Delta hard man would be uber-focused right now, as the dark could play tricks on an operator's mind, making him see shapes and movement where there wasn't any. Outlaw would be verifying silhouettes by running his eyes around the edges of each apparent object. The edges of retinal vision were better able to adjust to night-time than the central point. And he would keep checking each shape to look for signs of movement. If the object was still in the same location on the fourth or fifth check, over a period of a minute and a half, or longer, then it was probably inanimate, and therefore not a threat.

He radioed into Outlaw and asked for an update on the target area.

'I see one vehicle, Nissan, brown. Lights off. It's been parked out front for the past two hours at least.'

'X-rays?'

'Negative. No sign of human activity.'

It was now 0005 hours. What was keeping them?

Coldrain felt the stock of the AK-47 sitting between his legs, muzzle propped against his inner thigh. He hoped he wouldn't need to use it. Discharging rounds in a built-up, foreign urban environment would open up a whole new world of shit. Just in case things did go tits-up, he had stocked up on ammo. Six mags of copper-plated steel 7.62x39mm M43 rounds for the Kalashnikov at thirty bullets apiece, a carton of three-inch Super X cartridges for the Saiga, twenty, and four spare thirteen-round clips of .357

brass for the Sigs. Enough firepower to face down a small army.

Suddenly there was a rap on the driver's window. Coldrain spun ninety degrees in his seat to see a bloke dressed in tattered rags with the whole top row of his teeth missing. There was a black hole where his right eye should have been. He was holding out his hands and trying to say something. Coldrain rolled down the window and copped a whiff of the guy's breath. He smelled as if he'd just sucked an elephant's dick. He kept saying something over and over in Kurdish. Coldrain didn't understand, didn't need to. The guy had the universal look of a beggar, and the personal hygiene to match.

Coldrain dished out a few shekels from his pocket and shoved them into the tramp's hands. His one good eye widened. His Christmases had all come home at once.

'Move on, mate,' Coldrain said.

As the tramp hobbled away, his peripheral vision caught sight of a sea-green Mercedes-Benz CLK Coupe slowly rolling up to the left of his position, parallel to him. It was just fifteen metres behind. The windows were tinted and Coldrain couldn't get a visual on the driver or passengers. The wheels turned slowly on the stony road. Now it was eight metres away.

Now five.

The Merc pulled up next to Coldrain, dark glass on the driver's side sliding back. Coldrain's window was already wound down, owing to the oppressive midnight humidity. He saw an olive-tanned face he recognised. Goatee from yesterday, out the front of the Kafe. He was holding something in his hand.

TWENTY-TWO

here was a pause of no more than one and a half seconds, but it was enough for Coldrain to realise that something was about to go horribly wrong. The outstretched hand held a dark object. His stomach tightened.

Goatee was gripping an Uzi, the Micro model. Short, slim and weighted with tungsten to reduce the super fast discharge rate. The jet-black nozzle was pointing up at him at a five-degree incline, ready to spit 1,250 rounds per minute of 9x19 Luger madness into Coldrain's body. He had a split second to react.

Coldrain pushed his foot down hard on the accelerator. The Hilux growled and lurched forward. He willed the Toyota to speed up. If he didn't get enough distance between himself and the shooter, Coldrain was toast.

To his eight o'clock he saw the Merc coupe receding. He was putting yards between them.

Then it was suddenly too late.

He caught a quick flash from the retreating Uzi. Didn't see the puff of smoke spit out to the rear, but felt it, warm air tunnelling around him. There was a piercing din as glass shattered. Rounds thumped against the metal framework, a frantic burst, high-pitched and rattling, followed by a supersonic roar that sounded like a train entering a tunnel. Even against the thunderous grind of the Hilux wheels, Coldrain made out the metallic clink of the spent cartridges tumbling onto the cobble-stone.

Another burst. There was a massively loud metallic bang as the rounds tore an explosive route through the aluminium monocoque structure, carving routes through the Hilux chassis. The heat on Coldrain's back was intense. His ears exploded. This was a sustained burst, ten, maybe eleven rounds. Could be twenty in total. But his lugs were ringing from the awesome sound of metal clanging against metal and he just couldn't tell how many had been discharged. It was like a million hammers simultaneously banging against lead pipes.

Coldrain kept his foot down on the gas. The Hilux chewed up road as it surged forward. He was five, ten, twenty, thirty, forty metres ahead of the Benz. As he hit fifty metres the speed dial passed fifty miles per hour. Coldrain eased off the gas and wrenched the steering wheel to the extreme left. As the Hilux power slid to ninety degrees into the U-turn he slammed down hard on the brakes, kicking up violent plumes of dust and sending gravel pinging down across the chassis, until he was a hundred and eighty degrees turned, level opposite the Merc, forty-five metres away.

He heard more rifle reports. These ones were further away.

Outlaw was putting rounds down on the car. Each single-burst round smacked into the Benz. The front right tyre burst. Then the rear. The Benz sank on its side, rendering it immobile. Coldrain had to admit, Outlaw was surgical with a fucking gun.

Coldrain saw Goatee fiddling with his weapon. An Uzi mag held just twenty rounds and the momentary lapse in discharge told Coldrain that the guy was out of ammo, needed to insert a fresh clip. Even if Goatee was a shit-hot reloader, the pause still gave Coldrain enough time to do all the damage in the world. He pointed the AK directly at the windscreen, pulled back the trigger, closed his eyes and let rip.

He rattled off a three-round burst. Shattered the windscreen. Then Coldrain used the muzzle of the AK as a rake, driving it out from the large crack and slashing off the rest of the glass. A shower of glass shards fell into his lap, each fragment glistening. Clearing away the glass was essential, because firing through an automobile windshield could deflect a round by up to thirty inches over fifty metres, as well as suck the energy and momentum out of the round, reducing its ability to penetrate and puncture other surfaces. If he wanted to zap Goatee, he needed to have an obstacle-free trajectory to the coupe. Coldrain felt the warm taste of blood on his mouth. Shards of glass had rained down on his head, scratching his temple to shit.

With the glass cleared, Coldrain realigned the iron sights on the Kalashnikov and vittled a six-round burst. He heard the rounds tear through the Merc's front windshield. Then he churned out an eight-rounder, just for good measure. Up ahead he saw Goatee jerk and spasm in the front passenger seat, as if someone had pressed a couple of electrodes against his balls. The driver was out of sight, ducking away from the trails of gunfire.

Goatee was fucking taking it.

Coldrain flung open the Hilux door and debussed. Pounded towards the Benz. Fifteen metres to the vehicle and he got a good look at Goatee's gopping wound. He was in rag order. One of the rounds had smacked into his forehead. The wound itself was small, but the hypostatic energy from the round on impact had smashed his eyeballs right into the back of their sockets and shattered the top of his jaw. His front teeth were missing. Coldrain saw a few of them lying out on the dirt track, bloody and messed up. Goatee was toast.

As he neared the motor, Coldrain clocked the driver climbing out of the other side of the Merc. He swung open the driver door and a thick plume of tar-grey smoke spilled out behind him, a noxious mix of cordite and diesel fumes that shadowed him like a long cloak. The guy was packing an MP5 Heckler & Koch. He aimed it in Coldrain's general direction and fired recklessly, every round missing. Coldrain squatted behind the opposite side of the Merc's cut-up chassis, well aware that it only took one stray round to enter at an awkward angle and it'd be game over. The driver circled to the front end of the Merc, forcing Coldrain to move to behind the boot and maintain cover. He unleashed another few loose rounds and then started pegging it down the road. Up ahead Coldrain saw Outlaw chewing up pavement, thirty metres away. He'd decided to join in the party and was armed with the 12-gauge shotgun, swinging the Saiga like a police baton. He meant business all right.

Outlaw was quick, a proper racing snake, caning it like the Duracell bunny.

'How many?'

'Two down.'

'The driver getting away?'

'Not today he ain't.'

Coldrain broke into a run, surging ahead of Outlaw.

He sped down past the left side of the Merc. The driver had a hundred-metre head start on the two operators. But Coldrain, never the slimmest or nimblest, had the advantage of big calves and a powerful stride. He was chewing up the road. Hunting down his target.

The driver's run for freedom was more like a limp. Blood was gushing out of his leg. With every step he took, more red gushed out. He wouldn't get very far like that.

As Coldrain passed the Merc he felt a snap of hot air brush over his head. A round had just missed him. There was noise to his right, something clattering. Coldrain turned. *Fuck.* The rear passenger door was flung open. There was a third guy sitting in the back, and Coldrain had failed to spot him.

It was New York. One of the stray rounds from Coldrain's AK burst through the windscreen must have deflected into the rear of the car and deposited itself in the guy's arm, because there was a thick dark-brown stain next to New York and his forearm had a long gash down its length, several inches deep, as though the bullet had burrowed a trench through his flesh. His left arm, the good one, was pointing another Micro-Uzi in his direction.

New York had a look on his face that said he just didn't give a fuck. The guy knew he was history and wanted to take someone else with him. Coldrain was in direct firing range, highly exposed.

And he knew New York could depress the trigger quicker than Coldrain could bring his AK to bear on the guy.

Coldrain was knocked back to the ground and heard what sounded like a massively amplified nail gun being fired. His eardrums throbbed and his muscles shook violently. For a moment he thought he'd been shot, braced himself for the impact of hot lead, but as he arched his neck to his right he clocked Outlaw unleashing a four-round burst of 12-gauge bore ammo into the car. New York took the blasts. Chunks of his chest and face flew up into the air like slices of apple pie. He screamed. Half of his good arm was blown off, showering the Merc's swish beige leather upholstery with charred bone and torn slabs of muscle tissue. The guy was zapped ten times over. Outlaw let him have another single round just for shits and giggles.

'Fucking get the driver,' Outlaw said. 'I'll cover you.'

Coldrain launched himself to his feet, springing up on the backs of his feet, and grabbed his AK. The driver was still able to run despite his injured leg. And he was making a beeline for a network of shanty huts that had cropped up at the end of the road on the left. Coldrain cast his eyes over the buildings. They were similar to the corralling grids that protected insurgents in Fallujah. He bet there was a labyrinthine chain of alleys and paths that the driver could use to shake Coldrain. It was critical he apprehended the runner before he hit the other side of the road, roughly twenty metres from his position.

After-burners time. Coldrain urged his body to close the gap. He widened his stride, bounding across the road as quickly as his quads could power him, taking deep draws of breath, working his calves like his life depended on it.

Thirty metres from the target.

The driver edged closer to the alleyway. Fifteen metres, tops.

Raw air stung Coldrain's lungs. He ignored it. Pain is just your body flushing out weakness. That was what the

Marines taught you. You had to break through the barrier if you wanted to win.

Twenty-five metres. He was gaining ground.

The driver glanced over his shoulder and spotted Coldrain charging towards him. Spun around and suddenly Coldrain found himself examining the business end of the MP5. His instinct was to duck for cover. But his training fought against his base fear. Told him that the guy's hand was unsteady, he couldn't use a two-hand grip on account of his gash leg, and the MP5 was primarily designed for close-quarter battle. Its effective range was a maximum of one hundred metres and, depending on weather conditions and lighting, was sometimes as low as twenty-five metres.

The nozzle of the MP5 flashed and two, three rounds smacked into a watery pothole in front of his feet. The biggest danger now was allowing time for the driver to readjust his aim and get off a second, more accurate burst.

Coldrain was already raising his AK. He adjusted his aim off-centre; he didn't want to kill the driver, just make him think twice about making a dash for the hills. He depressed the trigger and vittled seven rounds into the gap between the target and the alleyway. Two of the rounds struck the door of a battered old Nissan Sunny.

The driver didn't take the hint. He unloaded another wild four-round burst in Coldrain's direction. This time Coldrain surged forward, not allowing himself to think about the rounds whizzing past him, not letting his body get overcome with fear at the sound of the MP5 being discharged. He was fast approaching the driver's position. Now fifteen metres away. The driver was ten from the alleyway. He was ditching the MP5K and scrambled towards the apartments. He knew that the game was up.

Nearly there now.

Just six more big strides and I've got him.

At the lip of the alleyway, Coldrain finally tagged the driver, dropping the AK to the ground, leaping forward and rugby-tackling him from behind. The force of his dive threw them both to the ground and suddenly Coldrain was on top of the target. The driver tried to crawl away in a last desperate attempt to escape. But Coldrain saw the danger and responded with a good old-fashioned boot to the middle of his back, dropping the target to the pavement. Still the fucker tried to scramble free. Coldrain dug out the Sig from the band of his combats. Brought the butt down on the back of his head and gave him a hoofing whack. The driver's head fell forward. He was kissing dirt.

Gripping the wanker by the back of his shirt collar, Coldrain hauled the driver up so their heads were level. He was severely battered. The nose was crooked and one of his eyes was puffed up. It looked like he'd just been in the Octagon cage with Kimbo Slice. He was mega fucked-up. He was impressed with the damage possible with the butt of a Sig Sauer, a hard surface and a spot of violent improv.

'Where's Dogan?'

The guy's eyes were out on stalks. He was whiter than a snowstorm. And yet still he didn't answer. His lips quivered, but the words weren't spilling out.

There was no time to fuck about. Coldrain needed to know. In about ten minutes half the place would be crawling with Turkish military and police forces. Even in a crap town like Van, the racket of AK and Saiga rounds being fired off was bound to have the neighbours calling the police. He had to get the info, and get it quick.

Fixing the driver's ankle with his left hand, Coldrain took his right index finger and pushed it deep into the entry wound. He squealed in agony as the fingernail entered the hole. Coldrain kept his digit inserted and waited a beat to see if he had relented. But the driver was proving a stubborn arsehole, so Coldrain pushed his finger in deeper. The pained squawk turned into a throaty, guttural moan. At one point he closed his eyes and Coldrain wondered if he was going to slip out of consciousness. That would be the disaster dressing on the fuck-up sandwich they'd chewed on this evening.

Coldrain slapped the driver about the face a bit to keep him zoned in. There was a real danger he'd drift off and at that point their last chance of finding Dogan would be up in smoke. But he also kept up the pressure. He was having a right old fiddle about in the entry wound, which was now about twice its original size. His finger was in up to the second knuckle, twisting around inside the temporal cavity the 7.62mm round had freshly carved out. A new wave of pain seared through the guy's body as he let out an ear-piercing howl.

'Enough! Enough! Please!'

But Coldrain didn't stop. He did the exact opposite of stopping. Ratcheted the fucking pain meter up to eleven. There was no point letting him off until he'd given them the all-clips.

'Tell me where's Dogan. I won't fucking ask twice.'

'I swear on my brother, I don't know!'

Not the answer he was looking for. Coldrain plunged

his digit all the way into the wound, past the lower knuckle. The guy screeched.

'Okay, okay,' he sputtered out between heavy draws of breath. Tears were flowing down from his bloodshot eyes, his nose was covered in snot and shit, and his long black hair was dripping with sweat. 'He in Iraq.'

'That's a big old country, mate. I'm gonna need something a bit more accurate.'

The driver spat bloody mucus and phlegm onto the ground.

'Sadr City,' he said. 'It is a house on al-Quds Street. All I know.'

Coldrain believed him. A man gets to the edge of his pain threshold, he becomes physically incapable of bullshitting. And not only that, but it made sense too. *The Thomas job was in Baghdad*, he thought. If Dogan was behind that, it made sense he would be holed up there. He unplugged his digit. It was covered in thick red blood and beads of small round black and purple gunk. A slice of muscle resembling a flesh-pink elastic band was caught dangling from his nail cuticle. There was a dark, wet patch on the driver's jeans. The tosser had pissed himself in fear and pain.

He took the Sig and pushed the barrel right up against the base of the driver's skull. Kept a boot pressed down hard on the middle of his back to hold his body in position. The driver knew what was coming. 'Fuck you, man,' he spat.

No, Coldrain thought. *Fuck you*.

Coldrain pulled the trigger. A single round tore into the driver's head. The body shuddered as the energy from the bullet rippled through his body like a shock wave. He stilled.

Outlaw was waiting for him back next to the Merc. He was in surveillance mode, checking the streets to see if anyone else was coming to join the party. Coldrain nodded to the Hilux. Passing the shot-up Merc, he allowed himself to pause and admire his handiwork. The Merc was riddled with exit holes, five-inch-thick perforations dotted along the chassis. Bloody good work.

Suddenly his BlackBerry sparked up. The display said the number was withheld. Coldrain let it go to voicemail then checked the message. 'Daniel, it's been twenty-four hours and you have failed to report back. I must remind you that there is a lot of pressure on this assign—'

He zapped the message. The Sandman could wait.

'You feeling okay, chief?' Outlaw asked.

Coldrain's ears were bleeding from the AK firestorm. His hair was smouldering, and the man wig on his chest was burnt from where two of the empty cases had bounced off the windscreen and slipped down the front of his shirt. His eyes were watering from the blowback, but none of that mattered. They had got what they had come for, a clear path to Dogan, and they needed to act on it before the trail went cold.

'Sod it, I'll live. Fancy a little day trip, mate?' Coldrain asked.

'Shit, D. For a white boy, you're one merciless mother-fucker.'

'Iraq?'

'Shit. Baghdad?'

'Yeah.

'*She-eeeeet*.' He drew out the word across four or five seconds. No operator liked to head back to the most dangerous city in the world. It wasn't a place that was brimming over with happy memories. But the trail to Dogan led all the way there. They would have to get a move on.

As Coldrain hit the accelerator and turned off the boulevard, they could hear the faint roar of police cars in the distance.

PART THREE

TWENTY-THREE

They raced down the Mosul–Baghdad highway, flying at a ninety clean. Driving slow wasn't an option here. The area was notorious for bandits rolling in white Nissans and Nasr Sahins, who cut in front of other drivers, forcing them to pull over by prodding an AK-47 out of the window. Only one guy had tried that in the hundred and forty klicks they had traversed so far, and as soon as Coldrain clocked him, Outlaw popped out the Saiga and aimed the shotgun out of the window. The target in the Sahin hit the brakes and fucked off.

IEDs were more of a problem but Coldrain had learned from his time in the Afghan that there was next to nothing operators could do to protect themselves. As a Bootneck, he had been on patrols which were mind-numbingly slow, as every potential IED object, be it a pile of rocks dumped in the road, the rotting carcass of a dead dog or even freshly dug earth, meant the team had to grind to a halt, get out the bomb-disposal bloke, usually some pissed Estonian who had a devil-may-care attitude and breath that could skin a dog, and then wait until they got the all-clear to move on. Covering just a few short kilometres could take anything up to twelve hours. It was boring and stressful at the same time. Personally Coldrain had it down that you could spend all day straining your eyes looking for signs of IEDs, and still miss the one object that would ultimately zap you. If it was your time, it was your time. There was no point mincing about in a place like Iraq or the Afghan if you weren't prepared to accept the risk.

The road was the colour of fag ash and one long earthquake simulator, a continual stream of mortar rounds and airborne projectiles conspiring to dig it up like a rugby match in the middle of January. It was more cut up than the Somme. In places, Coalition forces had attempted to relay the road, but they must have had an asphalt shortage, because half the replacement road was just a load of wet brown soil patted down and smoothed out on top. It summed up some countries' contribution to the war. Do some half-arsed repairs on a few key access roads then fuck off home for croissants, cappuccinos and threesomes while the Brits and Yanks got the shit blown out of them.

Getting across the Turkey–Iraq border had proved easier than Coldrain and Outlaw had figured. They had driven to Silopi, a town in Şirnak Province nudged away in the south-easternmost corner of Turkey. The town was just a collection of bazaars that fed off the nearby Habur Frontier Gate, the only border crossing between the country and neighbouring Iraq. The Hilux joined a queue of trailers and trucks that stretched from the border point back half a click. Most of the drivers stood outside their vehicles, brewing tea and smoking cigarettes, like they were used to the hold-up.

'This is nothing,' one of them shouted to Coldrain from the side. 'Sometimes we are here one week.'

When they reached the front of the line, the border guards simply waved them through. No checks, no questions, no sign of anyone giving a fuck. Probably, Coldrain guessed, they were more worried about the lorries coming in from the other direction, many of them loaded with heroin and bound for the streets of London.

Traffic had been light so far, mostly oil tankers and lorries. To their right, lined by tall reeds and barren stretches of desert dotted with vegetation, the steel-blue sludge-pool known as the River Tigris slowly ebbed, transporting excrement and spilt oil. It had been tracking them all the way from Silopi. As they crossed the bridge over the Tigris, Coldrain saw a couple of Iraqis on a fishing yawl in the middle of the river, using nets to try and drag something to the bank. It took him a few seconds before he was able to identify the shape as a human torso. He remembered someone telling him that every day dozens of dead bodies were caught up in iron nets designed to trap plants and rubbish. Most of the corpses had been tortured. Eyes pulled out, noses cut off, finger- and toenails removed and genitals dismembered. The combination of raw shit, tonnes of rubbish and rotting flesh had made the Tigris, previously a good source of potable water and fishing, unusable.

Coldrain had been driving since the border crossing. Outlaw, the eyes and ears, Saiga on his lap, face brushed by the cool air lapping in from the rolled-down window, DMX playing on Outlaw's iPod plugged into the main stereo.

As they neared Baghdad the landscape shifted once more. They had crossed Mosul without fanfare, sticking to the basic rules he learned on the circuit. Never stop the car, always keep moving, maintain a low profile and obscure any weapons from view. Public shows of force tended to provoke hostile reactions from the locals.

'Goddamn beautiful country,' Outlaw said. 'Can't think why I ever wanted to leave.'

Once they had crossed the bridge stretching from east to west across the river like an artery through the heart of the city, Coldrain pointed the wheels south until they had emerged from the city via the south-western quadrant. Both he and Outlaw breathed a sigh of relief as the city shrank in the rear-view mirror. In 2004, an insurgent had stepped into a dining hall at FOB Marez located within the city, killing nine US soldiers and wounding another thirty-four. The dicker had disguised himself as an Iraqi security serviceman. Mosul was not the kind of place for a white Western male to be loafing around in.

Now the road was swelling with vehicles. They passed US up-armoured Humvees kitted out with side- and rear-armour plating as well as a ballistic windshield to protect against forward-propelled shrapnel and low-velocity rounds. The armour had been fitted out only after the original Iraq invasion. When their US counterparts saw Coldrain and a few other Bootnecks rocking about Basra in Pinzgauers with welded-on bits of scrap metal to create modified GPMG frames, they decided to ape them, cooking up hillbilly armour plating on their own vehicles.

The soldiers in the Humvee gave a wave as they slid by. The Toyota Hilux was a dead giveaway, being the vehicle of choice for pretty much any security adviser stationed in-country.

The guy manning the M249 disappeared down inside the belly of the Humvee for a moment, then jumped back up. He was hoisting a red and white horizontal two-bar pennon with a patch of blue on the left and a star in the middle. The Texan flag. Coldrain nodded back. Thought, *Better put that thing away soon, mate, or it'll be raining bloody RPGs any minute now.*

Next stop, Baghdad.

TWENTY-FOUR

It was red pigs in Sadr City when they rocked up at 1450 hours, drenched in sweat as they moved through Baghdad's cauldron-like streets. All told, they had travelled more than three hundred and sixty miles since they'd left Van. Coldrain was hanging out of his arse, so shattered that he had gonked out for the last quarter of a mile. Just driven blind. But he wasn't about to pitch up at an Esso for a power nap. Sadr City was going to be roughers in daytime, but neither he nor Outlaw fancied sticking around after nightfall, when the security presence evaporated and the insurgents were left to roam free. They were going to have to dig out for the next few hours, at least until after they had filled Dogan in.

In his mind, Coldrain was wondering if he should fess up to Outlaw about Dogan's involvement in Jamie's death. He felt bad about withholding that nugget of int. I'll tell him later, he thought. *Maybe after I've wiped the floor with Dogan's fucking brains*.

Gaining access to Sadr City had taken some time. The Hilux finally hit a checkpoint on the south-western end of the district along a highway that Outlaw explained was called Route Pluto. Al-Quds Street was a few streets north of the artery. There were two types of vehicle riding the blacktop, rusted old civvy cars and US Humvees and infantry fighting vehicles (IVFs) which banged a right off the thoroughfare along a dust-soaked shoulder that ran along concrete T-walls, the blast-proof barriers placed outside embassies, hotels, airports, restaurants, UN bases and just about anywhere that the insurgents thought made a good target. The civvy vehicles just drove straight on. *Wise choice.*

'Fourteenth Cavalry,' Outlaw said, pointing to an M2 Bradley IVF up ahead of them. The rear ramp on the Bradley was lowered and six dismounts were busy bundling into the troop compartment, while a seventh guy manned the 22mm M242 chaingun on the top-left bang box and provided lookout along the roads. They were ready to pop rounds at any vehicle that behaved suspiciously. Stowage racks fixed to the left and right sides of the laminate armour plating which normally held TOW anti-tank missiles had been shredded. A banner on the roof of the rear chassis announced 'STAY BACK OR WE WILL SHOOT'. Some Arabic squiggles below, which he guessed was the same message but in the local lingo. The debussed soldiers were wearing wraparounds and modular tactical vests (MTVs), aka cool-as-shit ballistic body armour.

The nearest soldier raised his hand, indicating to the Hilux to stop. Coldrain hit the brakes. These guys didn't play games. If Coldrain carried on driving the Cav lads would surely vaporise the pickup in the blink of an eye. Shoot first, ask questions later. The time-honoured Yank way of war.

'That's the second squadron, the Eyes and Ears. I know a few of these guys. They worked support and logistics for us on Task Force Orange. I'll go talk to them.'

'Fill your boots, mate.'

Outlaw debussed from the Hilux and Coldrain scouted the area. The immediate block was a row of crumbling tan buildings and alleys strewn with bundles of desiccated debris, old TV sets, tangled wires, bits of anonymous metal, the cracked shell of a fallen mortar round. A merchant shop run by a bearded old geezer with an eye missing was selling fresh fruit and tinned shit by the side of the road. Business was slower than a pothead reading Shakespeare.

Two hundred metres away, deep in the bowels of Sadr City, stood two tall housing blocks, maybe twenty storeys high. Banners hung slackly from the high-up balconies. One of them in particular caught Coldrain's attention. It was a black banner with stark white Arabic writing at the top that he couldn't read. But the central picture was a portrait of Mohammad Sadeq al-Sadr, the Grand Ayatollah who had defied Saddam and in whose honour the city was named. Sadeq was also Moqtada al-Sadr's old man. People had long memories in Sadr City. They didn't forgive, and they sure as hell didn't forget either.

There was a constant flurry of activity on the rooftops of the low-rises. Kids ran about, waving at the soldiers, old men stood around muttering to one another and smoking aromatic fags. Perfect vantage points for sniper or surprise RPG assaults on troops negotiating the compact grid of roads, Coldrain thought. *It must be a nightmare carrying out house-to-house here.*

Coldrain was just considering buying himself a can of Jihad Cola from the merchant store when Outlaw dashed back to the Hilux.

'Guys are heading up past Al-Quds themselves,' he said. 'Said we can come with, if we want.'

Coldrain's eyes widened.

'What, in that death-trap?'

'If we want.'

'Right.'

'I know what you're thinking,' Outlaw quipped.

Coldrain had a thing about being inside a crammed vehicle during an attack. His theory was, you were better off out in the open, because at least you had room to manoeuvre. Being stuck inside an APC as RPGs cooked off around them wasn't his idea of fun. Besides, Coldrain had been trained in the art of rolling false flag, low profile. Like all good British operators, working off the radar was as natural to him as breathing. He wasn't down with this Yank, Look-At-Me, I'm-Hard-as-Fuck attitude. Coldrain wasn't looking for a fight, he was aiming to get in, nab Dogan and get the hell out again with as little fuss and bloodshed as possible.

'Tell them, thanks, mate, but no thanks. We'll just roll behind them. I was planning on keeping my meat and two veg.'

Outlaw smirked. 'I'll let them know the first part. But you tell 'em the second bit yourself.'

The Cav guys finished loading, the rear ramp closed up and the Bradley sputtered into life. It couldn't happen quickly enough for Coldrain. Sitting in a static vehicle, astride the most notorious district in the most dangerous city in the world was hardly his idea of fun.

A few minutes later they were rumbling into Sadr City.

The pace was slow. The Bradley had a top speed of around forty miles per hour but it was presently doing about half that. Streets normally five metres wide had been reduced to just half that length, owing to the reams of junk littering them. Twice the Bradley had to stop, three of the Cavs dismounting and setting a small primer charge to detonate man-made roadblocks, crude blocks of cement with lengths of pipe jutting out like straws in a bowl of ice cream, designed to delay the convoy so that prowling rooftop snipers and RPG jockeys could do their worst. Each time the Bradley came to a halt Coldrain would keep the engine running on the Hilux, foot poised on the pedal, scope the rooftops and alleyways along a hundred and eighty degree field to the left of their position, with Outlaw scanning the area to his right. He spotted nothing out of the ordinary, but the two burnt-out Coalition vehicles down an adjacent street were a stark reminder that others had not been so fortunate.

As far as slums went, Sadr City was gash-grim. It made the Elephant and Castle look like the fucking Maldives. The deeper into the district they drove, the more dilapidated the scenery. They passed a convoy of V-shaped trucks with grille shields over the narrow window slots, 4x4 rear-wheel suspension and a couple of jerrycans tacked onto the back, kicking up thick clouds of dust in their wake.

'This the new toy of the US military?'

'MRAPs,' Outlaw said. 'Mine-resistant, ambush-protected. DoD bought a shit-ton of these little beauties after the IEDs got out of hand. They're meant to stop the guys inside getting some.'

'Do they work?'

'I never rode in one, and I don't have any desire to find out.'

'Don't blame you, mate. The day the bigwigs invent an invincible vehicle is the day soldiers get a proper pay.'

'True.'

The constant stress of knowing that they might encounter an IED with their name on it at any given moment was one of the reasons Coldrain was glad to be out of the close-protection racket. Being a human sandbag had its perks, but the random lottery of driving through hostile streets was definitely not one of them.

Overhead Coldrain could hear the heavy thrum of a paraffin pigeon. He looked up and saw the shadow of an Apache moving in front of the sun, looking to sink a few Hellfire missiles into any insurgent dumb enough to try and have a go.

'When was the last time you were in Iraq?' Outlaw asked.

'Not for a year, mate. Back then old Moqtada al-Sadr's Mahdi army militia had just stood down. No more engagements within Sadr City. That was the official line at least.'

'It don't look like much of a ceasefire has been in place.'

The scars of battle were everywhere to be seen. The walls of every home displayed a dozen or more bullet holes, 7.62mm rounds, the Iraqi equivalent of pebbledash. Spent jackets were to be found everywhere. Several buildings had been reduced to dust and there was a putrid smell of shit in the air as they entered the heart of Sadr City.

The filth in Sadr City was gopping. Honking big heaps of excrement were lying right outside people's front doors, the old dirt track disappearing under a thick black quagmire, browntop instead of black. Peering down a side street, Coldrain saw a soccer field overflowing with rotting sewage and rubbish. There were elderly women and young children picking their way through the mountains of garbage, fishing out blackened fruit, dead rats and bits of this and that.

'It's not really al-Sadr's boys who are the problem any more,' Coldrain explained. 'There's a dozen splinter factions, maybe more. Most of them operate out of Sadr City.'

'I'm guessing they're free to roam too.'

'Yeah, the locals are too terrified to say anything.'

'Don't surprise me. When we inserted back in '03, I kept saying to my bosses, we can kill as many bad guys as we want, we can build all the fucking hospitals and factories in the world, but the people are still going to hate us. You know why?'

'Surprise me.'

'Because someone rolls into your neighbourhood who doesn't belong there, you'd rather *sell your soul* than work with them. It's like honky cops running around all-black neighbourhoods back home.'

'Honky?'

'White folk.'

They passed a network of streets that were pure rubble.

'Holy shit,' Outlaw said. 'Looks like someone went to town.'

'That's the Dukan market. Or at least it used to be. About a month back some insurgent dicker detonated a vehicle. Right in the middle of the market. More than fifty people were killed. Had a mate who was two streets away when it went off.'

The convoy stopped at an intersection separated by a twelve-foot-high concrete block. Coldrain guessed it was designed to blunt mortar attacks on the Green Zone. If they were within shelling distance of the GZ then he made it that they were in the very centre of Sadr City, the partition separating the northern district from the southern residential enclave.

The convoy ground to a halt. The Yanks dismounted

from the Bradley and one of the soldiers approached the Hilux. He was a thickset Hispanic guy. Sweat dripped down from his ballistic bone dome and he was chewing on a wad of tobacco. The name tag on his front pouch said RIVERA.

'This is us?' Outlaw quizzed.

'This is you.' Rivera pointed to the partition wall. 'You'll find the residential addresses over the other side.'

'Thanks, mate,' Coldrain said. 'Any idea how we get around?'

Rivera looked back at his comrades. They were entering a small compound twenty metres to the north, surrounded by HESCO bastions and concertina wire. A puppy leapt out of the Bradley, a small white thing. It wagged its tail excitedly and followed the Cav lads into the compound. Coldrain could hear the buzz from inside. Smelled the hot mugs of coffee being dished out. In the middle of this shithole, a place for the lads to hole up and have a brew, it must have seemed like heaven on earth.

'Well, there are two ways into al-Quds. You can drive another two, three hundred metres east, cut across the intersection, and hope some godforsaken asshole doesn't decide to treat you to a slice of RPG pie along the route.'

'What's the second option?'

'See this block right here? Technically I'd have to shoot anyone who tried climbing over. But for about a half hour I'm gonna be busy writing my girl. And technically speaking, I ain't seen shit.'

Coldrain and Outlaw exchanged a look. They didn't want to mince about. Having come this far, both men were itching to get their mitts on Dogan and fill him in good and proper. The only bummer was that if they abandoned the Hilux, every working part would be dismantled and stolen within minutes. In the thief-ridden environment of Sadr City, that was guaranteed. But they would worry about evac later.

It was time to pay Dogan a visit.

TWENTY-FIVE

Coldrain grabbed the AK-47 and the Saiga 12-gauge and threw them both onto the top of the concrete block, along with two spare clips of 7.62 brass. Outlaw shoved a fistful of 12-gauge cartridges into his pockets. They were fat slugs with a red wax casing supported by a thin brass base and to Coldrain they resembled lipstick tubes. He and Outlaw climbed onto the Toyota's front hood, elevating them up to a standing height of nine and a half feet.

Coldrain was first to the wall. Faced with a flat surface, and only one obstacle to scale, he opted to employ a mantling technique, lifting up his arms, placing both hands on the ledge, and hauling himself up until his chin was higher than his fists. He was focused on engaging his lats, shoulder and back muscle groups. Once his head was clear of the wall, Coldrain directed his energy downward, pushing his upper body weight onto his hands. He rotated his palms and swung his right leg over and up onto the ledge, allowing him to transfer some of his body weight onto the leg and give himself ample balance with which to manoeuvre across. Then he hoisted up his other leg and lay flat on the top of the wall to present a smaller target to any potential enemy combatants skulking on the other side. His lats burnt deeply. The palms of his hands were red and the joins beneath each finger were blistering up from the climb. He scanned the road.

Al-Quds Street was more squalid than the road the Yanks had patrolled down. Bits of old mortar rounds lay scattered on the ground. There were no market stalls or convenience stores on this side of the tracks. Caved-in buildings flanked a razed cobblestone thoroughfare with a big pool of murky sewage to the left that half a dozen rats and dogs were feasting on. The street was shrouded in darkness from the two tower blocks that sat a hundred and fifty metres to the north-east.

It was eerily quiet. A ghost town. The cut wires hanging like old rope from the electricity pylons suggested it wasn't because everyone was indoors watching Iraq's version of *The X Factor*. One thing was for sure: the American cloud punchers had fucked this place up.

Coldrain kept one eye fixed on the street as he grabbed the AK-47 and eased himself down the other side. A few moments later Outlaw joined him, wielding the 12-gauge. They both checked the rooftops for movement. It was difficult penetrating the shadows cast by the tower blocks so he focused on trying to look for the glint of a metal gun barrel.

To the left of the worn cobblestone a half-metre-wide stream of effluent slowly dribbled by. The smell was so rank even a full NBC suit and respirator wouldn't have kept it out. There were flies everywhere, so many of them that Coldrain could hear their wings beating. They attached themselves to his eyes, crawled up his nostrils and along the corners of his mouth. He saw three Iraqi boys in knackered old kicks, shorts and bloodied tees playing American football. With a dead cat. They ignored Coldrain and

Outlaw, like it was every day you saw two guys in mufti rig walking through the streets kitted up to their eyeballs. Coldrain and Outlaw ignored them back, like it was every day you saw dirt-poor kids playing sport with the carcass of a domestic animal.

A crude slab of concrete announced Dogan's house. Two rudimentary windows looked out onto the street, one on the ground floor and caked in a solid inch of soot, the second on the first floor, the glass fully blown out of the window frame. A satellite dish poked out of the rooftop like a miniature radar dish. Bullet holes peppered the side of the property, and lumps of the roof perimeter had been carved off, along with half of the gutter piping, but, in comparison to the building next to it, Dogan's pad had got off lightly. The next place along had been flattened, just a messy stack of burnt cinderblock, melted plastic and bent metal frames. It looked like a giant fist had pounded down on top of it.

They moved quietly through the street, Coldrain keeping his eyes trained on the door and the motor, Outlaw providing backup and scoping out the surrounding rooftops and streets. A high-level target like Dogan, someone might be watching. The PKK people had been vigilant in Van, protecting their asset. He doubted somehow they would make it any easier in Baghdad.

Coldrain approached the motor, a facelifted Peugeot 406 sedan in brown. Or maybe it was white, he thought, and the owner hadn't gotten round to washing off the bird shit and mud for a long time. Peering through the rear window, Coldrain clocked a back seat full of explosive equipment, primer charges, det cord, a dozen blocks of C-4 plastic explosive, two jerrycans, bags of wheat flour, a bundle of percussion detonator caps, the lot. The soap bars of plastique alone were sufficient to blow a tunnel down to Oz.

The front door was twelve metres further down. The two operators edged towards it, taking care not to let their Tims scrape against the gravel, sidestepping empty plastic bottles and scraps of paper, anything that could disturb the quiet of the street. As they bent down, moving under the sooted window, Coldrain tried to catch any sounds coming from within the house. But he heard nothing. Not the din of a TV, the whirl of a fan or the sound of water boiling in a pan. No wonder these people were pissed off, Coldrain told himself. If he didn't have electricity he wouldn't be jumping for joy either.

They reached the entrance, a light wooden door with six raised panels down it, Arabic stencilled writing on each. Coldrain gave the black doorknob a rattle. It was loose. He took the right side of the door, Outlaw positioned himself left. They took a three count and Coldrain indicated using hand signals he would be the Number One and go in first; Outlaw would follow in behind him ready to engage with the 12-gauge. Coldrain had long experience of house-to-house warfare from the early days in Basra, when insurgents were freely taking potshots at squaddies from around the city and the Royals had to come in and vittle the bad guys up.

A lot of people back home thought that war twenty-first-century-style was a hi-tech business, like playing a video game. Identify an enemy target, radio in for fast air and sit back with some popcorn and watch the fireworks light up the sky. But urban fighting was dirty, emotional, adrenalin-pumping, in-your-face nauseating and when it came down to it, you were bursting through the fatal funnel of fire, the area of the room that defenders were most likely to aim at, and it was a high-risk game of Russian roulette. One side would get lucky and shoot the other first. It was controlled aggression, and little else.

His breathing was erratic. Heavy. He fought to control it. Coldrain was facing a high-pressure entry, with no dit on enemy strength or numbers, or the layout or features of the combat zone. It was like shoving his cock into a hole and hoping for the best.

In a blur, Coldrain smashed the butt of the Kalashnikov down against the doorknob. The handle made a loud clink as it dropped onto the frayed cobblestone. Then he plunged his right boot into the frame, and the door swung open. He was in.

TWENTY-SIX

She made sure she stayed back far enough that they would not spot her, and as she climbed over the wall and landed on the other side she was briefly pleased with herself. It wasn't every day that she tailed specialist operators, after all, and the fact she had done it so effortlessly proved a point. To herself, more than anyone else. Truly, Ischenko was a top-class field journalist, whatever malicious gossip that crusty old idiot Jancko had circulated around the newsroom.

Travelling in her car, she'd been able to remain calm, as though the tranquil, air-conned atmosphere of the Honda insulated her from the dangers of the world outside.

But now she was on foot, Ischenko was all too aware of the precariousness of her situation. *I'm in the middle of Baghdad, alone, no protection, on what is, basically, just a hunch.* When she mapped it out like that, it sounded like she had taken leave of her senses, and there had been moments during the intervening twelve hours when she had questioned whether this really was a smart idea. Perhaps Coldrain and his friend were really just a couple of freelancers. God knows, Ischenko had met enough of them in Berlin, back from adventures in Afghanistan and Iraq, all eager to tell their tales over a beer and a bratwurst, and, if you believed everything they said, Osama Bin Laden had been killed, captured and tortured a million times over. They exaggerated their stories, mostly, she suspected, because they thought it would improve their chances of sleeping with her.

On that score, they were very wrong.

No one knows you're here. The voice seemed to come from the back of Ischenko's skull, quiet as a whisper at first, now gaining decibels with every beat of her heart. *If something happens to you, God forbid . . .*

No. I won't entertain such thoughts. She scooped heaps of denial onto the voice, burying it before the fear and anxiety could work their way through her system. Ischenko was a tough cookie and had a tighter handle on her fear than many a man in the newsroom.

She glanced constantly behind her. There seemed to be no one on the street except for those poor children, and a couple of women sticking close together. But Ischenko was aware of how incongruous she looked in tight jeans, shirt and a basic shawl. She scrutinised every alleyway, rooftop and window. Everyone knew the stories of journalists finding themselves in bad situations, and the ones who had security advisers tended to live. Dietmar Bilt, with whom she became acquainted with when they did shifts on the production floor learning the tricks of the trade, was one of those who neglected to have a security detail on his first trip to Baghdad three years ago. It also turned into his last, after he was dragged from his car into a nearby house and beheaded. Ischenko recalled the news being broken to Bilt's wife. She shuddered at the memory.

Well, no point worrying about that now. She was already here, wasn't she? All she hoped was that the story would be worth the hassle. *Even if it is*, the voice inside her chided, *you have to be alive at the end of the day to tell it*. That was also very true.

As she approached the building the men had entered, she wondered two things. First, whether she should go in, admit to them she had pursued them all the way from Van, and ask if she could accompany them. At least that would afford her some protection. And second, how things would play with Coldrain. No doubt he assumed she had deliberately flirted with him to tease information out of him. To believe that, however, ignored the fact that throughout her career Ischenko had had to fight doubly hard, to prove her abilities on TV and in the newspapers, to demonstrate to everyone that her alluring good looks had nothing to do with her success.

Perhaps that's why you flirted with him. Subconsciously. For the sake of the story.

Not a hope in hell, Ischenko told herself. Try as she might to dress it up otherwise, the bottom line was she'd been attracted to Coldrain from the start. After all, it fitted in with her pattern of relationships. She liked damaged goods.

And they don't come any more damaged than your man Coldrain.

TWENTY-SEVEN

It was uber-dark in the room, a shock transition from day to night. He couldn't see shit, much less make out any shapes. For all Coldrain knew, there could have been six X-rays in the room. He was momentarily disorientated. Squinting, he tried to focus around the edges of the objects in his direct line of sight. It was too dark. But it was also too late to turn back.

He moved forward into the blackness. The AK-47 was raised in a high-ready stance, holding the firearm in a shooting grip, with the stock resting on the inside of his elbow. The barrel was level with the bottom of his chin so Coldrain could look across the top of the gun as he cleared the room, able to shoulder-mount the weapon quick as a flash.

Close-quarter battle – CQB – was always the most stressful kind of attack. Your adrenal glands were pumping overtime, endorphins were being released throughout your body, and it was a struggle to keep yourself in check. The temptation was to let rip with a few warning rounds once inside, because you were highly exposed, but CQB training had drummed into Coldrain the emphasis on not wasting bullets in a close-combat environment. Missed shots could injure unaccounted-for civvies.

His eyes began to adjust to the objects in the room, shapes attained dimensions and definition. This was a sort of communal living area, yellow sofa to the left, small widescreen TV opposite, a coffee table in between and a row of three naff pictures on the walls, flowers and shit, except the middle one, which was an oval-shaped mirror encased in a gold-painted frame. He couldn't see any moving objects. There was a staircase at the rear of the lounge. It looked about ten metres away. A couple of metres to the right of the stairs was an arched portal. Coldrain figured that was the entryway to the kitchen. He felt Outlaw's breath on his neck to the left as he shifted forwards, flitting his line of sight between the staircase and the portal.

Coldrain motioned for Outlaw to tag left and tackle the staircase at the same time as he himself would hit the room to the right. Timing and coordination would be everything. The two men were putting total trust in each other's abilities.

Coldrain leant against the portal wall, held his breath and listened intently. Outlaw knelt beside the staircase. Both men were tuned to hear the faintest sound. A slight draw of breath, a foot scraping across floorboards, the working parts of a gun or loose ammo clinking against each other, all could help pinpoint the enemy presence.

There was chatter coming from the kitchen. It was indistinct, a lot of gibberish to Coldrain, but the voices were heated, like they were arguing about something. He heard two marked, separate voices trying to shout over each other. Dogan had company. And they weren't happy about something. Maybe they were squabbling about whether to paint the walls beige or light blue.

With no grenade to pop into the kill zone, Coldrain bent

his knees and swung round into the door frame. He immediately dropped to a kneeling position, making himself a smaller target. His finger was already halfway depressed on the trigger. He didn't even have to think about it, his muscle memory and training just told him that he needed to be ready to discharge a round within half a second of identifying an X-ray.

He was looking at a dank kitchen, five by eight. The tiled floor had a big stain on it, some brown shit. An old wooden table to the left. Ashtray overflowing with cigarette ends. Radio. The source of the old boys nattering away, he realised. Coldrain wasn't totally surprised. Iraqis didn't do hushed tones or polite conversation.

But no X-rays in this room. Coldrain spun around and saw Outlaw moving up the stairs. He turned back to the kitchen for another scan, in case he had missed anything first time round. And that's when he saw it.

Four copper wires snaked along the kitchen top, down onto the floor tiles, and led into a set of black containers, each one the size and dimensions of a shoe box. There were blasting caps, resembling long, golden electrodes fitted to the ends of the copper wire. Without even looking closer, Coldrain could guess what was inside the boxes.

Home-made explosives rigged to detonate at a moment's notice.

There was a spill of small white bobbles on the floor, like tiny bits of Styrofoam. Ammonium nitrate-fuel oil, aka ANFO, a combustible HE usually employed to blow open mine shafts.

Safe to handle, easy to transport and able to be filled in boreholes thanks to its free form, there was a big demand for ANFO and the Yanks churned it out quicker than porn. With so much ANFO flooding the market, it was only a matter of time before the jihadists and the crackpots got their greasy mitts on it too. Now it had become the explosive of choice for the discerning global terrorist. And a bunch of the stuff was crammed into those boxes, probably alongside a few sticks of dynamite or Tovex, a water gel explosive, as a booster charge to guarantee a big bang. Coldrain's eyes followed the copper wire paths. He needed to know where that shit was coming from. The wires ran up the kitchen wall and slid out of the window.

Bollocks, he thought. *The whole house is one big fucking IED.*

Coldrain spun around and faced Outlaw. He was halfway up the stairs. To the right of the stairwell was a small ventilation grille, no bigger than an envelope. Worming its way out of the grille was a neat bunch of copper wire, held together with a plastic rat belt fastener. The bunched-up wires ran down the wall from the grille, along its cracked white paint, and fed under the stair treads.

Two steps high from Outlaw.

House-borne improvised explosive devices, HBIEDs, had become an increasing problem in Iraq. Coldrain had heard about these booby traps from guys in the Royals. In house clearances, the insurgents knew that Coalition forces would have to clear every single house on a block. They also learned from observation that the more houses they cleared, the more careless and frantic soldiers were likely to become, as the stress of urban combat began to exact its supreme physical and psychological toll. It would be the last house, or the second from last, that would be selected for the HBIED. As soon as the soldiers stepped into the home they would be entering one giant rigged device. The HBIED could be activated in a number of ways, either through a tripwire positioned inside a doorway or remotely detonated by a dicker observing the assault from another position.

Or they could use pressure plates.

When the foot pressed down on the plate with force, an electrical charge would be transmitted up along the copper wire and into the blasting cap, which was packed with mercury fulminate as a primary charge. The current channelled down the wire would melt the bridgewire, creating an exo chemical reaction that would detonate the blasting cap and ignite the secondary, larger explosive materiel contained in the black boxes. A set of home-made bombs, properly rigged and mixed, could flatten the entire building, incinerating everything within a thirty-metre radius.

Boom, and you wouldn't just be browners. You'd be a million fucking pieces of history.

Coldrain could see Outlaw ascending the next tread. His right foot was in the air, poised to land bang on top of the pressure plate. There was nothing he could to do stop it happening, Coldrain was already too far away to make a grab for him. He shouted at Outlaw, but even as the big ex-Delta operator stopped, his foot was already falling onto the plate buried under the black and white goatskin rug.

Outlaw's foot hit the floor.

'BOMB!' Coldrain shouted breathlessly. 'Get out, NOW!'

Outlaw did a one-eighty.

Coldrain was already bracing himself.

Waited for the world to swallow him up.

TWENTY-EIGHT

He was going to die. He was certain of it.

It was two seconds since it had been fused.

Now three.

Outlaw was bundling down the stairs, racing towards the door, the two men moving in giant leaps, kicking hard like two sprinters poised to hit the finish line. As the seconds crept by like water dripping from an old tap, Coldrain wondered how much of him would survive. How badly it would hurt. Knew that the force of the explosion would rip him from limb to limb.

Like a tree being torn apart in a hurricane.

Coldrain's only chance was that Dogan had made a botch job of the wiring, left it a little loose, or the wires were the old copper variety. That could delay the primer charge reaction. It was a slim hope on which hung his life, but war was all about the inches, the tiny margins. A bullet smacks into the wall where a moment earlier a soldier's head had been; a knife misses a mate's heart and lungs by millimetres; a bomb doesn't blow because the charge is wet. That was the difference between living and dying in a combat zone.

Four seconds passed. *Fuck it, if you're going to blow up, just get it over with. Don't make me fucking wait.*

They were hurtling out of the door.

Into a mouth of sluiced white light.

That was five seconds, Coldrain thought, or was it six?
He couldn't tell.

His heart skipped a beat as they dashed across the
cobblestone. The detonator would kick off now, surely. In
his mind he visualised the massive concentration of energy
surging down the wire and into the primary charge. The
sudden colossal energy build-up would cause the explosive stuff to compress, and with the temperature increasing,
the materiel would send out a supersonic shock wave, and,
a few moments later, the burning explosive following
behind it, echoing the shock wave and creating the conditions for multiple waves of detonation. It looked nothing
like a Hollywood fireball, but it was ten times more devastating.

He willed himself on to reach the other side of the street,
where a half-demolished wall stood. Coldrain beat a quick
pace towards it, hoping the cover would be enough to
protect them from the blast. The amount of ANFO stashed
in the kitchen was more than enough to total the house.
He wondered how big the blast radius might be. *You don't
know. It could be ten metres. Might be twenty. Just get a fucking
move on and hit the doorway. Get behind that wall. It could save
your life.*

Yes, but then again it might just crush you. Your ribs
would be snapped like balsa wood. Unable to breathe,
you'd choke to death on the fumes in a few minutes. Each
draw of breath would feel like a knife piercing your heart.

Fucking hurry up. You want to live?

He hit the doorway and rolled through, Outlaw behind
him. Slid up against the wall, the AK-47 by his side, the
cold metal muzzle prodding into his sweating armpit.

Seven seconds.

Longest of his life.

Then the whole world shuddered.

He felt the powerful release of the initial shock wave.

When a supersonic wave erupts, it fans outward, discharging faster than the speed of sound. Anything caught in that first wave is pulverised. Then the flames spew out and toast the remains. They were outside the eye of the blast, but remained within a potentially lethal kill zone.

First came the cloud, an accelerating fog of hot dust and a million rock-sized concrete and metal fragments spinning through the air, penetrating the doorway and punching against the metre-high wall Outlaw and Coldrain were crouching behind. Day turned to night as the air was swamped. It was like being submerged in a dark, polluted body of water. Everything went silent, the world slowed down. Debris spun through the air like it was spinning in treacle.

And then came the sound. Roaring wind, crushing lead, crumbling brick, crackling air, the whole devastating symphony pounding his eardrums, banging repeatedly against the sides of his head. It was sensational and terrifying and felt like it would never end, like being in the middle of a volcano going berserk. He felt a chunk of something smash into his left shoulder. A slice of wall, maybe. His shoulder blade throbbed. Piping hot fragments peppered his hands and face.

It seemed like it would never end.

His ears ached and his eyes watered over. His throat was so dry it hurt to breathe, like swallowing glass and vomiting it back up again. His face was covered in salty tears and dust. Coldrain took a blackened hand to his face and wiped it with the back of his wrist. He expected his sight to return to normal. But it did not. There was a swaying trace of each object, like the motion-shadow on a tuning fork.

Beside him, Outlaw was hocking up some thick black shit. String mucus dangled from his lips and nose. A little bit of pavement pizza came up too. He was keeling over, hacking away like an old man on a sixty-a-day habit. From top to toe, Outlaw was caked in lime and grey-coloured ash, so that he resembled a neglected statue. He looked like crap, but Coldrain guessed he didn't look any better himself.

'Boom,' Outlaw joked in a harsh, throaty voice. Coldrain wanted to laugh, tried to, but when he did, he found himself coughing violently, bats flapping in a frenzy in his ribcage, and he thought maybe he had suffered a crushed rib.

He blinked and wiped away the tears streaming down his face. Found himself staring in a daze at the crater where the house had been. The black hole was twelve metres wide, eight deep. Smoke wafted skywards, three or four small fires breaking out amidst the tombstone-sized slabs of mortar and the spaghetti of wires and twisted metal rods. It was difficult to accept that a house had stood there a couple of minutes before. The whole place had been totalled. Coldrain was glad he and Outlaw had made it out in time. Dodgy fusing, junk wires, he didn't give a fuck. They had been inside for a couple of seconds more, there would be nothing left except for a small pile of cremated bones and hair, and another reason for his parents to wallow in misery and booze.

And then down the street there was noise. The ringing in his ears was persistent, and would last for some hours, giving everything a hollow, distant quality. But there was no mistaking this sound. It was urgent, screeching. Like a knife piercing his skull.

Thirty seconds later, or was it a minute now, it felt more like an hour. Through the cordite fog, he saw the lights. Red and blue flashes. Then he caught sight of the car. Wide saloon with a bulky grille and shiny sky-blue bonnet. Strip of white beneath the headlights. The white flecked with brown dust.

The cop cage pulled up twenty metres from the blast site. Doors were flung open on the driver and passenger sides. Two men stepped out. One was early twenties, skinny as a rake, dressed in a long-sleeved light blue shirt and black combat trousers. He had a dark blue baseball cap pulled low over his head, the tongue shadowing his features, the word POLICE emblazoned on the front in bright white lettering. On the upper left sleeve an Iraqi flag badge had been sewn on.

The older man was short and stocky, broad-shouldered and dark-skinned. He was wearing a black and blue digi-cam uniform, a dark blue beret and a pair of tan boots. A third-generation Glock G20 pistol was holstered on his utility belt, along with a pair of handcuffs and a black walkie-talkie. The Glock glinted as it caught the thin beams of sunlight breaking through the smoke.

His face was indistinct, the smoke like a veil pulled over his face, but as he stepped closer the cloud lifted and his features became clearer. His eyes were small and green. They lacked intensity, had a weary, morose sheen. Like he was very afraid of something. The man's eyebrows were low and bushy, and his face was unshaven, the jawline smothered in curly black stubble. He looked back at Coldrain and Outlaw as if he knew who the two men were.

'Come with me, *kafir*,' he said. 'I have a friend who wishes to speak with you.'

Coldrain looked towards the police car.

Slumped in the back seat was a tearful Ischenko.

TWENTY-NINE

He smoked his way through a couple of extra-long Marlboro Reds and said his name was Khalid. Coldrain did not ask him why a serving Iraqi police officer had conveniently arrived in the wake of the blast and arrested the pair of them, because it was obvious Khalid was the type of guy whose bread was buttered on both sides.

'You are all the same,' he waffled on from the front as they drove through the streets. 'All you fucking Americans and Brits. You come to Iraq like it's some fucking adventure. Same as the *sharmut*,' gesturing to Ischenko, sandwiched between Coldrain and Outlaw. 'You never ask what price our people must pay. I see men like you every day, killing Iraqis because they drive too close to their car. Drinking in the hotels. Raping our women.'

Coldrain and Outlaw sat in the back of the police saloon car with their hands tied behind them with lengths of plastic rat cord. The confiscated AK-47 and Saiga 12-gauge were stashed in the boot. Coldrain watched Khalid wrestle with the steering wheel. He noticed that Khalid's middle finger on his right hand stopped at the first knuckle joint, the result of one too many times mucking about with bang-bang powder.

When they tried to arrest Coldrain, he fought back, pushing away the skinny officer. In retaliation, Khalid struck his temple with the Glock butt, knocking him sideways and opening up a half-inch gash. As the pain rang out through Coldrain's head, like the world's worst voddie-induced hangover, Khalid had pounced on top of him, fastening the cord of rat belt so tight he could feel the blood flow being cut off.

Khalid lit another fag and blew the smoke out through his nose while the skinny kid drove. He turned to face Coldrain, and grinned, revealing a set of jagged yellow-brown gnashers. A thick tuft of black hair poked out from his nostrils and ear lobes. Beneath the beret, his black hair had turned grey at the back and sides.

'You followed us the whole way?' Coldrain said to Ischenko.

She snorted. 'Don't act so surprised, soldier. It's not as difficult as it looks.'

Coldrain pushed out his bottom lip pensively. Initially he'd been raging mad when he clocked Ischenko. Now that he weighed it up, he saw she had to have real balls and determination to pursue them across the border, into a country where a lot of journalists wouldn't so much as set foot without a four-man security detail.

'Don't worry,' Coldrain said. 'We'll figure a way out of this mess.' He tried to smile, reassuring Ischenko. 'Maybe then we can finish the rest of the rum and have that chat.'

'I'd like that,' she replied. 'And maybe after the rum we could—'

'You only speak when you're spoken to,' Khalid ordered, fag hanging from his lip. Ash drifted from the end of the tab. 'Tell me. You are Special Forces of some kind, yes my friend? SAS? Delta Force?'

Coldrain stayed silent. Ischenko stared at him. He looked out of the window, staring at the barren streets like they were a hot fucking tourist attraction. Beside him, Outlaw buckled forward and spewed all over the floor. His technicolour yawn was dark, almost black. Coldrain spied droplets of blood and he worried that Outlaw had ruptured something internally when escaping the ANFO blast.

'No. Perhaps not. How about CIA? MI5?'

He kept his gob shut. Refused to even look at Khalid.

'Then I say you are mercenaries. Or, how do you say, "security advisers". I like that name. Because it pretends that you help make my country safer. But you do not. You take the money and get rich. The Iraqi people, we pay in blood. It is the only currency we have left.'

The driver was racing through the streets, pulling off the kind of sharp turns that belonged in motorsport, the car dipping violently with each mortar crater, chassis rising then falling low to the tyres.

'You come looking for Dogan. Don't worry. You will meet him soon. And then you will die.'

As they cleared another corner, the driver lost momentum, turned too hard, skidded along the road, jerking from left to right, carried by the energy in the rear wheels. For a moment it looked like they were going to collide with a tin-roofed hut. The skinny kid's forearms gripped the steering wheel hard, and then suddenly they were pulling free again, smoothly settling into the road.

Some old geezer cussed them in Arabic.

'It has been a long while since we have captured Americans and British. Before, we would sell you for lots of money. Maybe to Taliban. But not this time. Now, you are more valuable to us dead than alive.'

'You were waiting for us,' Coldrain uttered. It still hurt to talk. His throat was powerful sore, like he had swallowed paper. 'You were on the scene as soon as the bomb kicked off.'

Khalid chuckled. His jowly cheeks wobbled. 'Perhaps you are not the complete idiot, British. Not like your monkey friend here. Or the whore. But really, it was not very hard to find you. We know you come, because our friends in Van say it is so. And then, your girlfriend, the *sharmut*, makes it very easy to follow. Pity it is not always this easy when it comes to finding *kafir*.'

Ischenko looked down at her lap, ashamed.

'Do you know why you are after Dogan?'

'He's a killer.'

That laugh again. Those juddering cheeks, vile teeth, flaring nostrils. 'Very good. Yes, according to President of United fucking States, Dogan is terrorist. But according to people of United States, your last president was fucking terrorist. So who am I supposed to believe? It is not as simple as that, *kafir*.'

'He blows up innocent people. He's a coward, not a freedom fighter.'

'And you drop bombs from planes so high in the sky that our children cannot even see them. I do not think that is very brave either, my friend.'

'Bullshit. Dogan deserves to die.'

The smile disappeared from Khalid's face in a flash. He leant in closer to Coldrain's face. So close Coldrain could almost taste the noxious smell of tobacco on his breath. Could hear the torrents of air rushing out of his nose. See the beads of sweat lining his greasy face.

'But you say these words with the passion of a lion, not the coldness of a *kafir*. This is strange.' He narrowed his eyes, like he was trying to read Coldrain's mind. 'I think there is something else between you and Dogan. Some personal business, perhaps.'

Coldrain wanted to say that Khalid was bang on the money, that Dogan was responsible for Jamie coming home in a wooden box, that when you took away all the bullshit and looked at the facts, Jamie would still be smiling and playing rugby and chasing girls and beating him at pool if that Kurdish bastard hadn't rigged an IED.

But for now, he made do with, 'Go fuck yourself.'

'Yes, I forget, you British are the masters of English language.'

The chassis vibrated as it veered sharply to the left, underneath a low, crumbling arch, and onto a T-road. There was a low factory plant at the end, fifty metres away. To the left were row upon row of shallow trenches, old irrigation ditches that had fallen into disuse, and on the right, a stack of old Soviet mortar rounds. The two faces of modern Iraq, on one single stretch of road.

They came to a halt by the front of the factory. Khalid threw open the rear door on Coldrain's side.

'Get out.'

'Not until you tell me what's going on.'

He shook his head. 'Out of the car now, or I kill you all. Starting with the girl.'

Coldrain looked defiant. It was important not to show that he was scared even though, deep down, Coldrain was shitting himself.

'Out of the car now,' Khalid said, jabbing the Glock into Coldrain's face. He felt the cool tip of the barrel sink into his cheek. Coldrain relented. Shuffled out of the car. Outlaw followed suit. With the barrel pointing at him, Coldrain walked towards the factory, Outlaw and Ischenko in tow behind.

THIRTY

It was humid inside. A high corrugated iron roof with more holes than a lump of Swiss cheese cast sunlight onto the grubby factory floor. Coldrain tasted stale air.

The factory was a dusty expanse, thirty metres long and twenty wide. A set of metal stairs at the back led up to a blacked-out office and a few dead light bulbs dangled from the ceiling. By the west wall, a rack of four two-sided meat hooks was suspended from a lead pipe, eight feet off the ground. The lower hook tips were polished red, and on the floor beneath each hook was a thick, dry stain.

Blood.

A tenner says it ain't goats being strung up here.

A workbench on the east side paraded a set of well-maintained bench vices, a collection of hammers, saws and nails, and a shiny new hand-powered meat mincer. Two wooden chairs were positioned next to the bench. They were dark red, and Coldrain suspected it wasn't a paint job. Couple of rusted Kalashnikovs, serious Eric the Red jobs, lay in a corner, bathed in a spool of light.

We're in an old Ba'ath torture shop.

Coldrain had heard some of the gruesome rumours surrounding torture at the hands of Saddam's security forces. During his time in Iraq, locals couldn't wait to regale him with tales of how such and such a rellie got the old crocodile clips treatment. Saddam's people got up to some suck shit. People having nails hammered through their skulls. Women getting their tits crushed in vices. And men having their fingers shoved into meat grinders. Some lived until the eighth or ninth finger, or so the stories went.

Khalid shouted up to the blacked-out office. There was banging coming from inside, and then a figure emerged.

He was shorter than Coldrain imagined.

Although his face was indistinct, Coldrain recognised the eyes instantly. Ink-black pupils, wide and intense, stared back at him. Arching stripes of whitish skin sat high above the sockets, like someone had waxed his brows, and he was decked out all in black, black shirt, black trousers, then scuffed white kicks and a red and white *keffiyeh* strapped with black agal to cover the lower portion of his face. But Coldrain would have recognised those eyes anywhere. They were sinister. And they belonged to Dogan.

He came down the stairs and approached Coldrain. There was a tattoo on his left wrist. It looked like some kind of a wolf.

'Who are you?' he asked. His voice was soft but laced with violence.

'We're your worst nightmare, mate.'

Dogan laughed.

'This one must be English. He has sense of humour.'

Then his eyes narrowed.

'Special Forces?'

'Unlikely, brother,' Khalid replied. 'They are only carrying Kalashnikovs, no radio system.'

'What about you, African?' Dogan said, eyeballing Outlaw. 'Do you want to talk?'

'Kiss my ass.'

'American and funny. A rare breed. And the whore?' he added, pointing to Ischenko.

'Worse than a whore. A journalist. We caught her following them to the house.'

'Always I am amused when I see women doing important jobs in the West. It must be clear, to everyone, they are not suited to positions of power or influence. A female journalist does not report, she merely causes trouble.'

Dogan walked across the factory floor and ran a hand over the vice grips. 'I know from reading many newspapers and books that your country does not permit the killing of people outside the field of battle. It is not allowed in your constitution. So you do not come here to kill me on behalf of your countries. Another has sent you, and another will regret it when they learn your bodies are floating in the Tigris.'

Coldrain watched Dogan closely. A single thought crystallised in his mind. *This is the bastard who killed Jamie.*

He remembered the two figures on the motorbikes. Dogan had watched Jamie die, then slunk off into the sunset, and Coldrain had been left to look on helplessly as the clear-up team collected all the little bits of his mate. Every flap of skin and shard of bone had to be accounted for, bagged, numbered and sent home. Twenty-four hours earlier, Jamie had asked Coldrain to be the best man at his wedding, which caught Coldrain by surprise.

'But you haven't got a girlfriend, mate.'

'Details, Danny, details.'

Dogan produced a folding pocket knife, dug his fingers under the titanium lock bar and flipped out a three-inch Damascus steel blade that Coldrain IDed as a Chris Reeve Sebenza model. The handle was engraved with Arabic lettering. Gripping the Sebenza, Dogan strutted over to Outlaw's kneeling figure and kicked him in the middle of his back, sending the big man to the floor. Then he pushed his foot down on Outlaw's spine and reached down with the blade.

Fuck me, Coldrain thought. *He's going to lop our heads off with a baby blade.*

But then Dogan was dragging the Sebenza down to Outlaw's bound hands, and slicing through the plastic rat cord. It took just one quick up and down slash with the knife edge to shred it. Damascus steel was hardcore; the Arab swords made out of that shit back in the day could cut through the old European blades like a knife through hot butter.

In an instant, Dogan and Khalid were dragging Outlaw across the floor, struggling to control him. They hauled him over to the workbench. Outlaw fought back ferociously, kicking away Dogan's hands and rolling his shoulders from side to side. Dogan smacked him point-blank in the face, and then Khalid was cocking his weapon and Outlaw relented.

Khalid dug the Glock into the middle of Outlaw's back and he doubled over, his gut resting on top of the bench. Pinning him down with his left forearm against his neck, Khalid grabbed a nine-inch nail from the mess of toolbox next to the meat grinder and held it in place between his left index and middle fingers, poised over Outlaw's outstretched right hand. With his free hand Dogan picked up a heavy rubber mallet, and in one clean blow bashed the nail on the head. It sunk a couple of inches into the big American's hand. Outlaw's fingernails dug into the workbench, trying to absorb the pain shooting through his body.

'*Son of a fucking bitch!*'

'It will be the other hand next,' Dogan said coldly. 'Now, tell me, who sent you?'

'Put that shit in my other hand, I'll tear your head off and shit down your neck.'

'Threaten all you want, monkey. Your helicopters cannot help you now.'

Outlaw tried to control the pain. He didn't scream. But he was sweating like a paedo in a prison riot. Coldrain thought to himself, *He's not yet reached his pain threshold.* He could see Dogan thinking the same thing. He dug the nail out with his right hand. The tip had bits of white and purple muscle dangling from it. Dogan tossed the nail to one side and pushed Outlaw along the workbench. To the bench vice. Held Outlaw by the scruff of his neck and shoved his head into the gap between the fixed and parallel jaws. The last user had left the parallel jaw unscrewed with a gap of ten inches between them.

With Outlaw's head set in place, Dogan began to spin the screw on the parallel jaw clockwise, moving it along the plane. Outlaw's bone dome started to turn bright red. He started to scream as the vice pressed against his skull. Dogan kept turning the screw. The fucker had a big smile broadcasting on his face, like he was enjoying this sick shit.

'Fucking cunt,' Coldrain shouted. 'He doesn't know anything, leave him be!'

Dogan took a time out from the torture marathon, strolled coolly over to Coldrain and delivered a round-house kick that struck him square on the jaw. He fell back, spat blood onto the floor and shook his head.

'What's going on? Who are these people?' Ischenko pleaded. Tears had smudged her mascara along her high cheeks, rivulets streaking down to the corners of her trembling lips. She looked like a teenage goth.

'They're just a couple of nutcases with anger management issues.'

Dogan was back manning the vice grip. Outlaw's skull began to make a cracking sound. Like Brazil nuts being split open. His scream transformed, in a snap, to a nasal wail.

And then he was trying to say something. Dogan leant in to catch it. Outlaw's face was maroon. The veins on his forehead bulged, and his eyes were popping out of their sockets.

'Yes, African. Tell us.'

'Enough,' he whispered. 'Please. No more.'

Coldrain knew that Outlaw was playing the role of torture victim perfectly. In the movies, people were defiant under torture, refusing to buckle to the pain and goading their torturers. In the real world, operators were told to display the pain they were suffering, and exaggerate it whenever possible. If a torturer thinks someone is resisting their techniques, he is only going to do one thing: increase the pain. But if he is making the victim scream and beg for mercy, he will think twice about taking the torture any further, because the object of torture is to get information out of someone, not kill them. By pleading with Dogan, Outlaw was being clever.

And it worked. Dogan spun the screw anti-clockwise. As the grip loosened, Outlaw fell to the ground. He clutched his head.

Exchanged a glance with Coldrain.

The look said, *Get ready to do it.*

They would have one chance to overthrow their captors. If they got it wrong, they would end up dead.

But the way Dogan was carrying on, all three—ashing
would wind up bobbing down the Tigris soon—g being
than later. Doing nothing was as good as si— —ve hear
own death warrants.

THIRTY-ONE

'**Y**ou're next,' Dogan said. 'Perhaps you will be more cooperative than your friend.'

He slashed Coldrain free.

Time to act.

Coldrain wiggled his fingers, feeling the blood pumping back into his hands. Instantly dropping his right shoulder, he formed a fist with his right hand, delivering a hefty slug into Dogan's midriff, with his white-numb knuckles. Wind gushed out of his mouth, shock registering on his pain-stricken face.

Coldrain climbed to his feet, gripping Dogan's soggy shirt.

Smashed his knee into his face.

To his right, he clocked Outlaw getting medieval on Khalid. Dogan's man was lying on the floor, on his back, waving his hands desperately in front of his face as Outlaw unloaded a torrent of knuckle sandwiches.

'The kid,' Coldrain shouted. He was out front and, once he heard the noise, would be coming in any moment. Outlaw nodded and, kicking Khalid in the goolies, rushed over to the AK-47s in the corner. He took the less rusty one.

Meanwhile, Dogan groaned and started th[...]
about, trying to roll over and escape the hi[...]
dished up, but Coldrain's grip was steady. He g[...]
another knee bash. Dogan grunted. Coldrain pulled him
upright. Leaning back, clenching his teeth and strength-
ening his neck muscles, he headbutted Dogan, his forehead smacking into the area just above the eyebrows. It
was a perfect butt. The forehead on the skull was hard
and a blow to that area would hurt Coldrain more than
Dogan, but lower down on the facial area the bones were
softer and easier to break down. It made a satisfying crack
as his temple crashed down hard.

When Coldrain leant back again he got an eyeful of the
damage his bone dome had done. Dogan's nose was in
bits. He was properly filled in. There was blood and bone
and shit everywhere.

Outlaw opened the front door, AK raised, ready to
pump rounds into the kid. He returned a moment later.
'Kid's bugged out,' he said. The kid had probably crapped
his pants, decided a career in the police force wasn't for
him.

He tossed Coldrain the other Kalashnikov. He conducted
a quick systems check. There were only about eight moving
parts on the rifle. Cleaning rods, a cleaning kit stored in
the stock, gas chamber, piston, recoil spring, and, yeah,
that was basically fucking it. Simple but effective. He pulled
back the action shutter and checked to see a 7.62x39mm
round lodged in the chamber. The spring was coiled and
the piston ready to shunt the bullet out of the muzzle and
fuck someone up. It wasn't zeroed and he guessed the
aiming would be off, but it'd have to do.

THIRTY-TWO

Coldrain retrieved the two spare box mags for the AKs. Chucked one to Outlaw and tucked the other down the back of his combats. That made two mags each. Sixty rounds per man. He approached Dogan's keeled-over body and gave him a kick to the family jewels. He rolled over the floor in agony. Dogan wouldn't be slapping the old salami for a while, that was for sure.

'A little taste of your own medicine, mate.'

'Shit. You messed him up bad,' Outlaw said, his voice purring in admiration.

'Bad or good?'

'Oh, *bad*, for real,' he grinned.

'You didn't do such a bad job yourself,' Coldrain replied, nodding to Khalid.

'All I've done so far is slap that bitch around. That's what I call the entrée. The main course awaits.'

Coldrain cocked the AK and pointed it at Dogan's forehead. There would be no question time, no pissing about. It was time to waste this piece of shit once and for all.

But Dogan was cackling away.

'You don't want to ask me something first?'

Outlaw flashed Coldrain a quizzical expression. Behind he heard Ischenko, still bound up with the rat cord, struggling to break free. She'd have to wait.

'I remembered your face as soon as I saw you,' Dogan continued. 'It was, let me see, three years ago. Is that correct? I have taken the lives of so many, it's becoming harder to remember who died and when.'

'Fuck you.'

'Then pull the trigger, if you wish me to die so badly. But I know why you are really here. You wish for answers.'

Outlaw frowning, 'What's this asswipe talking about, Danny?'

Dogan ignored Outlaw. He eyeballed Coldrain, and something like a smile broke out on his face. 'A brother-in-arms, yes?'

'Shut up.'

But Dogan persisted. 'I'll tell you all the details, if that is what you wish? We needed to create a new type of bomb arrangement. Set up dummies using obvious cache sites and then hide a camouflaged explosive device nearby. The dummy serves as the distraction and draws the soldiers' attention away from the real threat.' Dogan's smile had mutated into a full-on grin. 'It worked, as you no doubt recall.'

'You killed Jamie.'

Dogan shrugged. 'It could have been any of those soldiers. You, maybe, or another, maybe. It was unfortunate that it was someone so close to you, but this is, how you say, the realities of the war. You are a soldier. You know what I talk of.'

'That's bollocks. If you hadn't put that bomb there, no one would have died.'

'But it was necessary, you see.'

'Necessary for *what*?'

Dogan was silent.

Suddenly Coldrain was flashing. He couldn't control his temper any longer. He was out on his chinstraps, knackered and tired of being fucked about like a squaddie in a souk. Coldrain swung the AK-47 like a baseball bat, the stock slapping against the side of his dome. Dogan wheezed and fell onto his side, blood oozing out of a two-inch wound above his ear.

'What are you talking about? Answers. Now! Or I fucking ice you and your mate.'

'Go ahead, *kafir*. Death is only ever a matter of time. I am prepared.'

'Do it,' Coldrain instructed Outlaw.

'Shit, no,' Khalid whimpered. They were the last words he said. Outlaw pumped three rounds into his gut, one after the other. The shots echoed around the hollow factory. Dogan watched in horror as the rounds tore into his bent copper mate. He briefly shuddered, like someone had attached a couple of jumper cables to his chest. He stilled. Dogan was about to curse Coldrain when he felt the cold tip of the AK-47 muzzle press against his cheek.

'Just try it.'

Dogan's reaction was weird and unsettled Coldrain. He started chuckling. Not an evil, manic laugh, but a hearty, full-bodied giggle that made Coldrain feel like he was the punchline of some secret joke. He pushed the muzzle harder against Dogan's cheek, but it made no difference; if anything he laughed harder. It went on like this for several seconds, before he finally calmed down.

'What's so bloody funny?'

'You have no idea who you are dealing with, soldier.'

Coldrain blinked. He was in a difficult situation. Half

of him wanted to zap Dogan right there and then. Get this over with. But the other half needed to know why Jamie had died. Why Dogan was up there that afternoon on the ridge. There had to be a meaning, something that could help him rationalise it. At least, that was what he had prayed for all this time.

Coldrain struggled with the senselessness of Jamie's death the most. The idea that his best friend died randomly. For nothing. Strip away all the hero tags, and, at the end of the day, Jamie didn't have to die. He made the ultimate sacrifice, but it didn't result in a battle being won or the capture of an enemy, or any tangible sense of victory. He was just the wrong guy in the wrong place at the wrong time. And now Dogan was hinting that there was more to his death than met the eye.

'Do you really think,' he was saying, 'that we kill those politicians just because we like to?' He rubbed a hand over his temple. A bunch of purple bruises were forming. 'They all made the same foolish mistake. Asking questions, just like you and your friend. Speaking to people they did not need to speak to. When a person asks too many questions, it is right to silence them.'

That all depends on what they're asking, Coldrain thought. 'The guys in Kabul, Baghdad, you mean they knew something?'

'They knew some things. Not the whole story. No one knows that. Only myself, and one other.'

Coldrain looked across instinctively at Khalid's body, but that only prompted a snigger from Dogan. 'Please, do not be so insulting.'

A voice inside him. Impossible to quell, picking away at something that he had never answered, never thought about, until this moment. *Up on the hill. Dogan looking down.*

Watching Jamie get blown to bits. And something was not quite right.

'That day,' Coldrain said. 'There were two of you. The other man.'

'You do remember.' Dogan's smile revealed blood-painted teeth, as if he'd sucked on a raw steak. 'It is always the way. The days when people die, we do not forget the details. I have found it is mostly the opposite. Death enshrines memories, protects them.'

'Who was he?

'His name,' Dogan said, 'is Gustav Markarets.'

THIRTY-THREE

'**W**ho is he?'

Dogan's voice was assured and he held eye contact with Coldrain. He gave Dogan the eyeball treatment, trying to see if he was spinning a gen dit or talking a load of made-up buzz. Coldrain remembered something an old Royal Sea Daddy had told him in Iraq back in the day.

'How do you know an Arab's lying? Whenever his lips move,' the veteran Bootneck had said.

'The world is built for men of action,' Dogan said. His words were assured, clipped, like he was dictating his memoirs to a typist. 'Today, everywhere is a battlefield. We are in a permanent state of conflict. If you wish to change the world, you must change it by force. The world did not listen to al-Qaeda before the Twin Towers fell, but it listens now to every word from its leader. When al-Qaeda speaks, the news reports it. But for some people, this is only the beginning. Men of action, like myself and Markarets, are planning even bigger changes.'

'Grand-scale terrorist attacks,' Coldrain suddenly felt powerfully thirsty. He licked his cracked lips.

'Not for us. Nothing as crude as that. The problem with

al-Qaeda is they produced something so amazing, the whole world stood still and watched in fear and awe. It is impossible to create the same impact again. Madrid, London, Bali, these will go down in history as footnotes to the main event. We do not seek to be footnotes. That is not our fate.'

Coldrain listened, but took everything Dogan said with a fucking fistful of salt. In his experience, wannabe terrorists were up there with marketing managers and politicians in their ability to spin bullshit and inflate their self-importance.

'So Markarets is your boss?'

'We are business partners,' Dogan said smugly. 'I am the brains of the operation and he brings the charisma. We both want to change the world. Individually, we know that each of us can only do so much. Separately, we could kill one or two infidels. But there could be no ultimate victory in Iraq or Afghanistan, where the weight of military power stands tall against us. Only the poor uneducated Yemenis and Pakistanis believe they can beat the Americans and British. The genius of myself and Markarets was to understand that another kind of victory can be achieved. By joining together we could ultimately triumph.'

Coldrain heard activity outside. Car engines. Gravel being crushed.

'I'll deal with this,' Outlaw said. He gave the mag on the underside of the AK a hefty slap and chambered a round. Stepped to the left side of the door, ten metres back, dropped to one knee with the rifle pointed midway up at the door, nudged it slightly ajar.

'What's the score, mate?'

'Two cars,' Outlaw said.

'How far?'

'Coming up the road now. Hundred metres. Maybe one-twenty.'

'Support?'

'Not that I can see.'

Coldrain turned back to Dogan.

'Friends of yours?'

'You underestimate the strength of your enemy. And that is a grave mistake, for which you will pay with your life.'

Voices. Car doors slamming. Bad guys. Outlaw zeroing the sights on the AK. Peering out of the door.

'X-rays are on the move,' Outlaw said, 'I count seven of 'em. Fully tooled up. Body armour too. Range, eighty metres.' His voice was firm but urgency crept in. The average person cleared just north of a metre per second walking. At a brisk pace, with large strides, that went up to almost two metres per second. Eighty metres gave them just over a minute to get their shit together.

'If you let me go now, I will instruct them not to kill you,' Dogan said.

Bollocks, Coldrain thought. Soon as we let him go, he'll turn the guns on us and we'll be fragged. He weighed up the situation. As a Royal he had been paid to make critical decisions on the spot, in the most stressful of circumstances, but as far as big calls went, this was the hardest one of all. On the one hand, he and Outlaw had a couple of chad Kalashnikovs, plus whatever else they could rustle up from the factory, against seven enemy soldiers, with unknown levels of back-up. That kind of firepower and manpower imbalance weighed heavily against them. Even though they were two of the best operators in the business, the odds were not in their favour and they could easily be over-whelmed.

On the other hand, Dogan was offering a way out of a potential clusterfuck situation. But he was a terrorist and a murderer, and the olive branch he was extending could well be a load of bullshit.

'Forty metres,' Outlaw said.

'You're running out of time,' Dogan said.

He wanted to kill Dogan so badly it hurt.

But when he closed his eyes, and shut out the rage, he knew there was only one thing to do.

'Get to your feet,' he ordered. Dogan stood up uneasily. 'Now fuck off.'

Dogan, unbelieving, slipped out of the door.

'Danny, what the *fuck*—'

'No choice, mate. If we keep him here, it's a Mexican standoff at best. Worst-case they call every insurgent in a ten-mile radius and we're carted off and strung from the nearest lamp-post and set alight.'

'I don't like it,' Outlaw said, shaking his head.

You and me both, Coldrain thought. He kept his sights trained on Dogan's back. Part of him prepared for an attack. The other half reasoned that, with nothing left to claim, and Dogan a trigger pull away from death, his buddies wouldn't fancy their chances of an assault. Dogan spoke with two other men, identikit Iraqis in sweat-patched shirts. They talked loudly, gestured extravagantly, looked back to the warehouse and nodded. Thirty seconds passed, and it felt more like thirty hours. Finally, the men stepped into the vehicle and breezed out.

'They're leaving,' Outlaw reported.

Coldrain spoke to Jamie in his head. *I'm sorry, mate. I wanted to zap the fucker for you. I've let you down*.

'Danny,' Outlaw began.

Coldrain stared at the ground. He looked back to

Ischenko. Stood up and moved over to untie her, his body language limp, his heart deflated. He had let himself down. His mucker too.

'D,' Outlaw repeated, his voice urgent.

'Yeah.'

'We got trouble.'

Coldrain snapped out of his trance. He was never very good at feeling sorry for himself. Self-pity was best left to the guests on daytime chat shows. 'What kind of trouble?'

'Those cars? They're heading back our way.'

THIRTY-FOUR

Coldrain sprang into action. There was no choice. No time to lose. It was stand back and die. Or fight fire with fire.

Lying next to the AK-47s was a bundle of Russian grenades lifted straight out of the Imperial War Museum. Shaped like pineapples, the grenades were known to military nerds as the F1 hand grenade, a *limonka*. But whatever name it went by, the grenade was devastating in its impact. And it could also be turned into a crude booby trap.

'I need wire and stakes,' he told Outlaw. He pulled back from his position by the door and checked the workbenches. He came up trumps, and dropped a four-metre length of metallic wire and two eight-inch-long wooden stakes into Coldrain's hands.

'You mind telling me what the hell you're doing?'

'Springing a little surprise, mate.'

Holding a *limonka* in his left hand, Coldrain placed one of the stakes next to it and then wrapped the wire around the two objects several times, until they were fastened tightly together, with the sharp point of the stake sticking out below the bottom of the hand grenade.

He approached the factory door and drove the stake into a patch of earth to the left of the doorway. The concrete floor was flaky and cut up easily, like sodden turf.

While Outlaw kept watch, Coldrain threaded the wire through the *limonka* safety pin, around the protective cap, and then down and once around the fly-off lever. He dragged the wire across the foot of the entrance at ankle height, and wrapped it around the other stake and drove it into a similar spot of earth on the other side of the door. He dug the stake in and out several times, modifying the distance so he could wrap more of the metallic wire around it, increasing the wire's tension until it was absolutely at its maximum tautness without forcibly ejecting the pin. All it would take would be the merest brush of some poor fucker's leg against the wire and that pin was dropping.

'They're nearly on top of us, chief.'

'Gather weapons and ammo. We'll head up the stairs.'

'What about the girl?'

Ischenko had fallen mute in the corner, white with fear, as if someone had smothered her face in chalk.

Coldrain approached Ischenko, crouching beside her. Something flashed in his mind, a vision. Him beside Melanie, in an almost identical posture, at her pod in her office. Only a few days ago, but it seemed like a post-card from another universe. Ischenko tentatively raised her eyes level with Coldrain and his feelings for the German and Melanie smashed in the middle, crunching his guts. He didn't know what was right and what was wrong about the way he felt. I haven't betrayed Melanie, he thought. That's important. Counts for something. *But you can't betray yourself*, another voice countered. *You're sacrificing Ischenko for a relationship with holes in it. What are you going to do, spend the next forty years papering over the cracks?*

He offered his hand to Ischenko.

'Rough day at the office, huh?'

'Something like that,' her voice croaked. She swallowed dust. 'Thank you.'

'Forget about it. You know, a lot of civvies would've cracked under the pressure back there. Not you. That takes some doing.'

Her eyes smiled. Coldrain experienced a powerful urge to kiss them.

'Tell you what, when this is over, we'll do that story. On condition that I'm anonymous.'

'That sounds great,' she said, taking Coldrain's hand and rising to her feet. As she stood fully upright, their noses brushed against each other and Coldrain found himself moving in to kiss her. He stopped himself at the last moment, the guilt in his belly going into overdrive and forming a lump in his throat, and he gave her a quick peck on the cheek.

'Danny, we have to be history, man. Fucking now.'

Coldrain tilted his head at Ischenko.

'Follow me,' he said.

Coldrain focused on a shadow blocking out the small ridgeline of light between the bottom of the door and the concrete. Someone was outside, waiting to breach the interior. Outlaw was training his AK on the door. Coldrain took another *limonka* grenade from the bundle and grabbed Ischenko's arm. Then he nodded to Outlaw. Walking backwards, an eye on the main door and ready to engage, they backed up the metal staircase. Someone grappled with the doorknob, twisting it clockwise, anti-clockwise.

The door resisted, shook. Relented. It opened as Coldrain hit the upper risers, and eight metres from the office, Coldrain heard the faintest sound of a pin breaking from the fly-off lever and dropping to the ground.

THIRTY-FIVE

It took five seconds for the F1 hand grenade to detonate. Coldrain pushed Ischenko in front of him as he charged up the stairs, AK swinging freely in his right hand. Ischenko tripped up on the last step, crashing to her knees on the landing. That delayed the chain leading up the stairs. *Come on*, he raged at himself. *Get a fucking move on.* Three metres behind him, Outlaw had his back turned and was facing down and to his right. He was only three-quarters of the way up the stairs and was still within sight of the front door and living area. Outlaw discharged a single-burst from the AK towards the door.

It was a small room with a table in the middle that had maps and laptops spread out on it. The windows overlooking the factory floor were smeared with dirt. Coldrain waited for the blast. He was cursing the chad grenade. *Maybe it's a dud*, he thought.

A second later the *limonka* detonated.

There was a short, deep thud.

The walls shook.

Screams, and the sound of a million burning pieces of mortar and glass tumbling through the air.

'I think they need a second round, mate.'

'One is never enough. Let them have it.'

'Give me some covering fire.'

'I'm on it.'

Coldrain took the second *limonka* and manoeuvred back down the stairs, Outlaw behind him, tapping out single rounds, the muzzle pointing directly into the billowing ball of smoke. Coldrain tasted hot metal on his mouth. Smelt crisply barbecued flesh. He had to move quickly, careful to avoid stepping on stray bits of shrapnel drizzled along the treads, large, thin strips whose edges were sharp enough to slice open a man's gut, like slashing open a car tyre.

Coldrain had to kick a load of shit off the steps. It was as if a cloud had showered gravel and plaster over the factory. He kept one eye on the stairs, watching where he trod. Looked ahead to the factory door as the smoke dissipated. Revealed a scene of total carnage.

He clocked three bodies.

Make it two and a bit. Eight metres inside the factory, one guy had been cut in half. His torso was missing, his legs and arsehole erect, like a statue sliced in two at the hips. There were guts and entrails and bits of stringy shit all over the place. He was more than fucking history, he was obliterated.

'Second grenade,' he reported.

'Ready,' Outlaw said.

The second and third X-rays were a couple of metres closer to the doorway and Coldrain figured that Mr Arse and Legs had caught the brunt of the grenade's explosive force. The other two men were lying in crumpled heaps on the floor, their faces awash with their mate's blood and guts. Frag shards jutted out of their chests, arms and legs. One guy's left foot was blown clean off. The other guy's jaw had gone AWOL, leaving a big black void where flesh and bone should have been.

Coldrain pulled the pin on the second *limonka*, let it cook off for one and a half seconds in his grip, then tossed it into the zone between the two X-rays. It landed to the right of one of the guys, and he tried to lift his slashed and singed right arm up, in a vain attempt to throw it away. It was a forlorn effort. He knew he was zapped.

Coldrain bugged out back to the office and let the *limonka* do the good work. There was a scream, followed by a loud bang, earth and metal and shrapnel cutting through the air, bits of it nicking the stairs. They turned their attention to the door.

THIRTY-SIX

Two rounds struck the floor next to Outlaw's feet. He could hear the supersonic report as the bullets flicked concrete into the air, like tiny firecrackers kicking off.

Outlaw tried to get a couple of bursts off but had to pull back behind the doorway as tracer rounds zipped past at head height and clattered into the southern factory wall. Whoever it was doing the shooting, they were far more experienced than your run-of-the-mill local insurgent. Tracer rounds, the shit that Western forces used to zero in on targets, that wasn't how the Iraqis rolled.

'I need you to keep your head down and wait here,' Coldrain said to Ischenko. 'I'm getting you out of here, I promise.'

Ischenko nodded, knitting her brow at the deafening clatter of gunfire.

'Cross your heart?'

'And hope to die,' Coldrain said.

'Be careful.'

He was surprised at his strength of feeling for her. How it had grown so quickly, from a tiny seed into something much deeper. And yet he knew that, when push came to shove, he'd leave Ischenko, because that was the way his world functioned.

He bounded towards the doorway, stepped around Khalid's mangled corpse, and took up his position to the left of the door. Swept a load of shrapnel away from his position and dropped to one knee, keeping his body behind the wall. More rounds smacked against the floor. The reports were smooth, quick. Shallow. An AK-47 firing was loud and hollow because there were so many moving parts banging into each other when the trigger was pulled. These Gucci rifles were way more advanced.

'Danny!'

Outlaw's voice implored. He looked at the Yank and followed his eyes, his ears picking up the groaning sound before he'd angled his head and clocked the guy on the ground, still breathing. His right arm was shredded, one leg torn off at the knee and the upper joint black as charred timber, the other in rag order, blood and crap all over the floor and up the factory wall. The guy had been flung through the air like a rag doll. His face looked like a Halloween mask.

Pistol in his hand.

Pointed directly at Coldrain.

Outlaw went to aim, but the half-dead guy was already depressing the trigger. Coldrain envisaged the trajectory of the bullet as it penetrated his flesh, hot lead ricocheting through his body like a pinball in an arcade machine. He knew he was shit out of luck.

Ischenko sprang out from the corner of his vision, clutching a monkey wrench snared from one of the work-benches. The wrench had already seen action, judging from the red splatter marks on the holding jaws. She swung it like a hammer down onto the half-dead guy's skull. The guy shuddered, dropping the handgun. Ischenko smacked him again, making a massive divot in the base of his skull. His arms flopped, and he went over to the dark side.

Coldrain and Ischenko exchanged a brief glance. She was wide-eyed with fear and adrenalin and she lingered over the freshly dead guy, her shoulders rising and lowering with each draw of breath. He went to say something to her, but Outlaw hollered that they needed to focus on the door. He was right.

'Switch to fire and movement,' Coldrain instructed.

'Our only way out of this mess, that's for sure. You want to go first or me?'

'Honour's all yours, mate,' Coldrain replied, controlling his breathing, hypnotic and supremely focused.

'Had a feeling you'd say that.'

'On a three count, then.'

'One . . .' Outlaw's neck muscles tensed like thick rope.

'Two . . .'

'Three.'

'Covering fire!' Coldrain shouted above the crashing clatter of gunfire.

Keeping his back straight and his head behind cover, Coldrain flicked the AK-47 to semi-automatic and vittled off two four-round bursts outside the door at chest height. He couldn't see where he was shooting, but that wasn't the point. The aim of his suppressive fire routine was to pin down the X-rays, interrupt the volley of bullets so that Outlaw could get a clear visual on the target positions and put down some accurate fire.

The secret to good covering-fire technique, Coldrain knew, was to maintain a consistent rate of fire, with no lapses in the stream poured into the kill zone. Once the enemy was pinned down, you had to keep them there. If the bad guys thought another round was on the way, they wouldn't move. He let off a third burst, two rounds, and then a fourth. Keep the bastards guessing. And when they finally did pop their heads up, Outlaw would be ready to put one between the eyes.

In his head Coldrain counted the number of rounds he had left in the box mag. He had used twelve, so that left eighteen. Plus the spare clip, and Outlaw had another tucked in his waistband that he could sponge. Still, he couldn't afford to put a never-ending stream of suppressive fire. In real life, there was no infinite ammo cheat to get more bullets. Once he was out, he was out.

Coldrain pumped out a final three-round burst. Outlaw looking at him, eyes trained on the AK, observing Coldrain's posture and body language, ready to spin out and get his shots off the very instant Coldrain was finished. That way there would be no delay, no chance for the enemy to get their bearings. It would be bang, bang, dead. At least, that was the plan.

He withdrew the AK and in the same move, almost like it was choreographed, Outlaw was stepping into the breach, in the standing position, rifle stock tucked into his shoulder, one hand on the trigger, other on the belly of the barrel, head straight, legs shoulder-length apart and treading on hot brass, one eye closed, the other staring down the sights.

Coldrain counted the shots. One, two, three.

Tap, tap, tap.

'Got two of 'em,' Outlaw reported coolly.

'Nice work, mate.'

'Ya'll see that first guy? Dropped him like sixth grade French.'

'Fall back to cover.'

'Got it.'

And that was how people died in war. Nothing dramatic, no slow-mo shots or extended deathbed speeches. Just the crack of a gunshot, a split second of silence, and then one guy confirming he killed another guy. No dramatic screams, no close combat with knives and fisticuffs. It was in such moments that Coldrain realised how easy it was to get zapped.

He vittled off a couple more three-round bursts. The barrel of the AK shuddered with each report. It was a struggle to keep the assault rifle under control. From the firing angle, Coldrain had to solely engage his right shoulder and arm muscles in order to absorb the kick from each round. His biceps burnt and his wrist was on fire, like a cigarette lighter was burning underneath. Nine rounds left, he thought.

'Almost out.'

'Got a refill?'

'Yeah. But I can't keep them pinned down much longer. Ten seconds at most.'

'Forget it. They're already falling back.'

Outlaw pumped off two more bullets with Gucci written all over them.

'Score both.' And then, 'Just call me fucking Rambo.'

'In your dreams, mate.'

Coldrain was threaders. He was sweating worse than an Arab at customs. His throat stung with each breath of air, and his muscles throbbed. He could barely lift the AK, let alone walk on his legs. It felt as if he'd run a marathon. The psychological stress of combat was matched by its physical exertion. The fury, the intensity. The alertness to new threats.

In his mind, Coldrain kept turning over the name Gustav Markarets. If he had been up there on the hill that day in

Ghorak, then Coldrain held him equally culpable for Jamie's death. He knew, deep down, that he would not be able to rest until both Dogan and Markarets were buried six feet under. Coldrain believed in an eye for an eye, a tooth for a tooth, and the fucking eye had been snatched from him.

Something else bothered him, too. *If Dogan can call on seven, eight men to rescue him, how many others are on his payroll?* There could be hundreds, he realised. He needed to find out what they were up to. Whatever it was, it would not be good news.

But first things first, he told himself. *We need to get out of Sadr City alive.*

Easier said than done.

More cars rocking up to the party. Voices, urgent and foreign. And recognisably not Arabic. Spanish, or Portuguese. Some kind of Mediterranean lingo. *What the fuck?* Coldrain thought. *Things are just getting weirder by the minute.*

'Danny, I hate to bring you bad news, but . . .'

'More company. Shit. We can't keep holding them back.'

'You thinking what I'm thinking?'

'Time to bug out, mate.'

'Where to?'

'Back door?' Coldrain U-turned. Clocked a rear exit at the far end of the factory. It was an old, rusted door, the paint stripped off and replaced by an all-over coating of Eric the Red.

'Good idea,' Coldrain said. He beat a path to the door, thinking, *I'm not waiting around for these fuckers to come knocking.* On the way back, he gathered Ischenko. She had ditched the wrench, shivering as if standing on a chilly peak in the Scottish highlands. Coldrain snapped her out of her trance. As they hit the door, he suddenly realised he was holding Ischenko's hand. She gripped tight, her smooth fingers enveloping his calloused palm.

'He was . . . I saw the gun . . .' Ischenko gulped, like the words were a hairball lodged in her throat.

'You did great,' Coldrain said.

'But I killed him.'

'Trust me,' and he held her gaze, 'you did the right thing.'

At the door now and Coldrain gave the crusted handle a tug. It was stiff. Outlaw joined in. The two-man wrecking crew finally dislodged the door. As it eased open, Coldrain thought that if the enemy was badly trained, they would amass at the front entrance and just pour in. But if they had been schooled properly, the X-rays would be surrounding the building, securing all the exits – including the back one.

He was blinded by the sunlight. A bleached street presented.

Coldrain hoped the bad guys weren't as good as their guns.

THIRTY-SEVEN

Coldrain was first out. The factory backed onto an eight-metre stretch of cobblestone street that flowed from east to west. That was the first problem. Left and right. Two potential funnels of fire. The second became apparent a moment later. He was facing a row of low-rise houses that provided excellent sniper cover. A shooter from a window could easily pick them off. Make it three fire channels. For Coldrain, that was three too many. It was like stepping into the middle of a shooting gallery. Maybe he should have taken the front door option. Just blown their way out. *Yeah, and how long would you have lasted then?*

Not very.

Too late to turn back now. Just get the fuck out of there.

'Checking left.'

'Checking right.'

'All clear left,' Outlaw said.

'X-rays at three o'clock. I see three of 'em.'

The targets were twenty metres away. Two were standing. The third knelt down, busting an RPG launcher, the tube pointed ten degrees above eye level. Coldrain spotted the RPG just in time to witness the smoke flooding out of the back and the sound of the grenade firing, like

241

the hiss of an angry python. He could make out the nose of the projectile in the centre of his line of vision, its fins rotating as the grenade homed in.

Coldrain flung himself into the middle of the street, his left arm tugging Ischenko towards him in a desperate attempt to clear the line of fire. Behind him, Outlaw stood in the entranceway, unaware of the grenade poised to thump into them.

The grenade smacked into the ground in front of Coldrain. He closed his eyes.

Nothing.

It hadn't detonated.

He opened his eyes and saw the rocket motor burning ferociously at the back.

Coldrain figured that the RPG had travelled a shade or two over the twenty-metre mark necessary to ignite, but he didn't give a shit about inches. He was just thankful the fucker hadn't kicked off.

Rolling over onto his chest, Coldrain adopted the prone firing position, making sure as much of his body maintained contact with the ground as possible for added stability. He bent his knees slightly to transfer his balance to his core and pushed the AK stock into his right shoulder. With no bipod to maintain aim, he had to improvise and use his elbows as weapon supports, keeping his left forearm at an angle of thirty degrees to the barrel. Hunching his shoulders forward a little, Coldrain sparked off three rounds in quick succession.

He wasn't aiming for the RPG bearer but the second guy, who was busy loading in another warhead. The first two shots missed the target, fizzing into the ground just ahead of the standing figure. The third nicked the wall next to the target, flinging mortar dust into his face. But the guy kept his cool, slapping the warhead into the front of the launch tube.

No time for Coldrain to unleash a second burst. From start to finish the X-rays had taken fourteen seconds to reload and lock the RPG on Coldrain's position. *They're quick*, Coldrain thought. Sort of speed he was used to witnessing in specially trained forces.

They needed to find cover, sharp.

'Where do we go from here?' Ischenko asked, shouting above the din.

'See that pile ahead,' Coldrain nodded at a chest-high mountain of concrete and wire-mesh rubble on the opposite side of the road. It wasn't ideal cover, but it was the only defensive shield on offer.

'I see,' Ischenko said.

'I'll go first. Follow my lead. And Anika,' now looking in her eyes, the desperation and fear in them replaced by a determination that seemed to radiate in the whites of her eyes, as if she'd stared directly into the sun. 'Stay at least four metres away from me, you understand?'

In case I get fragged, he neglected to add.

She nodded. Yes, she understood. Added, with a wry smile, 'You're a dangerous man to know.'

'So I'm told.' Coldrain straightened his face. 'I'm gone!' he shouted, jumping out from cover.

'Covering fire!' Outlaw boomed.

To his four o'clock he saw Ischenko scrabbling forward. Coldrain turned around and clocked Outlaw rattling off a couple of rounds. The bullets seemed to rip through the sky, like hands splitting apart a length of cotton fabric. Spent jackets popped out from the right side of the barrel.

'Got him,' Outlaw said remorselessly as the third X-ray, to the left of the RPG bearer and reloader, dropped to the ground. Then he fled across the street and dived next to Coldrain and Ischenko behind the rubble. He was just in time.

The second RPG flew in Outlaw's wake. It was so close that Coldrain swore he could hear the fins gently brushing against the back of his down gilet. Then it passed by and whacked into the wall.

This time the warhead fused.

Amber fire spewed out of the grenade on collision. The ground shook. Slabs of debris loosened up, threatened to dislodge. The burning fireball was swallowed up by a huge, swirling cloud of smoke that erupted from the wall and surged across the street, carrying with it a furious din. Glass shattered, bricks crumbled, metal clanged, a blizzard of molten carnage suddenly on top of Coldrain, Outlaw, Ischenko. Coldrain closed his eyes and tried to hold his breath. His senses were knocked.

Just as quickly as it had expanded, the thick wave of smoke began to contract, leaving an opaque white cloud. Coldrain sneezed and shifted from around the rubble. Even though he was on the receiving end of the RPG round, Coldrain was still impressed by its destructive capacity. You had to hand it to the Soviets, they knew how to make one hell of a weapon.

Coldrain wiped a grubby forearm across his eyes. His vision was blurred. Everything was out of focus. The roof of his mouth was burning. The cloud was clearing. He looked ahead and saw two indistinct shapes fumbling with the tube launcher. Getting ready for round three. It was six, seven seconds since the second warhead had fired. Ischenko was prone on the ground, shaking. Outlaw was still getting his bearings, coughing up black shit and searching for his rifle.

'That fucker with the RPG has us pinned down good and proper. One more rocket and we're toast.'

'What do you want to do?'

'Don't think we've got any choice do we?'

Outlaw's face hardened like cement. 'You're not going to do it.'

'It's our only way out, mate.'

'You'll get dropped in a second.'

Coldrain thinking, *The odds aren't great. But what choice do we have*? He tensed his body and wiped dirt from his eyes.

'Danny.'

'See you in five.'

'*Dan.*'

But Outlaw's protests fell on deaf ears.

Coldrain rushed forward.

THIRTY-EIGHT

Coldrain bounded over the rubble, pushing his left palm down onto the highest point, a five-inch wide slab of concrete, and using his arm as a pole vault, clearing the debris in the kind of leap that earned civvies Olympic medals, but merited him the right to stay alive for a few more precious seconds.

He landed flat on the soles of his feet and transitioned into a kneeling firing manoeuvre, dropping his right knee to the ground and keeping his left leg forward. The accuracy of fire from such a position wasn't great, but that didn't matter. Coldrain needed to get rounds down on the X-rays and he needed to do it in the next three seconds, or they were all toast.

Peering down the line of the AK's front and rear iron sights, Coldrain steadied his grip, locked his shoulders tight, took a deep breath and made sure he exhaled as he peeled off a two-round torrent. Thinking, that leaves seven bullets. The rounds clattered into the ground a metre or so in front of the two figures.

Bollocks to it, Coldrain thought. He flipped the selector back up to automatic, next to the safety setting, and squeezed the trigger again, but this time kept it depressed, knocking out the rest of the mag. There was a hyper-fierce dull rap as the last seven rounds left in the box mag were rapidly discharged.

Coldrain ejected the empty box mag and fetched a spare from the band of his combats. The cobblestone around his feet was littered with spent brass. Then Coldrain fed the fresh mag into the tray, and gave it a hard tap from beneath with the palm of his hand, to make sure it was fully inserted. He pulled back the spring loader and depressed the trigger. Kept that bitch depressed. Rounds peppered the area around the two X-rays. They had dropped the tube launcher. Coldrain felt like the contact was turning in their favour. He had the baseline established. Now it was a case of kicking on and gaining ground.

Right on cue, Outlaw was manoeuvring alongside Coldrain. He was four metres away at Coldrain's three o'clock, upright and darting ahead.

'Decided to join in the fun, mate?'

'You know me. If there's a party on . . .'

'I'll fire. You move.'

'Got that right.'

'Go!'

Now it was time to close the distance on the enemy. Outlaw surged ten metres forward and adopted a kneeling position. As he started pumping 7.62mm NATO rounds at the X-rays, Coldrain followed in Outlaw's wake. They were covering the street in bounds. This was how they would win the battle. One guy firing, the other pressing. Coldrain sprinted past Outlaw, moving forward and to the right, until he was twenty metres away from the enemy. He dropped to one knee and started chopping away.

Tap, tap, tap. The noise was incessant, relentless. Remorse-less.

After he unloaded his second mag and fished for his third spare, Coldrain saw something flash in the sky, like a mobile shard of light. It seemed to hang in the air for a second, then increased its speed as it came towards him. The light shard zipped past him. He turned and saw dirt splash up just a few inches to the right of Outlaw.

They were firing back.

Both X-rays had whipped out rifles. Coldrain felt badly exposed. The figure on the left was on semi-automatic mode and was primed to discharge rounds directly at him.

Coldrain held his breath and let some slack into his shoulders as he fired off a single round.

The bullet smacked into the shooter's head, right above the eyes. A puff of blood erupted from the back of his skull. His body fell limp, like he'd slipped into a deep coma.

'Still one X-ray left.'

'On him.'

The second shooter took one look at the vittled-up sack of bones and shit lying next to him and decided he didn't fancy joining his mate in Satan's backyard just yet. He let off a desperate pray-and-spray burst and then caned it across the street, ducking and diving, weaving his way into a narrow lip of an alleyway on the right, twenty metres away. From behind the cover of the alleyway he prodded out the rifle barrel and sent a wild volley of rounds, twelve, fifteen of them, flying in Coldrain and Outlaw's general direction. A few whizzed past their heads, others slapped into the ground around them. Two landed a few metres away but that was as close as the shooter was going to get aiming blind.

They would have to assault the alley if they were going to take the X-ray down.

Outlaw stayed down on one knee and adjusted his position until he was facing the alleyway at a forty-five degree angle. Then he fired off a quick report. Bullets creamed into the wall edge, flicking jet streams of mortar and dust into the air. The black tip of the shooter's rifle disappeared deep into the alleyway.

'Reloading,' Outlaw said, reaching for another clip.

Coldrain let off six shots at the alleyway, keeping the target pinned down. He was aware of the ammo situation. Down to his last mag. Twenty-three rounds left and he'd be out.

Another burst from the fucker hiding out in the alleyway and Coldrain decided to go hell for leather and finish the job. Fully reloaded, Outlaw was putting good rounds down, turning the alleyway entrance into a lethal killing zone. He was twenty metres away from the alley mouth.

Now fifteen.

Ten.

As he closed in, Outlaw stopped laying down suppressive fire and in a flash the shooter's barrel was out again, spitting 7.62mm fury in a long, drifting arc. Standing back thirty metres wasn't a problem, but, at such close range, Coldrain was taking a huge risk. He presented a much bigger target. Given the short distance between himself and the X-ray, the fucker could be a chad-as-yer-dad shot and still get lucky.

Eight metres.

The next moment was critical. Coldrain flung himself to the ground. A second later he heard Outlaw unleash another barrage towards the alleyway. The back of his shirt rustled as the supersonic rounds passed a few inches above him. Coldrain didn't panic. He had complete trust in Outlaw's firing abilities. In that situation, he had no choice.

Coldrain counted six rounds in a deliberate burst. That was the signal. He sprang to his feet and broke left, his AK tucked under his shoulder. The alleyway came into view. It grew deeper and wider as he shuffled sideways, opening up, but all he could see was a grainy well of darkness. No sign of the shooter. He tried to focus on the blackness, but he couldn't make out shit in the alleyway. Sod it, he had to push on. He'd already come this far.

And then, a moment later, the X-ray scrolled into view.

Coldrain didn't give him time to react. He just depressed the trigger. Pulled on it hard.

The AK-47 rounds punched a symphony of holes in the X-ray. Blows were scored on the shoulders, stomach, neck and thigh. Each bullet struck with a satisfying thump. The guy stumbled back, catatonic shock registering briefly as he realised he was supremely fucked, and Coldrain fed him another salvo of brass just for good measure. Eyes, foot, hand.

He collapsed onto the ground, blood and shit seeping out of his wounds. The air already stank of cordite and burnt skin.

Coldrain turned back to Outlaw.

'Maybe you are Rambo after all, mate.'

'Right. And who does that make you, Chuck Norris?'

The street was empty. Fair enough. No one in their right mind would be outside right now, not with all the rounds chopping the place up. But something was missing.

Coldrain realised what. Panic spread through his system.

'Where's Ischenko?'

Outlaw turned behind him, looking at the heap of rubble. She wasn't there.

'Oh, no.'

'Shit.'

Coldrain sprinted down the street.

He saw the figure in the distance.

And he clocked the sniper on the rooftop, setting up his scope.

THIRTY-NINE

He was a slip of a target, so small that he barely filled the notched rear tangent on the AK-47's iron sights. The range was forty metres. Throw in a drop of fifteen plus to the brink of the rooftop, and at a forty-five degree angle to his position, and you were looking at a difficult shot, with maybe twenty per cent chance of a kill.

On a good day.

The sniper was shrouded in black, a blurry silhouette, the faint sun slung over his shoulder. Any other day, he could have been one of a million curious Iraqis sitting on their rooftop, smoking fags and filming gun battles on their mobiles, but for the Chinese QBU-88 assault rifle in his hands, the distinctive ridged barrel propped against the quarter-metre-high ledge running around the rooftop.

The muzzle leered at Ischenko. The shooter peered down the QBU's telescopic mount, locking on.

Preparing to take his shot.

Coldrain adjusted his aim so that he had the ledge dead centre in his sights. It was an awkward angle and height to fire an unadjusted AK-47, and the best he could hope for was to aim low and vittle off a controlled three-round burst on semi-automatic. There was heavy recoil on the

AK, caused by the urgent release of gas in the piston forcing the bolt lever to slide all the way back. All that movement produced a lot of wobble and meant that the first successive rounds would jump a little. If he simply fixed the shooter in his sights, the rounds would skip over and up into the sky.

The shooter had the look of a pro sniper. He wouldn't miss.

Taking a deep breath, Coldrain pulled the trigger.

And got the dreaded double click.

The bolt lever didn't move. It was stuck rigid.

Stoppage.

Coldrain frantically slapped the mag with the palm of his hand, then tried recocking the weapon. The bolt lever was still jammed hard. He ripped out the box mag, shook the weapon and tried again, tugging the bolt lever. As he pulled it back, the jammed shell popped out. With the chamber clear, Coldrain reinserted the mag. Brought the weapon to bear on the target.

He was too late.

There was a short, sharp crack.

Up ahead, he saw a small puff of red spray emitting from the back of Ischenko's head. And then she was falling, like she had tripped on something, and then she wasn't moving.

God, no. Please.

No no no no.

As his mind screamed, Coldrain reacted on instinct. He vittled rounds at the shooter, four, five, six, he lost track of how many. He saw the first two slamming into the brown-grey ledge, punching fist-sized holes in the brickwork. Round number three was the money shot, penetrating the sniper's neck.

He dashed over to Ischenko.

Her wound was crude and obvious. And fatal. Even before he knelt beside her, Coldrain knew it was over. She was utterly lifeless. The round had struck at behind her left ear, creating an entry wound the size of a golf ball. Her hair glistened around the wound, matted, glistening. Coldrain could tell from the point of impact that her skull would have been crushed. Energy release and fragmentation from the bullet would have severely fractured the cranial area and travelled through the brain, killing her instantly. Blood oozed out of the wound. It ran through the cracks between the granite setts, forming tiny rivers that flowed out in every direction.

He overdosed on rage. Could hear the blood rushing through his head, reaching a crescendo as it swirled around his temple, raging like a violent storm at sea.

First, Dogan had snatched vengeance away from him.

Now this.

He closed his eyes and the rushing sound amplified. Sounded, to his ears, like whitewater rapids, his emotions crushed like sticks bashing against the rocks.

And through the fire and flames raging in his skull, Coldrain had one clear thought. *Dogan and Markarets did this. They killed Jamie at Ghorak, and now they've slaughtered an innocent woman in Baghdad.*

And then: *I want to find Dogan. Waste him. Then find Markarets. Kill him too.*

Someone once said if everyone took an eye for an eye, the whole world would be blind. Coldrain wasn't planning on taking that many eyes. But these two, Dogan and Markarets, he was prepared to make a lot of people blind in order to finish them.

'Motherfucker,' he heard Outlaw mutter behind him. 'It's one thing to drop a soldier. But a woman?'

'She wasn't . . .' His voice trailed. She wasn't what, he thought. Armed? A soldier? A target?

These things, yes. But ultimately, Ischenko wasn't meant to be snatched away from you.

He cast his eyes over her body and felt someone strike a match against the side of his heart. Melanie had vacated his thoughts these past few days. Drifted away almost imperceptibly until she became nothing but a vague, distant figure. He'd waged a quiet war against his feelings, but something had grown in him since Van. A sense that, despite his innate cynicism, a future with Ischenko might be possible. That white-hot glow in her eyes. The way she gazed at him, like a child marvelling at their first sparkler on Guy Fawkes' Night.

'These bastards are merciless, Danny,' Outlaw filling the silence. 'They just don't give a fuck.'

'Neither do I, mate.'

Coldrain reached down and felt into Ischenko's pockets. Fished out a wallet. She had a stack of business cards and debit, store and credit cards, blood donor, gym membership, the usual stuff. Among the wad of receipts and shekels, two photographs, folded in half. He opened them up. One was a black and white shot of a girl, three or four years old, playing in the garden. The scene looked rustic. Old. Her mum, he figured, or maybe even her grandmother. The second was a picture of Ischenko herself, leaning against the barrier along the Niagara Falls. There was a man next to her, slightly older, arm draped across her shoulder. The crease line on the snap ran along his face, distorting his features.

'This Dogan guy. He killed your brother?'

'Adopted. We were more like best friends.'

'Well,' Outlaw said, lighting a blunt. 'It's obvious as hell that he needs to die, real fucking bad.'

'I was going to tell you earlier.'

'Chief, it doesn't matter if you told me today, yesterday or whenever. If this guy killed someone close to you, I get it. You know I lost my best buddy in a contact in Iraq back in Fallujah. Fucking haji said he was surrendering inside a house. My buddy goes in, he takes one in the chest. Took him a half hour to die. The shit was, he couldn't even speak, you know?' Outlaw's voice drifted like the wind. 'Just mumbled and shit his pants. Then he died.' He spat on the ground. 'And I owe you. Don't think I ever forgot about that shit in Madagascar.'

'I was just doing my job.'

'Bullshit. If you'd have just done your job, I'd have been history. Seriously. On this one, I'm with you all the way. Sandman or no Sandman, it's irrelevant. But do me a favour and promise me something.'

'Yes, mate.'

'We nail Dogan, and Markarets, and then we put all this shit behind us.'

'What do you mean?'

'I'm saying, we take the paper and we fucking hang up our guns for ever. Move to Nicaragua and start up a fucking bar or some shit.'

'Nicaragua?'

'Or where the fuck ever. The place isn't important. The idea is.'

Coldrain nodded. A clean break sounded like the best idea in the world.

His BlackBerry was buzzing. Coldrain dug it out from his pocket. The screen was cracked in three places, the N and M keys had fallen off and there were a few little nicks and scratches. But it was still in decent enough nick. He knew who was calling even before he glanced at the screen. Coldrain hit the green key. He couldn't avoid the caller any longer. And he wanted to ask some questions of his own too. He heard the voice start to waffle down the other end of the line, but Coldrain cut him off.

'Who the fuck is Gustav Markarets?'

FORTY

He imagined the Sandman squirming awkwardly in his chair, the black executive model with the five-thousand-quid price tag. The office reeking of old leather and lies. 'I have no idea who you're talking about,' he said.

Coldrain gave it a few seconds. Waited for the Sandman to say something else. But he kept shtum. 'Funny,' Coldrain finally said, carving up the silence.

'What?'

'You're a thousand miles away, but I can still smell shit.'

'No, Daniel,' he replied in a voice deep-fried in condescension. 'This is not the way it works. I pay you, not the other way round. As long as that remains the case, I do not need to tell you anything. Not what I had for dinner, not what my favourite colour is, and not fucking whether I know someone called Gustav Markarets. I ask the questions. Do I make myself clear?'

Coldrain was burning up with fury. He wished he was talking in the same room as the Sandman, not down some fucking phone. Give him ten minutes alone, a wire coat hanger and a cigar and he'd make the Sandman sorrier than he'd ever been in his whole bloody life.

'Now, have you found Dogan?'

'We did. But he got away.'

There was a pause. Coldrain thought he heard a hissing noise. Or maybe it was the phone. Then:

'What happened?'

'We found Dogan all right. But not in Van.'

'The Baghdad bombing.'

'That was him.'

More silence.

'But you let him escape.'

'It wasn't like we rolled out the red carpet and wished him the best, for fuck's sake. He had a bunch of mates racing to his side, soon as we nabbed him. And then he started banging on about how we didn't know who we were fucking with, and this bloke Gustav Markarets.'

'I don't quite follow.'

'Dogan said that all those diplomats were being iced for a reason. Not terrorist goals, nothing like that. More because of what they *knew*.'

His voice was drowned out by the drone of an engine, interspersed with the sound of air being chopped up. Coldrain arched his neck and looked up into the sky. An AH64-D Apache Longbow hovered overhead. A Bradley trundled along towards them.

Coldrain figured the second squadron had heard the shit hitting the fan and decided to check it out. For once Coldrain was glad to see the overt display of force, happy to clock the soldier manning the M242 chaingun, primed to deliver 22mm-shaped good news to any insurgent who wanted some.

There was a long pause. Coldrain looked at the screen. Maybe he'd lost the signal. But there were still three bars on the display panel. He pressed the BlackBerry close to his ear, plugging the other with his finger, as the Apache hovered low over the street, the powerful thrum from its twin turboshaft engines getting louder and louder.

'Markarets. I want to go after him.'

'You forget our little chat,' the Sandman snapped. 'I pay you to kill people. Not to make decisions. That's my business.'

'Look, you wanted me to hit Dogan, and we came within a fucking inch of completing the mission. But it's you who fucked up, not us. We had no int on the back-up. The blokes who came to rescue Dogan, they weren't standard insurgent shitters. I'm talking proper soldiers, with proper weapons and training. And the way Dogan was going on about Markarets, it sounded like something big was going down. Yeah, you're right, you do pay me, but I'm also paid to do the job right. And unless we sort out Dogan and Markarets, both of them, this ain't over.'

The Sandman snorted down the phone and was quiet for a long time.

'Wait there. I'll get the file on Markarets.'

He hung up.

Coldrain figured that, even for someone with fingers as slippery as the Sandman, it would take him an hour or two to dig out information on Markarets. Or he was just going to sit there in his office, pretending to pull out a report while he led Coldrain on a merry dance. When it came to the Sandman, you could never rule anything out. He parked his anger.

Outlaw was shooting the shit with Rivera. The sturdy Hispanic Cav nodded ruefully, blowing cigarette smoke into the sky. Coldrain joined them. Rivera offered him a tab.

'No thanks, mate. Don't smoke.'

'Me neither,' Rivera replied.

No one said anything for longer than a little while. An outsider might look at them and think they were contemplating shit. But they thought nothing. Like boxers after a twelve-round slugfest, they were too dazzled and shook up to think. At last, Rivera spoke softly, slowly, 'Was the girl with you guys?'

Outlaw shook his head but Coldrain said, 'Yeah, she was.'

'I'm sorry.'

'Reality of war, mate.'

'That don't make it any easier.'

'Do me a favour, can you?' he asked, taking one of Rivera's tabs after all, his first cigarette in six years.

'Sure, buddy.'

'Make sure she gets sent home okay.'

Rivera patted him on the shoulder.

He asked if he wanted to hitch a ride in the Bradley. Sure, he said. As it happened, the boys would be heading back to the Green Zone and Camp Victory. He could grab some hot scran and cold limers. Maybe a cool shower too. Begin to get his head around today, and think about tomorrow.

FORTY-ONE

The red light on his BlackBerry was busted and Coldrain only realised the email had come through an hour and a half later, as he and Outlaw sat in the canteen.

'Look at this shit,' Outlaw said, pointing to his plate. 'Burritos, hot dogs, steak, fries, pasta, burgers. It's like I've died and gone to heaven.' Camp Victory food rocked.

'Nothing beats the Green Zone, mate.'

'It's four years since I been here, but not a thing has changed. I even saw the same guy outside selling bootleg DVDs,' he said. 'When they pack up this camp, that's gonna be the motherfucker of all operations.' Outlaw belched and made no effort to hide it. 'Next top is the PX store. Heard they got iPhones going there for less than a hundred bucks. You want me to get you anything?'

Coldrain blinked. His body was numb. Like he'd over-dosed on codeine.

'Dan?'

'Uh?' Snapping out of his half-coma, 'No thanks, mate. I'm good.'

Coldrain's plate was half empty. He picked at his bright yellow fries lacquered in salt, played with them rather than ate. He wasn't really feeling hungry. Not after what had happened to Ischenko. It was Jamie all over again. He blamed himself for her death. For not looking out for her. For not protecting her, when she really needed him the most.

His BlackBerry sparked up.

It was from the Sandman and the subject line read GM FACTFILE.

The email was epic. Coldrain rolled the pearl down with his thumb, reading carefully, while he picked at his chips. They were salty and yet somehow sugary too. Smelled better than they tasted, but in his experience that was true of most camp nosh. He thought he might try out the ice cream once he was finished.

THIS IS ALL I COULD FIND OUT. READ THEN CALL ME, the Sandman had written at the top of the email. The rest of the email comprised a forwarded message, the original sender's email address deleted, typical cautious, paranoid fucking Sandman.

Coldrain read on.

Gustav Markarets, the report stated, was born in Belgrade in 1959, in what was then known as the Socialist Federal Republic of Yugoslavia, back in the days before the Bosnians, Croats, Macedonians and the rest decided they fancied having a go at the whole independence lark. His uncle had been a member of the Chetniks. Coldrain had heard a little of them. They were some kind of paramilitary force with a skull-and-crossbones flag, which collaborated with the Nazis in the Second World War. Apart from that, Markarets' early life had drawn a blank.

According to his file, at the age of twenty Markarets enrolled at the University of Belgrade, studying stomatology, which the file helpfully described as being a branch of medicine that relates to diseases of the mouth. After that he trifled with this, that and the other. A short stint working for some obscure branch of the Socialist Federal politburo. Dabbled in journalism and writing for a few nationalist pamphlets and newsletters. Nothing that indicated a man of any great direction, or distinction. Just another party bitch.

Then, in 1988, Markarets' file suddenly started to get interesting. He was specially selected for the 1389 Group, a secretive offshoot of the Unutrašnja Državna Bezbednost. The UDBA, Coldrain knew, was the old secret police in the Yugoslav Republic, and linked to dozens of assassinations and kidnappings during its years of operation. The 1389 Group was named after the Battle of Kosovo, where the Serbian Empire was crushed at the hands of the Ottomans. The battle, the report noted, was a hugely significant date in the Serbian nationalist calendar. Sort of their Waterloo, except they fucking lost. The 1389 Group was charged with protecting the integrity of the Yugoslav state.

Markarets was one of the Group's overseas agents. And one of their most promising young killers. He operated undercover throughout Europe and South America, eliminating dissidents. A French Bosniak academic was shot dead as he walked to his car in the front of his apartment block. In Buenos Aires, two Croat secessionists trying to acquire firearms were pushed out of an aeroplane. A Montenegrin ambassador was found hanging from the light fitting in his hotel room in Copenhagen. The list went on. Eighteen murders in total. And every time Markarets managed to slip through the authorities' nets, despite being on Interpol's hit list and making the FBI Most Wanted roll-call too. No doubt about it, he was the ultimate professional.

But Markaret was operating in a climate of uncertainty. By the late 1980s, the loose Yugoslav federation was beginning to disintegrate, triggered by the power vacuum created by the death of Tito, aka Mr Yugoslavia. The appeal of Communism was fading, and each part of the federation was pulling in a different direction. Then Ivan Stambolić, leader of the Serbian Communist Party, sent a delegate to Kosovo in 1987 to quell Serb protestors complaining of persecution by the Albanian population. The official was supposed to stamp out nationalist outcries, but the official performed a dramatic U-turn, endorsing Serb nationalism and declaring himself defender of the Serbs. The man's name was Slobodan Milošević.

With the disintegration of the Yugoslav state, the 1389 Group saw its priorities change. Overseas assignments were no longer a priority. In 1988, Markarets was recalled to the fatherland and specially assigned as a bodyguard to Milošević. As far as the intelligence agencies were concerned, he was unworthy of attention again until January 1999, when he was reported to have engineered the massacre of eighty-seven ethnic Kosovo Albanians in the town of Novo Krsto, a small village outside Pristina.

The massacre at Novo Krsto was not any ordinary bloodbath. After the incident a UN observer by the name of Jim Casement stumbled upon the village. He was so horrified he wrote a report on his findings the next day and immediately filed it with his superiors marked for urgent attention.

It had been Markarets' intention that no one survive Novo Krsto. First he gathered the firstborn of each family and offered the father of each a simple choice: kill the child or cut off their own right hand as payment. Every father chose the hand, and the soldiers gathered them into a pile in the middle of the village. To show people the meaning of sacrifice.

Then he had the children killed anyway. To show the people the meaning of pain.

His soldiers were ordered not to waste bullets, so Markarets had his men execute people with their bare hands. Most were strangled. Others were not so fortunate. One boy, just five years old, was slammed against a wall until his head was pulp. Another was forced to swallow knives while the soldiers watched and laughed. A woman had her unborn baby cut from her womb and cooked in her oven. She bled to death, watching the men eating the cooked foetus. Markarets presided over this orgy of depravity, and, to ensure his men carried out his orders without question, he had the family of each man bound and gagged, with the threat of murder should any of them disobey direct orders.

When they were done slicing off the breasts of teenage girls; when they were finished prising out the eyeballs of old men; when they had made a man eat his own fingers and burnt off the toes of an old woman; then they committed the ultimate indignity and left the bodies to rot out in the open. 'We should not hide our handiwork,' Markarets was reported as having told one of his men. 'The world will see what we did here today and tremble at our cold hearts. They will fear us, like they have never feared another.'

To commemorate the event Markarets insisted that each soldier had a tattoo of a Tibetan wolf on his right bicep.

At that point, Gustav Markarets was just another rabid Serbian nationalist with a wanted poster and a fast-track ticket to hell. The massacre at Novo Krsto had elevated him to the level of psychopath, well known as a demented

nutcase within the corridors of the UN and other humanitarian organisations. But little to suggest he wielded any
real influence or power.

The file indicated that was the last verified information
on Markarets. The next reports were unsubstantiated. MI6
water-cooler gossip. According to CIA field agents on
undercover operations in Pakistan and Saudi Arabia,
Markarets had spent the past few years reaching out to
influential pro-Taliban sympathisers, the sort with deep
pockets and an even deeper hatred of the West. Similar
rumours floated in Central and South America. Nine
months earlier, he had managed to procure a loan from a
creditor called White Wolf Holdings. This wasn't a case of
Markarets popping down to his local bank so he could
upgrade the family motor. White Wolf had loaned him a
cool US $20 million. A month later, a disused military
airstrip on the outskirts of a town called Windar in
Balochistan Province, forty kilometres north-west from
Karachi, changed ownership, to a British Virgin Islands-
based company called Panteri Assets. For precisely $20
million.

The report ended. Coldrain handed his BlackBerry to
Outlaw, who licked the burger sauce and grease off his
fingertips before scrolling through. Rivera looked at
Coldrain's plate of ketchuped chips.

'You gonna eat that, *esa*?'

'Maybe.'

'What do you think?' Coldrain asked Outlaw.

'Hard to say. If it's all true, I ain't going to be adding
Markarets to my Christmas list anytime soon.'

'No doubt, mate,' Coldrain said. Across the mess hall a
soldier threw a tray at a tall guy with eyes close together

and so much muscle he probably mixed roids with his Cheerios. Muscle Guy stormed forward, grabbing the thrower by the collar and pointing a finger in his face. A dozen soldiers whooped and hollered and separated the men before things turned ugly.

Coldrain chewed on the file's contents. But he couldn't quite join up the dots. There was Dogan, blowing up diplomats who, apparently, all knew something that he was desperate to keep under wraps. And then there was Markarets, a Serbian sociopath with connections, money and delusions of grandeur. Something was missing.

He called the Sandman.

'I've read it.'

'It is an interesting file, as you can see. I have since learned that Panteri Assets has just one share. Issued to—'

'Let me guess. Gustav Markarets.'

'Not quite. An associate, an old friend from his security days who now runs a Silicon Valley blue-chip company, Savo Ćurčić. Too close to be a coincidence, I would say.'

'That's all super-interesting. But what's Dogan got to do with all this?'

'Before I say anything else, let me be clear. I want you to go.' He paused, reluctant to continue. Coldrain was confused. 'We have both been duped, Daniel. My contacts in Whitehall claim never to have heard of Gustav Markarets. Given all that has happened with Dogan, I find that a little hard to believe.'

'I'm in.' He didn't even need to think about it.

'Good. But on one condition. You bring Markarets in alive. That's non-negotiable. The fee I'm offering is three million apiece.'

'Fine. But Dogan has to die.'

'Do what you wish with him. Markarets is the one who

interests me. If my instincts are correct, he has enough information to severely embarrass the British government and perhaps even force the lot of them to resign.'

Coldrain listened impassively. He didn't give a fuck about politics. Had never voted and believed that Government was full of pen-pushers and stuck-up university graduates who all thought they knew best.

'Where will I find Markarets?'

'I'm not sure exactly,' the Sandman said. 'But most probably Mogadishu.'

Coldrain did a double take. 'What the hell are they doing in Somalia?'

'Again, it is hard to get a complete picture. But as things stand, it seems very probable that they are trying to engineer a *de facto* takeover of the whole country.'

FORTY-TWO

'When you need answers, always track the money.' The Sandman's mini-lecture was succeeded by information that blew Coldrain away.

'The funds diverted into the airstrip in Balochistan were not intended for local regeneration purposes, Daniel. Quite the opposite. Satellite images from the area indicate a fully functioning airfield, with heavy fuel loads being transported inside, and a fleet of at least four C-130 Hercules aircraft.'

'Bound for Mogadishu?'

'It appears that way. Dogan and Markarets, it seems, are transporting soldiers and arms to the coast, with the intention of organising a hostile conquest of the city. Markarets supplies the money, and Dogan provides the resources. As you well know, there are plenty of young men in Iraq who are desperate for money and have a track record in the insurgency. It would be very easy for Dogan to sign them up as salaried soldiers.' Coldrain thinking, *That ain't a whole lot different from my own job title.* 'The men who rescued Dogan, I presume, constitute a very small part of the force that they are able to call upon. And I can see no other reason why they would send supplies to Mogadishu unless it was to work in collusion with the Islamic Front based in the city, to overthrow the regional government and establish a radical Islamic stronghold in the Horn of Africa.'

'That's fucking insane.'

'It is something, although I'm not sure your choice of words quite hits the spot.'

'And the diplomats, Thomas and the other guy. They knew about this?'

The line crackled with background interference. 'I'm afraid I am not close enough to Thomas to confirm that. However, Watts' own background would seem to indicate that, if anyone in the UK was to be aware of such a strike, it would have been him. A simple glance at his CV is enough to demonstrate that. Prior to taking up his role in Kabul, Watts was the Special Envoy to Ethiopia, and deeply involved in the high-level negotiations between Ethiopia and the Somali militia over sending troops to prop up the new government in the latter state. Watts, it transpires, was also born in Kenya.'

Somalia. Mogadishu.

Coldrain thinking, *This just gets worse.*

A lawless hellhole and an anarchist's wet dream. He'd never been there, but Coldrain remembered speaking to a couple of guys from the Royals who were part of Sneaky Beaky teams working off the coast, hunting pirates. It wouldn't be a walk in the park. Not unless a morning stroll with the dog involved fifty blokes with machetes hacking your bollocks off and burying you alive in the desert with nothing but a sack full of baby scorpions for company.

He thought about it some more and came around to the idea. Either he squashed this shit now, or went back to his life feeling empty, Jamie and Ischenko unavenged, Dogan and Markarets free to cause misery and destruction wherever they roamed.

Go hard, he thought. *Or go home.*

'I'll need a plane for a HALO drop.'

'Fine.'

'Weapons too.'

'Consider it done.'

'And extra men. If he's packing a shitload of insurgents, an army of two ain't going to do it.'

'Is that a little humility I detect, Daniel? You're not turning soft, are you?'

'Fucking do one.'

'Charming as ever. Your mother must be so proud. I'll arrange some support.'

'And anything you can find out on Markarets before we land, I need to know. Weapons, soldiers, whether he pisses with the seat down or up. Anything.'

'Of course. But I say again. There is a precondition to my greenlighting this assault. You must bring him in alive. You're a good soldier, Daniel, but you have a terrible temper. Be warned. If you are careless with Markarets, the deal is off and you're on your own. Am I perfectly clear?'

Crystal, Coldrain, thought, but he didn't dignify the Sandman with a response. Let the old bastard sweat a little. He hit the red button on his BlackBerry just as it ran out of power, and popped a fistful of chips into his mouth. They'd gone cold, soggy from the ketchup and mayo. Tasted floury. He managed a couple more before pushing his plate away, longing for nothing more than good old battered cod and chips, with a side order of his favourite dish, jellied eels.

'Help yourself,' he told Rivera, noticing his eyes on the food, like he was ready to fucking propose to it. Rivera ravenously attacked the leftovers, scooping the slop onto his plate and shovelling junk into his mouth. The man was a walking food depository.

'Everything all right?' Outlaw asked.

'Yeah, mate, good,' he said, but his voice was distant, as though he was underwater. *You're more tired than you realised*, he told himself. *All the Red Bull in the world can't help you now. You just need some Egyptian PT.* Coldrain excused himself from the canteen and went to find a bathroom. He passed the table where the fight had broken out, Muscle Guy and his rival sitting together, having kissed and made up.

Coldrain took a long piss. His urine was dark, putrid yellow and smelled tangy. Then he clocked his mug in the mirror. His eyes were baggy and bloodshot. There was about an inch of thick dust on his face, and Ischenko's blood was splashed up and down the front of his combats. He was tired. Most of all, he just wanted to go home.

Was he really going to go through with this? It would not be easy. *Yeah, like it had been a bloody cakewalk so far.* But things were going to get a lot hairier once he landed in-country. Coldrain had done several tours in Africa. Angola had been his most recent contract, a year ago, and he remembered it only as one massive human shit pit. Compared to Somalia it was the dictionary definition of a calm, civil country.

He didn't know how long he stared at himself in the mirror like that. Watching the hot tap running in the sink, the water swirling around the plastic plughole.

First things first. He finally snapped out of it, and produced the business card Ischenko had handed him. Stashed away in his pocket, her blood had seeped through and stained the card a dark pink. The same colour as her lipstick, he mused. He went back into the mess hall and asked a jumped-up jarhead where he could find a phone. The kid was all of about eighteen years old and spoke in a raspy voice, like his balls hadn't dropped. He pointed Coldrain down the corridor and went back to telling his mates how he couldn't wait to kill him some Arabs.

Coldrain took a deep breath and dialled the work number on the card. Four rings in, he got Ischenko's voicemail. It was in German. He hung up, called the second number, and was put through to the main switchboard. He tried to speak, but found the words difficult to form. Finally, with the woman on the other end growing frustrated at the silence, he answered.

'I need to speak with the boss of Anika Ischenko,' he said.

PART FOUR

FORTY-THREE

The wave pushed him under, submerged him. Coldrain felt tonnes of energised water crashing down on his skull. He lost his grip on the Zodiac and, fuck it, now he was drowning, salty water flooding his nostrils, and when he opened his eyes a stinging, iodine void was in front of him, shapeless and scary. He couldn't tell which way was up or down. Had no sense of time or space. Then he caught something. Slivers of moonlight resting on the surface. His heartbeat jumped. He tried to push towards it, except he couldn't. Something tugging at his legs.

He peered down. Saw a length of nylon para cord tangled around his lower half, from his thighs to his ankles. Dragging him under.

Coldrain kicked frantically, one leg after the other, but instead of rising up, he was sinking deeper and deeper below the surface. He could get no purchase. Felt the cord tendons working against him, binding his legs together. He was struggling to break free and the ocean was coaxing him below. His blood cells cried out for more oxygen, his head felt loose and giddy and any second now he was going to lose consciousness. *At sea, most people don't drown, they pass out.* He clawed at the light with his fingers. But the sea would not yield.

He was certain then that he was going to die.

And then suddenly his head was above water. He took in shallow, hysterical gulps. Moist air filled his lungs. Christ, that tasted good. Like fine wine. Coldrain shivered and watched as beneath his feet the disentangled chute foil sank into the depths of the Indian Ocean, cords dangling below it, like a dead jellyfish drifting downwards. He had broken loose.

A hand shot out in front of him, open, inviting. Waiting to be clasped. He seized it. Clocked Outlaw hanging over the starboard edge of the Zodiac, arm extended, knee propped against one of the airtight chamber tubes. He was reeling Coldrain in. To his right, Coldrain clocked Pete McGrady in the water, arms wrapped around the Zodiac's glass-reinforced plastic hull, his Fairbairn-Sykes dagger between his teeth. Coldrain suddenly understood. McGrady must have dived in and cut the cords.

Hauled in, head propped against the gunwale, Coldrain gagged up seawater.

'Bloody hell, lad, you're meant to be the one who's used to mucking about in the water. Or is that just another Green Death myth?' McGrady grinned as he clambered back into the Zodiac, the craft's freeboard dipping as the weight distribution shifted. His face was redders and he had a crazed look in his eyes, the look of a man who wanted nothing more from life than a bottle of Jim Beam, a cheap motel and a couple of Thai prossies. With his tea-brown teeth, he looked more like the alcoholic down Coldrain's local than a hard-as-nails ex-Para with a Military Cross, earned for lobbing grenades into a Taliban mortar nest in Afghanistan while his mates were pinned down by heavy enemy fire. 'How are you feeling, lad? All right, I bet.'

Coldrain spat out some more salt-plus-water. It was like someone had pissed directly into his mouth. 'Never been better, mate,' he said.

'Yeah, you'll be all right.' McGrady nudged the bloke next to him. Valentin Belkevich, size of an elephant and whiter than dhobi dust, traditional Marine washing powder. Next to the six-foot-six, eighteen-stone frame of Belkevich, McGrady, five-seven at a push, looked like a midget.

They were six nautical miles east off the Somalia coast, on a westward bearing towards Mogadishu new harbour, only marginally less shit than the old one. Coldrain checked his Breitling: 0330. Twenty-four hours ago he had been in Baghdad, washing Ischenko's blood off his arms. It felt like a lifetime away.

The Sandman had arranged for a C-130 Hercules, shipping out of Baghdad twenty-four hours after Coldrain and Outlaw pitched up at the base. Coldrain had been aching to go the same night, but logistics dictated otherwise, and besides, his body was crying out for a rest. So he spent the day doing what every soldier does trying and take their mind off things. He ate a bucket of chicken wings and fries at a take-out, played pool and caught up with the latest mess-hall gossip on the Afghan.

But Coldrain could not put himself at ease. The following day he was going to have to hunt down Dogan and Markarets. The terrible twosome, as Outlaw had begun to refer to them. Later Coldrain hit the base gym, tried to better his one-rep max on Romanian deadlifts and squats, got to 120kg on the former and 190kg on the second. Busted out some crunches and felt a little better for it. Then he went for a run around the base perimeter in the cool of dusk. But he was restless. More than anything, Coldrain wanted to get it on.

The plan, like all good ones, was stupid-simple. They would insert into Somali waters in the dead hours, between 0100 and 0300, when the majority of the local population would be tucked up in bed and deep in sleep. Flying into Mogadishu itself was out of the question. The city's official airport, a trophy for warring clans, had changed hands more times than dodgy bank notes, and, anyway, an endless barrage of mortar attacks had decimated the two landing strips. The only available runways belonged to private businesses, warlords, or the blokes making the daily delivery of *khat*, some kind of evergreen plant shit, grown on the hills of east Kenya, that the local population chewed. *Khat* got them high as a kite. Coldrain didn't blame them for taking drugs. If he had the rotten luck to be born in Somalia, he'd be smoking everything in sight.

Since Mogadishu was closed by air and far from any bordering territory, Coldrain's team would be dropping into the Indian oggin in the early hours of the morning. From the drop point they would make their way to the first RV, a rusted ship half buried on the beach, on a bearing of two degrees latitude and forty-five degrees longitude, sandwiched between Mogadishu new harbour at the south-west and the Alifuuto Nature Reserve to the north-east.

From there they would assemble and observe harbour activity.

'We have no intel on the ground situation in Mogadishu. Not since the aid agencies withdrew their support in the face of escalating clan hostilities. But I have a tip-off that an unusually large concentration of vessels has been sighted at the port,' the Sandman had told him on a briefing update that morning. Coldrain's BlackBerry had finally packed in and run out of battery power, so he spent a few notes acquiring an iPhone from the PX store. Went for the 16GB version, a snip at $149. *God bless war*, he thought as he handed over the shekels.

'Normally, there would be no more than a handful of small fishing trawlers at the port. It's mostly empty these days, thanks to the pirates attacking any nearby foreign vessel. Unless there's a humanitarian disaster, boats should not be unloading there.'

'I thought there was always a crisis in Somalia.'

'Of course. But not the kind that gets media attention. Any aid package is strictly low-key. And this is something different. What we are hearing about, Daniel, is a large fleet of vessels, involved in some kind of on-shore transport.'

'Attack crafts, you mean,' Coldrain said, thinking of the small raider-type boats that pirates sometimes got their hands on.

'Bigger than that.'

'Christ. And this is Markarets and Dogan?'

'It would appear to be the case.'

It was sorted. They would go looking for trouble. And like an Essex wide boy prancing along the Southend seafront in a Ford Escort, they would not have to go very far to find it.

After a fitful night's sleep, Coldrain was awoken by a guy kicking dirt in his face. He was about ready to pop a fist when he recognised the face. Jim Westfall, former Marine Corps jarhead, who had fought alongside Coldrain in the Iraq War. During the invasion of the al-Faw peninsula, Westfall had slotted a Bootneck, Dave Cahill, in a blue-on-blue friendly fire incident. Cahill had been a good drinking buddy of Coldrain's, and the Royals had never forgiven Westfall, nor believed his dit that it was an accident. The fact Westfall never even apologised to Cahill's family and friends also left a bad taste in the mouth.

Westfall was one of the Sandman's 'field agents', blokes the old wanker paid specifically to cut budgets and refuse requests for new equipment, making an already difficult job near impossible for a field operator.

'Wakey, wakey, dipshit,' Westfall chided.

'Fuck off.'

'Top of the morning to you too, buddy. The Sandman tells me you're to head out tonight. Here's hoping you make it back in one piece.' His voice sarcastic, his manner superior, like he crapped out pure gold. 'Anyway, the Sandman said you might need some tools.'

Now Coldrain's interest was piqued. Flipping the bird at Westfall's back, Coldrain and Outlaw followed Westfall to BIA, past the hangar where the C-130 was being refuelled. Engineers performed maintenance checks ahead of the flight. They stopped at the smaller hangar next to it. Westfall unlocked a padlock on the door and ushered them in, all the time sniffing, wiping his nose.

'Still snorting half of Bolivia, then?'

'Funny guy. You should give up the day job, hit the comedy clubs.'

'Not my game,' Coldrain replied. 'You just keep on giving me such good material. Mate.'

Westfall fell silent. He was fuming mad, but sod him. Westfall flicked on a light switch, and Coldrain suddenly felt like a kid in a candy shop. A candy shop filled with very, very big guns.

He was looking at a rack of M4 carbines, A1 variant, with all the Gucci bells and whistles, including flash suppressors, M68 Aimpoint red-dot reflex sights, and best of all, meaty M203 underslung grenade launchers (UGLs) that fitted on a rail beneath the main barrel to provide extra destructive capability.

Next to the M4s stood a Dragunov SVD sniper rifle. With a range of over a thousand metres, the gas-operated short-stroke rifle was the daddy of all modern sniper rifles, dating back all the way to the early sixties. It was the all-black polymer version rather than the wooden furniture edition, so the weapon would more easily blend into the natural environment. On a mission that required stealth and adhering to the golden rules of shape, shine, shadow and silhouette, a non-reflective black coating bested wood every time.

Rounding off the kit were Kevlar ballistic vests and Browning Hi-Power handguns, the classic 9mm pistol that was as old as Coldrain's granddad and dated back to the Second World War. But it was a dependable weapon, easily maintained, and it would not let them down in the field. A box of L2A2 hand grenades lay in a crate beside the primary firearms. Nothing better than lobbing one into an enemy bunker and watching everything in a ten-metre radius get blown to fuck.

In the centre was the crème de la fucking crème, a Zodiac combat rubber raiding craft, of the type used by US Special Forces groups. The Zodiac was placed on a wooden pallet and ready to be loaded into the back of the Hercules. How the Sandman managed to organise stuff at the click of his fingers, Coldrain would never know, but given the speed he operated at, and the resources he could call on, he certainly had to have his fingers in a lot of mucky pies.

'This is everything we have. Take what you need,'

Westfall said, his face locked in a grimace. It really pained him to help Coldrain out like this.

'Cheers, mate. Here,' he said, digging out a couple of shekels from his pocket, 'go buy yourself a cup of tea or something. Oh, that's right, you don't need charity. You already got a job kissing the Sandman's backside.'

Westfall turned, muttered a 'fuck you' under his breath, and left them to it.

'Who was that asshole?' Outlaw asked.

'Some Yank tosser.'

'Hey.'

'No offence.'

'None taken. I think.'

To the right of the Gucci guns were Bergen backpacks and basic supplies. Some foul-tasting meals, ready to eat, which came in brown foil packets and could be eaten cold or reheated using Hexi blocks, some sterile stretch gauze, basic first-aid kit, high-protein sugary chocolate bars, binoculars, extra ammo clips, some string, a Leatherman tool, plus a length of det cord, explosives, detonator, cam cream, a GPS navigator, water purification tablets, anti-malaria pills, box of matches and a torch, with a Gore-Tex smock for sleeping on. As it was a night-time mission, they were also given monocular night-vision goggles (NVGs), a headset which would slip around the forehead and fix a single lens over the right eye to provide a thermal image, and infra-red optics for the M4 carbines.

Coldrain was in the middle of testing his NVGs when he felt someone tapping on his shoulder.

He turned around to see a short, stocky bloke introduce himself as Pete McGrady, in a Geordie accent thicker than cold porridge. His clipped hair was ginger, but the horse-shoe moustache was salt-and-pepper, blond and dark brown patches, with spots of rust. It looked like someone had rubbed their arse cheeks up and down his face. Beside him was an absurdly big bloke, wide as he was tall, shaven-headed, with a pair of tiny Arctic-blue eyes that stared back. But he didn't appear intimidating or angry. Just indifferent, like he didn't give a shit. Like he had been fighting wars all his life. Russian, Coldrain guessed, and McGrady confirmed it, introducing him as Valentin Belkevich, ex-Spetsnaz and 'Bat' to his mates.

'The boss said we might find you here,' McGrady said, speaking for the two of them.

'And you are?'

'The cavalry, lad. Coming to your rescue.'

FORTY-FOUR

Coldrain left Outlaw to pack the rest of the equipment and grabbed a coffee with the two new recruits. He brought them up to speed on everything that had happened so far. The hunt for Dogan in Turkey, shit kicking off in Van, and the pursuit across the border to Baghdad. The shootout, and, when he retold it, it sounded like the gunfight at the OK Corral. McGrady listened intently as he sipped from his paper cup, nodding at each development like an old timer. His face was worn and blemished and Coldrain put him at thirty-five, maybe a little older.

As they talked, Belkevich scoffed up a plate of eggs and sausage meat, slowly chewing on each mouthful as he stared ahead into the middle distance. When he was done with his plate, he went up for a second helping. By the time Coldrain had finished giving them the gen dit, Belkevich had polished off four epic plates of scran.

'Let me get this straight, lad. You mean to say there's two right evil muppets up to no good in Africa, and we're to go there and nick the bastards?'

'In a nutshell, mate. Bit harder than just strolling through the streets. If the Sandman is on the money with his int, there could be hundreds of bad guys over there. We're not talking chad-as-yer-dad insurgents, but hardened fighters. A whole bloody army of 'em.'

'Sounds a bit like mercenaries.'

'Except these ones are bad guys.'

McGrady leant back in his chair. Belched. Picked at his teeth.

'So what's your story, mate?'

'Ah, not much of one. Sixteen years in 1 Para, all told. Joined straight from borstal. Quit last year. I'd had enough, me. Seen Norn Iron, Kosovo, Iraq. Afghan. I did my time and then some, lad. Then I heard my mates making big money on the circuit, like.'

'Got a family?'

'I've got me a couple of bairns. But the slapper, aka their so-called mum, says I'm not fit to be their pa. You know what it's like in them courts. It's your word against hers. A man's got no chance. So I get them one weekend a month and they show me all the fancy gadgets and computer games their new rich daddy has bought them. Just goes to show, a man's got to have a big house and a flash car to snare a lass these days. Well, good luck to her, I say. You talk about family? All the boys in the maroon machine, lad. That was my family.'

'And now?'

'Now, this grand old toon. The gaffer put us here on a contract to train the Special Forces. Special needs, more like,' McGrady cracked.

Both McGrady and Belkevich looked unhappy about the gig. Training up military units was fraught with danger and not the kind of frontline gig that most operators signed up for. They were looking for a job where they killed bad guys, not trained them, McGrady said. Coldrain knew exactly what they were talking about. More and more insurgents and al-Qaeda militants were making it their business to infiltrate local law enforcement and army units, thereby gaining access to a treasure trove of intelligence, combat techniques and weaponry. Understandably, guys like McGrady and Belkevich weren't too keen on handing over the keys to the palace. Dark arts were supposed to stay dark.

Coldrain's iPhone sparked up on the way back to the Herc.

'There have been some developments,' the Sandman croaked. 'I am getting in reports of an increased number of refugees from Mogadishu, fleeing north along the Jubba river.'

'Maybe they're hungry,' Coldrain replied.

'If there was a crisis, the UN and the World Food Programme would be on the phone to donors as we speak. That is certainly not the case. It could be Dogan and Markarets, although we cannot rule out a total breakdown of order in the city.'

'I thought it was already broken.'

'Nearly. But not quite. The situation in Mogadishu is highly unstable. After fifteen years of anarchy, the Somalis entered into a fragile transitional government. It held as long as the Ethiopians used military power to suppress the warlords. But Ethiopia has withdrawn from Somalia, and the southern half of the country is now controlled by Islamic insurgents and Mogadishu is by and large controlled by the warlords and their various clans. It's not beyond of the realm of possibility that the internecine warfare has simply increased lately.'

'But why now? If they've had the last fifteen years to leave.'

'Somalis are very good at reading the runes. Perhaps it is an approaching storm.'

'Or it could be linked to our mates.'

'Then you had better find out. I don't pay you to sit around,' the Sandman snapped, and suddenly the line was dead.

'Is he always this nice?' McGrady asked.

Their Bergens packed to the brim, they spent the hour prior to take-off breathing pure oxygen, flushing any excess nitrogen out of their bodies. Freefalling left a man susceptible to hypoxia, where oxygen supplies in the bloodstream became so low that the operator would fall unconscious, hence unable to release his parachute.

Kitting themselves out in neoprene wetsuits and with their parachute foils strapped on, Bergens below the main chute, they headed out to board the C-130. Dressed in mix-and-match digi-cam, US Army trousers, Royal Marine shirts, Timberlands, plus their firearms, they stood out from the crowd of jarheads and MPs. They were bandits, gunslingers. Renegades outside the system.

Coldrain had ridden in a Herc dozens of times. It looked like the inside of a space station, all padded walls and exposed cables. He had usually flown when the bulkhead was crammed full of sweating and farting Royals waiting to go to war. With just the Zodiac for company, the bulkhead was much colder. They sat on red webbed seats fixed to the walls. The Zodiac was pushed deeper into the plane's belly.

Taxiing along the runway at BIA, the Herc's engines droned so loudly Coldrain thought his ears would bleed. The hull was like a wind tunnel, loud and clammy and dark. Climbing to a height of 25,000 feet, the Herc would make its way along a route over Saudi Arabia southwards, down along Yemen, and then bearing east over the Indian Ocean, taking care to avoid flying over mainland Somalia.

All told, the journey took three hours. The flight passed

slowly. Outlaw produced a pack of cards and cranked up a game of no-limit hold 'em, but Coldrain found it hard to concentrate. A million things were running through his mind. He thought about what was waiting for them in Somalia. They were going into the unknown. All he wanted to do was find and neutralise Dogan, nab Markarets and get the fuck out. But he couldn't help feeling depressed about the events of the past two days. He kept playing out Ischenko's murder in his head, wondering if he could have done things differently. Stopped it from happening. It was only now that he remembered thinking the same things after Jamie died. The pity and self-doubt. The over-whelming sense that he was somehow to blame.

He'd spoken to her boss. Guy called Henrik Ribbech.

Anika's gone, he'd said.

Gone where, Ribbech had asked, chewing something, sound of a foil wrapper being scrunched.

No, you don't understand. She's gone.

You mean—

Gone.

And then Ribbech stopped chewing and Coldrain heard the squeak of a chair leg as Ribbech dragged himself closer to the phone, demanding to know what had happened. Coldrain explained. The tears followed. A trickle at first, a sniff on the phone and a tremble in Ribbech's voice until he finally released a scream that carried down the line and pricked his ears like a syringe.

The last words Coldrain said were that he'd achieve justice for Ischenko.

Do that, Ribbech said. Do it.

The red-light countdown began. Coldrain felt sick. He hated HALO-ing. The first time he performed a high altitude, low opening jump, he had been totally fearless.

But the next twenty-eight drops had gradually got worse, and now he was a massive bundle of nerves. Experience had taught him that there were all kinds of things that could go wrong on a HALO jump. Maybe the weight wasn't distributed correctly and he wouldn't be able to balance out. Maybe his chute would fail. Maybe he'd slip into a coma.

All those thoughts crowded up at the back of his head as the loading ramp lowered, revealing a midnight blue canvas that graded grey on the horizon, beneath a bright full moon and starlit sky. The Indian Ocean. It looked polished. To the west he could see a murky strip. The Somali coastline. And then Mogadishu. Only a few faint lights flickered. Lack of electricity. Classic symbol of a failed state.

And then the countdown began.

'Ten . . .'

Each man had carried out last-minute equipment checks, monitoring their oxygen levels, making sure their altimeters were correct. Praying that they wouldn't end up flatter than a pack of dead batteries. As well as firearms, they were tooled up with ammo supplies, surveillance gear, basic medic kits, rations and cooled water packs built into their Bergens. They were going in with hardcore shit, and that was good, but the extra weight was at the cost of an emergency parachute should their main one fail. And that was bad.

'Five, four, three . . .'

The wind was kicking up. Coldrain could see thin streaks skimming along the ramp's edge.

'Two . . .'

He knew a guy who died on a jump. Chute failed. Reserve failed. He was just eighteen, and a great lad.

And dead.

'One.'

Outlaw and Belkevich were first, Outlaw in front and smiling as he jumped, actually fucking enjoying it, the bastard, Belkevich gripping onto the back of Outlaw's pack, undaunted. Like he was popping down the local boozer for a cheeky half. Not jumping out of the back of a plane tens of thousands of feet in the air. The two men were there.

And then they weren't.

Coldrain and McGrady were next. He shuffled forward. Could feel McGrady leaning on his Bergen, his grip powerful. He was scared to let go. Funny how HALO manoeuvres turned even the hardest old salt into a terrified kid. He fought the fear and leapt forward. *That chute had better fucking open.*

Midair and the noise was crushing. He was hurtling down at terminal velocity, wind punching into him at a hundred and seventy miles per hour. He felt like he was in the middle of a tornado. It was bone-achingly cold. He tried hard not to panic, not to think about the height he was falling from, just focused on stabilising himself. Adopting the starfish position to ensure his body was balanced, the wind abruptly calmed. His anxiety began to subside as well. The four-man team assembled into formation and checked their altimeters, but restricted hand movement to a minimum, because the more times they moved their hands, the greater the risk that one of them might stray off course and end up landing a distance away from the rest of the unit.

At 4,000 feet they deployed their chutes, one man after the other, so they wouldn't become entangled. When they reached 3,000 feet they were under their canopies, their Bergens released on to eight-foot strops which dangled below their feet.

A little over two minutes later, they were slapping against

the water. They waited for their chutes to collapse before cutting themselves free from the rig. Then they swam towards the floating Zodiac. Coldrain knew there was no good reason to be flapping; landing at sea was meant to be as safe as houses, especially as the procedure had been updated a few years ago, in place of the old early-release system, after one too many jumpers had a nasty accident. But still, as he touched down, Coldrain breathed a massive sigh of relief. From start to finish, the insertion had taken less than ten minutes. It had seemed more like an hour.

That was when he tried to disentangle himself from the nylon parafoil, and felt the cords tie themselves in a chaotic wrap around his legs. Like tentacles. He had been close to death. Not just knocking on death's door, but shouting through the letterbox and threatening to smash the windows in. Fucking close. He didn't want to think what would have happened if McGrady hadn't reacted as quick as he did.

But he'd live. As he wiped chunks of rainbow pizza from his lips, Coldrain's eyes followed the tide. The water was slimy and blackness percolated from the sky down to the sea, like a leak had sprung up somewhere. On the horizon things were clearer. He could see the foamy edges of the wave licking at the shoreline. Glowing purple, washed by moonlight.

Mogadishu.

FORTY-FIVE

The Zodiac's jet propulsion system guided them towards dry land. They did not need to strap on their NVGs just yet. The moon shone like the world's most powerful Maglite down on the sea, stars glinting like raw diamonds, illuminating the horizon.

Seated on the wooden board at the stern, Outlaw steered the pumpjet engine using a tiller arm, a pair of cast-steel hydraulics clamped around the rudder stock. Propped up beside him, Coldrain acted as the navigator, using a handheld GPS navigator for reference points.

Two and a half miles from the coastline Outlaw killed the two-stroke propulsor. They went old school for the last leg of the journey, each of the four-man crew working a paddle and operating in pairs. Rowing was a bitch on the shoulders, wrists and arms, but it was as quiet as a wet fart and running the engine this close to the shoreline was bound to attract unwanted attention. Somali pirates didn't worry Coldrain much. The thought of some fuck-off ships docked at the port was a far bigger concern.

Coldrain wiped the face of his Breitling Seawolf Chrono. It was now 0357 hours. The remaining two-plus nautical miles would take a half-hour to complete, if

294

they maintained their current rowing speed of four knots. So they would be hitting the ship RV point, lying on a narrow band of beach straddling Wajeer District, by around 0430.

Plenty of time to debus, sort their rig out, ditch the Zodiac and find out what the fuck was going down at the harbour.

As they closed in on the shore, they spotted a two-man fishing boat, its black keel jutting out of the water like a shark fin in a low-budget horror movie, bobbing up and down with the congealed tide. They rode on and encountered six or seven Arab dhows, also overturned, their primary red and blue bellies floating in the water, torn lateens draped over them. Coldrain parked his paddle and stared out across the thrustboard. Something rising and dipping a few metres ahead, brown and oval-shaped, waves slapping against it. More than one of them. Seals, he wondered for a moment. Then the moonlight brought them into knife-sharp focus and he found himself looking at four bodies, bloated and face down.

'Mebbies some pirates messed up on the *khat*,' McGrady said.

'I'm not so sure,' Coldrain said. 'Multiple boats, dead bodies. This isn't the work of pirates. They loot and ransom. It's generally not in their interests to slot people.'

He was interrupted by something blinking in the distance.

It came from the sea.

There was a shard of silence. Coldrain felt drawn to the light. It was bright and unreal. Visceral. Just as rapidly as it had appeared, it was gone again, like a light being switched off, and Coldrain found himself peering into a pitted blackness.

And then the sound came after it, like the wind flailing

behind a speeding train. It zipped past. *Phhht*, it went, confirming Coldrain's worst fears. And then he heard another noise, a human voice squealing, gasping, and he knew that they had found trouble.

FORTY-SIX

Coldrain clocked Outlaw's finger hanging off, like an axe had fallen on it.

'Who the fuck's shooting at us?' McGrady shouted.

'I don't know and I don't care, mate,' Coldrain replied, scanning the blackness, thinking, *Might as well look up my arse for all the visibility we've got.* 'Just put as much distance between them and us as possible.'

Trying to pinpoint the shooter's position was like playing pin the tail on the donkey. He knew it must have been a boat, because they were still over a mile out at sea, definitely too far for a land-based shooter to score an accurate hit. Best guess, a patrol boat looking to secure the perimeter beyond the breakwater. *But that doesn't make it any easier to get away.*

Outlaw was lying prone on the high-pressure inflatable floor, his right hand, already bandaged from the nail wound Dogan had inflicted, gripping his left wrist and holding his blood-coated hand as though it belonged to somebody else.

'Show me your wound."

The finger was ninety-five per cent lacerated. Reaching into his Bergen, Coldrain fished out the medic kit, applied some antiseptic wipes to the wound, then wrapped a thick tourniquet tightly around his index and middle digits. The makeshift compression pack was quickly soaked through.

'Son of a fucking *bitch*.'

'Hold it above your heart,' Coldrain said. 'That will help minimise the blood loss.'

Both men knew that the tourniquet was only a short-term measure. Sooner or later, Outlaw needed proper medical attention, otherwise the wound could become infected and possibly septic.

A second shot whistled through the air, followed by a loud thump. *Phhht*. Coldrain rolled over onto his back and darted his head from right to left, looking for the point of impact. Belkevich and McGrady were both lying on the deck.

'Anyone hit?'

'Negative. But they're getting fucking close.'

Then he caught a hissing noise. Furious. *Pressure being released*. One of the Zodiac's air tubes had taken a hit. The need to get out of range became critical.

Coldrain turned back to the stern and fired up the engine. *Sod low-profile*, he thought, *we've got a man down*. And, anyway, it was pretty clear they'd raised the local alarm already.

'So much for the covert landing,' McGrady grunted.

No plan ever survives contact.

The Zodiac lurched forward, skidding over the waves. Two more lights winked at their ten o'clock.

Phhht, phhht.

Coldrain crouched to make himself as small a target as possible. But he couldn't lie totally flat; he still had to have a line of vision in front of him, otherwise he would be steering the boat blind. One of the rounds whooshed in front of him, smacking into the water on the starboard side.

Bad guys saying hello.

The second round was muffled by the sound of the propulsor cutting through the water.

'What the hell was that?'

'We got a puncture,' McGrady said. 'Second chamber. If we take a third, we're wet toast. We need to get the hell out of here, Coldrain.'

'I'm working on it.'

There were eight airtight chambers fixed around the Zodiac, interconnected by internal valves, which meant that if one chamber leaked the air could be bled from an adjoining chamber, equalising the pressure and maintaining the balance of the boat. McGrady was fiddling with the repair kit, working on the pressure gauge. Still almost a mile out from land, swimming to safety from here, especially with a wounded comrade. Well, Coldrain didn't want to even think about it.

No plan ever survives contact with the enemy.

Yeah, but I'll bet the guy who said that still had a better plan than going on an op with nothing but instinct and a few guns.

'Keep the fuck down!' he boomed. 'STAY DOWN!'

More rounds vittled over them. From his position at the stern, Coldrain was pressed into action as emergency coxswain. He worked the tiller, shunting it hard to force the boat right and went full throttle, fifty-five horsepower. The boat jerked and shook and tilted, the Zodiac was sideways, and for a terrifying, stretched-out second, he felt the turn was too hard, they were going to go under. In his mind they were already capsized, scrabbling in the open waters. And then, suddenly, the Zodiac was returning to a horizontal plane and one more round was fired, missed them, he could hear it whizzing into the water behind them, and they were getting away. They would be landing a few miles north from the original RV point, but fuck it. As far as Coldrain was concerned, it was still game on.

His victory face didn't last long.

There was a loud crunch, a jolt, and the boat stopped dead in the water. The propulsor screamed.

'Shit!'

'What is it?'

'Engine's jammed.'

'We've struck something.'

'Can we get past it?'

'I can't see. We'll have to row backwards. Fucking now!' Coldrain yelled at McGrady and Belkevich. Their eyes were glued to the engine. 'ROW!'

They picked up their paddles out of the sleeves and started reverse-direction rowing, trying to free the jet engine from whatever it had struck.

As McGrady and Belkevich grunted, pushing their paddles hard into the water and straining every sinew, Coldrain inspected the propulsion system. He tried to remain calm, even though he heard other boats revving in the background, somewhere in that claustrophobic darkness, heading for their position. His biggest fear was that the prop would be shredded and twisted by the object it had collided with. If it was badly bent, he lacked the necessary repair kit to straighten it out and get the fucker running again.

It was not that bad.

The propeller on a Zodiac has a shrouded impeller instead of the open prop type found on most commercial motor boats. Shielded props were good for two things. One, preventing tired or clueless operators from accidentally turning their hands into mincemeat in the water. And two, it meant that if the props impacted against something hard underwater, there was less chance of significant damage to the blades. The system had worked a treat on this occasion.

'How's it looking, Marine?' McGrady asked.

'A few nicks on the props, nothing serious. I've seen worse.'

'Lucky bastard. I should ask you for six numbers.'

'I'm not that lucky, mate. If I was, we wouldn't be getting fucked at in the middle of the ocean.'

'True that.'

Coldrain leant over the stern to see what the propulsor had ground against. When he saw the object, he fought a strong urge to gag. A mangled corpse rose to the surface like an apparition. The props had chewed up the body, innards diced and chopped, entrails slithering out of the stomach lining. Only the arms and head were identifiably human. The main body was just mush. Holding his breath, Coldrain used his paddle to push the body away. He went to fire up the engine. The same words rang through his head. *Get the fuck out of here.* The corpses, the bad guys, the pirates. Somali waters, he was fast learning, were like the gates of hell. He almost missed Helmand Province.

Get the fuck out of here now.

But now was too late. Coldrain felt a burning light spread over the Zodiac like a rising sun. Turning everything monochrome, the whiteness was so pure. He spun around and saw a flash directly in front of the bow. *Another bullet,* he thought. Only this flash was much bigger, much brighter. And it did not disappear. *Bigger gun,* Coldrain wondered. But no, the flash was still there and if it had discharged something, they'd all be browners by now. Him, Outlaw, McGrady, Belkevich. Bobbing along in the sea, singed hamburger. Just like the mate they'd bumped into.

Then it became clearer. The light swung back at the thrustboard and his eyes adjusted to the ghostly image around it. Spectral. Dark. He saw the outline, picked out details.

Spotlight.

FORTY-SEVEN

At first Coldrain hoped it was a fishing trawler or a passing merchant ship unwittingly caught up in this shitstorm. But it was too small to be a trawler, there were no nets or winches fixed to the stern and it was painted all in black. It was sleek and mean-looking. Not a pirate vessel. There were four bodies on deck, behind the spotlight, decked out in Gucci fireproof assault clobber, all-black, state-of-the-art combat rifles and NVG headsets that looked like souped-up Bluetooth packs. Two of them were wielding MP5s, the third controlled the spotlight.

The fourth crewman operated a gun from a free-swinging pedestal with armour plates fastened to the left and right of the weapon. It was an Oerlikon 20mm cannon, and, if the guy pulled the trigger, the 450-round-a-minute barrel would vaporise everything in sight. The boat was thirty metres long, and Coldrain guessed it was some kind of fast attack craft.

The kind used to hunt pirates. Not driven by them.

'We got incoming!' he shouted to the others. 'At our bow, twelve o'clock.'

'That ain't no small-time trawler.'

'Hold on, lads, I'm going to swing us across.'

Coldrain's first instinct was to shift the Zodiac at a ninety-degree angle, kick up some surf and make a run for it. But as he hand-extended to the tiller, he felt another spotlight cast over him. He turned around and saw an identical craft to the starboard side.

'We got ourselves a wee problem,' McGrady said. He was facing port side, where a third attack boat had homed in on their position. They were squeezed on three fronts. Coldrain looked aft, wondered why he was even fucking glancing in that direction, as if they could dig out of this world-class lash-up, row backwards at top speed, escape the ninja crafts and the wrath-of-God guns and somehow ungash the mission.

'We're in the rattle big time.'

'No way out,' Outlaw said. 'Nowhere to fucking run, neither.'

'What do you want to do?' McGrady piped up. 'Hands in the air time?'

No way out.

Nowhere to run.

But he was a Royal through and through. And Bootnecks never gave up.

'Keep your hands where they are,' Coldrain said. 'And get ready to give them hell.'

He reached for the tiller and gave the Zodiac engine a rev. McGrady and Belkevich began popping lead from their M4 carbines. They aimed for the spotlights on the port and starboard lights, nailing them first time, plunging the boats into darkness.

Muzzle flashes lit up the sky, like a million thunderstorms kicking off at once. Ahead Coldrain saw the jerky motion of the cannon swinging on its arc, tracking the Zodiac as he made a run for the gap between the fore and starboard vessels. It was in-your-face, do-or-die shit. His team could put down as many rounds as they wanted, but either the Oerlikon would hit them or it wouldn't, simple as.

The cannon spat bullets, smoke gushing out of the barrel and rounds the size of Coke bottles bouncing off the deck and into the sea. It sounded like the power drill from hell, one round after another, and Coldrain was scared shitless. One of those 20 mils hit him, his whole body would collapse in on itself. Nothing left except some rags and bones and shit. All around him the sea kicked up as the rounds impacted, throwing up water like bags of exploding flour. He kept going forward, eyes on the gap and tried desperately not to think about the Oerlikon. Wanted to close his eyes. Told himself to man the fuck up.

The cannon bellowed again. Geysers of water flung up into the air.

Keep going.

And then suddenly they were through.

Coldrain swung the tiller around, trying to force the Zodiac forward in a zigzag manoeuvre that would make it harder for the Oerlikon to nail them. All the while, trying to keep them heading towards the beach. McGrady and Belkevich were at his shoulders now, left and right of him, pumping out more M4 madness on the attack crafts. His ears were ringing with each discharge.

'Go, fucking go!' McGrady shouted.

The Zodiac was intact. So were the team.

They were approaching the beach.

FORTY-EIGHT

Grains of sand stuck to Coldrain's Tims as they waded up the shallow waters where the tide clung to the land. The sand was wet and squelched underfoot, leaving dark purple prints that glinted in the pre-dawn haze. A thin fog lingered around their ankles.

In the distance he could hear cracks of gunfire peppered with the occasional crump of mortar rounds, like a thousand heavy metal drum solos all being played at once. More battles.

'Bloody hell, it's all kicking off tonight.'

'They're coming from the west,' Outlaw said. 'I'd say half a mile away. Maybe more.'

'How do you know that?'

'I trained as a fire support specialist before I joined Delta. Back when I was normal person.'

'If it's that far away,' McGrady said, 'that places it in the middle of the city.'

'About right.'

'That's one party we need to get ourselves to, lads,' Coldrain said.

'Let's get a fucking move on then.'

Toxic black smoke drifted upwards, suffocating the purple-orange sky.

Coldrain could hear engines from out at sea.

The attack crafts were on their coat-tails.

'Determined fuckers, aren't they?'

'We have a minute, tops.'

'Not enough time to get off the beach.'

'Then we'll stand and fight.'

Ditching their heavy Bergens and retaining only their primary and secondary firearms and grenade belts, canteens and knives, Coldrain led the way, running fifty, sixty metres up the beach, towards an old edifice half consumed by the sand. The rusted frame of a building with its insides hollowed out. A factory or warehouse, back in the day, a time before Somalia went tits up.

It would do.

Coldrain crawled down into a shallow scrape behind two rusted metal blocks on the north side of the structure. He was facing south, seawards, his M4 directed beyond the scrape, at the surf. Finger on the trigger.

McGrady and Outlaw joined either side of him in the scrape. Belkevich was unslinging the Dragunov and adjusting the thermal optics. He went down on one knee with a metre-high rectangular metal sheet for cover.

Moist sand stuck to Coldrain's nose and lips. He felt granules rub against the cuts on his forehead, irritable, like salt in an open wound.

'How's the finger?' Coldrain asked.

'Fuck, you know what they say, right?'

'Better lose a finger than a dick.'

'You still got some puke around your mouth.'

'Yeah, all right. I've seen better days.'

'You and me both.'

Coldrain spotted the edges of the attack crafts approaching the beach. Frantically assembling his NVG monocle, Coldrain observed the anticipated entry point. Night-vision brought the world to dappled, verdant life.

'First craft's hitting the shore. I see the crew dismounting. Two of them approaching.'

The two figures were glowing white-hot and beating a path straight towards their position. With the tide lapping around them, one X-ray dropped to his knees as the second stood to his immediate right, assault rifle raised, elbows tucked tightly in.

'Let's fucking take them down, lads.'

'Happy hunting,' Outlaw quipped.

FORTY-NINE

The trigger on Coldrain's UGL rail attachment was located on the underside of the M203, just ahead of the standard 5.56x45mm magazine feed. Using the M4 mag as a grip for his firing hand, Coldrain flipped up the rear leaf sights. UGLs needed their own sighting mechanism because the M4's standard scope system was not aligned to the trajectory of the round. Acquiring a target with the UGL leaf sights meant using a different aiming principle, taking into account the grenade's flight path. He had to line the relevant notches on the leaf sights. The notches were graded from 0 to 250 metres, although, for a window-sized target, the M203 was really only good for approximately half that range.

Pointing the weapon at a fifteen-degree angle, so the lowest marking on the leaf sight was level with the target's head, Coldrain depressed the trigger.

The projectile made a tinny popping sound as it flew out of the barrel and arced through the air, slow enough that Coldrain could follow it with his own eyes. It landed with a thud in the sweet spot, right behind the two X-rays, then expanded into a six-foot-high ball of smoke. Jet-black in the centre, tar-grey on the outside.

Boom.

Fucking have some.

'Scratch two bad guys.'

'I see four more on the way. And another craft landing too.'

The round was an M406 HE, a 40x46mm high-explosive shell with a kill radius of five metres, but Coldrain wouldn't fancy his chances from twice that distance. As it impacted, the explosive energy fragged the enemy. It was like a nuke had detonated behind them. The men screamed as the extreme pressure sucked their lungs clean in, crushing them along with a tangle of other organs. Flaps of skin landed not far from Coldrain's feet. That was how it was done.

Four more soldiers debussed from the craft as a second vessel pulled behind it. Coldrain pumped another HE round into the killing zone and watched as their bodies were blasted to shit, bits of arms and legs tossed into the air like a French salad. It was as though they had each swallowed a live grenade. Coldrain got two strikes with his second UGL round, and McGrady and Outlaw were on the money with their shots, zapping the other two bastards before they could vittle off some bullets and launch a counterstrike.

His third UGL round was off target and fell short by a couple of metres, but it was still close enough to lop the nearest fucker's head off. Now Belkevich was getting in on the act. He was a surgical son of a bitch with the Dragunov, taking deep, controlled breaths. Discharging lethal single-burst shots. He struck a guy clean in the neck. Guy staggered backwards, slipped and rolled down the beach until he stopped by the tide, waves licking at him as he desperately tried to plug the haemorrhaging wound.

Good luck with that, mate, Coldrain thought. Another X-ray tried to head for cover behind a low coral feature, but Coldrain lobbed a projectile into the area and waited for the inevitable boom. Amid the swirling gases, he clocked a pair of legs.

'Shit. That guy's got no torso. That's just fucking mean.'

'Two birds, one stone, mate.'

Adrenalin was surging through his body now. He was getting some, big time, and if he was honest, he was loving it. Forget all the bollocks about there being no atheists in foxholes. The rush from being in combat was like sex times a million. He had missed this. Missed the firefights and the tense atmosphere. Missed the camaraderie and the sense of brotherhood from being in the same shit as the guy next to you. This was why he had signed on the dotted line as a Bootneck in the first place. And this was why he had put up with shit pay and crap living conditions and monotonous training routines.

To get some.

The guys from the third boat were smarter than their mates. They stayed low, using the craft bow for protection, vittling off two- and three-round bursts, and then advancing forward by one or two metres. Coldrain could see that if they kept that up, they would be on the team's position within minutes.

'Switch to grenades!' Coldrain yelled. McGrady, Belkevich and Outlaw all removed a hand grenade from their belt and pulled the firing pins. Chucked them overarm towards the ground between the closest two X-rays and the three men at four metres' remove. The action was synchronised, like they had practised it a thousand times before down the ranges. No doubt about it, Coldrain and his team were in the zone today. If ever there was a good time to be outnumbered and outgunned, this was probably it.

The grenades exploded one after the other, and, as a dirty cloud of shrapnel poured shit down on top of the bad guys, Coldrain switched back to the M4 carbine and sprayed lead. He caught two guys with a six-round burst, one right in the kisser, the other a two-shot delivery thwacking into his stomach. The victim made a shrill cry as he floundered forward. The wails increased as he tried to stop his bowels from slopping onto the wet sands.

The last of the boat crew was zapped.

There was barely time to catch his breath.

'Something you ought to check out,' Outlaw said.

Coldrain rolled over in the scrape, lying on his back so he was facing the north, towards the mainland roads forming a belt around downtown Mogadishu. There was no cliff-face on this patch of shore. The sand simply ended and gave way to rows of low-level whitewashed buildings pockmarked with bullet holes. The nearest structures were three hundred metres away and from this distance Coldrain could see very little, even through his NVG monocle.

Outlaw handed him the pair of binos, Bushnell 2.5x42 model. He pulled the monocle up, resting it on his forehead and looked through the binos. Switched on the infra-red illuminator to enhance the image.

'See the mosque?'

'Got it.' The tall white minaret was immaculate.

'Now look west a little.'

His view was partially obscured by a couple of bombed-out classic Italian-style buildings. What he did have a visual on was a section of the road pointing west towards the old port and then, half a mile further down, the new harbour. There were no cars in sight. He wasn't surprised. If you were a civilian driving a vehicle in a place like Mogadishu, you needed your head examined.

'Wait. Keep your eyes on the road.'

And then, a few seconds later, it appeared, blurred and out of focus, but the general shape was enough to unsettle him. He saw it only for two seconds tops, and then the tea-green object was gone again. Coldrain could scarcely believe his own eyes. But he was not mistaken.

'You have got to be fucking joking,' he said.

'Either that was T-90, or I need to stop eating them happy pills.'

'It's a Russian tank, all right. I can even make out the smoothbore 125 mil on the front.'

'Looks like Dogan and Markarets brought more than just soldiers with them.'

A figure crossed Coldrain's field of vision. The binos automatically adjusted to bring the target into focus. He was a short man, five-five, narrow, hunched shoulders, wearing a pair of desert cargos and a leather jacket over a dark woolly sweater. A beret sat on top of his head, with a bushy dark beard smothering his jawline. Around him formed a group of men in a semi-circle, doing a good impression of looking like bullshit security guards.

Coldrain had no doubt it was him.

'I see Markarets.'

'At the mosque?'

'Standing by a jeep. No sign of Dogan though.'

'Shit. Where the fuck are they buying all this equipment from? T-90s don't exactly grow on trees.'

'China, Russia, India, who the fuck knows? They're here now, mate. That's all we need to worry about.'

'What's the asshole doing now?'

'He's pointing this way.'

'Fuck.'

'More X-rays coming. I can see a T-90, one of 'em. Plus sixteen infantry.'

'*Fuck.*'

And behind the T-90, Coldrain saw a GAZ-2975 Tiger, a high-mobility vehicle similar to the US-produced Humvee. Two occupants. A driver, and, next to him, Dogan.

He handed the binos back to Outlaw. 'Look who else has joined the party.'

'Finally. A chance to say hello to this motherfucker.'

'We'd better go and give him a proper welcome, then.'

Outlaw stashed away the binos. He tensed up when accidentally bashing his bandaged fingers against them.

They're coming, Coldrain thought. *You'd better be ready then.*

I will be.

'I got the feeling this is gonna be a long damn night.'

'Don't hate the player, mate. Hate the game.'

FIFTY

He had one eye on the T-90 and the other on the det cord. The Russian beast crashed through two shack homes like they were made out of papier mâché. A shallow brae was situated at the edge of the road, like a skating ramp, and a drop of three or four feet on the other side to the beach. Picking up speed, the T-90 jumped forward, several inches off the ground, then crash-landed, sending a shock wave along the shore

'We're running out of time,' Coldrain said. 'Put some suppressive fire down!'

McGrady and Belkevich started putting rounds down on the advancing parties.

'How's that det cord looking?' Outlaw asked

'Almost there, mate.'

'You know how to rig that shit, right?'

'If I don't then we're fucked.'

Det cord was a very long, thin bomb. It resembled a white nylon clothes line and was loaded with PETN, a compressed explosive that could trigger detonations at two kilometres per second. Holding the cord tense, Outlaw observed Coldrain working the main explosive charges, a

315

couple of slabs of dynamite, two inches wide and encased in a protective neon-yellow coating.

Coldrain had used his survival knife to chop each single two-foot-long dynamite into six-inch payloads, burying them at metre-long intervals in a column next to the scrape. That would give him a total lethal zone of eight metres, which was still small by explosive standards, and utterly useless if the tanks and troops took a detour along the north face of the shore. Under the circumstances, though, it was the best he could do.

'Two hundred and closing,' McGrady announced.

'Already?'

'That T-90's faster than it looks.'

He heard the jangle of gunfire as McGrady discharged rounds towards the tank. Belkevich was using his grenade launcher in stand-alone mode, the mad bastard. The M203's HE rounds were not armour-penetrating but the clouds of smoke might at least distract the crew from the dynamite trap being set for them up the beach.

Coldrain was wiring the end of the det cord into a blasting cap. The cap would act as the primary charger, triggering the first block of dynamite to explode before the charge continued flowing down the det cord, igniting each separate explosive in succession, so quick that to the naked eye it would seem as if they were all detonating simultaneously.

'Hundred metres, lad, we need to bug out!'

'Nearly done. Just give me a few more seconds.'

'Time's almost up, Dan. Wire that shit up.'

Sinking the cap into the leftmost plastic dynamite mix, Coldrain dug up fistfuls of sand and poured them over the blasting cap. It was crude, but a little camo might help conceal the caps. *Worth a shot.*

'It's set. Fall back and establish a baseline.'

'On it.'

With a lot of dynamite in a tightly packed zone the explosion might expand sideways rather than vertically. Dynamite was made from nitroglycerine mixed with sawdust to dilute some of the explosive energy. Bottom line, though, it still had a critical diameter of about an inch, and that made it a highly unstable, combustible explosive. Minus a controlling influence, there was no way of knowing how the blast would develop. In a standard detonation they would pack sandbags around the explosive to control the direction of the blast, otherwise shit would fly everywhere. But this was not a standard situation. No sandbags.

Just hit and hope.

Gripping the dynamo trigger mechanism in one hand and his M4 in the other, Coldrain led the team's displacement, pepper-potting back to a baseline sixty metres southeast of the booby trap. They arranged themselves in prone firing positions beside the corpses of the boat crews. The air stank of burnt, rotten flesh and Coldrain could no longer hold it in. He felt acidic, sickly fluid in his throat and he retched. Pure water.

The turret on the T-90 swivelled to face them head-on.

'Seventy metres.'

The 7.62mm coaxial machine gun opened fire, sending columns of torched sand skywards. Coldrain tried to get a bearing on the operator, but he was effectively concealed behind the armoured plating. The rounds were getting closer. If they stayed here any longer, they were bound to take casualties. Already the det cord was at full stretch. Bugging out once more was not an option.

'That gunner is killing us,' Outlaw seethed. 'We'll be wasted before the tank even hits the explosives.'

'Take that fucker DOWN!'

Coldrain barked the order at Belkevich; the Russian listened and coolly retrieved the Dragunov. Unfolded the bipod as rounds skimmed past him. The coaxial operator knew what Belkevich was doing, so he concentrated his fire on his position. Coldrain, Outlaw and McGrady all gave the gunman hell, unloading continuous streams of brass in a volley so furious Coldrain could see sparks flare up on the plating as each round impacted.

'Fifty metres,' McGrady said.

At this close range there was no need for Belkevich to engage the optics. Instead he was peeking below the scope, in the gap between the optics and the receiver, using the iron sights on the barrel to settle on the target. Regardless of distance, and the hardcore qualities of the Dragunov, the odds were against Belkevich making the shot. Only a fraction of the operator's head was exposed, a four-inch gap above the coaxial and between the plates. Difficult enough on a stationary target. Ninja hard when the target was atop a bumpy, fast-moving tank.

7.62 rounds lit up the environment. Impacted closer to their position.

'Fuck-shit-cunt!'

McGrady.

'You get caught?'

'My ankle. I took one clean.'

'Outlaw, take a look. I've got you both covered.'

'We have got to bug out, chief,' Outlaw shouted above the crackle of gunfire. 'No stopping that gunner.'

Coldrain emptied half his mag into the turret. It was like pissing in the wind. He might as well have thrown rubber darts.

'You hear me, Danny?'

'Not yet, mate.'

'Shit, anyone ever tell you you're a persistent son of a bitch?'

'Women, mostly.'

The gunner gave up trying to zap Belkevich and turned his attention to Coldrain, turret rotating in super slow motion, slow enough for Coldrain to have time to think about it, and he was pausing, not firing, his brain screaming *Discharge, you bastard*, and then he remembered his clip was out. He needed to reload, but there was not time.

My luck's got to be up, he thought. *No getting out of this one.*

There was a single, clear-cut report.

And then the operator flopped forward, hands dangling at the sides of the coaxial. Coldrain saw Belkevich blinking blowback gas out of his eyes. The Russian had nailed him.

'Gunner's down!'

'Yeah! Get some!'

'Good job, boss.'

They were the first words Coldrain had ever heard Belkevich speak.

'No time to celebrate. T-90's almost on top of the det cord. Infantry behind.'

'Detonate that shit now, Danny!'

Coldrain activated the dynamo.

The earth shuddered.

FIFTY-ONE

Smoke gushed out in every direction, flinging clumps of sand and shrapnel from the front end of the T-90 in a three hundred and sixty-degree sweep. Coldrain raised a forearm to his eyes, protecting them from the swirl. He heard screams, several of them, the grinding of metal on metal, and then the fog settled, debris and bloody sand cascading down, a metal and dirt waterfall.

The uncontrolled direction of the blast had worked in their favour, as the detonation had spread out over a wider field than the enemy expected. Every guy was flattened, most of them missing an arm, a leg, a head. Sometimes all three. The tracks on the tank were shredded, immobilising the vehicle.

'Dan.'

Outlaw. *McGrady*.

'How bad is it?'

'Never been better, lad.' He had a length of thick gauze dressing wrapped around the ankle and hobbled on his one good leg. A guy like McGrady might have been down, but he was never out.

Coldrain was already bounding forward.

Thirty metres behind the crushed T-90, he located the

Tiger. It seemed intact, too far away from the kill zone. Voices to his six o'clock.

'Dan! Fucking hold up! Some of those X-rays could still be alive!'

'Not this time, mate. This ends now.'

With the M4 raised, Coldrain made his approach.

'Wait, you crazy son of a bitch!'

'Leave him,' he heard McGrady say. 'The man's got a death wish.'

Two bodies in the Tiger, driver and front passenger, plus a shitload more corpses on the ground, the wounds covered in sand, as though they had been lying there for a little longer than a while, gathering dust.

The front passenger had a slice of T-90 buried in his cranium. Coldrain tossed the limp body to the sand.

The driver's bloodied head was resting against the wheel. He pulled it back. Guy was missing an eyeball and half his jaw, but he was still breathing, blood bubbling around his mouth. Reaching for his pistol. *Nice try.* Coldrain pumped two rounds into his chest, point-blank, tap-tap, and followed through with a boot. The guy groaned and fell backwards out of the door, blood spraying the seats. Fuck him. Fuck everyone.

Forty metres away he saw Dogan. Running for his fucking life.

Not this time.

Two cracks of the carbine and Dogan was hit in the leg. He was dropped.

FIFTY-TWO

He was face down on the sand, and, when he stood over him, eclipsing the moon, he merely looked up and smiled, and he saw that his teeth were coated in blood, his chin too, blood all down his front.

The first shot had struck low on his calf. The second had entered higher, penetrating his lower back, moving up through his body, rupturing his spleen and tearing his right lung. He could see the exit wound, located to the left of his sternum. The massive internal bleeding he had suffered from the second bullet would kill him, eventually. But he did not want justice eventually. He wanted it now.

Lowering the M4 muzzle, he aimed it directly into his mouth. The smile transformed into a panicked grimace. He was scared of dying. Everyone was, when you cut past the machismo and the hype. He was facing death, and there was nothing he could do about it now except wait in silence, or protest, but, in either case, the result would still be the same. Dogan had no more room for manoeuvre.

'I didn't kill your friend,' he pleaded. 'It was all Markarets.'

Coldrain said nothing. Held the muzzle millimetres from his mouth.

'I swear on Allah it is true. He planned each experiment. It was he who decided that we should kill those who tried to break the silence. I always said that they could be bought. Everyone has their price, yes?'

'You were there that day. In Ghorak.'

'Yes.' He was panting heavily. Blood dripped from his chin into a neat pool between his legs.

'You planted the bomb.'

'Yes,' he said, and he closed his eyes and sensed that his closing argument was lost. He did not need to be disappointed. There was no way he could ever have won. Almost willingly, he opened his mouth and allowed the muzzle to be pushed in. The tip of it pressed against the roof of his mouth, aiming upwards so the round would cause the maximum hypostatic damage as it carved its way through his skull.

There was nothing else to say.

He pulled the trigger.

FIFTY-THREE

Coldrain's ears pricked up at the sound of a jeep revving up in the distance. He looked up from Dogan's corpse towards the mosque. Markarets was boarding the vehicle, along with a couple of his henchmen. The wheels leaked trails of smoke. Whoever the driver was, he sure didn't know how to handle a military cage.

Coldrain heard the gears crunch as the driver kicked it into drive and strangled the throttle.

Markarets. He's getting away.

I know.

Ignoring Outlaw and the others, Coldrain jumped into the jeep. There were two injured soldiers lying on the sand, reaching for their weapons. One of them got as far as raising his assault rifle at Coldrain, before two short, sharp cracks reported through the air and the figures fell back again, guns dropping from their hands.

Outlaw covering his back.

He fired the Tiger west along a derelict main road parading nothing but rubble and buried hope. Rocketed past the old shallow drift harbour, where the ghostly shells of Norwegian supertankers were anchored. Into the bowels of Mogadishu.

The sun was rising now. Coldrain tore off the NVG monocle and watched as the city coloured in. Like a lot of old Navy Wrens, it looked better by night.

Eyes focused on the jeep. Markarets had a hundred-metre head start on Coldrain, and to make matters worse the road was marred with potholes that seemed to drop all the way to the centre of the earth. But the Tiger ate chad roads for breakfast. On the right, the rusted carcass of an ancient Italian P40 tank parked up on a mound of earth in front of a bombed-out university building. Last symbol of the legacy of the colonial horror show that had been Italian Somaliland.

He kept his foot pressed on the gas, making sure he didn't get danger-close to the jeep. If he ventured closer than fifty metres, one of the henchmen in the back would slam a few rifle rounds in his direction. It had already happened once, and, although Coldrain didn't give a shit about getting hit himself, he worried about the Tiger taking some hot lead in the wheels, paralysing the vehicle. Allowing Markarets to ride off into the sunset scot-free. And something deep inside told Coldrain that if Markarets escaped now, unlike Dogan, there would be no second chance to snatch him.

Up ahead the jeep banged a hard right, bearing north into the city centre. Coldrain almost missed the turning. His eyes were distracted.

The new harbour scrolled into view on the left, catching the first rays of the sun. It wasn't much. A rundown dock-yard, timberwork breakwater that extended out into the Indian Ocean, some empty containers. Rubbish-strewn wharf. And, just as the Sandman had claimed, a set of boats.

Boats way, way bigger than the small attack craft they had evaded during the insertion.

They wouldn't have looked out of place at Plymouth. Shiny grey vessels, like steel obelisks floating in the water. Coldrain was spying on a fully fledged naval fleet. He counted a dock landing ship used to transport marines and hovercraft, a Newport-class tank landing ship for carrying and unloading tanks, APCs and soldiers, as well as four La Fayette-class stealth frigates and a pair of Pauk-class patrol corvettes equipped with anti-submarine rocket launchers and SAMs. Markarets had a navy larger than those of a few NATO countries.

A ramp was lowered from the bow of the Newport and more T-90 tanks rolled down onto the wharf, along with APCs, BMP-1 infantry fighting vehicles and, sweet Jesus, even Pantsir S-1 surface-to-air missile launchers. At the stern, a gate was opening up and a hovercraft was launching into the port waters. A shitload of tanks and Tigers and other military vehicles were parked on the wharf. Dozens of soldiers minced about. It looked like something out of a commemorative D-Day documentary.

A fleet that size, with that kind of armament, a man could conquer almost any port in the world, let alone the jetty of a city and people descended into anarchy.

An alarm shrieked in his head and he looked back towards the road. Saw a goat twenty metres ahead, stationary in the middle of the road. He flung the Tiger hard right, just nudging it as he slid by, the goat bleating, both Coldrain and the animal equally grateful for the Tiger's impeccable handling.

The road abruptly stopped, bending north. Makrarets' jeep was out of view, so Coldrain put his foot down and banged the right turn, and up ahead he caught sight of the jeep. The bastard had gained distance. A hundred and fifty metres of shitty dirt track lay between them. He kept pushing the gas, going through the gears. It was time to see how fast this bad boy could go.

They played cat and mouse through block after block of adobe houses with glass and tin roofs, the poorer ones resorting to crude palm-leaf finishes. Internet cafés were stationed on every street corner. Old government buildings and UN compounds had been reclaimed and converted into makeshift housing units, the lawns covered in goatskin tents, clothes lines rigged to each rusted window. Sickly sewage scuttled up his nostrils.

A voice scratched at the back of Coldrain's skull.

There's something wrong with this scene.

Something missing.

He had no time to process the thought any further. The two henchmen riding in the back of the jeep were lobbing grenades onto the road, holding them for an extra second to cook before releasing. Coldrain slammed on the brakes and hoped the Tiger's wheels were packing some A-list traction. Three grenades were flung into the street, one sinking into a crater, the other two skimming along the uneven track like pebbles on water. They rested in gutters filled with steaming effluent. The Tiger stopped ten metres before the nearest grenade. The last to explode. Shrapnel whipped against the windshield, cracking it in several places. But the screen held.

Markarets' jeep was tearing off again.

FIFTY-FOUR

Coldrain flicked the wipers on. Silicone blades spread a filthy, shit-flecked smear across the glass.

He raced past roaming camel herds, their skins taut and ribcages protruding from empty bellies. Overloaded telephone poles, a million wires wrapped around them, threatened to topple. The old People's Arch of Triumph was a bullet-riddled shell. Whitewashed testament to aborted independence.

The streets all looked the same. Shit. But no matter how hard Coldrain pushed the Tiger, he could not gain ground on the jeep. It was tortuously close, less than a hundred and fifty away. But not close enough.

Another burst from the jeep shooter. Rounds struck the Tiger's engine and something crunched inside. The Tiger growled, and then pure white smoke billowed out of the hood blocking Coldrain's view. He had to slow down, swerving past blocks of cement, knackered old cars and goats.

A buzzing noise.

At first he thought it was the engine hitting a new low, some kind of wheezy signal that it could take no more and was about to die. Then the buzz became distinct. It

328

gained in noise until it was dominating the wounded Tiger motor.

Coming from above.

Coldrain craned his neck and searched the sky, half of him knowing what he would find, the other half hoping that he was really fucking wrong. There, a glimpse of it, so close he could almost reach up and touch it. Skating across the scattered cloud. He had been really fucking right. Then it was gone, dipping behind a dilapidated three-storey adobe block and he dragged his eyes back to the smoke and the road while he tried to weigh up what he had seen. *Could it really have been?* And then, *It's been such a weird day, you can't trust anything any more. Maybe not even your own eyes.*

The engine stopped coughing and thank God he could now see clearly again, the road and the jeep and the sky.

Up ahead, the jeep suddenly stopped. There was a pause where it seemed to be suspended, and then it tipped forward, dangling on a precipice. Swaying over a deep crater in the road. Rear wheels spun madly, but the vehicle was too elevated at its rear to win sufficient grip on the track. The wheels spurted up loose stones and grit. But the jeep would not budge.

Above it he saw the gunship.

Dust blew across the street in great swirls, as though a tornado was rolling into town. Air streams blasted downwards from the tips of the rotary blades to the ground.

The Mil Mi-8 hovered sixty feet in the air, like it was suspended from an invisible wire. High enough for the jeep to pass unmolested beneath. Low enough for Coldrain to see the tips of the rounds in its nose-mounted 12.7mm machine gun. He could make out the individual markings on the rocket pods fixed to the outrigger pylons.

Coldrain zigzagged manoeuvre, swerving hard left then hard right to avoid the machine-gun fire. The road in front of him was ablaze with bullet marks. The Mi-8 lowered even further in the street and hissed as two rockets were fired. They flew over Coldrain's head and pounded into the buildings behind him. Holding the wheel one-handed, Coldrain used his spare hand to empty everything he had in the M4 carbine towards the helicopter. He was aiming for the cockpit, hoping to score a hit on the pilot or co-pilot.

The pilot freaked out, pulled the Mi-8 high into the air and went into a circling manoeuvre. But it would be back for more, Coldrain knew. Sticking around the streets was definitely a no-no.

The decision was automatic. Coldrain was going to ram the jeep and crush that fucker Markarets. With a bit of luck he could knock the bastard unconscious and snatch him with no fuss, evac out of the city and trade in an ex-Serb war criminal for a three-million-quid cheque. Things were never going to be that simple, but he figured everyone was allowed to dream.

He slipped into fifth gear, asking the diesel for one last push before it died.

In the back of the jeep, two of Markarets' henchmen took aim at Coldrain and unleashed. He prayed that the Tiger was as brutal as the sales blurb promised. If the armour plates were not combat-effective against 7.62mm rounds, he was browners.

Coldrain was eighty metres away.

Bullets ricocheted off the hood, the wheels. Coldrain was driving into a wall of lead. He heard a bang on the Tiger's left side, felt the chassis lurch dramatically, unbalanced, knew that the front tyre had been popped. Hoped that the other three would hold.

Forty metres.

The windscreen was struck several times. It resembled one giant crack. Another round smashed against the shield and this one made it through, sinking into the headrest of the front passenger sheet. Foam flakes drifted across his line of vision.

Twenty metres.

A streak of light flashed towards him and then it was gone. A second later he felt a dull pain, like someone had punched him on his arm. Then he felt something wet. He'd been shot.

The entry wound was on his bicep. He had barely noticed it, he was so maxxed out on adrenalin. It felt warm and the pain was gradually building up, throbbing. But it was not so bad yet. He could still drive.

The faint drone of the Mi-8 picked up again. There would be no second chances against the Russian bird. Those rocket pods weren't the forgiving type.

Arms wrapped around the steering wheel as he clung on for dear life, the front of the Tiger walloped straight into the rear of the jeep. Glass shattered. Headlights, brake lights and every other kind of light a car had. Clatter of fragments breaking loose. Distressed metal parts clanging and creaking. Motors sizzling. Engines wheezing.

As the energy of the impact flooded through the Tiger, Coldrain sensed a formidable force thrusting him forward. He tightened his core muscles and locked his shoulders in place. His arse was lifted off the seat, he was thrown forward, his head colliding with the glass-splashed dashboard, steering wheel slamming into his gut with the force of a two-ton truck.

He shook his head clear. More like semi-clear. He felt punch-drunk. Engine smoke teeming out of the front of the jeep like a hot summer's day barbecue obscured his view. But he saw enough to know that one of the jeep shooters was sandwiched between the Tiger and his own vehicle. He was coughing up blood and shit. Everything below his waist seemed to be trapped between the two motors. It was a grisly sight, his bollocks and legs squashed to a pulp. Coldrain retrieved his Browning Hi-Power handgun from his waistband, used the barrel as a scrape to clear out the rest of the windshield, and slugged the guy a mercy shot right in the centre of his forehead. Put the bastard out of his misery.

Then he cranked the door open. Stepped out of the Tiger.

FIFTY-FIVE

Harsh sunlight blinded the driver as he staggered out of the jeep.

He was clutching a PP2000, a state-of-the-art Russian sub-machine gun that turned organs to mush. The weapon hung limply from a hand stickered with glass. Coldrain watched the man collapse at his feet, face down in a brown puddle. He leant in and pushed the tip of the Browning hard against the back of the henchman's skull. Pulled the trigger. The body spasmed, like he'd been administered an electric shock, and then it was static. Wiping the brain-smeared barrel up and down the guy's back, he nicked the PP2000, a Gucci addition to his arsenal.

Voices to the left. He instinctively ducked behind the jeep's frame, just in time as a volley of bullets whizzed overhead.

Markarets. Had to be.

As the last shot sounded, Coldrain sprang to his feet, Browning poised in a two-handed firing stance. But he was aiming at shadows, two of them, darting into a two-floor structure with a hole punched in the ground-floor wall.

He was in a marketplace of some kind. Street stalls abounded. Some with fresh goat meat hanging from hooks.

Others were little more than rickety tables displaying slapdash wares, individual cigarettes, bottles of Coke and Pepsi, any shit local people could lay their hands on. Then that half-thought he had earlier returned, itching to be completed.

What's wrong with this scene?

People, that's what was wrong. There were no people. Coldrain didn't see any hustlers. They had all abandoned their stalls.

Nobody's here.

Yeah, another voice countered, but a place like this, you don't expect it to be overflowing with people. Hadn't the Sandman mentioned something about a mass exodus as well?

Empty streets just as Dogan and Markarets roll into town.

Coldrain moved round the jeep and got his answer. Slouched against the wall perpendicular to the hole he was angling towards, a line of bodies, thirty or more, three rows deep, nothing visible of the corpses buried at the bottom except for a hand here, a leg there, or a strand of blood-matted hair. Piles of spent brass lying next to them. Blood streaked up and down the wall. Thick, jelly-like pools of it around the corpses, decanting from every orifice. Eyes, noses, ears, arseholes, exit wounds, the lot.

They were not the only corpses. As he looked up, Coldrain made out a carpet of children's bodies, their head cavities split open. Women too. So thick were the bodies splayed across the street that you could walk down the road without your feet ever touching the ground.

Rabid dogs feasted on their limbs, tearing off elastic tendons. Coldrain had heard about the existence of rabies-infected canines in this part of the world. Wild, neglected, disease-infested animals that resorted to eating human flesh, and then acquired a taste for it that developed into a thirst. Like zombies. He had dismissed it as so much mess-hall BS, but now he saw they were fucking real. It was a brutal death for these kids, shocking even to Coldrain. Next to them was a stack of AK-47s arranged in a tepee shape.

The conclusion was crystal-clear now.

Markarets was in control of Mogadishu. Not just combating the militias, but actually conquering the place. And slaughtering civilians as a shock tactic.

Everything began to make sense. This was an old-fashioned invasion, Nazi-style. Take what you want, and kill anyone who dares stand in your way. That much Coldrain could understand. But he couldn't see why Dogan and Markarets were launching it on an anarchistic hellhole like Somalia.

He stepped towards the hole the two figures had ducked into. It was a door, Somali-style, leading into a bare living room. Making his approach from the right side of the hole, Coldrain deposited the Browning in the rubble and switched to the PP2000. His left bicep screamed and he twisted his arm so he could inspect the wound. The round had entered through the front of the upper arm, bursting out to the rear, through his triceps brachii. *Bastard*. At least the round had exited, rather than lodging inside the muscle. Whenever he bent his arm or straightened it, an intense jolt of pain hit him, like someone sticking a million syringes into the muscles all at once.

He buried the pain. Silenced it. Forced his bruised, sticky fingers on his left hand to bind themselves around the smaller front-hand grip, used his right to hold the pistol grip, and tucked the stock into his right shoulder. A red-dot laser was fixed to the top of the receiver. That would come in handy when he burst into the room. His left arm still caned, but at least he was in a position to discharge bullets. The agony, he could live with for awhile.

Coldrain took a three count. Drew long, deep breaths. His lungs throbbed. Breathing in hurt. Breathing out hurt. Shit, everything hurt. He hoped the Sandman's contract included health insurance.

A step forward, then another, and he entered the room.

FIFTY-SIX

He saw five figures huddled in the middle.

A family. Old man dressed in a wraparound sarong and shirt, his wife much younger and supermodel-hot, a green direh covering her flowing underdress and a hijab pulled over her head. The three kids all wore football tops and scuffed jeans. The family didn't seem much scared or shocked by the guy standing in their makeshift front door wielding a Russian sub-machine gun. One of the kids, a Liverpool shirt covering his bloated belly, tried to stand up and reach out for the PP2000, and his mother quickly threw an arm around his chest, clamping him tight to her bosom. The old man was chewing absent-mindedly on some *khat* leaves.

A few tired flames flickered from an old stove, casting their shadows onto the red clay walls. The living room also doubled up as a bedroom, with a single large mattress in one corner, the label still attached, and a few posters on the walls. A shawl was laid out to the right with several objects placed on it in a neat row. Old screwdrivers and hammers, some pairs of glasses, a few first-generation Nokia mobiles. This guy must be one of the market sellers, he thought.

The dirt floor was spotless.

There were three doors connected to the living room. One at the far end, one to the left and one on the right-side wall. Coldrain figured one door led to the kitchen, and one was for the bathroom. The door at the rear of the room was made out of some sort of animal hide, and two more kids came dashing through it as Coldrain entered. He smelled coconut and pepper. Kitchen.

The kid finally wriggled free of his mother's clutches and ran up to Coldrain. Stood not two feet from him, staring up at Coldrain's sweat-smeared face. The kid's high Nilotic forehead and razor sharp eyes lent him an adult complexion. Probably the kid had seen more shit than most people did in their entire lives. The kid ran his eyes up and down the man in front of him. They fixed on the gun. Coldrain felt sorry for him. He was not sure what to do, so he asked him for his name.

'Ahmed,' the kid replied.

'Dan,' he said, extended his hand. The kid shook it. To Coldrain it weighed no more than a paper ball.

'Ahmed, do you want to play a game?'

The kid nodded.

'The game is called Find the Bad Man.' Ahmed watched him carefully. 'Do you know where the bad man is?'

The kid pointed to the right-sided door.

'In there,' he said.

'Good boy.'

The kid was suddenly scared and ran back to his mum. Coldrain moved tentatively forward. He didn't want the family kicking up a fuss, and he was mindful of showing respect to their dwelling. Put a finger to his lips and the child nodded enthusiastically.

Coldrain stopped at the side of the door and pressed

338

his ear close to the clay wall. Breathing softly through his nose, he tried to phase out the background noise, mostly made by his own body. He was hyper-sensitive, could hear his heart pumping and the blood rushing through his ears. But from the other side of the wall, he heard nothing. Coldrain's palms were clammy. He wiped his trigger hand down his trousers. He hated the idea of opening the door, exposing himself to an unknown funnel of fire. If he simply pulled at the door, chances were someone would be lying in wait on the other side. Ready to fill him in. There had to be another way.

Or maybe not.

Coldrain looked back to the family. The wife was staring at him, not terrified, but fascinated. He pointed to the animal-hide door. She looked towards the kitchen, at her kids, then back at Coldrain, as if seeking his permission to move about in her own fucking home. He nodded, *Yes, get the hell out of here*. The girl was smart. She took the hint, gathered up her sprogs and pulled the old man at his elbow. Paralysed from the waist down, he pushed himself forward on the palms of his hands, dragging his useless legs along the dirt floor behind him. As he reached the hide door, he turned and eyeballed Coldrain. Nodded, as if to say, get it done.

Alright then, I will.

The family were out of sight. Time to act.

As he prepared for combat, Coldrain asked himself what he was fighting for. He knew it had evolved into something other than pure vengeance. Jamie's killer was already dead. Markarets was an extension of that bloodline. More than that, he was remembering why he had taken up arms in the first place. Coldrain had answered the call of duty because he genuinely believed there were bad people out there, and, like rabid dogs, they needed to be stopped. True, he was more cynical these days. Jamie's death had rammed home the fact that bad things happened to good people, and the world was a truly fucked-up place. But there were still some causes worth fighting for. Like taking down a warlord only interested in invading weak, foreign nations and massacring the locals.

Besides, it wasn't fun to let the bad guys win.

Raising the PP2000 level with his lower chest, both hands on the firearm, Coldrain orientated himself so he was at the door face-on, but still to the right of it. Then he took a deep breath. Shifted along, kicked the door off its hinges and it fell back, revealing a gloomy brown stairwell. Vittled off several rounds into the opening, before flinging himself onto the wall on the opposite side of the door, to the left. Blowback gases and smoke gathered around his ankles. Little hot dust clouds. The last of the Parabellum cases dinked as it dropped to the dirt floor. But there was no return fire.

He heard footsteps. Fuck it. *Got to get up those stairs.*

In an instant he was bursting through the opening, machine gun pointed upwards. His pace was slowed by the staircase, adobe-brown and uneven, with an eight-inch riser between each tread that made bounding up them impossible. As he reached the top of the staircase, his peripheral vision was working overtime. Thinking, wall to the right, open window looking down over the street. Left, room with some kind of a calendar on the wall. A low exit cut into far end, leading out to the rooftop. Pool of sunlight, splitting the darkness in two.

And a black object. Left corner.

Metallic. Glinting.

Assault rifle.

He threw himself to the ground as bullets smacked into the wall behind him, readjusted himself, and, using the red-laser dot on the sight posts to guide his aim, unloaded an ear-splitting torrent of lead into the area around the rifle barrel. The PP2000 was venomous. Fast and accurate, the kickback was minimal, the rate of fire awesome. In a single depression he had unloaded the rest of his mag.

The assault rifle clattered to the floor, flecked red, the gunman's face and his mouth open in a kind of rictus grin.

Coldrain turned to the rooftop. He crouched by the low opening as a shitload of cartridges smacked into the ground, fifteen, twenty rounds. Two or three kicked up again, lodging in the flat rooftop and the opposite wall. He ejected the empty mag from the PP2000. Flipped out the spare magazine-slash-stock and slapped it into the housing unit on the underside of the pistol grip. Found the exposed end of the bolt carrier, on the upper-front section of the gun, and pulled it to charge. He was ready.

FIFTY-SEVEN

'**Y**ou have a problem,' Markarets said. He had a voice that could skin a rat and boil it for breakfast, and he spoke with a slight lisp.

'So my bird tells me,' Coldrain shouted back. 'But you're the one who should be worried right now. Your time is up, mate.'

Markarets laughed. It was a humming sound, sealed inside him, like he had a hive of bees in his belly, and told of a man who found death and war amusing in some perverse way. It was hard to tell if Markarets was laughing at Coldrain's crack, the gash situation he was in, or both.

'I like English expressions. Always they are distinctive, and you cannot easily find them in the language of my people. This special one. *The boot is on the other foot!* It means there has been a reversal of fortune, no? One moment you believe you are on top. The next, someone else is on top of you. Very good. So. You might want to look out of the window and see the boot.'

Coldrain shuffled backwards to the window, finger on the trigger, eyes on the opening. *Fuck the Sandman*, he thought, *if Markarets pops his mug round the corner I'm firing. Payday or no payday.* A bad feeling was brewing in his gut.

He slid up next to the window and peeked out. Only for a second, in case Markarets had a sniper waiting on a neighbouring rooftop ready to scalp him.

A second was enough.

Two APCs were pitching up next to the mangled Tiger. Woodland camo BTR-90s, Russian vehicles dating back to the Cold War. Nine soldiers clambered out of each BTR, dressed in black fireproof fatigues, ballistic helmets and body armour with studs on the front for extra pouches. Respirators on the faces, lead soldier wielding a riot shield, the man behind him sporting a chain of flashbangs that dangled from his body armour.

They would be pouring through into the living room at any moment. He was truly fucked.

In desperation he lay flat on his belly and discharged half his second mag into the opening at the bottom of the staircase. He hoped a round would ricochet off and strike one of the soldiers, maybe make his mates think twice before storming the treads, and buy him a precious few seconds to formulate an E&E plan. He also hoped the rounds wouldn't deflect into the kitchen and injure the parents or the kids.

Barely had the final brass bounced down the stairs than he clocked movement to his three o'clock, twisted on his core to find Markarets stooping down low, entering the room. The sunlight was blinding behind him, like he was caught in a solar eclipse, silhouetting the Serb. Coldrain had the red-dot resting on the spot between his eyes, half of him desperate for the bastard to try and have a pop. But Markarets wasn't packing. The gun was nowhere to be seen and his hands were empty, open, by his sides. He stood at the top of the staircase. Saw the dead guy in the corner and gave him a kick. Checking the dead guy was dead.

He glanced at Coldrain. Glazed eyes shaped like dagger slits looked him up and down, pure black pupils. His grey beard was immaculate, each hair clipped and straightened to equal length. Up close he seemed somehow taller than from afar. And younger too. According to his file, Markarets was fifty-one, but he did not look a day over forty. No crows' feet or creased brow. The patches beneath his eye were mottled, as though he suffered from a rash of some kind. He did not look much like a man of war, except for the knot of reddened skin where his left ear should have been.

'Tell me,' he said, crossing his arms. He looked away from Coldrain as he spoke. 'Are you familiar with King Leopold II?'

He produced two cigars from his breast pocket.

'The finest Cuban Cohibas. The story behind this cigar is an interesting one. One of Fidel Castro's bodyguards, a man by the name of Bienvenido Pérez, would suck on a very aromatic cigar in the presence of his great leader. Castro himself was struck by the smooth flavour. So one day he pulled Pérez to one side and asked him what brand of cigar this was that he smoked and was so delicious. Pérez replied that a friend of his rolled them. And so it became that this friend was asked to personally roll Cohiba cigars for Mr Castro. This was a task that was performed with great security and only Pérez was permitted to handle the cigars. Because, at the time, the CIA had considered the possibility of killing Castro by creating an exploding cigar.' He smiled. 'I liked this story very much. We used it to kill the Englishman in Kabul.'

Markarets bit the end of the cigar off with his teeth and spat it out onto the ground.

'Biting is considered a sin by tobacco experts,' he opined. 'They say it damages the binder and filler. Myself, I like the taste. And I am a man who believes the rules are there to be broken. Do you agree?'

Coldrain shrugged and watched Markarets strike a match against his beard. Gripping the cigar around the band using his thumb, index, middle and ring fingers, he raised the flame to just below the end of the cigar. He was careful not to let the cigar touch the flame. Then he slowly puffed on the Cohiba, blowing out thin pockets of smoke, rotating the cigar with his fingers as he did so, until the outer rim glowed. Now the smoke drew easily, blanketing his face.

He took several long puffs, then neared Coldrain and offered him the second cigar. Coldrain hesitated for a second, weighing up the situation. He was, in effect, a hostage. X-rays downstairs and a wannabe warlord for company upstairs. The outlook was gash-grim. If cooperating with Markarets would buy him a precious few minutes, then it was worth doing. Coldrain took the Cohiba and lit up. The smoke was silky-smooth and gently stroked his parched throat.

Markarets continued.

'The story of King Leopold is an interesting one also. You see, in the late nineteenth century, many of the great European empires were fighting over Africa. Every country wanted to exploit the raw wealth and opportunity. Gold. Diamonds. Copper. Leaders were drunk on the riches on offer. Yet those nations chose to stay close to the coastlines. Places like Italian Somaliland, you see, because accessing the interior of Africa was very difficult. Supply lines were almost impossible to maintain, the risk of malaria or sleeping sickness was great. King Leopold sensed this neglect of the heart of Africa, and seized his chance. He was a very skilled showman and persuader, and by manipulation of the political channels he succeeded in convincing the great European countries to transfer ownership of the Congo to him, personally.

'One man in control of an entire country. King Leopold was Congo Free State's sole shareholder and chairman. The country did not belong to Belgium, or the monarchy, but to Leopold himself. It was a big accomplishment. To this day, I do not know how this was ever possible, that a man could declare himself owner of a country that he had not even seen, and a people whose language was not his own, and that the world powers would accept such a situation. Incredible, do you agree?'

It was something all right, Coldrain thought. He had a four-letter word to describe it better.

Keep your gob shut, he told himself. *Play along until you've figured out your exit strategy. Because, right now, you don't have one.*

FIFTY-EIGHT

Markarets waffled on.

'Owning the Congo presented Leopold with a difficulty. You see, the running costs were very high. He had to pay the soldiers, the officials, and arrange for transport. All this needed money, and so Leopold began to exploit the great rubber and ivory wealth of the Congo Free State. And if the people of the Congo could not meet the quotas, they had to pay the white agents the difference in severed hands. Soldiers were required to present one hand for each bullet they had spent, to prove they did not waste ammunition on shooting wild animals.

'In this way, Leopold turned the Congo into one of the world's leading rubber producers.'

'Sounds like he turned it into world-class slaughterhouse too,' Coldrain said. He couldn't resist. Markarets appeared not to hear and went on, underterred.

'Everything in life costs something, costs a part of us. A man wishes to create a great rubber industry, he cannot do it with smiles and kindnesses. No. It is done through guns and tears. *"The great questions of the day will not be decided by speeches and resolutions of majorities, but by blood and iron."'*

'Otto von Bismarck.'

'You know your history. That is good. Today, of course, if you choose to study King Leopold's Congo, you will only read of humanitarian disaster and the struggles of the villagers. Stories of children having their hands smashed to bits by the butt of a white agent's rifle, and of unruly gangs passing from village to village and cutting off the hands of each man, woman and child so they can meet their payments to the state officials. But that is to focus on the pain, rather than the consequence.'

Coldrain looked down at the PP2000. Half a mag left, that worked out to fifteen rounds. If he popped two into Markarets, that left thirteen for the death squad downstairs. With the kind of firepower they were packing, he would be massively outgunned. *Maybe I can make a run for it across the rooftop. Markarets' weapon should be out there too. I could ditch the PP, get the new firearm and go rooftop-hopping.* Then he remembered that half the buildings around here were palm-leaf roofs and wouldn't support his weight. And the chopper was somewhere out there too.

'It is possible to change the world with a gun, but only if you have the genius to match its deadly nature,' Markarets was saying. His back was to Coldrain. He could pop the rounds off now, no problem. But something inside was stopping him from following through.

'I have big plans for Somalia, like Leopold had for Congo. First, however, I must control the country and in this world you cannot barter for the ownership of a land with those imbeciles at the United Nations. You must take it by force. Mogadishu falls, the rest of the country will fall with it soon enough. Eliminating the gangs has been easy so far. They are weak and we are strong. I have pulled men from the best militias in the world, and they are more than a match for the local forces. FARC guerrillas, insurgents from Iraq, Chechen freedom fighters. Tamil Tigers. They are all in my army, and ready to fight.

'We work on a single rule. Any Somali who protests is killed. It is a simple message for a country schooled in barbarism. Once we have the country we usher in a brave new age, the age of the political strongman. No more weakness, no more bargaining and shoe-horning and calling it democracy.'

'You're fucking nuts.'

'It is the nature of genius that at first glance it seems insane.'

'Is that what you told the mug bankrolling this op?'

That laugh again. 'To adopt a saying from your country, where there is oil, there is a way. There is plenty of oil in the Puntland province in the north of the country. They say as many as ten billion barrels of it. That is cause enough for some countries to go to war. It can sometimes be enough for countries to look the other way.'

Sod it, Coldrain thought. *I've got to ice this psycho, even if I take one myself. He's lost his marbles and he's in control of a fucking evil army. Hand-picked terrorists from around the globe, running amok in a lawless state off the global radar. If I don't kill him now, there's no telling what kind of destruction he might wreak.*

'Join me,' Markarets said, turning back to face Coldrain just as he was reaching for the PP2000. He was so stunned by the offer his hand froze near to the weapon. Markarets seemed not to notice the movement. Or maybe he did, and he just didn't care. 'We are men of action, not words. I saw how you killed Dogan. That was unfortunate, but with him it was merely a matter of time before it happened. All that blood spilled. Either you would do it, or at some point someone else would. It was as inevitable as the rising of the sun. But you were impressive. Bold, yes. Fearless, yes. I could use a soldier like you.'

Coldrain spat the cigar out. The Cohiba rolled across the dirt floor. 'Sorry, mate, but I'd rather cut my own hands off than work for a piece of shit like you.'

Markarets nodded solemnly, eyes lowered. 'I give you one more chance.'

'Maybe you didn't hear,' Coldrain snapped. 'Fuck off.'

'Kill him!' he shouted, voice projecting downstairs. Then he stood over Coldrain. 'Now, it is you who have the problem.'

Markarets made for the opening and as Coldrain wrapped his hand around the PP2000 grip, he felt something brush against his left leg. Looked down and saw a black cylindrical tube with holes down the side and a clipper on the top and knew it was a flashbang. It had rolled to a stop right next to his knee. There was no time to react.

Every operator in the trade knew that, although flashbangs were classified as a non-lethal weapon, they could still cause some serious damage. When the volatile mix of aluminium and potassium perchlorate detonated, it created a pressure wave of over 30,000 pounds per square inch, and although the tube body stayed intact, some of that explosive compound emitting from the holes could cause horrific burn injuries. It was like a small bomb going off.

He tried desperately to kick it away, but at the same time he saw Markarets disappearing through the opening, back out onto the rooftop, taking one last look back at

Coldrain, and he had a split second to decide – pop a round into the bastard's back or kick away the flashbang – but he could not choose, and then, suddenly, he was out of time.

FIFTY-NINE

His world melted away into a scorching white nothing-ness.

Coldrain did not even hear the flashbang detonate. There was the grenade resting by his kneecap, and then suddenly everything seemed to burn up. Light, and a shrill, irre-pressible ringing noise in his ears that drilled all the way through to his brain. He did not know where he was, he did not know his name, or how he had got there. A thousand headaches criss-crossed his skull all at once. The whiteness seemed to stretch for ever.

And then cracks started to appear. Faint lines, colours, blocks. His head was throbbing and the ringing continued, but he knew his name. Dan Coldrain. He remembered he was in a house in Mogadishu, Somalia, and that he had been after a killer, though he could not quite recall who. It was like waking up from a bad dream and not yet sure what was real and what was fantasy.

Sensations poured through the cracks. He felt a stinging pain on his knee joint. Could smell burning flesh and fabric, and figured that the flashbang had melted away the skin around his kneecap. To the cut forehead, bullet in the bicep and the aching shoulders, throw in a burnt knee. He could make out shapes now. Dirt floor. Clay walls. Opening that led out to a rooftop. Someone had escaped through there. The killer? He wasn't sure, but he thought so.

Body in the corner.

And another coming up the stairs.

The figure was eight metres away when Coldrain saw him. At first he identified the head. Black ballistic helmet, anti-flash goggles protecting the eyes and a nomex balaclava layered beneath, respirator gas mask covering the mouth. Then he noticed the combat assault rifle beneath the mask, pointed directly at Coldrain.

He remembered something else. He had a weapon. Yes. The PP2000. Where was it? He still could not see properly, half the world was bleeding white, and he hurriedly felt around the floor with his fingers like a blind man. Found something cold and round.

The barrel. *Grab it.*

The weapon was heavier than he expected. No, the gun didn't weigh more. His left arm was weaker. That was it. The blood loss from the exit wound taking its toll. Coldrain had to summon all his energy to drag the PP2000 onto his lap. By instinct he found the pistol grip with his right hand. The figure was almost at the top of the stairs now, just four feet away, and Coldrain couldn't make the aim true with the red-dot sight. Mustering all his strength, he just about managed to align the barrel vaguely in the direction of the X-ray.

He unleashed a four-round burst, back of the weapon jabbing into his stomach with the kickback. And, miraculously, he was on target. The figure jerked, dropped the assault rifle and fell backwards down the stairs, blood speckled along the red-clay treads. Coldrain was conscious enough to curse himself for wasting four whole fucking rounds on the bad guy. One or two would have done the job. That left him with eleven bullets, and he knew there were at least eighteen other X-rays downstairs. Maybe more. Even if he was the most shit-hot marksman in human history, there was no way he was getting out of this clusterfuck in one piece.

Coldrain made his mind up there and then. He would go down fighting. Take as many of these wankers down as possible. He was a soldier. A Marine. *Bootneck*. Taught never to give in, never to surrender.

Two more X-rays launched up the stairs, side-stepping their zapped buddy, weapons poised. Ready to kill. Coldrain lowered the PP2000. Used his busted left arm, half numb from the extreme blood loss, to flick the switch and change his weapon to single-shot. His training was taking over. *Conserve your ammo. Wait for a lull then pick up the dead guy's assault rifle.*

He fired once at the target on the right.

Missed.

Second shot. Caught the X-ray through the goggles. One moment they were clear, see-thru, and the next they were filled in red. He stumbled back, shaking his head frantically, trying to remove the respirator as he choked on his own blood. Coldrain smoothly twisted the barrel to the right and took aim at the second X-ray. Fired, and missed again. Shit, he really couldn't afford to fuck this up now. The guy had his finger on the assault rifle trigger. Coldrain pumped out a single shot. It struck the guy on his hand. He dropped the rifle. It clattered to the ground. He went to pick it up and Coldrain was working the PP2000, depressing the trigger, slamming a second round into the back of the guy's head. He collapsed. Lifeless.

Coldrain thinking, four shots expended, when he could

have used just two. What a fucking waste. What a pathetic way to go. Not only caught in a firefight, but unable to properly perform the actions he had been taught hundreds of times in training. That, somehow, disappointed him more than the fact he was about to die. He had let himself down.

Now three more X-rays were testing their luck, backed up by two more behind them, and Coldrain knew that, in his state, his remaining seven rounds would not be enough to take down five bad guys.

He fired three shots in quick succession at the figures as they leapt up the corpse-laden stairs. All of them missed. Little bobbles of red clay were flicked through the air. He spent the last four 9x19mm Parabellum cartridges. One struck the closest guy on his ballistic helmet and skidded off. A helmet scratch, and sod-all else. The other three smacked into the legs and groin of the leftmost target. He howled in agony and clutched his mangled ball sack, his fingers covered in gooey green shit, but his mates weren't rushing over to help him. They were far more concerned with putting one through Coldrain's head.

In a last act of defiance he threw the PP2000 itself towards the figures. Used the good strength in his right arm, and the chad strength in his left. But there was not enough leverage on the throw and it fell short, landing sadly at their feet on the last tread. The closest X-ray kicked it away and took aim with his assault rifle.

It was over.

SIXTY

He closed his eyes and did not expect to open them again. Thought, *This is it. Well, fucking bring it on then.*

Did not expect to open them again and was surprised when he could. For a second he did not know what to make of it. *Maybe I've taken one to the head*, he thought. *Maybe this is what it is like to die, to be nearly dead. You're shot and you don't even feel it.*

Then he felt an incredible weight crushing against him. His body giving in, finally, belatedly, to the fatal wound. He'd never experienced a pressure like it before. It felt as if a building was falling on top of him. He felt the life force slowly seeping out of him. It was an excruciatingly slow process, this dying. He'd assumed it would be over in the blink of an eye, not some sort of agonising, drawn-out hell.

He heard more gunshots. These ones were muffled, as though being fired from a great distance away, but he recognised the ferocity of each discharge. Not combat assault rifle reports. The low thud and the dense rumble, it was unmistakably a Browning .50 cal heavy machine gun. The rounds were fired in slow, methodical bursts. He counted twelve of them, each one separated by a rolling echo like a lightning-bolt strike, and a gaggle of panicky voices. Screams. Just as quickly as they had erupted, they finished. There was silence. He waited to die.

Suddenly, there was light. He felt the weight on his body lighten. He could breathe, barely. Took in deep, desperate drags of air. Rubbed his eyes. Thought, *I'm not dead. I can't believe it. I'm not dead.*

And then he heard voices and looked up. There was a man standing over him, dragging the X-ray's contorted, limp body off of him. At first he couldn't understand, couldn't even begin to process what was happening. But recognised the man, remembered who it was, clocked the sinewy frame and wraparound shades and tight lips. And he began, very slowly, to understand.

SIXTY-ONE

'You intending to lie there for ever?' Outlaw said. He offered a hand for a gimme-up. Coldrain seized it. He slowly rose to his feet. The pain in his left knee came into sharp focus. He looked down at the wound and saw that his knee was in rag order. The flesh burnt away, as though acid had been poured onto it, exposing pinkish-red tissue. It was painful to look at it, and it hurt a million times more to flex it. He caught Outlaw inspecting the wound.

'Getting my Halloween rig sorted,' he croaked.

'Two's up,' Outlaw replied, gesturing to his fingers. The tourniquet was dark red. 'At least we'll be the freakiest motherfuckers on the town.'

'You're bleeding bad. We need to get you to a doctor.'

'First, chief, we got to get the hell out of here.'

Hobbling down the stairs, arm slung across Outlaw, they kicked aside the bodies. One bad guy was still writhing on the floor, half-conscious, and Outlaw paused, watched him struggle and then popped a round into his skull.

No mercy.

There were bodies everywhere. Eight in the living room, nine if you counted the random severed arm and entrails splashed liberally across the dirt floor. He looked towards the animal hide door, and saw a young pair of eyes peering out from within. Ahmed, staring blankly back at Coldrain. Dead bodies in his living room and the kid wasn't even upset. It was a hard life out here, that was for sure.

Crawling out into the street, Coldrain was heartened by what he saw. McGrady on a pick-up truck in the middle of the road, with a .50 cal Browning 'Ma Deuce' mounted on the back.

'Like my new toy?'

'Where the fuck did you get that?'

'Fell off the back of a truck, mate. Or we slit the throat of the guy operating it. What do you think?'

Loading the .50 cal and making sure the feed tray cover was down and the bolt forward, McGrady fed the ammo belt with the double-loop side first past the belt-feeder prawls, making sure that the engraving on each round was facing up. Placing his hand palm up on the charging handle, he gave it a firm tug and slid the bolt forward. Then he pulled back on the charging handle and released it as the bolt slid forward again, locking the bolt latch down to set it to automatic fire mode.

'I see X-rays, three of them, to your two o'clock,' Outlaw shouted.

'Got 'em.'

McGrady vittled some rounds against a trio of X-rays positioned in the mouth of a bombed-out building to the right of the street. The standard rounds on the link were M33 ball, no armour-piercing or incendiary properties, nothing fancy. But still deadly as fuck.

The first M33 rounds were fired off, creating a massive shock wave so deadly that anyone standing within five feet of its trajectory would have their arm blow clean off.

Coldrain could feel his bones vibrate as McGrady rattled off round after incessant round. It was dark in the mouth of the building, like someone had draped black tarpaulin over it, so Coldrain could not see how much damage the .50 cal was causing. But he got a sneak preview after five rounds, when a human head, jaw blown off, rolled out into the street.

'Now you see them, now you don't.'

Five metres to his right he saw Belkevich, leaning against the mauled front wheel of the Tiger. Keeping his head behind cover, waiting to pick off X-rays with his Dragunov. Coldrain tried to say something to him, but felt nauseous and coughed up blood.

Something buzzed overhead. Coldrain arched his neck and scanned the sky.

The Mil Mi-8, its five blades slicing up the air.

SIXTY-TWO

The 127 MIL canon whirred into action. Everyone ducked down behind cover. Rounds tore up the street, bullets striking the dead bodies. The sound of the gun, and the dead flesh being punctured. That was their universe. They could not see, or hear, anything else.

An air-to-surface missile cruised into one of the APC carriers, tossing it through the air like a toy model. It landed, flipped upside down, the chassis burnt black, on the other side of the road.

'Think they're trying to send us a message?' Outlaw cracked.

'Something like, "Our guns are bigger than yours."'

'Whatever the fuck it means, we're not getting out of here until that chopper is neutralised.'

'If we had an RPG, I could take it down in one hit straight to the rotary blades.'

'Yeah, but we don't. Got fucking M4s and nothing else.'

Belkevich stepped up to the plate.

'You cover me,' he said. It wasn't a request.

Before Coldrain could even respond, the burly Russian was taking aim with the Dragunov, resting the muzzle on the Tiger hood.

Coldrain vittled off some more rounds to distract the pilot.

'Help me out here, lads,' he shouted to Outlaw and McGrady. 'Give the chopper everything you've got.'

Belkevich seemed to take for ever to aim, all the while the Mi-8 circling through the air, banking left and right, floating high then drifting low, avoiding their M4 sprays with ease. Coldrain finished the clip and fished for another. The mag scalded his skin.

'What the fuck is he doing?'

'I don't know, mate, but whatever it is, he'd better do it quick. I'm on my last clip.'

Finally, the helicopter was coming in for a second run. It spun around at the far end of Bakara Market, angling to face them, and steamed forwards. Any second now it was going to unleash a fearsome barrage of rockets and bullets. They were about to be torn gopping big new arseholes.

Belkevich pulled the trigger.

His right shoulder jerked slightly. For a split second, Coldrain thought Belkevich had missed. Nothing had happened. The bird was still coming towards them, Belkevich was still aiming at the helicopter. He wondered what the hell was going on.

A split second later and a second fireball filled the sky. Not a rocket being launched. It was bigger, like the sun itself had landed in the middle of fucking Mogadishu. The bird was on fire, spinning through a frantic three hundred and sixty-degree arc, losing velocity, losing control, losing everything. It slid down by the side of a housing block, the rotary blades hacking against the adobe wall.

Then it crashed to the ground amid a cacophony of

twisting metal and flying sparks and exploding parts. The blades cut up the street, slicing up protruding limbs.

They slowed.

They stopped.

'Smart-ass son of a bitch,' Outlaw shouted out. 'You went for the rocket pod, right?'

Coldrain punched Belkevich on the shoulder.

'Fucking well done, mate,' he said.

He didn't respond.

'Cheer up, I'm buying the first round tonight, mate.'

Nothing.

His neck was swollen and drenched in greasy blood. There was a hole about an inch and a half high by an inch and a quarter wide, located directly in the middle line below his chin. He had taken a 127mm round clean. Between the pumps of blood he could make out gristle and bone belonging to his cervical column.

Air entered through the hole. Coldrain knew that wasn't a good sign, because it meant the bullet had torn a large temporal cavity through Belkevich's neck. He rolled Belkevich onto his side, not easy with a limp body that big, and inspected the exit wound. There was a violent, misshapen rupture at the lower rear of his nape, in the area between his clavicle and shoulder blade, big enough to place an orange in.

Coldrain switched to CPR, giving the chest a couple of pumps and then started breathing into Belkevich's mouth, pinching his nostrils as he did so. When he blew into his mouth Coldrain could see blood bubbling in the nose and around the entry wound. Pumping the chest was difficult because it increased the blood gushing out of his neck.

Outlaw rushed over. Knelt down beside him, pressing his hands down against the wound, trying to stem the bleeding. His hands dark red, and occasionally blood would squirt up into his face.

The mouth-to-mouth quickly became impossible. Belkevich, unconscious, vomited, clogging his airways. Coldrain had to roll him back onto his side again to try and eject as much of the sick from his mouth and lungs as possible. He was drowning in his own blood.

Coldrain checked for a pulse again.

'He's bleeding out.'

His arms were coated in dark, glistening blood from his fingertips all the way up to his elbows.

The ground around his knees was awash with blood. He tried to continue with the CPR but the air just kept getting blown back up at him from Belkevich's blocked lungs, and Outlaw was losing his battle with the wound, pressing down so hard that his hands were in danger of crushing the ribcage. The blood still flowed.

Coldrain finally gave up the ghost.

Belkevich was dead.

SIXTY-THREE

He watched as the last bad guy made a run down the street, weaving between the Somali bodies. Coldrain took Belkevich's Dragunov, aimed, and fired a single round in his direction, bang on the money, and the guy's head exploded like a water balloon being pricked. Something deep inside Coldrain was satisfied. It didn't count for much, and it wasn't exactly revenge, but zapping that last guy felt bloody good.

A sudden wave of exhaustion hit Coldrain. He dropped the Dragunov, rested his head against the ground, and dreamt about an ice-cold water pitcher. His lips were cracked and bleeding sore, and white shit had collected at the corners of his lips. His vision was blotchy.

When he looked up again he saw Outlaw was on mop-up duty, strolling through the rubble, shooting anyone still breathing. It wasn't exactly Geneva Convention shit, but this wasn't an everyday kind of war.

Coldrain reached over to examine the body of the closest X-ray. He pulled back the sleeve on the fireproof assault top and checked out his wrist. Sure enough, a tattoo. Tibetan wolf. Black outline of a vicious-looking fucker. The same one that was painted onto the arms of the soldiers at Novo Krsto.

His phone range. Coldrain was surprised the thing still worked.

He answered.

SIXTY-FOUR

'What's going on?'

The line was distressed. The voice screeched.

Coldrain's ears, ringing from the tumult of battle, struggled to pick up the voice at first. He was disorientated. Badly. Felt as if someone had shaken him inside a mini-globe, his senses confused, his brain scrambled. And it hurt to breathe, like a boa constrictor had him in its grip. He spat out bloody spit and wiped sweat from his forehead. The head mist cleared a little.

'You won't believe what's going on here,' Coldrain said. Thinking, *Fuck it, not even I can believe it.* 'It's all kicking off. Battleships, tanks, APCs, militia . . .' His voice trailed. 'The fucking lot.'

'Yes, yes, I know,' the Sandman said, irritated. There was some interference, squawking on the line, and Coldrain had to hold it away from his ear. 'Hello? Daniel? Are you there?'

'Yeah.' He said no more, waited for the Sandman to continue.

'Where is Markarets?'

'He got away. A bunch of his cronies didn't.'

'Good. Your orders are to head to the evacuation RV immediately.'

'But what about Markarets?'

'Forget it. We'll deal with him later. It's more important you get out of there alive.'

Coldrain licked his lips. He wanted a glass of water more than anything else in the world. A thought broke the spell. *Since when did the Sandman place the safety of his men above the value of the mission?*

Easy. Since, well, fucking never.

'You don't want Markarets dead, do you?'

The Sandman didn't answer, so he repeated the question. Slower, just in case the old fixer was getting hard of hearing.

'I do not decide the targets, Daniel. You know full well that I have my own people to answer to.'

'The ones who write your cheques.'

'That is none of your business.'

'I thought so. But let me get this straight. Whoever asked you to hunt down Dogan doesn't want us to wipe out Markarets. Is that it?'

'They have their reasons,' the Sandman said. His tone was muted.

'You should see what he's done here. Bodies everywhere. Innocent people. What sick bastard would let Markarets get away with it?'

The Sandman was quiet again. The line crackled, like someone was screwing up paper next to the speaker. Coldrain shifted, the signal increased, he listened out for the Sandman.

'Are you there?' he said.

'They have their reasons,' the Sandman replied.

SIXTY-FIVE

Killing Markarets is off limits, he had told them, and they had groaned collectively. After all, they were ultimate warriors, the elite of the world's forces, and it was a mark of their dedication and skill that, even though they were all three injured, and the fourth man KIA, they still preferred to get the job done rather than bug out to the RV and leave Mogadishu to go to hell in a handcart.

We can't kill Markarets, Coldrain continued, *but that doesn't mean we can't cripple him.* We'll hit him where it hurts. Sink those ships. Destroy those tanks. Give the local militias a fighting chance, and scupper Markarets' grand strategy. He would live, but the twisted dream he harboured would be left in tatters.

Suddenly Outlaw and McGrady were beaming. They agreed it sounded like a good plan.

And, besides, Coldrain couldn't shake the image of the kid. No one else was going to look out for him. If the tanks came rolling in, the kid was finished. Coldrain knew nothing about the kid except his name, but he knew that he wouldn't let Ahmed down.

The Black Hawk was waiting for them at the RV, ten miles north of Mogadishu, in some dry scrubland, long-bodied, asparagus-coloured, its two distinctive, large blades slicing up the air a hundred feet above. Coldrain and his team needed to remove a pile of rocks directly in front of the landing platform. The rocks were heavy and it was a task that had him truly hanging out on his arse. He shook the pilot's hand. Asked for his name.

'Jake La Frentz.' He spoke with a drawl. It took him ten years to say each word.

'What sort of armament you packing today?'

He grinned, almost as if he could read Coldrain's mind. 'Got the 7.62mm minigun mount, got the 70-mil rocket pods, got the Hellfire air-to-ground missiles too. You know how I do. This is a Black Hawk, brother. Bells and whistles war machine.'

'Well, Jake, I hope you don't mind, but we'd like to take a little detour.'

La Frentz chewed on his gum.

'I'm not due for any detour. Orders are, evac you boys back to Mombasa and call it a day.'

Coldrain nodded.

'Where are you from, Jake?'

'Houston, Texas, and damn proud of it too.'

'How would you feel if a bunch of Taliban and guerrillas invaded Houston, mate?'

'I'd fucking waste 'em,' he replied eagerly.

'See, there's a bunch of insurgents and militiamen down at the harbour, and they've got similar plans for Mogadishu. Take it over, kill the locals, help themselves to whatever the country has to offer. Now, that doesn't sound right to me. And I'm hoping it doesn't sound right to you, neither.'

'It don't. But orders is orders.'

'Fair enough, so why don't you do the detour, fire your

missiles, and then afterwards you can tell the Sandman I had a gun to your head for the whole trip. I'll take the can on this one.'

La Frentz's eyes were out on stalks.

'You sure about this, pal?'

'Yeah, why the fuck not.' He was going to add that he seemed to have developed a conscience, but he knew the others would just take the piss and call him a pussy. So he kept that little thought to himself.

They were on the harbour in less than five minutes.

The boats sat fastened at the port side. Tanks lined on the docks, soldiers milling about.

Sitting ducks.

'Lock on,' La Frentz said coolly.

The Black Hawk edged forward, like a plane making its final descent, gradually nosing downwards until the sky disappeared and all Coldrain could see, peering in from the rear, was a wide bank of bright blue sea, with the Newport-class tank landing ship dead centre in their field of vision.

The first Hellfire was launched with a sharp, brief hiss as it ignited, released from the side rails, fire stream spilling out from the back of the unit. Coldrain watched, transfixed, as the AGM-114 glided on a downward trajectory, fumes spilling out from the back of the missile. Soon it became a glowing orange-white tip against the cloudless sky. As a thermobaric round, it was guaranteed to smash any tank in the world. Atmospheric oxygen would initiate the explosion, using heat and overpressure to obliterate the target. A lethal weapon heading straight for the tank lander.

Below, a few X-rays had spotted the Black Hawk and the Hellfire and ran for their lives. One optimistic prick let off a couple of cracks of his assault rifle skywards.

'That's not gonna help, mate,' McGrady wisecracked.

Suddenly a massive bright orange fireball erupted in the middle of the ship. An expanding mushroom of smoke and debris belched.

La Frentz released more Hellfires.

Each ship took a direct hit. Flames licked at the sea. As they passed over the sinking fleet, McGrady took the side-mounted 7.62mm minigun and caned the area with lead. They were a hundred feet off the ground and the X-rays were the size of insects, but their deaths looked real enough as they scrambled, jerked, toppled. They crawled for cover, but when death comes from above, there's nowhere to hide. The Black Hawk had no concept of mercy. Only of overwhelming destruction. As the men jumped out of the boat and into the orange-shaded, greasy waters, Coldrain thought they looked like ants escaping an ant hill. Reminded him of days spent in the summer holidays with Jamie, finding ant colonies and pouring hot water into them.

The carnage was incessant. Unrelenting. Rounds slammed. McGrady was a man on a mission. The Black Hawk returned for a second sweep, and McGrady kept the minigun rolling, Outlaw feeding rounds into the belt. On the second survey they totalled the remaining struc-tures, the gunfire so intense that flames licked the end of the minigun and travelled down the barrel. McGrady emptied the belt feed anyway, just as the flames reached midway down the barrel and singed his hands. He released the minigun and collapsed into a heap on the floor. Phys-ically spent from unleashing hell on the forces below. Mogadishu harbour, from this height, looked as if an atom bomb had been dropped on it. Structures bled flames and smoke the colour of arsenic. The smell of burnt human flesh reached Coldrain's nostrils. Like barbecued pork smeared in shit.

La Frentz banked the chopper south, straddling the brilliantly lit coastline, and Coldrain watched the harbour retreat into the distance, small pockets of fire flickering around the boats, a shit-ton of X-rays motionless on the wharf.

Outlaw pulled out a blunt.

'Give me one of those,' Coldrain said.

'My advice. Stick to cigars. Got a better taste to 'em than cigarettes.'

McGrady was propped up against the side of the fuselage.

'So what happens to Markarets?'

'Fuck him, mate,' Coldrain said. 'He's in the Government's pocket.'

McGrady's eyes widened. 'Ours?'

'British or American, it doesn't really matter who. Point is, someone high up the food chain is looking out for Markarets' arse. He mentioned something about oil. My guess is that whoever was bankrolling his mini-war here, they were hoping for a share of the spoils. Cheap oil, mate.'

Coldrain asked La Frentz if he had any water. The Texan gestured to a jerrycan lying amid a SPIE rig, ropes and shit. He figured it was treated stuff, probably river water mixed with a purification tablet. It smelled horrible but tasted better than the finest wine. He took three long, satisfying gulps and felt half alive again.

'But I thought our governments wanted Dogan out of the picture.'

'Dogan, yeah. But they never mentioned Markarets and even denied knowing about him outright when the

373

Sandman first mentioned his name. At least, that's what he told me.'

'So maybe there was a rift between Dogan and Markarets. One side playing the other.'

'Something like that. Thing is, Markarets wasn't exactly upset about me killing Dogan. I reckon he was going to get whatever happened. Probably Dogan had gone behind Markarets' back and tried to strike a deal over the oil with another country. China, India, who knows. Loads of nations would peel their eyelids off to get access to some cut-price oil, no matter how illegitimate the source.'

'So the US and UK do a deal with Markarets and Dogan, bankroll some fucking invasion of Somalia, then agree to take the oil at a discount in return. What kind of fucked up is that?'

'All kinds, mate. But I guess if no one knows about the link between HMG, the Oval Office and guys like Markarets, then the benefits outweigh the risk. All they need to do is recognise the new Somali government, and put some puppets in charge with no real authority. Lean on their mates in the EU and NATO to do the same, and, hey presto, you can start doing business.'

Outlaw shook his head. 'That's messed up.'

'Defo.'

'I mean, real fucked in the head.'

Coldrain tied himself to a lanyard, propped himself up at the side exit of the Black Hawk and let his feet rest on the side rails. A cool wind blew across his face. He looked back at the harbour. The shoreline was idyllic and could have passed for some luxury beach in Mexico. Except for the arsenic smoke spewing out of the harbour and billowing skywards, like a metal volcano erupting.

He nudged his brain; reminded himself that he had a

phone call to make when they landed. Coldrain dug the card out of his pocket, the dark pink square with Ischenko's name printed on it. On the reverse, he had written down another number in biro. Below the digits he had noted 'RIBBECH'. He'd give the German the news of the Somalia operation. Expose the truth. Anonymously, of course, and under the condition that the story was credited fully to the late Anika N. Ischenko. 'N' rather than her middle name, because everyone had their secrets.

She was mine, Coldrain thought.

She always will be.

'What'll you do when you get back?' Outlaw asked him as Coldrain gave his pang of guilt the cold shoulder. 'You know for sure the Sandman ain't gonna pay. Especially after we just spunked away a few million on them Hellfires.'

'I dunno. I'd say sort my life out, but that sounds too much like hard work, and to be honest, I'm not about to get down on one knee for my bird.' He took another draw on the blunt. 'That just ain't me.'

'Back on the circuit again?'

'Who knows? It'd have to be for the right reasons, mate.'

'I'm not sure there is one.' Outlaw felt for the dressing on his gash finger. 'You either do something or you don't. Ain't no rhyme or reason to it.'

Coldrain shook his head. Gestured towards Belkevich's corpse.

'You're forgetting the big man,' he said. 'Poor bastard didn't have to be out here, doing this shit. But he saved our bacon today. He made the ultimate sacrifice.'

'Just like Jamie,' Outlaw replied.

'I suppose so, yeah.'

He looked back out of the chopper. Was it about sacrifice? He hadn't given much thought to it before. But Jamie dying, out there, when he looked back on it now it didn't seem so futile. Any soldier, in any combat zone, had to be prepared to lay down their life. Stick around long enough and it would come and get you in the end. Jamie's number had been up before his own. Boil it down and that was what you were left with. Well, Coldrain told himself, maybe the only thing left to do was start over.

No more eye for eye.

He was a soldier at heart. Could no more run away from that fact than he could outrun the wind. Maybe it was time to face reality.

And, yeah, maybe he'd reenlist.

ALSO AVAILABLE IN ARROW

Bullet Proof

Matt Croucher GC

AFGHANISTAN, FEBRUARY 2008: in an out-of-control, dangerous country torn apart by war, Lance Corporal Matt Croucher trips a booby-trapped grenade whilst on a covert patrol behind enemy lines. His instincts kick in and he throws himself beside the explosion, covering it, figuring that saving the lives of his three comrades is worth the chance of losing his own.

Miraculously, Croucher survived, and mere hours later was taking part in a shoot-out against insurgent fighters, demonstrating a raw, unique courage and devotion to military duty that would later see him awarded the George Cross – a distinction bestowed only on those who perform acts of the greatest heroism in circumstances of extreme danger.

Croucher's is an incredible story, from this one terrifying incident and beyond to the battlefields of Iraq: a searing, vivid, non-stop account of one man's heroism and courage under fire, in the most gruelling combat environment since the Second World War.

'Breathtakingly told' *News of the World*

arrow books

Firefight

Chris Ryan

Former SAS Captain Will Jackson is a man with nothing to lose. A veteran of the most dangerous missions the Regiment could throw at him, his life was torn apart the day a terrorist attack killed his family. Now he leads a life of grief-stricken obscurity, the world of warfare nothing but a distant memory. People higher up the chain of command have other plans, however. They make Jackson an offer he can't refuse. An offer that will take him straight back into a brutal theatre of war.

Only one person can help prevent the disaster that is waiting to happen, and that person is being held by the Taliban insurgency in the depths of a harsh Afghanistan winter. As Will reluctantly prepares to undertake this final mission, he does so in the knowledge that it will stop a devastating terrorist attack – as well as achieve an ulterior motive of his own.

But someone, somewhere is playing a game with him; nobody can be trusted. Sometimes, you just have to fight fire with fire.

arrow books